MOSCOW GOLD

A Novel of Twentieth-Century Spain

DOUGLAS L. FIELD

MOSCOW GOLD
A NOVEL OF TWENTIETH-CENTURY SPAIN

Copyright © 2022 Douglas L. Field.

All rights reserved. No part of this book may be used or reproduced by any means, graphic, electronic, or mechanical, including photocopying, recording, taping or by any information storage retrieval system without the written permission of the author except in the case of brief quotations embodied in critical articles and reviews.

Certain characters in this work are historical figures, and certain events portrayed did take place. However, this is a work of fiction. All of the other characters, names, and events as well as all places, incidents, organizations, and dialogue in this novel are either the products of the author's imagination or are used fictitiously.

iUniverse books may be ordered through booksellers or by contacting:

iUniverse
1663 Liberty Drive
Bloomington, IN 47403
www.iuniverse.com
844-349-9409

Because of the dynamic nature of the Internet, any web addresses or links contained in this book may have changed since publication and may no longer be valid. The views expressed in this work are solely those of the author and do not necessarily reflect the views of the publisher, and the publisher hereby disclaims any responsibility for them.

Any people depicted in stock imagery provided by Getty Images are models, and such images are being used for illustrative purposes only. Certain stock imagery © Getty Images.

ISBN: 978-1-6632-0336-6 (sc)
ISBN: 978-1-6632-0337-3 (e)

Library of Congress Control Number: 2022903958

Print information available on the last page.

iUniverse rev. date: 04/18/2022

CONTENTS

Author's Note.. xi

PART 1: BAR MONTEAZUL.....................................**1**

Prologue.. 3
Chapter 1   Madrid: Tuesday, August 13, 1963....................... 7
Chapter 2   Madrid: Tuesday, October 20, 1936 23
Chapter 3   Cartagena: Sunday, October 25, 1936................39
Chapter 4   Cartagena: Monday, October 26, 1936 47
Chapter 5   Odessa: Tuesday, November 3, 1936................51
Chapter 6   Madrid: Wednesday, August 14, 1963................53

PART 2: ¡NO PASARÁN! **61**

Chapter 7   Berlin: Friday, November 6, 1936....................63
Chapter 8   Moscow: Saturday, November 7, 1936.............65
Chapter 9   Madrid: Sunday, November 8, 1936 67
Chapter 10   Madrid: (Later on) Wednesday, August 14, 1963.........77
Chapter 11   Carabanchel: Thursday, August 15, 1963 93
Chapter 12   Madrid: Friday, August 16, 1963 103
Chapter 13   Madrid: Saturday, August 17, 1963................109
Chapter 14   Madrid: (Later on) Sunday, November 8, 1936 123
Chapter 15   Madrid: Monday, November 9, 1936 129
Chapter 16   Leganés: Monday, November 23, 1936.............133

PART 3: SARDINERO BEACH **135**

Chapter 17   Carabanchel: Wednesday, August 21, 1963..................137
Chapter 18   Odessa: Tuesday, December 8, 1936 163
Chapter 19   Berlin: Thursday, December 10, 1936................167

Chapter 20 The Western Mediterranean Sea:
Monday, December 14, 1936..169

Chapter 21 Moscow: Friday, December 18, 1936 173

Chapter 22 Madrid: Tuesday, December 22, 1936.............................175

Chapter 23 Madrid: Thursday, August 22, 1963 181

Chapter 24 Santander: Friday, August 23, 1963 185

Chapter 25 Santander: Saturday, August 24, 1963 187

PART 4: OPERATION MARKGRAF 203

Chapter 26 Madrid: Thursday, February 11, 1937............................205

Chapter 27 Ciempozuelos: Thursday, February 11, 1937 207

Chapter 28 Ciempozuelos: Friday, February 12, 1937 213

Chapter 29 Ciempozuelos: Saturday, February 13, 1937................217

Chapter 30 Ciempozuelos: Sunday, February 14, 1937 221

Chapter 31 Arganda del Rey: Monday, February 15, 1937.............223

Chapter 32 Moscow: Wednesday, February 17, 1937 229

Chapter 33 Berlin: Tuesday, March 9, 1937....................................233

Chapter 34 Madrid: Thursday, April 8, 1937 237

Chapter 35 Paris: Monday, April 12, 1937......................................239

Chapter 36 Paris: Monday, May 3, 1937...245

Chapter 37 Paris: Wednesday, May 5, 1937 249

Chapter 38 Paris: Friday May 7, 1937 255

Chapter 39 Paris: Saturday, May 8, 1937..267

Chapter 40 Paris: Sunday, May 9, 1937..275

Chapter 41 Paris: Wednesday, June 30, 1937..................................281

Chapter 42 Berlin: Friday, July 2, 1937 283

Chapter 43 Moscow: Tuesday, July 6, 1937....................................285

Chapter 44 Paris: Friday, July 9, 1937 289

Chapter 45 Madrid: Thursday, September 16, 1937........................291

Chapter 46 Teruel: Thursday, December 16, 1937 295

Chapter 47 Teruel: Christmas Day 1937...299

Chapter 48 Teruel: New Year's Day 1938..301

Chapter 49 Teruel: Thursday, January 27, 1938 305

Chapter 50 Teruel: Wednesday, February 23, 1938 307

Chapter 51 Irún: Sunday, August 25, 1963 311

Chapter 52 Paris: Monday, August 26, 1963 315

Chapter 53 Paris: Wednesday, August 28, 1963.................................335

Chapter 54 Paris: Thursday, August 29, 1963 343

Chapter 55 Moscow: Thursday August 29, 1963 347

Chapter 56 Pullach: Friday, August 30, 1963 351

Chapter 57 Paris: Friday evening, August 30, 1963 355

Chapter 58 Saint-Cyprien: Sunday, March 12, 1939 361

Chapter 59 Perpignan: Monday, March 13, 1939..............................371

Chapter 60 Port Bou: Tuesday, March 4, 1939 387

Chapter 61 Port Bou: Friday, March 7, 1939 389

Chapter 62 Barcelona: Friday, March 21, 1939.................................391

Chapter 63 Madrid: Tuesday, April 11, 1939 393

Chapter 64 Madrid: Saturday, August 31, 1963................................395

Chapter 65 Paris: Saturday, August 31, 1963....................................399

Chapter 66 Madrid: Saturday, August 31, 1963................................415

Chapter 67 Madrid: Friday, May 19, 1939 421

Chapter 68 Madrid: Wednesday, May 24, 1939................................425

Chapter 69 Paris: Sunday, September 1, 1963....................................429

PART 5: EL AQUEDUCTO DE SEGOVIA **435**

Chapter 70 Paris: (Later on) Sunday, September 1, 1963................437

Chapter 71 Chalon-Sur-Saône: Sunday September 1, 1963 445

Chapter 72 Banyuls-sur-Mer: Monday, September 2, 1963 447

Chapter 73 Cerbère: Friday, September 6, 1963................................463

Chapter 74 Madrid: Tuesday, September 3, 1963 465

Chapter 75 Segovia: Saturday, September 7, 1963 467

PART 6: CARABANCHEL **481**

Chapter 76 Madrid: Monday, September 9, 1963 483

Chapter 77 Madrid: Thursday, December 12, 1940 495

Chapter 78 Berlin: Wednesday, December 18, 1940 503
Chapter 79 Carabanchel: Tuesday, September 10, 1963.................505
Chapter 80 Madrid: Wednesday, September 11, 1963 513
Chapter 81 Moscow: Thursday, September 12, 1963......................527
Chapter 82 Pullach: Friday, September 13, 1963............................529
Chapter 83 Carabanchel: Thursday, October 10, 1963...................533

PART 7: MONTIS INSIGNIA CALPE **545**

Chapter 84 Madrid: Sunday, October 13, 1963 547
Chapter 85 Algeciras: Wednesday, October 16, 1963......................555
Chapter 86 Pullach: Wednesday, October 16, 1963........................563
Chapter 87 Moscow: Wednesday, October 16, 1963.......................565
Chapter 88 Madrid: Wednesday, October 16, 1963........................567
Chapter 89 Gibraltar: Thursday, October 17, 1963 569
Chapter 90 Gibraltar: Friday, October 18, 1963 581

PART 8: THE SUNSET CLUB **595**

Chapter 91 La Línea de la Concepción:
            Friday, October 18, 1963......................................597
Chapter 92 Madrid: Monday, October 21, 1963 603
Chapter 93 Madrid: Wednesday, October 23, 1963.........................605
Chapter 94 Madrid: Thursday, October 24, 1963 613
Chapter 95 Madrid: Friday, October 25, 1963................................629
Chapter 96 Madrid: Friday, November 22, 1963.............................633
Chapter 97 Madrid: Saturday, November 23, 1963 637
Epilogue 651

Historical Background and Context 657
Acknowledgments 671
About the Author...673

*To my wife, a beautiful woman with a beautiful soul,
and to my grandchildren and beyond; should they ever
wonder who Sandy and I were, here is a glimpse.*

AUTHOR'S NOTE

The sweep of Spanish history in the middle decades of the twentieth century is complicated and convoluted. A short summary of the background and context of the historical events out of which the following narrative springs is in order. To promote greater ease of understanding I have prepared one. Since, however, this is a work of fiction, I have put the summary at the end of the volume. The reader is invited and encouraged to reference it early. But for the moment, let the adventure begin!

In Spain there is a lot of sun and an excess of light,
So that everything is all too clear. It is a country
Of emphatic claims and denials where doubt has
Been put to the torch—to that sinister clarity.
—Manuel Vincent

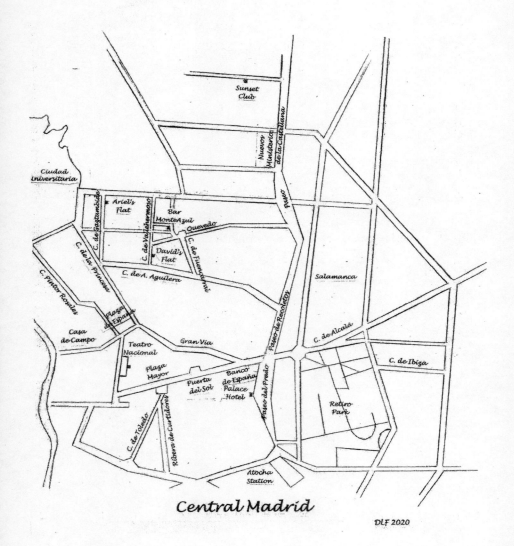

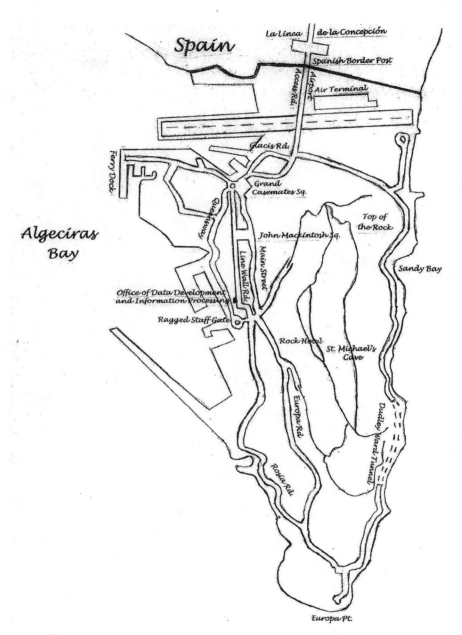

PART I
BAR MONTEAZUL

At times, a historical event will take on a life of its own. It comes to transcend its past. It exists in the present. It projects its influence into the future. It motivates actors and actions. It animates human relationships. It taints lives and reputations.

One such event is the disappearance in 1936 of several billion dollars of Spanish gold reserves in coin and bullion. These reserves are known to exist. They were sent to Russia for safekeeping during the crucible of civil war. What happened to them thereafter is less clear. Their subsequent history persistently survives as the story of the Moscow Gold.

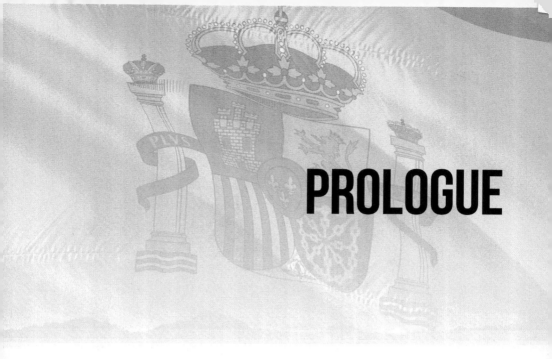

PROLOGUE

Paris: Saturday, May 8, 1937

Five young operatives from East Europe were gathered in the ticketing flat at Invalides Métro. They had a soccer ball.

Each had wrangled himself a blue-and-white-striped jersey of the Racing Club France soccer team. They could have given themselves French code names but decided their own Slavic given names would be adequate for this hit. Tickets already bought; they were loitering just past the entry barriers.

They dribbled the ball, kicked it off the wall, and passed it about. Working their feet and expending energy, they hoped to look and act French. It would distract their mark. The mark was late. That made them nervous and fidgety.

"We sure this is the right station?" Todor said to no one in particular.

"It's the right station and the right time," confirmed Auloy. "I checked it with the boss. It's confirmed by Agent Alois, the German. Boss got the information from the gardener over at their embassy. The gardener's information has been good before. Alois has his own separate assets here in Paris. They say so too. The mark'll be here."

"We grab shipment? Get away this time?" This by Zahn, the youngest but ablest soccer player of the group. He asked it as he juggled the ball in the air with his foot.

"Yes, idiot," Auloy snapped and shook his head.

"Last hit, boss tell us botch it. How that makes sense?"

"Just do your job, Zahn, and leave the thinking and planning to your betters. It's that kraut Alois. He wants some of the hits to fail. Since he's the one paying, the boss says he gets what he wants—good sense or not. Keep up your lookout."

Another three minutes of tense waiting passed. Then Boyko whispered, "Here comes the mark. Get ready to move. Look natural. You know the drill."

The mark was a smallish and wiry man, casually dressed, trousers, and a collared shirt. No tie, no coat, no beret, he was not French. He descended the stairs nimbly from the street to the ticketing booth, his movement purposeful but not hurried.

"It's him," said Auloy softly. "He's got the briefcase. It looks like he's alone. He'll head in the direction of Charenton-Écoles. The platform's to the right and downstairs. Head there, and we'll pick him up when he comes down."

The mark carried a medium-large briefcase that appeared to be heavy. It was secured to his wrist with a light handcuff and chain. No one would just grab the case and run.

The mark had correct change ready in his pocket. He passed it through the ticket window; collected his ticket, as was proper; and pushed through the turnstile. The footballers were no longer in evidence as he turned right and headed down to his platform.

On the platform, the mark positioned himself to board at the rear of the train. The Métro often put a first-class car in the middle of its trains. He had not paid the extra. He wanted to be inobtrusive. No sense jumping first class and getting caught by the transit police.

He now saw that there was a group of soccer team members. They were also waiting for the rear of the next train. They were chattering and kicking a ball around. They annoyed him. He hoped their ball would fall off the platform and onto the rails. There was no time for him to nurse his ill will. He felt the wind and saw the reflected light of the approaching train.

The team was gratified to observe, as they had anticipated, that the train was lightly populated but not empty. There were riders on board, but there were empty seats.

Perfect for their purposes.

Now for the delicate bit. They continued their minor roistering as the train eased to a stop. They crowded around the mark as the doors opened. More good fortune. No one exited. Zahn had picked up the soccer ball and was bouncing it on the platform. He and Bokyo were in front of the mark. They held back a fraction of a second until the mark pushed forward and until the remaining three could move in close behind him. The mark was distracted and surrounded. They all went on the train in a tight little scrum.

Auloy had his chloroform pad saturated and ready. Once he stepped aboard, he clapped it over the mark's face and held it hard. The mark collapsed as the train started to move. Todor and Petar took an arm each and set him on an open seat. All five then surrounded him while Boyko produced a small set of bolt cutters and sliced through the mark's chain.

Concorde station was next and close. No other riders took note of the team or their now unconscious mark. The doors opened. The team took the heavy briefcase and bolted off. The mark appeared to have fallen asleep with a soccer ball in his lap. He rode serenely on toward Charenton.

Out in Place de la Concorde, the team stripped off their jerseys and dumped them in a trash bin. They hastened down to the Quai des Tuileries and hailed a taxi back to their safe house and the boss.

"You succeeded, I see," commented the boss dryly as Auloy handed over the briefcase. "Any problems?"

"None. Perfect execution." Auloy answered for the rest.

"It was a perfect plan. The mark?" The boss said, raising an eyebrow.

"Never knew what hit him. Still riding around on the Métro taking a nice nap. What's in the case? What have we been stealing from these people?" Auloy continued.

"I think we can have a look," replied the boss as he hefted the case and undid the clasps. "Alois won't mind. If he does, screw him."

When the case came open, the team was dumbstruck. It was coins, hundreds of them. Gold coins. Neatly packaged. Of obvious immense value. They clinked together with the high-pitched timbre of complete purity. Some had a goddess walking among rays of sunlight on one side and an eagle in flight on the other. Others had what looked like a horseman killing a dragon and one monarch or another on the reverse.

The boss shook his head and closed the case. "Yes. Well done. All of you. The next operation is a go for tomorrow. Let's rehearse the details."

CHAPTER 1

Madrid: Tuesday, August 13, 1963

David Fordham needed to disappear—soon.

At least he had to get out of sight, maybe even leave Spain.

There was Isham. And then there were the cops and the doorman in his building and his wife—small stuff that, on its own, was little enough. Yet when he added it all, it sniffed like he was coming to people's attention. David didn't need to stand out. Standing out was not the indicated thing to do in a modern fascist dictatorship. The Spanish bureaucracy seemed benign. But it was like a sleeping crocodile; get too close to the water's edge, and it might lunge, try to bite. All of David's instincts told him it was stirring.

Thus was David preoccupied at nine this fine morning. For him, he was out early. He had gone over to Quevedo.

Already, painful August sunlight bounced off the bright white statue of the Spanish satirist Francisco Quevedo. Skeptical and constitutionally sarcastic himself, David liked to lean against the railing that led to the entrance of Quevedo's Metro station and stare at the statue. He would steal a few brief moments from his otherwise

MOSCOW GOLD | 7

busy life to commune with the great writer, ponder the profession and worldview they seemed to have in common, and maybe even share a concern or two.

What's going on here, Francisco old buddy? What bullet is coming around the corner at me that I don't expect?

Quevedo's *glorieta* and the area surrounding it, known locally as merely "Quevedo" and the whole Vallehermoso barrio were David's Madrid center of gravity. Here he spent his time, met his friends, and had his favorite haunts. Here he was known. It was familiar. He was comfortable. Important for today, here was where he got his inspirations and planned out his strategies.

He had been brought to Madrid a decade earlier in his mid-teenage years by his parents. His father had a long-term business assignment in Spain. The Fordham parents had settled into the comfortable Anglocentric expat community growing in Madrid.

David had elected a different path. He went exploring.

A Metro ticket cost the equivalent of an American penny and a half. No *rincón* or *callejuela* eluded the teenager's investigation. Within a fortnight, the plan of the city was engraved in his mind.

Unburdened by time or family, David had marched to urgent drums of wonderment and discovery. Even though it labored under a stern and uncompromising dictatorship, Madrid was wide open and free to her new and curious occupant.

David's new city had an easy and unconfined rhythm, day and night and night and day. David had seldom rested. He was there for all of it. All night long, the city bubbled. In the smallest hours, the previous day's refuse was washed away by fire hoses. Train consists were made up at Atocha and del Norte. Then before dawn, while it was still dark, deliveries started, as did the baking and stocking of public markets. Bars and cafés populated as the sun was coming up. Workers and craftsmen in blue jumpsuits and grit-faded berets came out early. They then were soon enough chased out by the suits, the office workers and functionaries, so very prevalent in the capital. In the young light of day appeared the maids and nannies with string shopping bags and the family's schoolchildren. Breakfast was late. Dinner was later, well into the afternoon. Business and commerce stopped for the midday meal and then an afternoon nap. Everything opened back up in the late afternoon only to close again for the day at early night. The whole city turned out for its *paseo*, the streets jammed, no room to move, seeing and greeting everybody they knew. So it was every night. Supper was taken leisurely at around ten, and off to plays or the *zarzuelas*, or the films. Finally, home just ahead of the street washers as the cycle began again.

Thus, the cycle had done this morning. David hadn't caught the early part of it today as he had wholeheartedly participated in the late part last evening.

David Langston Fordham was, to the inch, six feet tall. He had curly, dark brown hair and green-brown eyes that changed color with the clothes he put on, with the weather, and sometimes for no apparent reason at all. He had a square face and almost olive skin, resulting he supposed from what his family lore had as significant Native American heritage. It all went with a somewhat prominent chin, full lips, and a largish ski-jump nose.

In school, he had been fond of strength training and endurance athletics, could do physical work all day long, and remained strong as a mule. Curiosity and perseverance were hallmarks of his emotional and intellectual makeup. So was a free, independent, and cynical spirit that disliked being told what to do; was often snarkily sarcastic; and was averse to sustained work and effort. His fondness for the writer Quevedo was no surprise.

Quevedo stands astride the borderline between the Madrid barrios of Vallehermoso and Chamberí. He looks down from his high perch at the center of the glorieta that bears his name on the river of taxis and little delivery trucks and motor scooters that rush past his feet. The river that surges south from Cuatro Caminos into the broad Calle de Fuencarral before that street narrows to a one-lane standstill near the center of town. David imagined the fellow must have thoughts regarding the placement of his statue. More suitable would have been a leafy and quiet intersection in a moneyed and elegant part of town.

Oh well, nothing can be done about it now, old buddy. You are stuck where you are, and so am I.

Vallehermoso barrio was unpolished and worn. It had a certain anonymity that suited David. It was Madrid's old new section up in the northwest that pushed up against the expanse of University City. Laid out like a modern gridiron in the first half of the twentieth century, Vallehermoso felt free and open, not like the medieval tangle of alleyways and passages of the traditional center. David's barrio was comfortable, prosaic, uninspired, and most of all convenient to his preferences.

Vallehermoso and University City were, David knew, where, back in November 1936, the people's militias, with inadequate weapons and worse leadership, had barricaded the streets and bled to deny them to General Franco and his Moors. By 1963, the memory and ethos of the civil war still lurked everywhere beneath the surface of everyday life in Spain, palpable and unforgettable. David had been fascinated from the outset.

The civil war left Madrid a quarter of a century ago now, but not the sun or the coming heat and not David's worries. The still morning air did not yet move the chestnut leaves. The intensity of the light and coming heat increased David's tension. What to do about the attention he seemed to be getting bounced around in his head while he slouched against the entrance railing and squinted at the statue.

Madrid started later than other big European cities. David had a little time to make some decisions. Urgent ones they were, too, but maybe this was not the best morning for it. Yesterday evening coming home up Fuencarral from downtown, there had been many bars, several *vinos tintos* and then the brandies. This morning, he was vague, stiff, and slow.

Bad decisions last night. Need better ones this morning.

David bestirred himself. He walked west into the Calle de Magallanes. Magellan Street. The grayest and plainest of streets in a gray, plain corner of Madrid, it was not that much to honor the great around-the-world explorer.

What did Magellan expect? He's Portuguese. This is Spain.

The Bar MonteAzul is in Calle de Magallanes. An American journalist working in Madrid had to ensure that the sometimes gray and dismal town did not become depressing. David had a cynical and skeptical side, but he was neither gray nor dour. He liked it that the Bar MonteAzul relieved the drabness of the street. He gravitated toward it. The old MonteAzul was a friend and regular haunt.

MonteAzul was spelled out in individual blue block letters set in square backlit boxes. The "Z" had fallen off, lay askew, and had knocked out the light. Who knew how long ago? Who knew how long before it would be fixed? If ever. In English, it is the Blue Mountain. Colorful painted tiles outside, noisy within, the place was never without construction workers in their dusty berets, plus the odd suit and briefcase.

The MonteAzul was always a lift to his spirits and a favorite place to reflect and reason matters out. Once inside, he lit a Bisonte, blonde naturally. Spanish cigarettes were designated black or blonde. Years living in Madrid, and David had never gotten used to the black. So, a Bisonte and time to confront decisions.

Why the message from Isham? Malevolent bastard. Way too soon to hear from him *again.*

David had a continuing sense that his easy and agreeable routines were about to be set well out of joint.

"What will you drink?" asked the barman, Victorio. Victorio owned the MonteAzul. He was a transplanted Italian. He changed the spelling of his name by a letter or two to accommodate his Spanish hosts. Victorio single-handed the MonteAzul.

David should have ordered breakfast, Spanish style; black coffee; and a couple of churros.

"Brandy. Fundador," David ordered against his better judgment. Fundador is the popular local stuff. Not smooth nor elegant but of agreeable price.

The barman shrugged, flipped up a glass, and filled it.

David quaffed his drink at one go. He fished out a few coins and poured them out on the bar.

I'd like to have another. Brandy's not that great a decision to start a day of decisions. Maybe OK to have a little morning buzz on, but not wasted.

He grabbed his smokes and threaded his way toward the window.

The MonteAzul's front window was large and grease-streaked in perpetuity. Better for looking out than in. Made for a good lookout though. It overlooked Magallanes back up toward Quevedo. So, if he paid attention and avoided letting himself get distracted, he saw everything that entered the street.

There wasn't much this morning. Three elderly ladies stooped and doddering along arm in arm were dressed in the ubiquitous all-black uniform of Spanish widowhood. Plus, two *grises*, uniformed members of the Policía Armada. *Gris* meant gray. Gray uniforms with red flashes and piping. All was normal for a weekday morning. David could relax a little.

He wasn't worried about the grises anyway. You could spot them a block away. Avoidance was a snap. What you had to watch out for were the plainclothes, undercover agents, the Cuerpo General de Policía.

The plainclothes ones were cunning and skilled at melting into the crowds on the sidewalks and plazas and down in the Metro. If they wanted to talk to you, they would find you. There would be no warning. One got in your face. His partner lurked behind your left ear.

Two of them had materialized around him just late last week down around the corner on Calle de Fernando el Católico.

"Your passport, Señor Fordham." No *please*, demanding, entitled, right up to the borderline of rude.

"I must have left it in my flat."

"Then how shall we know who you are?"

"You already know my name. Not sure what my passport would add." *Give 'em a touch of American insolence.*

"Yes, mmm. How is your stay in our capital? Is the city to your liking? What is the purpose of your residence here?" Then more to the point. "You know that it is not permitted for an *extranjero* such as yourself to have a job for pay? You know this?"

Not interested in the answers to the questions, that day they were just making the presence known. *Never underestimate our vigilance, Señor.*

"I'm a freelance journalist—for the *International Herald Tribune.* They deposit direct to my account in the States. Something you also must already know. What's the point of this?"

"Ah, a fine newspaper." David's question was curtly ignored. "I shall have to look for your, eh, byline is how you call it?"

"Very kind."

"But you have no article at the moment? Yes, just so. And you are not otherwise working for money in Madrid, *sí?*"

"No. Of course not. *Jamás.* Never ever," David had fibbed.

"Be so kind as to remember to carry your passport at all times, Señor Fordham."

And then they were gone.

Until the past couple of weeks, the Cuerpo, as they were known colloquially, never had bothered David. The change formed a big chunk of his nowadays disquiet. Anybody who lived in Madrid lived with a level of government control. When the accustomed level of involvement changed, that's when you took notice. It had changed for him. David was taking notice.

His Spanish friends explained that Spanish dictatorship may be less harsh in 1963 than it was in the years closer to the end of the civil war. But down deep it was intact, undiminished, and oh-so-practiced. The harsh methods—the digging you out of your house in the middle of the night, the vicious beatings, the dumping you into some dungeon where no one would ever find you, the summary executions even, now, after a quarter century—were diminished. It now was more of a tender tyranny, they had said. No longer the *dictadura* (hard dictatorship) but, as they liked the play on words, the *dictablanda* (soft dictatorship). Now it was characterized by the surprise appearance, the unconvincing geniality.

We know who you are. We know what you are doing. We are tolerant, Señor, but be careful not to test the limits of our patience.

While the two in uniform who David could see out MonteAzul's window weren't a concern, the periodic and increasing hazing he was getting by the Cuerpo was. He knew he would have to figure out why and what to do about it.

David returned to the bar. He set the empty down. Victorio didn't even ask, just flipped up the big bottle and poured as David stood watching. Then David shouldered his way back to the window, past walls once painted white but now a deepening amber from daily clouds of cigarette smoke with a yellowing and curling bullfight poster from the San Isidro Festival of 1957.

The MonteAzul was always crowded. It offered about as much anonymity as was available in crowded Madrid. The other patrons he was squeezing by were all men—men of opinion, definite opinion; they had opinions about soccer, politics, the price of olive oil, American movies. In the MonteAzul, it was not the substance of your opinion as much as the absolute certainty of commitment and of conviction and of hand gestures and finger thumping to back it up. David wished he had such clarity and conviction today.

He often used the MonteAzul to hide and tune it all out. The place's routine varied little. Amid the clamor and clatter, he had his drink, and he smoked. He kept his eye on the world outside. And he could think.

It wasn't just the Cuerpo either. David was thinking about Isham. This morning David had known what it was in an instant. As he made torpid departure for Quevedo through the lobby of the building where his *pensión* was located, a letter had been handed to him by the *portera*, the doorman's wife.

"A letter for you, Señor David," pronounced /Dah*veeth*/ with emphatic accent on the latter syllable, she said with an affectionate smile that showed a couple of gold teeth. He imagined that she imagined his correspondent was a high US government official or, even better, a Hollywood starlet and that the letter would be most welcome to him.

But Isham's note was most *unwelcome*. Jack Isham wanted something, and David didn't know what it was. Well, he knew what Isham said it was, but with Isham, one thing always led to another. And *another* was what worried David.

In regular practice, there was contact once a month or so. This note was way too soon. It was only a few days ago that David had been sitting in a sidewalk café down on Calle de la Princesa. Suddenly Isham had slid in next to him, slick and stealthy. They had talked then. There should be nothing from Isham this soon.

Solomon John "Jack" Isham was associate editor of the *International Herald Tribune*, Madrid Bureau. He did the job but did not look or act the part. That's what troubled David. When he had first gotten back to Madrid and hooked up with the paper, there had been a different editor. The first guy had been demanding but friendly, with the odd word of journalistic encouragement.

Not Isham. Isham didn't talk or act like a newspaper editor. It was as if Isham was distracted. The man had an office, but he never used it. He always would set you up to meet somewhere else. Isham made David suspicious and nervous. David's impulse when dealing with Isham was to have ready a contingency plan—just in case.

This time the note said, "Café Gijón, tomorrow, 3:30." That was it. There was no reason given, no signature, no pleasantries. Just show up.

I just saw you last week. What now?

Café Gijón at 3:30. Now that made no sense at all. Sure, Isham loved to go there. It had all that pretension. Fortuitously located as

MOSCOW GOLD | 15

it was right on Paseo de Recoletos, one of the poshest boulevards in Europe, it was the most famous café in all of Madrid and doubtless the most expensive.

It had gold-trimmed, maroon awnings and was all paneling inside, leather and clubby comfort. Galdós and García Lorca frequented the place. It was opened in something like 1888. Rubén Darío used to go there too. All the literati, glitterati, artists, and politicos did.

Out of my league. Yours, too, Jack, when you come down to it.

But why 3:30? That was the middle of siesta. Nobody would be in there at all. Maybe that was Isham's point. Maybe he didn't want anybody to see them meeting. That would be strange though. Isham was a self-promoter. He always called attention to himself. A quiet meeting *a solas* would be a departure for Isham.

This was David's first decision. Should he even show up at Café Gijón? How could Isham leverage him if he didn't? David guessed that was the crux of it. He knew that Isham had influence. He just didn't know how much. Worse, he didn't know who with. There was influence with the paper for sure. Everything depended on the paper. David had done well enough as a stringer for the old *Herald* for near on to three years now. They bought his stories with acceptable regularity. He was able to live. Isham could leverage him with the paper.

David's hardheaded, unemotional decision would be to bag it. Go home. Land a job with some paper in the Midwest. Find a girlfriend. Get married. Pop out a couple of kids. Move up the ladder. That would be the sensible and orthodox decision. But his life so far had been anything but orthodox. So why change? Besides, Madrid was Madrid. So what if it wasn't Paris? Madrid was busy, the center of the action in Spain, and quirky. Maybe it wasn't the prettiest or most elegant big city, but it was his big city. It would be a tough decision to leave. He had too much invested. It would be better to find a way to get out of sight—lie low for a while. Let his trail cool a little.

Maybe Carabanchel was the answer.

A suburb that lay a few miles due south of the city center, Carabanchel was a new addition to David's Madrid equation. The paper paid him in dollars. When converted into pesetas, David's dollars went a very long way. They covered his regular expenses. About all that was left was financing his "lifestyle." Lifestyle included tobacco, alcohol, entertainment, the usual stuff.

David was floating his lifestyle out of Carabanchel by means of a side gig he had acquired by agreeable happenstance. He had met a Spaniard called Jaime Castellón at a cocktail party he'd covered for the paper. The little fête was in celebration of the twentieth anniversary of the founding of the American Library in the US embassy. Isham had detailed David to cover it.

A prim and proper affair, the party had been scheduled at fashionable eight o'clock one evening. Nobody *important* was there—just a few mid-level Spanish officials and their American counterparts. It was all goodwill and continuing friendship lubricated by a little Cinzano or sherry. There was little to report except the usual pabulum about the endurance of Spanish-American relations and the importance of the library as a cultural resource to both communities. David started out bored by the entire event.

Castellón had been there in the company of an attractive and confident Spanish woman he'd introduced as Señorita Muñíz. Castellón described the young lady as his aide. She acted aloof and unapproachable. The man had wanted to try out his English. David had humored him distractedly. His interest was greater in the pretty girl than in this Spaniard practicing his English. As Castellón chattered on, the girl affected complete disinterest in the young American journalist and wandered off toward the hors d'oeuvres table.

Disappointed, David had turned his full attention back to Castellón. David's indulgence was rewarded by an invitation to supper the next evening at a *parilla* over on Calle de Goya. After agreeing to meet Castellón there, David thought to chase after Señorita Muñíz in hopes of getting to know her better. He found her on a balcony engaged in conversation with an older embassy official. It would have been awkward to intrude.

Hard to get a Spanish girl to give you the time of day on the best of days, so leave it for another time.

It turned out that David was not sorry he accepted Castellón's invitation. On David's arrival at the parilla, his host offered a card. It identified him as the owner and operator of Doblaciones Cinematográficas Castellón, S.A. Business offices on the Calle de Jorge Juan in Goya barrio. Workshops in the industrial suburb of Carabanchel. As with large numbers of Spanish companies, its name was shortened to the acronym DOCICA.

As David absorbed these details, he could not keep himself from wondering at which location Castellón's aide worked. He was sure it would be good to get to know her better. She had an air of competence and independence. These were qualities rarely observed in young women in tradition-bound Spain.

Castellón was not quite fifty. He smoked constantly, Ducados in his case, the regulation black tobacco, the staple Spanish tobacco. This time, at the parilla, Castellón spoke Spanish.

"*Claro está*, your English is perfect," Castellón commented before getting down to the business. "I apprehend that your Spanish is as well," Castellón used the informal word for "your." "May we *tutear*?" he asked before pressing on. He meant dispense with the formal forms of address and speak as friends, equals—always a breakthrough in Spanish social circumstances.

"Of course, very kind of you."

"Languages interest me," Castellón proclaimed. "I have observed that a small number of *notreamericanos* who know Spanish have what we call a *don*, a special talent, an ability."

"We have that idea. It's called a 'knack.'"

"Exactly. Well, I, well, my company that is, provides translations of your American films into *el castellano*." In Spain the language known almost everywhere else as *español*, is called *castellano*, Castilian. "I

18 | DOUGLAS L. FIELD

think your word for it is 'dubbing.' We need an American English speaker with the talent to assist us with the difficult passages and with your American argot. There are many things about your country that we do not know. We need explanations."

"This is something then that you believe I would be capable of?" David decided to move things along.

"You are a very direct people, you Americans. I like that. And, yes, I am sure of it. Of course, you would be well compensated—30,000 pesetas per month."

Thirty thousand! Five hundred dollars! That'll cover all my reasonably foreseeable lifestyle for all the reasonably foreseeable future. And it gets me into Carabanchel.

He indicated desire to accept but pointed out that he had no work permit. He was disallowed to have employment from a Spanish employer, disallowed to take payment in pesetas.

Castellón waved off David's concerns. "You may trust me. There will be no problem. Payment will be in cash. All very discreet." He concluded with a vague and disconnected allusion to some government contacts that he maintained.

David signed on. Throughout the encounter David managed, but only barely, to resist the temptation to inquire further about the elusive Señorita Muñíz.

Be patient. Maybe you'll see her around the office.

Thenceforward, around the fifth of every month, he was, without fanfare, handed a white envelope containing the thirty banknotes, all quite large and tidily folded in half.

David had already speculated that Carabanchel might offer him a level of much-needed anonymity. It might afford him a place to run to ground. Starting his work at DOCICA bore his speculations out. Most streets still were unpaved, with many building exteriors crumbly and unpainted.

MOSCOW GOLD | 19

Ramshackle Carabanchel had a history that suited David's purposes. Spain had suffered after World War II. The late forties and early fifties were a time of extreme privation. They became known as *los años de hambre*—the hunger years. The crisis was worse in the countryside. Migration to the cities had been inevitable. They came in their hoards and settled in the outskirts.

Places like Carabanchel were besieged. There was insufficient accommodation. Newcomers built themselves *chabolas*—shanties out of whatever materials they could scavenge.

By the time David began to frequent the little suburb, there was a languorous gentrification going on in Carabanchel shantytown. Electricity and other municipal improvements had been brought in. Some chabolas were being sold by those who had prospered and were moving to high-rises closer in. Others were abandoned and empty.

Legitimate businesses like Castellón's had come in bringing workers who patronized the cafés and bars during the day and went home at night. Carabanchel was still a good place to fly low, keep your head down, and go unnoticed. The shanties and their relative anonymity were not all gone—not yet.

From the street, DOCICA's building evidenced a state of perceptible dilapidation. On the inside, the cagey Castellón had worked it up nicely. More than adequate were both the offices where they did and typed the translations and the technical spaces where they did the dubbing.

David avoided regularity in his visits. He varied days, times, and lengths. There had never been a hint that the authorities were on to the specifics of his daytime moonlighting. He sensed general suspicion on the part of the Cuerpo that he was getting a little extra from somewhere, but he figured they had no concrete idea as to where from. Recently, he had taken a keener interest in the Cuerpo's tactics. He made sporadic effort to avoid their attentions.

His DOCICA colleagues came to appreciate him. They saved their American language and cultural issues for David's regularly irregular visits. He had little fear of being denounced. Miss Muñíz did work in Carabanchel. He occasionally crossed a sterile and formal greeting with her. She gave him no encouragement for greater contact.

Now, as he ruminated in the MonteAzul, David had the job at the paper to think of, but there was DOCICA to protect too. Isham had a lot of curiosity. If David showed at Gijón there would be questions. If he didn't, there would be a lot more.

Better to show he decided, but he wondered if it might be time to disappear for a while. There was always Carabanchel.

CHAPTER 2

Madrid: Tuesday, October 20, 1936

"I've arranged my transport," said the rotund little man with a self-congratulatory smile.

"One hundred fifty-eight trucks. It wasn't easy either. A logistical triumph if I may say so. The military types don't want to let go of anything. Not transport trucks. Not even for a few days."

"Why would they, Juan?" replied the man with him sourly. "The rebel threat to the capital is real. We might lose Madrid—any day now. Transport is a critical resource."

"Resources indeed, Francisco. Resources are my forte. And resourcefulness is my gift. I've been getting them their tanks, fighter planes, artillery shells, all of it—since the uprising began. They should trust me."

"You're humble too."

"Humility won't get us what they need. Neither will resourcefulness or perseverance. What it takes is money, and my trucks are going to help solve our money problem."

"*Your* trucks, indeed!"

MOSCOW GOLD | 23

The round little man was not an economist or a captain of industry. He was no particular student of efficiency or administration, public or private. He was a medical doctor. Somewhat portly, he had a dark complexion and a prominent and straight nose. His eyes were deep set with a strong chin and a high forehead. His was the strong face of serious mien. It was a face that belied natural congeniality and cosmopolitan conviviality.

The doctor had been born in 1889. After several years in Germany as a medical researcher, he'd gained the prestigious chair of physiology at the University of Madrid.

A man of great appetites, Dr. Juan Nergín was known from time to time to dine twice and even three times in a single evening and, after that, to indulge an intense interest in women. Negrín was effervescent and secretive, confident and worldly. He was the Spanish Republic's minister of finance. And now he had his trucks.

Dr. Negrín was entertaining his colleague Francisco Largo Caballero, the socialist prime minister of Spain, at a late supper down on Cava Baja. Over dinner, they were putting finishing touches to the most significant initiative that Finance Minister Negrín had yet made in office.

Largo, earlier in the day, had given his unenthusiastic agreement to Negrín's proposed shipment. It had fallen to Largo to secure the consent of the consignee. This had not been difficult.

"Will they take it?" Negrín had asked over coffee.

"It's all arranged." Largo did not conceal his disgust. "They didn't take much persuading. Their venality overwhelms me. They will provide the ships, but we will have to pay for them. Your contact is that stooge Stachevski, their economic attaché. He'll meet you down in Cartagena. The brute left by train yesterday via Valencia. Should be there before you are."

"I am prepared to do this, Francisco. We must take the risk. We are in danger of losing everything as it is. Putting up with a boorish Russian or two is a small price to pay."

"It has been agreed." Largo sighed. "As you say, we will have a substantial current account with them. To obtain what we need. The cost is high, though, Juan; it is high."

"Does Azaña know?" Negrín changed the subject.

"No. The president would never agree. He would find the means to stop you. When he learns, he will be apoplectic."

"By then, it will be too late. We are staking everything on this, Francisco, and we have no other choice."

As finance minister, Negrín had unlimited access to the Bank of Spain. The bank resided in permanent quarters at Calle de Alcalá number 48. Its offices looked out across the Paseo del Prado and across the ornamental Plaza de Cibeles fountain toward the Palace of Communications.

Upon leaving Cava Baja and after midnight, Negrín's taxi dropped him at the bank's main entrance doors. Despite the lateness of the hour and with ceremonial deference, a uniformed beadle admitted him.

Negrín bounded up the main staircase of the bank to the governor's office, where Francisco Méndez Aspe, his undersecretary, awaited him. If a Spaniard could be Dickensian, such was Méndez, tall and sour with wisps of dark hair and a whitening goatee. A reserved and unsmiling man, he represented the perfect counterpoint to his bon viveur chief.

"Largo has fixed it, Méndez." Negrín dispensed with conversational niceties. "President Azaña is not informed. He would put a stop to the whole operation. No matter. I am the finance minister. I have determined what's best. We will do this my way. Are your people ready?"

"They are, Minister."

"How many?"

"Five hundred eighty strong and fit men." Méndez was ready with facts and figures. "By my estimate three and a half hours to load. It's already in place on the loading dock. If your trucks are prompt, you will be loaded and on your way well before dawn. The men have been

MOSCOW GOLD | 25

told nothing. There have been no questions. They are glad for the work. Yet they will wonder. The cargo is of quite, ah, distinct character, if not to say weight. And this *is* a bank."

"Word will get out. It's inevitable." Negrín shrugged. "All we need is sufficient delay. But the trucks, the trucks will be prompt, my friend; you will see. Gather your men."

Negrín choreographed his trucks through the alleys behind the bank building where, at this time of night, there was little activity. The crates had been trundled up from the bank's strong rooms under the Cibeles fountain. No truck could accommodate more than fifty boxes. They were very heavy. They were 7,800 in all.

There had been no attempt to keep secret or to advertise the contents. There would be ten truck convoys separated by sufficient distance to discourage curiosity.

Juan Negrín himself would travel in truck number 141. It was a big American Ford stake bed—one blessed with a silky-smooth flathead V-8 motor and burdened by a balky clutch and transmission.

The finance minister's mate turned out to be called Ignacio. In the carrying out of this matter, last names were unimportant. Ignacio wore his *boina* in the Spanish style, straight and square, its dimples permanent. Perhaps it was removed at night, perhaps not. The rest of his attire consisted of dark and shapeless pants and a rough, collarless cotton shirt whose sleeves were too long, under an unadorned black vest. Ignacio's colors were plain, the more so as he was dusty. His dust faded him into even greater anonymity.

Sitting in the Ford's ample cab, Negrín noted a faint odor of unwashed socks. He glanced at Ignacio's espadrilles. They were oil-stained and worn. The minister's thought was to go in one of the later convoys. So, he had chosen 141. He could assist with stragglers and monitor breakdowns, keep everything moving.

Ignacio backed 141 up to the dock at 4:45, near the end of loading but not quite at the last. Everyone was loaded by 5:30. Once loaded, the convoys were dispatched southeastward down the Paseo del

Prado. One hundred ten trucks were forthwith diverted straight into Estación de Atocha, the big railway station downtown. The remainder, including Negrín's, continued south.

This was all part of the finance minister's plan. The bulk, but by no means all of the shipment, would go under close guard by super express train. The rest would travel by road. Divide up the shipment. Gain just a little more insurance.

Or so Negrín imagined.

❧

The anarchist cell was also stirring early. They were holed up in the barn and stables of a now abandoned royalist finca situated near the tiny village of Copey just south of Cuenca. Dawn had not broken before the stillness of the night was shattered by the arrival of a fast motorcycle messenger from the capital.

"Look alive, assholes!" shouted Gato, the leader. "The stuff's on its way."

Notable among the simmering alphabet soup of acronyms that bubbled and fizzed in Spain before and during the civil war was the FAI, Federación Anarquista Ibérica. Of all the groups, associations, confederations, and congresses, the anarchist FAI were the most brutal, most unpredictable, most loosely organized, most undisciplined, and least ideological of all. They were in it for themselves, for the joy of it all, for the destruction and mayhem, and for the possibility of personal profit.

The Madrid battalion was divided into several independent platoons that the anarchists called *pelotones*. By someone's bit of conceit, the platoons were denominated only by single letters. Pelotón G, known to itself as La Vanguardia, was now waking up in Copey. For security, and anarchists being anarchists, they were known to each other only by code names. Everybody had a code name that began with the same letter as the pelotón. Thus was Gato the elected leader. Then there were Gallo, Gustavo, Güero and the like.

MOSCOW GOLD | 27

The troops were beginning to move. "Gallo and Gordo, load up the barricades. The rest of you, see to your weapons," Gato ordered. "I'll brief you while you have breakfast."

Breakfast was minimal—coffee and a few chunks of bread left over from yesterday.

Gato got started. "Madrid reports that the consignment left the bank very early this morning. They loaded it up on a fleet of trucks. Most of it went to Atocha and was going down by train. They put some of it on a convoy of trucks. The trucks are headed our way."

"How many trucks?" asked one soldier.

"Unknown, but a lot. Divided into groups of about ten," Gato advised. "The train will be impossible to hit, so we are going to try some trucks. We'll let the lead convoys go by and jump one or two of the last ones. Try to peel them off from the rest, grab the goods, and go."

"Where?" said one.

"Same place I showed you before. At the curve below the top of the hill out there. Move out. Let's make some money. Get the car ready." The departing royalist *patrón* had left behind a large and quite heavy 1932 Hispano-Suiza J12 Dual Cowl Phaeton automobile. Gato intended to appropriate it to the pelotón's use. The monster weighed all but three tons and could accommodate all Pelotón G and their equipment.

"I think our dear abdicated King Alfonso XIII had one of these." Gato sneered. "In his honor, we're going to use it to pinch some of the ill-gotten gains of him and his ilk. It'll make the perfect roadblock. Pelotón G, mount up! We go!"

∿

Negrín's destination was Cartagena, the ancient Spanish naval base located in the southeast about halfway around from Gibraltar to Barcelona. Cartagena lay 250 hard miles from Madrid. The route selected by Negrín ran out across the *meseta* plain—rolling, brown ground that dried and flattened away from Madrid. Late October, Negrín knew, would no longer be smoldering hot, but there had been no rain yet.

As he intended, his convoys raised great thunderheads of grit. The dust would mark their position from afar. But down on the road, inside the convoys, visibility would be decreased. The dust screen would provide a little extra protection.

There should have been mechanical failures and even minor accidents. Negrín had anticipated them. To his gratification, his Whites, Fords, Fiats, and Renaults all turned out to be reliable and their drivers adept.

The route resisted stoutly. It never permitted much over thirty miles per hour, sometimes not even that. It would be a twelve-hour haul, maybe more. After Madrid, in Cuenca Province, the route crawled over a broken and buff land. Scarps scored the brownscape. Dry washes abounded. All had to be descended, crossed, and ascended again.

Ignacio's management of his Ford was a ballet. Without cease, he employed both arms and legs, both hands and feet, shifting, steering, braking; grinding up; easing down. Number 141 was heavy.

But Ignacio was not so busy that he could not chat a little. The miles passed. His confidence grew. "The truck is heavily loaded, Señor Ministro," Ignacio proclaimed. "I perceive the others are too. Considering the location where we picked up these boxes, I am imagining that the cargo is highly valuable."

"I am grateful for your willingness to be involved with this effort, Ignacio, is it?" Negrín avoided direct response.

"Yes, Ignacio. Most people call me Nacho.'"

"Your dedication is noteworthy, *camarada*, and will, I think, be remembered by posterity. Have you traveled this route before now?"

"No, Minister. I anticipate we will require until sundown to raise our destination. I have never before traveled this way. The road, Señor Ministro, he has his reputation and his pride. He is reluctant to yield. He is resentful of our presence."

"All the better, then, that you are vigilant and persevering. Socialism will prosper in the hands of men of Spain such as yourself."

Nacho had confidence to probe a little. "I am imagining, Minister, that the importance of our cargo and of its secure arrival in Cartagena cannot be exaggerated."

"So it is," Negrín deflected. "And with diligence, we shall see it safe at our destination in time for a late supper. And you, Nacho, will have the satisfaction of knowing that this morning, you are performing an important service to the advancement and preservation of socialism in Spain."

Nacho couldn't give a flip less for the cause of socialism. He had been assigned to this job. Besides, he needed the money. In his view, the finance minister and his lousy socialism had wrecked Spain's economy and cost a lot of blokes like Nacho their jobs. "I am being well paid, for which I am grateful." Nacho concealed his true feelings and continued to affect self-effacement. "But if our cargo is as valuable as I imagine, Minister, have you taken thought for avoiding an ambush or some other attempt to waylay us as we move along?"

"You are persistent, young man." Negrín cocked an eyebrow.

Nacho hazarded pursed lips and raised eyebrows.

"Yes and no," Negrín finally answered directly. "It was thought dangerous to arm the drivers and their mates. Fear there was of mutiny and theft of the cargo, you know."

"With respect, Señor Ministro, this whole country's at war. There are stray guns and unsupervised gangs of thugs everywhere."

"All that was considered."

"Then there are no weapons in the convoy at all?"

"None I'm afraid."

"I'm not sure that was wise, sir," said Nacho, emboldened. "Should we perhaps stop for a break and plan with the other drivers some action to take in the event of trouble?"

"No, Nacho, no time. We are proceeding well. Please drive on."

⤜⤛

Pelotón G set up at the bottom of a steep hill where the road turned sharply left. The Hispano was nearly long enough to block the entire road but not quite. After some maneuvering, they got it located past the curve and blocking oncoming traffic. But there had not been any traffic, oncoming or otherwise, other than the previous groups of trucks. Gato had chosen a desolate spot. He expected nothing to pass until time came.

Gato's expectation was that the convoy would slow coming down off the hill and fail to see the Hispano until it was on top of it. There would be no choice but an emergency stop with all the confusion and uncertainty that went with it. The convoy would bunch up.

The rest of the plan was simple. With the trucks all stopped in proximity, the pelotón would jump out into the open, brandish their weapons, and extricate the drivers and tie them up. Team members would drive the trucks and their cargo back to the finca. Gato would toss the car key to one of the drivers. After they worked their way loose, the drivers could leave in the car. No sense in hurting other workers or leaving them stranded.

There were three single-shot rifles and a shotgun that belonged to the patrón. Gato had a pistol. Ammunition was limited, but it wouldn't matter. Madrid had advised that the convoy was unarmed. In addition to the firearms, there were two stout wooden clubs the anarchists had fashioned out of oakwood found back at the finca.

The pelotón failed to take notice that the dust at the bottom of the hill was deep. Back and forth movements of the big car had left visible tracks—ones differentiable from those of Negrín's previously passing trucks.

MOSCOW GOLD | 31

In accordance with anarchist practice, the organization of the pelotón was democratic—so much so that it lacked adequate command and control. If Gato had taken note of the tracks, and if he had ordered them swept, no one would have obeyed. In addition, no one made the effort to hike up the hill and verify that the roadblock was hidden by the curve.

The chosen area was barren of significant plant life, rocks, or other cover so the team took shelter in and behind the big Hispano.

Nothing now but to wait.

⁓

As he drove along, Nacho continued ruminating on the possibility that the convoy might be attacked. In number 141, he was second in line behind 140. Nacho had noticed that 140's driver seemed competent, but his driving was uninspired. He was not overly cautious, but neither was he aggressive.

One-forty crested a solitary hill, and the driver applied its brakes, reacting to the steep downgrade ahead. As he crested the hill, Nacho pulled into the oncoming lane to have a look forward. The road bent left at the bottom of the hill. One forty slowed more. Nacho had come up close to even with its rear wheels.

Now Nacho saw the wheel tracks in in the dirt at the bottom of the hill. Some vehicle had been maneuvering there but after the convoy next ahead had passed. A split second later, Nacho saw the glint of sunlight off chrome—the bumper of a car. Blocking the road just past the end of the curve. Nacho stomped on the accelerator. The Ford's big V-8 responded with a howl, and 141 leapt forward into the lead.

"It's a roadblock, Minister," Nacho shouted over the roar. Negrín could only stare wide-eyed at the unfolding scene.

Nacho careered down toward the curve, going too fast to make the turn. The rear of the Hispano coming into view. Men with guns in and behind it. One forty-one's speed and clouds of flying dust confused them. They reacted slowly.

Nacho went for the brake and double-clutched the transmission into his next lower gear. Still slowing, he saw he wouldn't make the turn, not without cutting the corner and hitting the car. Rifles and a pistol coming up now.

What the hell! Stupid bastards set up their roadblock where there's almost room on the right to pass.

"Hold on, Minister! It's an ambush! The idiots are all in and around the car. If I can pop the car just right, we might get by. We're going to hit," Nacho hollered.

Nacho aimed 141 at the right rear corner of the phaeton. It was a perfect shot. He hit with enough force to cue ball the car out of his way but obliquely enough to let 141 keep moving forward. The Hispano crashed forward into a dirt embankment on the left of the road. It spread its occupants and those sheltering behind it all over the ambush site.

One forty-one was damaged. Nacho ground on the accelerator. He still had good momentum even after the hit. The crash had slowed him just enough to make the turn without falling off onto the right shoulder. He caught another gear and roared forward. Desultory shots fired through the dust screen 141 had kicked up—not hitting.

Nacho looked back. One forty had got it figured out and had stayed with Nacho. He vigorously waved 140 past. One forty-one coasted to a stop and Nacho was out on its running board and then in the road, windmilling his arms, urging the others to keep moving, to pass on ahead. They all did, intensifying the small haboob that Nacho had created.

Pelotón G was in disarray. Two were pinned under the Hispano, and the three that had been in the car were knocked about. One bled from a head wound. The ambush had been a fiasco. Gato lacked the initiative to pursue. He called retreat. The pelotón abandoned the car and melted away into dusty landscape back toward the finca.

❧

As the dust began to settle, Nacho helped Negrín out. They sheltered behind 141's cab. Nacho could see the Hispano in the distance. It looked abandoned. The attackers had fled.

"Well, there was a little excitement," said an insouciant Negrín. "You were right. They tried to bushwhack us. We shall need to be vigilant as we continue our journey, Nacho. Your fast action and driving skill seem to have saved us this time. Thank you for protecting my shipment."

"We were lucky, Minister. The ambush was amateurish. Whoever laid it on was incompetent. We'd have never gotten by had it been done right," Nacho replied.

One forty-one's left fender was stove in, and its bumper bent against the wheel. Otherwise, damage was minimal.

"Help me bend this fender back, Minister, please."

Negrín complied, and between them, the two got the metal clear. A crowbar was produced, and with a strong heave by Nacho, the bumper was moved just enough to let the left front wheel turn free.

Back in the cab, Nacho got 141 going again, and he resumed his place behind 140. The convoy now motored on. Nacho noticed that Negrín was bleeding.

"You are injured, Minister," Nacho stated the obvious.

"I cut my hand on the fender," Negrín downplayed it, unflappable as ever. "I doubt that it is serious. I'm a doctor after all. I will show it off as a war wound back in Madrid—at the bank. I shall recommend us both for medals."

❧

As stolid 141 rattled onward, Negrín struggled to remain alert. He dozed occasionally. Then he startled awake.

"Spain is a high-altitude country," Negrín said as he looked at his map. "In Europe, only Switzerland can claim higher average ground. The meseta rises almost everywhere rapidly from the sea. It is so on our approach to Cartagena. The land will descend abruptly and deposit us into town. You will see."

Nacho did see. The road dropped them precipitously into the pretty little port town. There was a fine bay. Nacho drove down into the town center along the waterfront.

Far around to the west of Cartagena center, Nacho and Negrín made their destination. The stone fort called La Batería de Castillos and its inner sanctum, the Magazines of Algameca.

The unloading of the earlier trucks had proceeded with gratifying efficiency. One forty-one and its convoy were attended to and dispatched for the night. Negrín found the captain of the guard. "And the train?"

"Arrived about three hours ago. There were no issues. The train is unloaded. All has been secured here in the magazines."

"Excellent news! There is a last convoy of eight trucks following this one. When they arrive, that will be everyone."

"Very good, Minister. Was your journey without incident?" inquired the captain, trying to be polite.

'Oh, yes, quite. Nothing out of the ordinary," said Negrín airily. "No excitement at all."

Nacho could only shake his head.

As he had hoped, Negrín was in time for late supper. Leading away from Cartagena's port and its piers was a large, paved expanse marked off by numerous government buildings of upscale quality. These included majestic Victorian-era City Hall and the Pensión Oriente.

The Pensión Oriente was flamboyant. Painted brick red, it was white trimmed with little balconies and impossibly ornate railings. The dining room was reserved for guests and their invitees. On this evening, it was busy and cheerful. Period furnishings amid a genteel bustle of the waiters and the faint odor of the carnauba wax used to care for the parquet floors promised to operate in Negrín's culinary favor.

His dinner companion that Negrín liked arrived first. They had time to share a *jerez*. Capitán Vicente Romero de Tavares was a career naval officer. Captain Romero would be instrumental in the next phase of movement of the shipment to its destination. He and Negrín had been friends since university days.

"Is it here, Juan?" the Romero asked after they had embraced.

"Indeed. We spilt not a drop!" Negrín said with a touch of hubris.

"Where have you put it?" Romero asked without warmth or enthusiasm.

"La Batería de Castillos, in the Magazines of Algameca—all locked up and guarded by several drivers who are not returning with the rest."

"Juan, that's not enough. I will detail an armed guard with a subaltern and several dozen sailors of confidence to do the loading. It will take two or three days to get loaded." Captain Romero left the table, long enough to give orders to an aide stationed outside.

Negrín looked up and toward the entry. "Ah, the Russian arrives."

His dinner guest that Negrín didn't like was Stachevski. "May I present Captain Romero de Tavares of the Spanish Navy? Captain, this is Arthur Stachevski, Soviet commercial attaché. Señor Stachevski has arranged for the further forwarding of our shipment."

Romero stood to attention and gave a dour little bow. Negrín motioned them both to sit.

"The consignment is now present in Cartagena here?" Stachevski asked in Spanish that was accented, twisted syntactically, and grated on the ear.

Affecting blitheness Negrín responded, "Kind sir, that is a matter you must leave to me. The question is whether your ships are in port and seaworthy?"

The Russian's jaw clenched for a moment. Then came brief, unsmiling eye contact. "You well know that they are, Minister."

CHAPTER 3

Cartagena: Sunday, October 25, 1936

Since the Stachevski supper, Negrín had walked once or twice down to the Cartagena pier.

There he saw the ships. Nicholas II, the last czar of Imperial Russia had had four beautiful girls. These seagoing daughters of the revolution that had deposed poor Nicholas were not so fairly endowed. They were the *Neva*, the *Komsomol*, the *Red Pioneer*, and the *Novgorod*. Freighters of around 4,500 tons each, they appeared frumpy and plain. There was something about Soviet steel that allowed it to rust a bright orange. Prevalent streaks of this were these sisters' sole notable adornment.

Negrín commended himself on the stroke of genius it had been to insist on four freighters. Stachevski had objected, the parsimonious weasel. Yet his penuriousness had been no match for Dr. Juan Negrín's powers of persuasion.

It was not possible to insure this shipment, Negrín assured himself—not for anything near what it was worth. Like they used to do in the heyday of Mediterranean piracy, he spread his cargo among several vessels. That way, if he lost one, the rest would get through and he would not be ruined.

∽

Korvettenkapitän Josef Staupitz of the German Kriegsmarine had been in Cartagena for a week. His ardor for the Spanish revolt had been on the point of cooling. Until today. Eleven months he had been in Spain. He had welcomed the overture to go there when it had been made late last fall. Be seconded to the Abwehr. Have an opportunity to work for the mercurial Admiral Wilhelm Canaris.

He lolled on the verandah of Cartagena's Marina Club. Scion of a long line of middle-class salt merchants from the north of Bavaria, "Sepp" Staupitz was not the classic Aryan. Aryan or not, Sepp believed in Germany. Moreover, he was, without pause, loyal to the navy, to the Abwehr, and to Admiral Canaris.

Sepp had undertaken his intelligence duties in the Spanish war with energy and dedication. They were an opportunity to frustrate and impede the singular menace of communism. They got him onto the playing field of world events. He could have influence and, convicted as he was of a coming wider European conflict beyond Spain, he would gain invaluable experience and training. He relished having purpose and being in the fight.

Of under medium height, his wiry hair was black to go with large and intelligent dark brown eyes. Small-boned and delicate, he was nonetheless trim and healthy appearing. When he wore it, the blue-black *Kriegsmarine* uniform set off his olive skin. What he may have missed in physical stature he more than compensated for in streetwise commonsense intelligence and persevering curiosity.

Such attributes, a potential liability inside the Reich, well suited his clandestine brief in Spain. His reports were at first viewed at Abwehr headquarters with hesitancy due to his novice status as a spy. But he had native talent for the work. Soon the Tirpitzufer had accorded grudging appreciation for his work, and now it was anticipated with eagerness, although nobody would admit that eagerness to his face.

Upon arrival in Cartagena, Sepp fixed his attention on the Marina Club. It offered him a useful vantage point for surveillance of Cartagena's working port and for making innocuous contact—should the need arise. It was an ideal place for Sepp to indulge his natural curiosity.

In civilian clothes and affecting his cover identity as agent for Nijders en van Maalen, NV, a large Rotterdam maritime supply company, he had both motive and opportunity for spending a portion of this quiet Sunday afternoon in close observation of port operations.

Before coming to Spain, Sepp had taken a rudimentary course in tradecraft. There had been intensive language study. Sepp continued to speak Spanish with his natural German accent—an accent that everyone in Spain, as intended, assumed was Dutch. His knowledge of ships and experience of the sea enabled convincing and natural participation in most matters maritime, not to mention in the conduct of considerable genuine business for his "company." The company, in truth, was in and operated out of Hamburg. Its name and a cosmetic office were all that resided in Holland.

Sepp's cover was good. He had a natural affinity for clandestine work. Sepp had found spying for Canaris exhilarating, especially at first. Sepp was not a highly committed Nazi. His great ardor was reserved for the Abwehr and for espionage.

Sepp admired his chief. The admiral had a long history with Spain. He had been interned here while a submarine officer in the Great War. After becoming involved with clandestine work, he was reputed to have made numerous and surreptitious returns. Canaris's anticipation of the outbreak of the present rebellion had been dead-on accurate. His prescience had put him in position to manipulate the rising of the Spanish military to the Reich's and his own personal advantage.

It had been a good run for Staupitz in Spain. But as summer turned to fall, Franco's offensive on Madrid had slowed and now threatened

MOSCOW GOLD | 41

to stall. Interest in naval matters waned. Sepp languished a little. Then Berlin got a whiff of the Finance Ministry in Madrid co-opting unusual amounts of motor transport. Berlin dispatched Sepp to Cartagena to watch and listen. Observe and report had been his instructions. Take no independent action.

He'd been observing in Cartagena a week now. At first there was little to report. Then off the port authority's shipping list Sepp had learned of the impending arrival of four Soviet freighters from Odessa. On the second afternoon, he looked up from his beer at the Marina Club and saw the forlorn Russian rust buckets make port.

He had nosed around on the Calle de la Muelle. The Soviet sailors had not been granted shore leave. There was no chance of picking up anything in the quayside bars or brothels. From the Marina Club vantage point Sepp did see some of their unloading. Crates. Some sixty of them. Long and thin crates, of evident light weight. After that, fifteen more—these stubby and square, heavier and unbalanced as if all the weight were on one end.

Sepp reflected on the off-load. A dozen or more biplane aircraft it looked like. It was a fair bet, too, that the Russians would not deadhead back. He figured they would be embarking an important return cargo, but he had not yet ascertained what it might be

Then midweek there had been something of a *conmoción* in the city. Large groups of trucks ground into town and unloaded sub-rosa at La Batería. Units of the Spanish Republican Navy, two destroyers and a cruiser, arrived.

A gaggle of senior officers disembarked, but there was no leave for their crews either.

Orders were orders, but Sepp knew he would never solve the mystery of these shipments unless he took some action. Besides, Admiral Canaris was tolerant of his junior officers taking initiative.

He observed from the Marina Club the depositing at the freighters' gangways of average-sized but heavy boxes—lots of them. He needed to get in and have a look.

The crates came by truck during the day to a barbed wire–enclosed staging area. There were 500 to 750 crates in the staging area at any one time. The site was illuminated at night by temporary arc lights. It was bright enough, Sepp observed, but there were shadowed areas.

Sepp decided on Sunday night to early Monday morning between 2:30 and 4:00. He could brazen it out by laying hands on a Spanish enlisted navy uniform and crashing the front gate. He debated whether to carry weapons. In the end, he decided on maximum stealth and minimum violence.

The loading operations were taking place during daylight. The site, quiet at night, was guarded by a squad of armed Spanish sailors. In the darker places, crates would be arranged flat, and off-duty sailors would bed down on them.

The German spy dressed himself all in black and put on a black balaclava and gloves. He went armed with wire cutters and a cat's paw. The staging area backed up against a disused and rusty crane around which the dockers had created a junkyard for cast-off equipment.

First, Sepp had to get past the main gate. In the deepest part of the night, he approached on foot and hid in the shadow of the guard shack. There was a single guard. There was no trade at this time of night. The guard played a radio and, off and on, picked up and looked at a pulp novel. Sepp waited. Finally, the guard decided to have a smoke; he abandoned his shack and wandered a few yards onto the port grounds before lighting up.

Sepp slithered through the guard post and into the darkness beyond. Next, he jinked across the port and padded undetected and out of breath into the junkyard. He hid himself under the abandoned and rusty bucket of some sort of excavating machine. He now had full view of the loading site.

The midnight patrolling was not energetic—four sentries in two pairs. Once every ten minutes, one pair separated from the front of the enclosure, walked the perimeter, and met at the back. The other pair itinerated randomly through the interior. The four chattered and joked with each other and their resting comrades. It was not a high-alert situation.

As soon as the perimeter sentries had turned and started back, Sepp slid up to the fence, wire cutters already out. Slicing the barbed wire made a deafening snapping noise. At least the wire was not thick. He was through unnoticed in half a minute.

Sepp stayed low and sneaked across to the closest row of crates. There was no space in between rows to hide. He would have to lie on top, but here, there was a sleeping sailor. He would need to penetrate the enclosure further. Well inside, he climbed on top of a row of crates stacked two high. The row was long enough he could stretch out and mimic a sleeper. Just ahead of him was a single crate on the ground. The crates were heavy and wooden. Their lids were attached with numerous and stout nails; they were not intended to be casually opened.

Absolutely still, Sepp waited for his breath to even and his eyes to adjust. He needed to get out before the sentries came back around. They might spot the cut wire.

As he lay on his boxes, he could see the feet of another sleeper just to his left. He had to start. The cat's paw was out. The lid was down tight. His tool was not going in. He moved forward for better purchase and tried a corner. The pry bar went in a little. He hammered it in with his hand. It went slightly. Not enough.

His salty sweat stung his eyes. He worked the bar back and forth. Now he could pry up. The nails protested audibly. He stopped. No movement by the sleeper. The bar went in further, and he worked in a couple of fingers along with it. The lid came up a little. He got both hands in and lifted. The lid shrieked off. Sepp held still and then looked inside.

"*Scheisse*!!!" he breathed. Gold coins. Thousands of them. Glittering. Even in the low ambient light. All laid in rows. A huge fortune. Just in the one box.

It was time to get out. Sepp wrestled with his conscience. He picked one up. It would serve as evidence, he told himself. It went in his pocket.

The closest sleeper still hadn't moved. Sepp made no effort to reclose the crate. Unlawful entry would be suspected anyway come daylight when the cut wire was found.

He oozed off his crate bed and scuttled toward his hole in the wire. The sleeper there was stirring. Sepp had to wait till he settled. So far, neither of the internal sentries had approached, but this was taking too long. Now he heard the steps of the perimeter sentry crunching along the concrete. He lay down in the shadows at the foot of the box pile and tried to melt in.

The sentries met and exchanged comments in slangy Spanish that Sepp couldn't catch. Vigilance remained low. No alarm was raised. They retraced their steps.

Now he could move again. Crabwise to his hole, he went through it and back under the bucket.

CHAPTER 4

Cartagena: Monday, October 26, 1936

"There was an attempt last night on the shipment," Captain Romero told his friend.

"One of the sailors?"

"It is thought not. The perimeter wire was cut, and one crate broken open. If it had been the sailors, there would be no need to cut the wire. Nothing, or at least very little, was taken."

"When will the loading be complete?"

"Before siesta. We are expediting. Not taking a chance on another night on the dock."

After siesta, standing on the dock, his cargo now embarked, Negrín was content.

Just then, black exhaust urped up out of the funnels of the warships. Negrín watched them creep south toward the Mediterranean. The four Russian sisters also made smoke and groaned away from the quayside. The two little flotillas joined up and shaped course to the

MOSCOW GOLD | 47

southwest. They gave evidence of heading for Gibraltar and the open Atlantic beyond.

Sepp Staupitz also watched their departure. He congratulated himself with a sherry on the terrace of the Marina Club. The Spanish Navy was covering a huge shipment of gold—gold carried in Russian steamers, steamers that themselves had just dropped off important cargo.

As he composed his message to Canaris in his head, Sepp fingered a heavy American double eagle coin in his hand.

In this way did Doctor Juan Negrín López, Finance Minister of the Spanish Republic consign the great majority of his country's gold reserves to Soviet Russia. Then the fourth largest gold reserves in the world, the Spanish holdings consisted of 7,800 crates. It added to 500 metric tons, most of it in gold coin, Louis d'Or, British sovereigns, and United States double eagles. In 1936, it amounted to no less than 1,585,000,000 pesetas worth, well over three-quarters of a billion American dollars. The current threat to Madrid was acute. The gold needed protection—protection the Spanish capital could no longer provide. Besides, the Republic needed deliveries of men and matériel. These did not come cheap.

Madrid now had a considerable line of credit. Negrín felt his contentment was justified.

Captain Romero de Tavares made note of the freshening westerly wind as his ships left Cartagena astern and rounded Cape Tinoso. Distasteful as his current orders were, it was refreshing to be away from land. As torrid and arid as the south coast of Spain could be, the air was cool, wet, and sweet in the Straits. He was grateful for the respite

In accordance with arrangements made with the Soviet merchant captains while still in Cartagena, the four frumps assumed a box formation. Romero ordered his destroyers to take screening stations ahead of them. His cruiser brought up the rear, alert for straggling and other unwanted eventualities.

They plodded through quartering swells at nine knots and maintained a heading of 225 degrees until an hour after nightfall. With Cabo de Gata light on their starboard beam and when Romero felt that all appearances were that his convoy was headed for Gibraltar, he ordered a turn to port to a heading of 96 degrees, just south of east. On that heading, they ran all night direct for Algiers. At dusk the next day, thirty hours out of Cartagena, they raised the Algerian coast. The Spanish warships peeled off, reversed course, and made once again for Cartagena.

Captain Romero watched from the starboard wing of his bridge. The Russian buckets pointed up to a little north of east in the direction of Malta and disappeared into the eastern Mediterranean.

"A bad business this," he muttered in the direction of the binnacle.

CHAPTER 5

Odessa: Tuesday, November 3, 1936

Six slow days out of Cartagena, the four Russian freighters were home.

The voyage had been unremarkable. It had gone around Sicily and northeast to Turkey, up the Dardanelles, past Istanbul, through the Bosporus, across the Black Sea, and into Ukrainian Odessa.

Their story was not quite finished. Their ordeal was not quite over. Canaris's man in Odessa reported to his Abwehr officer that they had lain in the Odessa roadstead without docking and were unloaded by tenders at night.

The report was delivered to Admiral Canaris in Berlin. He noted it with interest and added it to a special file that he was maintaining in his personal office safe. The file already contained Staupitz's report from Cartagena.

A few ideas involving the Spanish gold shipment were bubbling inside the Abwehr admiral's fertile brain.

CHAPTER 6

Madrid: Wednesday, August 14, 1963

Café Gijón was empty.

This was as expected. Not even Isham had arrived yet. It was cool inside, even in the heat of the day. Must be the dark paneling. David sat near the back facing the door.

David hoped he wouldn't regret coming over here today. He knew he hadn't made a lot of good choices lately. He asked himself whether this one would change things.

There came Isham. He was taller than the average Spaniard, looking collected in an ecru linen suit, blue shirt, yellow bowtie, and Panama hat. Nobody would mistake him for a *madrileño*. He arrived empty-handed—not carrying the ubiquitous brown satchel that every other white-collar type in Madrid had. He breezed right in.

A hard guy to figure was Isham. The word that David had on him was that he was not an unintelligent man and had graduated from Cornell sometime before Pearl Harbor. It was said he did some nondescript staff officer job in the army in Europe. One never could get him to be very specific about that. It was a job that had let him stay in Europe after VE Day. He had participated in the occupation.

"Davey boy, thanks for coming down. What'll you have?"

"A Mahou." Good Spanish lager.

David didn't understand the cordiality. Isham didn't need it or a face-to-face to give David an assignment. He could demand whatever he wanted. *Why the soft sell?* David asked himself.

"What brings me here, Jack?" David let it out that he was not in the mood for chitchat. No waiter was in sight. Isham waved the barman over. He ordered David's beer and one for himself in passable but anglicized Spanish. It looked like the barman understood, anyway.

"In a hurry are you, boyo? C'mon, it's siesta. You know I know you don't have business somewhere else."

"My time's valuable, Jack."

"So's mine. And your point is? Don't you want to make like a couple of Spaniards? Some snappy repartee? Talk with our hands a little? You know. Two guys, three opinions? Lots of blah? No decisions? No action?"

David didn't bite. "Is there something about my articles? You've been putting them in."

Their drinks came. Isham drank off half of his.

"OK. Let's do it your way. We need more from you, David, lots more. Your stuff is workmanlike, but it's pedestrian, not exciting. Why *ever* would the good readers of the *Herald* be scintillated by production figures for lentil and garban*tho* beans?" He lampooned the peninsular accent, often mistaken for lisping, that turns some /s/ sounds into /th/.

David bristled, "They're staples of the Spanish diet, Jack. Good bean crops promote stability on the farms. That translates into reasonable prices in the cities. Franco's got a lot tied up in beans. Beans do well, and so does he. They go south, and he has problems. The government is pushing the agrarian economy. They want the people to stay on the farms, not flood the cities any more than they already are. Beans are a bellwether."

54 | DOUGLAS L. FIELD

"All well and good and all boring. Like I said, you're going to need to give us more. This pedestrian stuff you are into about the economy and business, we think it can form the basis for something better, more meaningful," Isham said, seeming not to get it.

David had thought more than once that Isham didn't see the story behind the story and that his journalist's instincts were not that good. Now he was acting ominous. David wondered who Isham was and what he was up to. Isham was not what David expected from his editor.

"Lemme get to the point. How do you like Franco?" Isham said.

"Franco? Sweet guy for a fascist dictator. He's their generalísimo—a general's general. Won 'em the civil war going away. What's not to like?" David looked around the café. Still empty. Good.

"You're smarter than that. Franco and the civil war are, in a way, two separate questions. By my lights, the bottom line on the Spanish Civil War is that both sides were ferociously vicious and breathtakingly inept. Leave out the ineptitude, and it wouldn't have been as violent or as long. Anyway, the side that was marginally less inept won in the end. Not much more to it than that."

"Did you want my evaluation of the civil war, Jack, or did you ask me here to give me a lesson in recent Spanish history?"

"*Your* evaluation of the civil war? Why would I want that? Let me get to Franco. Franco's a friend. Cunning little guy, but very brave. Fought like a fury in Morocco in the '20s. Don't fall for the conventional line on him. Oh, yeah, he did the dance early with Hitler and Mussolini. Hard to blame him. The civil war bled Spain. Hooking up with Hitler was a cheap way of getting a little revenge against Stalin for supporting the Republic. Franco wised up by '42; got and stayed neutral. Let us operate our agents, or, I should say, let the OSS run their people here. Even got that leftie twit Truman on board. Ike sealed the deal in '53 when he signed the Pact of Madrid with Franco. We got the bases in Rota and Torrejón, and Frankie got a ton of economic aid—a ton—aid he needed. Old Francisco's been pretty much an anti-Soviet stalwart since then."

"You want an article on Franco's foreign policy, Jack?" David faked innocence.

Now Isham bristled, "No. Like I said, you're smarter than that. Franco's a friend, and we want him to stay a friend. For that to happen, he has to stay in power. We can help. Did you read *ABC* this morning?"

"The Caudillo's personal news organ? Yeah. Matter of fact, I did. Look at it every day."

"'Madrid's leading monarchist daily' more accurately, David my boy," Isham corrected. "And what are they all lathered up about this morning? The pueblo of the year! Interior Ministry canvasses the whole country to find the small town of the year. Know who won?"

"Sigüenza. I had never heard of it," David admitted.

"Northeast of Madrid. In Guadalajara province, I think. Maybe Soria. Sigüenza, David, is the apotheosis of hardscrabble." Isham continued to pontificate. "That's Old Castile up there. Why is Franco's government plumping it like it was Provence or Tuscany?"

"It's not just Sigüenza or wherever it is," David interrupted. "It's all the provincial towns. They're trying to give small-town life enough cachet to keep the people there—stop them from crowding into Madrid, Barcelona, and Valencia. Related to why the bean crops are important. But he's not managing it."

"Bingo. I told you you were smart, kid."

"Just giving you the facts, Jack. That's what you pay me for."

"You're also a smart-ass. Franco's overextended. He can't keep the people out of the cities, and neither him nor his rich buddies have enough money to swing building them places to live."

By now, David's mind was wandering a little. Isham had a good handle on some of the realities of modern Spain. But David questioned whether Isham grasped the delicious irony of it all. Franco had made like a latter day El Cid and "reconquered" the country from the Republic, all to preserve the old order. Then it's Franco who ends up fulfilling the Republic's fondest dream of lifting the masses.

56 | DOUGLAS L. FIELD

"You invited me to Gijón and bought me a beer to sell me a flat?" David deadpanned innocently.

"Try to stay serious, David. You're smart, but don't overdo it. Like I said, Franco's a friend. We want him to stay a friend. Next guy to come in may not be a friend. The Iberian Peninsula secures the western flank in Europe. The British look after Portugal, and we're taking care of Spain. So, if we can do some little thing to help with Paco's problems, we should. We will."

David's suspicions were pricked, "Who's *we*, Jack? The *International Trib's* establishing a foreign policy? The new *realpolitik?* You want me to do some op-eds?"

"Op-eds? Of course not. You're an investigative reporter. *We*"— Isham made eye contact and raised an eyebrow—"are me and you, David. American patriots. Responsible citizens of the world and all that. Journalists in service of the common good. All that happy horse crap you learned in school. 'Journalism's a profession, not a business.' Remember? Want another brew? This is pretty good stuff. Must have been some Germans in in the woodpile here way back when."

"Belgians, Jack. The Mahou family is Belgian."

"That so? How do you know that? Smart lad, just like I said."

Isham got up and talked to the barman. Gijón was still quiet, cool, and empty. David realized that Isham had been in Spain a long time.

Isham's Spanish didn't seem all that bad. It looked like he knew the barman. David saw some tan-colored bills materialize from Isham's pocket, folded deftly in his hand, followed by a nimble, covert slip into the barman's pocket. Several hundred pesetas. Way more than a couple of beers. So that's why Isham talked so freely. He had just paid an installment on the barkeep's discretion bill.

Isham carried the beers back to the table himself. "Well, Davey boy, let me get to the point.'

David gave Isham a look that said, *At last!*

"Do you know about the 'Moscow Gold'?"

MOSCOW GOLD | 57

David did. "Sure. Everybody does. It was the primary asset of the Spanish treasury. Legend has it that it was sent by the Republic in 1936 to Russia for safekeeping and to pay for military supplies."

"Precisely. Spain had large gold reserves in 1936. Then in September and October of 1936, the Republicans loaded it out of the bank and took it to Cartagena—'for safekeeping' supposedly. But then it disappeared."

David added, "It went to Moscow to pay Stalin for military assistance. Why are you telling me all this, Jack? Sounds like you know everything there is to know about it."

"Not at all. Being friends, we understand that Franco could use that money just now."

"He's an hour late and a peseta short, Jack. All that's twenty-seven, twenty-eight years ago."

"Maybe. Maybe not. You are going to investigate it. Learn everything you can. Find out where the gold is. El Oro de Moscú they call it. Write the story. Get your byline out there. Win a prize or two. And there'll be a nice bonus in it for you—every journalist's dream. Just get it done and get it done right."

Isham affected blasé nonchalance most of the time. Now, in a moment, David saw that he changed. His expression turned flinty and his eyes cold.

"Two things before I go. The gold story is an order. Don't let it enter your calculating and devious little mind to blow us off. It looks to us like you have it good here in Madrid. Plenty of money. Plenty of play. Nice friends. We know what we're paying you versus how you live. I hear the Spanish cops are nosing around. Neither one of us would want them taking any extra interest in you, would we? Hate to see your gig spoiled or you get deported or worse, yeah?"

"What?!? You threatening me, Jack?"

Isham responded with a disdainful look. "And the second thing. Be careful, Bucko. Franco's not the sole interested party. Bad as you might think he is, anybody else is worse. That gold's hot. All kinds of people been trying to get their hands on it since the night it left the Banco de España."

The big man grabbed his hat and got up to leave. "If you want a hint, Largo Caballero and Negrín are dead, but Negrín's still got family somewhere in Paris. That pinko Portillo is there too. They were all involved."

Isham took a few steps toward the door and turned back. "And, by the way, we need it yesterday. As they say."

Then he was gone.

David stayed in his seat for a few minutes more. He finished his beer and reflected on Isham's conversation. On the pronouns primarily. Strange selection of first person versus third and plural versus singular.

David was left alone to reflect.

Who the hell are "we," Jack, and who the hell are you to threaten me? And over a cold story.

There were few alternatives. Two maybe. Smart money would pack up and leave Spain. Live to fight another day. Avoid risk. Leave all the unanswered questions behind. Put a stop to all the manipulation. Bag out. David did not like being leveraged this way.

But David knew Isham was right. David did have it good in Madrid. In some ways, the gold story could be tasty. David's only alternative was to go ahead and do it.

A few more patrons were drifting into the Café Gijón. Siesta was over.

MOSCOW GOLD | 59

PART II
¡NO PASARÁN!

CHAPTER 7

Berlin: Friday, November 6, 1936

Wilhelm Canaris waited for his Spain agent to arrive.

His office was ceremonial, with high ceilings, a monumental desk, Renaissance tapestries, heavy framed photos, and souvenirs gathered from a long and successful career. Mementos included a red-and-gold silk. Spanish flag with embroidered royal coat of arms that he collected when he had docked the *U-29* at San Sebastián in 1917.

A restrained tap sounded at the door. Sepp Staupitz walked in, stood to attention, and saluted. "I've been down in Cartagena, sir."

"A pleasant Spanish town that. I've been there. What do you have for us? Good stuff as usual. I've read your report, but I want to hear directly." Canaris waved Sepp to a seat.

"Yes, sir, it is," Staupitz began. "A large shipment of heavy crates. Thousands of them. My orders were to observe and report. I decided to interpret them liberally. Broke into their staging area late one night. Popped open one of the boxes."

"Your initiative in disobeying your orders is noted and forgiven." The admiral smiled. "And what was *in* these boxes?"

MOSCOW GOLD | 63

Sepp held up his American double eagle. "This, sir, and a very great many more like it." He set the coin on the admiral's desk.

"Beautiful! Keep it. A souvenir."

"Any idea where they landed it?" Sepp asked.

"Odessa. Lehrmann reports similar ships arrived there Tuesday. That's about the right amount of time for the trip. They unloaded at night and in secrecy. He couldn't tell what the cargo was."

"Negrín sent their gold. Negrín's a snake." Sepp stated.

"Thus, it would appear."

Canaris took a moment to mull the intelligence over. "Well, that gold won't do old Koba any good lying around the basement of the Kremlin. There may be a way for the Abwehr to convert this matter to its own interests, Sepp."

Sepp looked back at his chief—noncommittal.

"We will watch for it to be sold. The usual outlets, Paris, Amsterdam, Geneva, Budapest, Cairo. No need to worry about their trying to fence it here in the Reich, I think. When he starts to move it, then we'll know. I'd say he goes with a single location. Bastard's not very creative sometimes. I intend for the Abwehr to keep track of who they use to liquidate it. That intelligence will be revealing and useful."

Staupitz said nothing.

"Also, Sepp." The admiral paused for effect. "The Abwehr may in time like to have access to that money. The *Abwehr*, Sepp, you know what I mean—not the SS, not Himmler, not Heydrich, not the Reichsbank—the Abwehr. We, you and I, Sepp, will do what needs to be done."

64 | DOUGLAS L. FIELD

CHAPTER 8

Moscow: Saturday, November 7, 1936

Ioseb Vissarionovich Dzhugashvili stood, arachnoid, under cover in the Moscow Kremlin's Grand Courtyard.

Keeping well back and sheltered from the freezing rain, he monitored the final delivery of the Stachevski Shipment. "The Stachevski Shipment, my ass!" Stalin growled. "Who thought up that name? Maybe I'll put Beria on that one. I exiled that *nekulturny* oaf Stachevski to Spain so he would rot in the heat, and now his name is on *my* shipment."

It looked like a race as to whether the sleet or the crates would pile up faster. It was the last leg of a long journey. The work party handling the boxes were Soviet sailors all. This far inland even, all were sweating and straining in the cold.

Means the crates are full. This is good. Negrín sent it all!

Commander Yuri Letchkov, in overall charge of the transfer, approached deferentially. "Unloading is all but complete, comrade. The weather worsens. It will be preferable to secure the shipment indoors."

"Have it taken to the Goskhran, the State Depository for Valuables—direct. And, Comrade Commander, make a through and detailed inventory. Omit nothing. Not a single kopek, yes? Have the inventory brought to me straightaway in my office upon completion."

"Aye, aye, Comrade Stalin."

Letchkov did not withdraw.

"Was there something else, Commander?"

"Yes, sir. The Spanish ambassador. Inside. Waiting to see you."

Stalin turned and went in.

"Good afternoon, Comrade Chairman," said the Spaniard with a formal little bow. "I see that our consignment has arrived."

"Our consignment, yes," said Stalin with the lift of one bushy eyebrow.

"We need now to complete certain matters of, how shall I say it, documentation, no?" the ambassador went on.

"Documentation, sir?"

"Yes, Comrade Chairman. A receipt in full. A joint statement as to the agreed upon value of our assets in hard currency. The unit cost of the items we will be purchasing. Terms of shipment of them. Disposition and return of all assets remaining at the conclusion of our hostilities. It is reasonable that we would expect this."

"Of course, of course," Stalin prevaricated. "I will have my finance and foreign ministers be in touch with your embassy promptly." The Soviet leader turned and walked away.

Reciting an old Russian proverb under his breath Stalin said, "The Spanish will sooner see their own ears than ever again see their gold."

CHAPTER 9

Madrid: Sunday, November 8, 1936

Nacho Arjona was risking his life.

The battlefront had gotten all the way to the Paseo del Pintor Rosales—almost anyway. Pintor Rosales was where Nacho needed to be.

Arjona, a *rubio,* had reddish hair and light brown eyes that shaded to beige. The coloring was not unknown for a Spaniard but unusual, nonetheless. Not the greatest time, this, to be unusual.

Nacho compensated and did his best to fit in by dressing in a *mono,* the workers' uniform, a royal blue boiler suit. There was something of a pun there. *Mono* meant "single," referring to the one-piece, monochrome coverall garment, but it also meant "monkey." Arjona completed the effect with sleeves rolled above the elbows; *alpargatas,* the canvas, rope-soled shoes of the proletariat; and a greasy beret.

Nacho was part of the Nationalist Cóndor spy network. Nacho took his orders and made his reports to Cóndor himself. It had been Cóndor last month who had detailed Nacho to a driving assignment. It had been good fortune that the finance minister himself had ridden in Nacho's truck. Nacho had reported on Negrín's conversation and his attitudes and state of mind.

Cóndor was displeased to learn that the gold had been sent, but the whole point of spying was to get information, not just favorable information. Cóndor had intimated that his superiors were already devising what he called "means and methods" to get the money returned—something about international pressure. Nacho thought the whole idea fanciful. The gold was gone.

The rapid rebel advance in the late summer and fall across large chunks of the south and west of Spain had put intense pressure on Madrid. Moving around the city had become an art. The streets were choked with refugees from the provinces, their animals and possessions gathered to them in great obstructive piles. Intersections of moment were barricaded with lumber, bits of barbed wire, dressers, armoires and dining tables, donkey carts, and the odd sandbag.

Complicating it all were the *checas*. Every faction, party, and movement had them—roving bands of armed thugs. Escuadrilla del Amanecer, Dawn Patrol they called themselves, or the Iron Column. Formed of displaced Republican fighters from Extremadura and Toledo, they were irked, irritated, and itching for revenge.

Armed and angry, they were capricious and erratic. You could be arrested at the slightest whim or provocation. They dragged you before some hastily cobbled "tribunal." Then they shot you or let you go. Madrid under the warlords.

He had a cover story as a baker's deliveryman. Even so, it was dangerous. The more you were out and on open ground, the more you were vulnerable to checa arrest.

The *franquistas* were bombing and shelling the city. They purposed to terrorize the population into surrender—all except for Salamanca. Franco had wealthy friends in Salamanca barrio.

The less affluent, including Nacho, had taken to seeking refuge underground in the Metro stairways and platforms. Madrid had no air raid shelters. Whenever the sirens started, crowds mobbed the

Metro. Great *avalanchas* of humanity surged down. Nowadays, the hordes weren't going back up because the attacks were so frequent. Despite nonexistent sanitation facilities, no food, and no water, still, they stayed. Still the resistance held.

The rebel General Emilio Mola had stoked the fires of the defenders' hatred and bitterness. Tall, bespeckled, nondescript looking, but ruthless and dangerous, he had boasted back in early October that he would be having coffee on the Gran Vía by October 14.

Mola was approaching Madrid from the north with four columns of seasoned troops. When asked which of the four would reach the city first, he made a wry comment about a "Fifth Column" of secret Nationalist supporters already within the city.

The general did have a fifth column in Madrid. Cóndor was running it. Nacho, to his significant peril, was part of it. It had been stupid of Mola to have indulged his outsized ego and bragged about it. The Fifth Column remark backfired. After Mola made it, no one in Madrid was safe. Thousands of killings followed. Nacho's activities became more perilous.

Mola hadn't made his coffee date on the Gran Vía either. In a display of snark, the Café Molinero, located on that great boulevard, at all times kept a table *"reservado"* for him.

Day by day, the rebels got closer. Pueblo after pueblo fell—Illescas, Torrejón, Getafe—each one proclaimed to be "the key" to undoing Madrid's defenses. Franco announced that the "liberation" of Madrid was near. They got closer, but they didn't get all the way there.

For Nacho, living in Madrid under siege became more perilous by the day. His optimism waxed and waned. Waiting, hoping, doing what he could, he soldiered on with threat to his liberty and his life at fever pitch and growing daily as the rebel forces advanced.

∾

Ahumada's Bakery was located on Calle de Cuchilleros well down in the medieval rabbit warren of alleys, *callejuelas,* and passageways in the Old City. Easy to get lost in there. Easy to stay lost. Nacho arrived at the bakery before dawn. Ahumada had already made a good start on his day's production.

"I wasn't sure I would get this here," Nacho wheezed, and he slid into the shop and bolted the door. "I had to run part of the way. Checas don't like to see people out early."

Nacho lived in a pair of rented rooms on the Calle de Carretas south of Puerta del Sol. A bed and a basin, bathroom down the hall. Heat if he was lucky. To get to the bakery, he had to go through Plaza Mayor to access Calle de Cuchilleros. He could go by Calle Mayor or Calle de Alcalá. Calle Mayor was through Sol and busier, so he took Alcalá. The checas hid in the shadows of doorways and alleys, out of sight and the light of the streetlamps.

As he was entering the plaza, they shouted at him from behind to stop. They hadn't seen him until he was past. He ignored them and walked on to the Cuchilleros exit. They continued to yell at him. Once around the corner he tore down the steps three at a time. At the bottom he kept running till he got to Ahumada's. It had not seemed that they gave chase. They often were lazy and would not. You never knew.

"Good of you to show up," Ahumada groused, unsympathetic.

"Busy night. There's news we need to pass to Cóndor. Here's the message." Nacho handed him a small light blue scroll of paper.

"You should use white, Aníbal," Ahumada scolded. "Less likelihood of detection." Aníbal, Hannibal, was Nacho's clandestine network name. Cóndor acted as Ahumada's controller as well.

"Blue's all I had. No time to find white. Have to take the chance."

Earlier, in the middle of the night Nacho, as Aníbal, had encoded the message.

Cóndor had set him up with what was called a "one-time pad"—a simple substitution code. In this case, the code was based on Espasa Calpe's 1933 edition of the great Clarín's *La Regenta*. *La Regenta*, the nineteenth-century realist novel by Leopoldo Alas y Ureña, pen name

Clarín. Nacho did not much read writers like Clarín but supposed that, if his name had been Ureña, he would change it too.

The tedium of encoding was massive. As today was "11/8," he used page 118 of the book. A number was assigned to each letter of the alphabet, "A" was 1, "B" was 2, and so on. The numbers of the letters of the message were then added to the numbers of the letters of the text starting with the first letter on page 118. The sum of the addition was then translated back into letters. The code was thus produced. Mere reversal of the process yielded the reappearance of the original message.

Encoding and decoding was taxing and exacting work. Nacho kept his messages short. No one other than Aníbal, Cóndor, and the rebel forces' intelligence officer knew that *La Regenta* was the key. A one-time pad is unbreakable unless the breaker has the key. Almost anyone could be taught to use one. No special equipment or intensive training was required. It was good for making civil war on a limited budget.

The message, based on reliable Aníbal sources, advised that Franco's plan of assault on the capital and order of battle was known to the defenders in Madrid. Massive, frantic preparations to repel the attack were being made.

For clarity, the encoding appeared in large block printing on a piece of baby blue stationery. When he was finished, Nacho rolled his message into a tight little scroll. The scroll he further rolled together with some tobacco into a handmade cigarette. The "pregnant" smoke went tucked behind his ear.

Ahumada inserted the scroll into one of his yet unbaked loaves. He gave that loaf an extra score on top. For reasons long obscured by history and tradition, the Spanish call a typical large loaf of bread a *pistola*. The usual pistola had four scores. One with five was distinctive if you knew the convention. The extra slash was innocuous if you didn't. Most people didn't. This scoring expedient ensured that the message-bearing loaf would be the one delivered to its intended recipient. Foolproof. Numerous "fours" and the one "five" then went straight into the oven.

"Let's have a smoke while they bake. They should arrive today, no?" Ahumada said, referring to the rebel army.

"Don't be so sure. That's what this is all about," Nacho answered, tilting his head toward the oven.

~

Nacho fidgeted and chain-smoked while he waited. He knew that the opposition would even now be flooding troops and resources into the central city—no doubt in part acquired by the gold assets Nacho had helped transport out of Madrid.

It was imperative Cóndor got the word that the defenders had adjusted their defense. The assault on Madrid had to succeed. Now, here was real danger it would not. The war needed to be won in the next day or so; if not, it would go on forever. Whatever the risk, Nacho had to get the message through.

"They're done," rasped Ahumada. With a slim hooked bar, he slid his pans out of the oven and onto a cooling table. A dozen and a half loaves were segregated out for Arjona, including the one bearing the extra cut.

"OK. Let's get them loaded. I gotta go."

"Patience, Aníbal. Get in a hurry and get caught," Ahumada gruffed.

The delivery vehicle for the Ahumada Bakery was Nacho's bicycle. A lightweight platform had been welded to its fork and handlebars. On top of that resided a little canvas tent.

Ahumada loaded the loaves into the tent at his own pace. Nacho continued to be twitchy. The setup was for fast and efficient delivery to Ahumada's customers. Once in a while, they got to their destinations still warm from the oven.

If Nacho were stopped by one of the checas, he had the plausible cover of a bakery man delivering his goods. Unless you knew the sign, the loaves all looked alike.

"All right. You're set. Get outta here," ordered Ahumada.

By the time Nacho finally left the bakery, a faint lightening started in the eastern sky. He slunk through the old town. He avoided the Gran Vía and the Royal Palace. But now he ran out of back streets. It would be four long and open blocks on the wide Calle de Ferraz to Pintor Rosales.

That's where they got him. He was riding past the Sabatini Gardens at the north end of the Royal Palace, just entering Ferraz. The whole place looked deserted; it was not quite yet dawn. From behind a fountain at the bottom of the Plaza de España, they surprised him. Four of them. Unwashed, slovenly and smelly. Carbines slung over their shoulders. Muzzles pointed at the dirt. One in front, three spreading out behind. Nacho stopped and stood astride his bike.

"You're out early, *compadre*. What you got there?" This came from the one in front. His days-old beard didn't obscure an acne-scarred face. He was doubtless the duly elected leader.

Nacho cowered a little, "Ahumada's Bakery. Fresh bread. Deliveries up toward Moncloa."

"Lot of fighting around there yesterday, more today. Dangerous place," grunted one from behind.

"Pistolas for the fighters at the front." Nacho tried a little word play. "The defenders have to eat."

Not amused, Leader unshouldered his weapon. Nacho could hear the others do likewise. He resisted turning to look.

"Let's have a look, funny man."

Leader lifted the little tent with the point of his gun. "And if you're just another Francoite rat? Mola says the city's full of them, doesn't he, boys?"

Murmurs from behind.

Nacho stayed silent.

MOSCOW GOLD | 73

"We caught two. Day before yesterday. Turned them over to the militia. Heard they were shot."

Act subservient. They deal in terror and expect you to cringe. Don't disappoint them, but don't overdo it.

"Nothing more innocent than bread, camaradas. Smells good, no? I'll bet still hot out of the oven." Nacho looked down, avoiding eye contact.

Leader shifted the rifle to his left hand and jabbed it into Nacho's chest. With his right hand he reached inside. "Hands behind your head. Still warm all right. Where *is* Ahumada's Bakery? Ahumada? That's a capitalist name, I think."

Nacho shrugged, hands still behind his head. A bit of a silence. "Down on Cuchilleros."

Don't let it get uncomfortable. Now for the risky part.

"When do you guys go to breakfast?"

"Oh ho! A bribe. Just like a fascist pig," snapped one of the others.

"No, no bribe, camarada." Nacho acted dumb. "It's just that old Ahumada, he's a loyal Republican, you know. I don't think he would miss a small contribution to the defense of the city."

Just there and then, the whole encounter hung in the balance.

Nacho now looked the leader in the eyes and lowered his hands. He reached toward the back of his tent. Gradual deliberation. Nacho extracted a loaf. Four scores. Good. Leader seemed to weaken a little. Hard to tell in the low light of dawn.

The rifle juggled to the right hand. Leader reached for the bread with his left.

Now Nacho took out another. Once again, four scores. He hazarded a look behind. Tender accepted. Then another. "No, not that one. It's small. Here, this one and this." Nacho began to relax. "Are there other camaradas?"

"No. You need to be on your way," ordered Leader.

Nacho stepped on the pedal, got his bike in motion. He raised a clenched right fist and shouted over his shoulder, *"¡No pasarán!"*

As Nacho hastened up Calle de Ferraz, from mouths now full, he heard the ragged acknowledgment, "*¡No pasarán!*"

No pasarán. It was the everywhere slogan of the defenders of the Siege of Madrid. "They shall not pass!" The French had popularized it during the Battle of Verdun in 1916. Now the defenders of Madrid had co-opted it. It would forever be linked to their desperate defense of the capital.

Today at least, Nacho had succeeded in his mission. He arrived at the upscale residential building at Paseo del Pintor Rosales 59. He knew his options and prospects for further success were dwindling.

The portal was unlocked. The *portero* already at his station. He and Nacho knew each other by sight.

"To see Cóndor. Morning bread delivery," he muttered. Five scores.

"Sí, como no. I believe he's in. Go on up."

CHAPTER 10

Madrid: (Later on) Wednesday, August 14, 1963

David went out of Café Gijón and back onto Recoletos.

Madrid was stirring itself back to life after siesta for the finish of the day. Paseo de Recoletos is a broad plane and chestnut treelined boulevard that alternates several parallel sidewalks with vehicular traffic lanes.

The great boulevard pours out onto the Plaza de Cibeles at the very heart of the city. This afternoon, Recoletos conducted David south on one of the interior pedestrian ways past the used booksellers who were reopening their stalls. In the waning of the day, there was promise of a cooler and pleasant evening.

As he moved along, David brooded over the meeting with Isham. Ambivalence worked him forward and back between curiosity to know the full story of the gold and his innate and constitutional scofflaw resentment at Isham ordering him around. Arriving at Cibeles, he turned right and headed up Calle de Alcalá. On the far side of the street, where it had always been, hulked the Banco de España.

There, in a single moment, curiosity won.

All right. If this is a day for decisions, why not make one? I can start right over there. Right now. Somebody in here must know about the gold.

David jaywalked wide Alcalá at a full sprint. His momentum carried him through the main portal and into the grand entry hall— Spain's national bank. It was cool and quiet in the vaulted and ornate foyer. He looked for a directory.

On the far wall past the bank of filigree-adorned elevators stood a large marquee. It detailed the agencies located within. It was itself a virtual organization chart and a glimpse into the shadowed labyrinth of Spanish banking bureaucracy.

They included the Official Credit Institute., the Directorate General for Insurance, and the General Directorate for the Treasury and Financial Policy. David thought this one looked promising— Room 11 on the fourth floor.

When David got there, Room 11 was already open for the afternoon, but no one was at first in evidence.

"*¡Oiga!* Anyone here?"

Out of the depths of the office wafted a woman of not quite middle age and of just over middle height. Her hair had been coiffed to perfection. She wore a straight blue skirt and an expensive silver-gray knit blouse and sweater combination, often-darned nylon stockings, and in this case no rings.

She's every Spanish woman in the world, David said to himself

David waved his credentials. "Good afternoon, señorita." In Madrid you accorded *señorita* status to any woman, married or not, and not yet a grandmother receiving her old-age pension.

"David Fordham, reporter for the *International Herald Tribune.* This is my card. Doing an investigation and story on what's known as the Moscow Gold and looking for background."

An arched eyebrow and a sardonic look, "Un momentito, señor," she interrupted. "The deputy secretary of the directorate is in his office this afternoon. I will ascertain whether he might see you."

Moments later, in an interior office of sparse decoration, "Mr. Fordham, a very good afternoon. I am Federico Sáenz Hernández, deputy secretary of the directorate. I am at your service, please. Won't you have a seat?"

When he learned he might meet the deputy secretary, David had half expected morning coat and striped trousers, perhaps a polka dot tie and pearl stickpin. But Sáenz was attired in a very expensive business suit. The jacket was cut too short for American and British tastes. It was custom-tailored locally.

"Very gracious of you, Señor Sáenz. I am a reporter for the *International Herald Tribune.* Specialize in economics, agriculture, and finance, that sort of thing. Been doing a series of articles on Spanish demographics, crop yields. Perhaps you've seen one or another of them?"

"Unhappily, no. I do not read English, a difficult language for us Spaniards, you know. But your Spanish, señor, it is most excellent." Sáenz was the picture of bureaucratic graciousness.

David went right to the point of his visit. "Back in 1936, at the start of the civil war, there was a large transfer of Banco de España gold reserves to Soviet Russia, I believe."

"Alas, you have come to the wrong directorate. Matters concerning the currency, specie, and monetary policy are handled upstairs by the Ministerio de Economía y Hacienda. Here we handle matters involving the security and integrity of the banking system and the securities markets. Up there they set financial protocol. Here in Room 11, we are the bank's enforcement arm."

"Well then, I'll just go up there," David said. "They should be open. What room would it be then?"

Sáenz continued, solicitous, "Ah, the wrong office here perhaps, but, as it happens, the right individual. I am but days ago transferred here to this directorate from my former post in Economía y Hacienda. Thus, the sparse humbleness of my office surroundings. Please forgive them. As it happens, by favorable coincidence, I am somewhat well

MOSCOW GOLD | 79

informed about that which you inquire. I dealt with matters of that nature in my former post. What would you like to know?"

David's suspicions were aroused. Questions flooded his mind. *Wrong room but right guy? Just transferred? Enforcement arm? Do they have their own cops and guns? Is this just too easy? Man's accommodating for a money bureaucrat.*

"To start with, how much gold was there?"

"A very great deal. Perhaps close to US $1 billon at the exchange rate of the time."

"Is it documented where it went?"

"It was consigned to Moscow in Soviet Russia. Bank documentation confirms it was loaded onto transport for that location. There is extant no written receipt that we have found. Little doubt exists here in Spain that it got to its destination. The Republican military forces received military equipment and supplies. They got nowhere near full value."

"How much is left? Loads of other questions." David smiled.

The deputy secretary went on. "Some 20 percent of the total holdings were sent to France. That much was returned. But regarding the Moscow Gold, as our friends north of the Pyrenees say, *aucune*. None. Well, virtually none. Do you smoke?" A pack of American Kents materialized out of a purpose-cut interior breast pocket.

David did smoke, yes, thank you.

And so it went. What the young American reporter wanted to know took just under an hour. Thereafter, David took his leave amid clouds of mutual expressions of appreciation and gratitude.

॰ৎৢ

As soon as the elevator doors had closed behind David, Sáenz picked up the telephone.

"Señor Director General? Sáenz here, Room 11. The expected inquiry came just now. American reporter for the *International Herald Tribune*. Asking all about the Moscow Gold. All the agencies had been advised of the possibility of his appearance. They were instructed to call me. By luck or coincidence, he went directly to Room 11."

"Should we be concerned that he has inside information?"

"I think not."

"How long was he with you?" asked the director general.

"An hour or so, sir. He left only moments ago. I briefed him. Answered all his questions."

"What is your impression of this individual?"

"Favorable. He asked incisive questions that got to most if not all of the relevant information."

"The process we have been expecting appears to have begun, Sáenz—rather more quickly than I had imagined. You know your next steps?"

"On your authority, advise Inspector Jaso over in the Cuerpo. Emphasize that, for now, the subject is to be observed only. No contact. Subject is not to know."

"This is delicate, Sáenz. We're walking a fine diplomatic line here. Our friends want this information and think it will help us. We much prefer it were left alone, but we must appear to cooperate. *If* the gentleman develops valuable evidence, we will want to lay hold of it. I will handle coordination with our friends."

The director general rang off without waiting for any reply.

During the summer, the heat of the day in Madrid takes its leisure in dissipating. Evenings, as was this one, are perfect for walking and for café life. His ultimate destination the MonteAzul, David walked up Alcalá. The crowds were flooding out now in earnest. He maneuvered his way through the thronging paseo onto the Gran Vía.

The Café Nebraska, grand dame of the Gran Vía, elegant and popular at this hour, was teeming with people. Incongruously named after an American state that is little known in Madrid and for reasons long obscured by time, the café was normally excessive of David's budgetary constraints. After the successful interview with Sáenz, David thought, *why not?*

He shouldered his way to the bar. It was jammed to the gunwales, and the din was enormous.

"¡Hola, jefe! Gimme a draft beer and an order of *boquerones.*" David had to shout to be heard. He decided to treat himself to some of the tender white Spanish anchovies marinated in lemon juice rather than cooked in oil.

Over his snack and in the isolation of the crowded bar, he reflected on his spur-of-the-moment visit to the bank. The right guy in the right place at the right time. The fates of journalism were smiling on him.

Or were they? Was this just too easy? Everything lined up to get me full details on the gold within mere minutes of talking with Isham? How could Isham have engineered it? And that fast? He couldn't have known I that I would go straight to the bank. I didn't even know that I would till I started to walk past.

David experienced another momentary stab of insecurity. It was compounded by the fact that Isham was not giving him any choice.

❧

"Chema, some foppish-sounding *mariposa* from over at one of the money ministries. On the line for you. Name's Sáenz. Says you know him."

"Yeah, Fonsín, I know him. Sáenz. Currency security guy. Finance regulation and all that. He's OK. Sort of a money cop. Put him through."

"Jaso, here. Yes, Sáenz. Room 11, isn't it?"

"*Precismente.* Perhaps you remember the surveillance operation that you and I chatted about recently. Well, it now needs to begin."

"I remember. Subject's a journalist. American or British? I forget."

"David L. Fordham, American. He's known to you. Suspicion of working illegally. You've had him under observation, I believe."

"Yes. Yes. It's all coming back now."

"Good. Observation now becomes close surveillance. But no contact for now. And he is not to know. This is on the director general's specific orders."

"OK, we're on it."

"It's urgent," noted Sáenz.

"It's urgent? What isn't? Let me have your number again so I'll have it here on my desk."

Inspector José María "Chema" Jaso of the Cuerpo General de Policía, Spain's primary internal security agency, leaned back and put his feet up on his desk.

"Fonsín," he shouted at his assistant. "Get me what we've got on an American. David Fordham. Lives up on Calle de Vallehermoso or some one of those streets up there. Get right on it. That guy Sáenz is Room 11. Over at the bank. You know what that means. They want it yesterday."

"Got it, boss."

"And Fonsín, I don't think I like this American. He's a snotty piece of work. Needs to learn not to mouth off to us like he does. We're not to touch him for now. But tell the boys to watch him close. He even spits in the street, I want to know about it. He goes anywhere near illegal, and I'm going to have him over to the *comisaría* here for a little attitude adjustment."

The MonteAzul was brimming when David arrived there. He wriggled to the bar through air close to unbreathable with body heat and cigarette smoke.

"Fundador, Victorio, if you please." David mouthed the words and pointed at the lighted advertising sign that hung over the bar. No use in trying to make himself heard. Victorio knew what he liked anyway.

"Tenga." Victorio slid the *copa* down the marble to David.

David caught the drink and looked around. There should be a high level of anonymity inside the rush of activity in the MonteAzul this evening. He took his copa into the back and sat on a stool next to a narrow shelf by the pinball machine.

David decided to get some additional perspective. He maneuvered over to the pay phone Victorio had at the end of the bar. The call was quick.

After a quarter of an hour, he heard, "Look who! Paladín! And no one else!"

The greeting caused David to look up. A tall, youngish, and willowy man slid sideways in beside him. "Buitre! Just me. Just here. That's all. You? Thanks for coming down. Hope I didn't interrupt." David gave the newcomer a backhanded swat to the chest.

"Interrupt? Nah. Just had a date for drinks and dinner with the lovely Maribel. I called her and cancelled so I could come and see you. She was unhappy, but she'll get over it."

"Bullshit too. Good to see you, macho."

"Likewise. It's been a while."

David knew Juan Miguel Calvín, nickname Buitre, from school days. They maintained regular contact. The butt of perennial ribbing for being named after a French lawyer and protestant theologian, Calvín had gone on from the *colegio* to pursue studies in business management. Himself the son of a minor Franco government functionary, he had now risen to a middle-level position in the Ministry of Tourism.

When he had first come to Madrid, David's parents had thought it would be useful for David to be immersed in the Spanish culture and language. He was enrolled in the fourth form at the Colegio Carlos I on busy Calle de Fernando el Católico, just around from the MonteAzul.

The course consisted of six forms in total. "Carlos Primero," as the kids called it, was situated in the basement of a large building of residential flats. Forthright and proud in segregating the sexes, it was affirmatively not coeducational.

Classrooms were small. The air always musty and stale, the closeness was exacerbated by the long and narrow desks and benches that the boys slid into and at which they labored shoulder to shoulder.

The Spanish boys had been friendly and welcoming. The level of subject matter was higher than in American high school. The teachers, of course, were all men. They were to be addressed as "Don." Don Juan taught history, Don Alfonso taught Latin, and Don Diego, literature.

It had been Don José who taught math. Corporal punishment was allowed and was administered with cheerful liberality. Don José hated whistling in his class. He was about seventy, had burly hands, and was strong for an old man. José wore very thick glasses. Even with them he was effectively blind. His appearance had earned him the sobriquet "el Búho," the Owl.

"Remember the Owl?" David asked after a few pleasantries.

"Sure. How could I forget? The old fart never got either one of us, did he?" Calvín smiled wryly at the memory.

The fourth formers, almost to a man, were aspiring young bullfighters. The temptation to challenge the Owl's proscription against whistling was too much to be resisted. Most of the boys had adopted bullfighter style nicknames, fatalistic and leaning toward the macabre. David's circle included Buitre, the Buzzard; Murciélago, the Bat; el Tirado, the Gunshot; and Sombra, Shadow. Harking back to television westerns that enjoyed immense popularity, not only in the United States, but also in Spain, David chose Paladín.

Taking advantage of the Owl's poor eyesight, it was common practice to change seats within his classroom. Each man took his turn in the front row. Someone would whistle and the Owl would, without variance, screech, "Who whistled?" Unless there was an immediate confession, which there never was, he would take a vicious swing at the vague shapes in the front row.

Don José was ham-fisted. He wore a heavy signet ring. As the quarters were close, his roundhouse punches, like the goring slashes of a fighting bull's horns, required infinite coolness, courage, and lightning-fast reflexes to dodge. Those evasions, and the occasional failure, became the subject of much dissection and discussion after class.

MOSCOW GOLD | 85

"No, he never did. That ring! Cut Paco Almendariz's face pretty bad that one time," David recalled. "What did we call him?"

"Chasquido, Crack of the Whip," Calvín replied. "Remember when that cop caught us running across the Gran Vía by Callao? Chasquido told him he was the Mexican ambassador's kid. Implied it wouldn't go well for him if he turned us in. Even faked the accent. Ballsy guy even if Búho got him that once."

In those times, the nature and independent spirit of the Spanish, repressed as it was by the pervasive franquista dictatorship, came out in subtle but nonetheless satisfying ways. It was not for nothing that the Metro found it necessary to post the obvious, *"Dejen salir"* (Let exiting riders off) over every door on every car. Even with the admonition, David and his friends crowded aboard without waiting.

Together with his Carlos I *compañeros*, David became an inveterate transgressor of all rules and regulations minor and confining. No traffic light or crosswalk was ever obeyed. If the selfsame Metro said not to go down the up stairway, they went brazenly down. If the Parks Department wanted you to stay off the grass, you walked on the grass. If you were supposed to board a bus from the front and exit from the rear, you did the opposite. Minor contumacy became, and for David forever thereafter would remain, a way of life.

Juan Miguel somewhat resembled his school days' sobriquet. Tall with long arms and rounded shoulders, he often hunched forward. His habit in the cold months of draping his winter coat over his shoulders made him look a little like one of his namesakes landed on a log. He was blond with a whitish, almost pasty complexion. He had an already receding hairline. David had often thought that Calvín looked more like a Hungarian count than a Spanish hotelier. A large gold ring on one of his long middle fingers would have completed the impression.

He was, however, anything but lugubrious. Glittering blue eyes with a satirical and conspiratorial smile enlivened his face and warmed people to him. His countenance thus confirmed a first impression that he was thoughtful and bright, an individual of deep conviction and balance.

"What brings us together, Paladín? You want to have a few and then run down the stairs the wrong way on the Metro?"

"Working on a story about the civil war I want to tell you about. But first, how's the innkeeping?" David answered.

Calvín fessed up to. "Trying to figure out how to get ten million English, French, Belgians, and Dutch in down on the Costa del Sol as tourists every year. We need the foreign exchange. They're talking about some kind of shared ownership apartments—in Málaga mainly. Some new concept. Working out the details now. Big meeting on it today."

"That's the third time money's come up for me today, Buitre," David mused.

Calvín ignored him. "I need a drink. Look at that mob." He got up and worked his way to the bar. He squeezed in between two civilians nursing beers. He nodded at them.

Soon enough, he came back with a gin and tonic, Spanish style— gin, tonic, and a slice of lemon but room temperature. There was no ice or, at most, one little cube floating in the drink.

"How can you drink that bilge?" David shivered a little.

"Mmm. It's good," Juan Miguel mumbled sucking on the lemon. "Hate 'em cold, the way you all do 'em. All that ice dilutes the gin." He threw the lemon on the floor. "What story about the civil war? Everybody I know is trying to forget that massive excursion into folly."

"Remember I told you I've been doing a series of articles on the economy, crop yields, Franco trying to keep the people on the land and out of the cities? Well now my editor suggests I might like to get interested in what happened to the Moscow Gold." David elected not to mention that his work on the gold story would not be voluntary.

"The Moscow Gold? Sensitive issue, David. Lots of dough involved as I recall. Franco and his people harbor huge resentment that they couldn't get their hands on it. Or at least so they say. Maybe its loss is just a good excuse for them. Explains why their precious fascist economy hasn't done any better than it has."

"Such candor, Buitre. Careful," David chided.

"They can't hear anything in here. Not that they wouldn't like to. What's the story?" Calvín always exuded confidence.

"Isham, my editor. You met him once."

"Yeah. Tall. Pretty well absorbed in himself as I remember."

"One and the same," David went on. "Thinks he and Paco are friends. It would be appreciated in high places if I can figure out where all that gold wound up."

"*Me* be careful?!" Calvín exclaimed. "It's Francisco Franco Bahamonde to you, good sir. I doubt if your editor has met him. Access is tight. So my old man tells me anyway."

Calvín was not all bravado, however. He let their conversation peter out a little, squirmed on his seat, and glanced around the bar. "I'm done with my drink. Let's go down to the Benidorm on Fuencarral for another. You're into some serious stuff here. It's making me nervous. We'll talk on the way."

❧

"They're leaving," Cuerpo Inspector Zapatero muttered into his beer.

"Let 'em go," answered Monge his partner. "Recognize the contact?"

"No. A local though. Madrid accent," Zapatero whispered.

"They make us?" Monge looked toward the door, but they were gone.

"Don't think so. The contact came up to the bar next to me, but I think it was just a coincidence."

"Well," said Monge, "let's call it in. Chema said to locate and observe, not follow. Not yet anyway. Got any *fichas*?"

To their perpetual annoyance, Spanish cops were mandated to use public telephones to communicate with headquarters. Public phones required special tokens, fichas in Castilian—no coins allowed.

"There's a pay phone in the restaurant across the street," Monge remembered.

"Chema? Monge here. I'm with Detective Zapatero. We located the subject."

"Any doubt it's him?" asked Jaso.

"No. It's him. He's known to us. He's the one we suspect of working without a work permit."

"Right, the newspaper guy," Jaso dissembled.

"That's the one. He frequents a bar up here called the MonteAzul. He went right there—just like he always does. We found him easy. He made contact with another individual. We haven't identified the contact yet. They left the MonteAzul together just now. The contact may have made us, so we're not following."

"Were they discussing our project?"

"Couldn't tell, sir, a big crowd in there. Looked like they are well known to each other. It did look like the discussion was serious. More than partying and girls."

"Leave it for now. Come on back in."

❧

It was several blocks down Fuencarral to the Benidorm. Calvín had time to finish his thoughts. "You gonna do the gold story?"

"My first impulse was negative," David conceded. "But I've gotten into it some. Stopped by the Banco de España earlier this afternoon. Got in right away. The guy I talked to knew all about it."

"What's the short version?" Calvín asked.

When David had told him, Calvín said, "Interesting that the French gave theirs back. I imagine our delightful current regime resents it that they can't get their hands on the Russian part."

"Right. Sáenz said the gold belonged not to one side or the other but to the Spanish people. At the start of the war, the Spanish economy had been healthy. Loss of the gold explains the twenty-five long years of poverty since. Blah, blah, blah. It was all quite lyrical."

MOSCOW GOLD | 89

"He's right about some of it. We don't call the '40s and early '50s the Hunger Years for nothing," Calvín recalled. "I still can't eat lentils. That's all we had sometimes back then. Sounds like the guy is pretty passionate."

"Yeah. There was lots more. Twisting the knife in the Republicans. Since they sent the gold within two months of the beginning of the war, they knew from the get-go they couldn't win. Then they used some of the money to finance propaganda to influence public opinion outside of Spain with perpetual claims of successes that only delayed their much-justified demise."

"Not much of a surprise. Like I say, the gold's a hot topic. I guess I didn't know quite how hot. I counsel caution." Calvín turned pensive.

"Why would you say that?"

"You've just had a glimpse of the torrid emotions that characterized our civil war. They still bubble close to the surface. You get in the middle of this, and you're sticking yourself into someone else's quarrel. That's never a good idea, David."

"Couldn't hurt to do a little preliminary nosing around on the under."

"Sure, it could. Nothing's on the under here. Spain's still a dictatorship."

David said nothing, so Calvín warmed to his topic. "You have a sereno over there at Vallehermoso?"

"Sure, nice guy. Lousy job. Up all night. Pay's a pittance."

City dwellers in Spain never carried keys to the main entrances to their buildings. At night after the portero went off duty, the door would be locked, and each block had a sereno. When you came home late, you stood in front of your building and clapped your hands—loud and only twice. Within moments, the sereno would come running up, from where you never could tell, his keys all ajangle, and open your door for you. For this service, he received a couple of pesetas, and you were bid a warm goodnight.

Calvín had gone on. "Spain is full of serenos, porteros, beadles, all manner of watchers, attendants, and observers. Now why would that be? Letting you in every night isn't making any sereno a living. Some little additional is coming in. They're watching and reporting to somebody. And *somebody's* paying."

"Buitre, I find that gold, I'm a hero."

"Not that simple, David. You find that money, you may be a goat. I can think of some parties who won't want it found—inside and outside Spain. Do you know how to detect it if you're being followed?"

"Am I a spy? How would I know that?"

"You might want to learn," Calvín advised. "That gold's controversial. The amount of money involved is staggering. People and organizations of very high order will be interested." Calvín had always been direct. "Don't go all off, Paladín, on to your usual this'll-be-a-lark-I'll-just-sniff-around-a-little-and-see-where-life-takes-me attitude. Easy to get your nose bent."

"'This'll-be-a-lark attitude'? Ouch!" David acted hurt.

Calvín didn't bite. "I'm no friend if I'm not candid. You can be a bit of a dilettante, David. This gold story is a serious business. You better be ready to get real serious and stay real serious. Real fast."

"I think you're overreacting."

"Am I? Yours is not all that safe of a profession sometimes. There were half a dozen Spanish journalists and photographers killed during the civil war itself. And then there was that guy, forget his name, about five years ago who was looking into the Paracuellos Massacre. For *France Soir,* I think it was. Disappeared. No body. No trace. No prosecution. *Nada.*"

"That's different. Nobody died over the gold." David knew he was trying to convince himself more than Calvín.

"Like I say, I counsel caution," Juan Miguel persisted. 'There will be numerous interested parties—powerful people, big governments, big organizations, ones that have enforcement capability. Play at this level, be prepared to go all the way and to protect yourself. I don't

MOSCOW GOLD | 91

know if you are. You also better develop an ironclad backup plan that covers you from attentions that could be prejudicial to your health and well-being."

"It's just a news story, Buitre! Not a new one at that. Not one that anybody's ever gotten hurt over. Not that I've heard of anyway. If I do run it down, it'll be a big splash. Could be a Pulitzer in it for me."

"Do they award *posthumous* Pulitzers?" His friend looked hard at David.

"It can't be that dire. Isham's a jerk, but get one of his reporters killed? Besides, I have my pride. Can't let bad guys be chasing me off the field of battle, can I?"

"Make light of it at your peril. My last comment is that Paladín's no lover of hard work. You're wicked smart. You know how to leverage your intelligence into getting what you want without much effort. This story might cost you some real work."

"Work! Work! Buitre, why does it have to be *work*!?"

"Here's the Benidorm." Calvín was finished. "You're incorrigible, and you're buying. Payment for excellent advice rendered. Will it be heeded?"

92 | DOUGLAS L. FIELD

CHAPTER 11

Carabanchel: Thursday, August 15, 1963

Since midmorning, David was at his second-floor desk at DOCICA.

He held in his hands a copy of the English screenplay of a new David Lean film. Something about a medical doctor and the Russian revolution. That was rare, he thought, what with Isham now and the Moscow Gold. His thoughts strayed from Moscow in the teens to Moscow in the thirties.

"Hola, David, falta poco para la una. ¿Quieres un cafecito?" (Hi, David. It's almost one. Want a coffee?)

It was Ariel Muñiz, Castellon's pretty and capable factotum who David had met at the American Embassy library party just before Jaime Castellón had recruited him to DOCICA. Ariel had been cool to him at the reception. Since he had begun regular visits to Carabanchel, they would greet each other politely but coolly.

At first, she indicated little interest in David, but as time had gone on, they would exchange a word or two. Lately, though, and on occasion, about this time, she would offer to go down to the bar on the street level and order them both a coffee.

"Tide us over till siesta," she would say. "Jaime's treat, *como siempre*."

"In that case, yes, of course. Two sugars, yeah?"

"Be right back."

This was becoming a pleasant ritual for David. It broke up the morning's work. Ariel was intelligent, he was finding, and very agreeable company.

David took pleasure in watching her leave.

❧

While he waited for the young woman to come back, David let his mind wander back to the events of last evening and earlier today. Last evening, Calvín had been brusque. David had made light of his friend's comments, but at the start of the new day today he knew Calvín was right.

David had awakened conflicted. Calvín was not fainthearted. He was pretty much fearless but not stupid. Since Carlos I, he had, with dexterous hand, navigated the eddies and sandbars of finishing his education; starting his career; and managing, to his own benefit, the thickets of Spanish bureaucracy.

The light came late to David's room at Vallehermoso 18, in the Pensión Alonso. Doña Mari, wife of the aging Don Alonso ran the place. Located on the third floor of a seven-story stack of residential flats, David's room was at the back. It overlooked a central courtyard into which the light of day intruded only with timidity and never until after the sun was well up. Ideal circumstances to lie up a little and have a leisurely colloquy with himself.

David looked around his space and ruminated. His room was spartan but comfortable. Mari provided the bed, a bureau, and an armoire. The maids did his laundry. He had a few reminders from home, including a small portrait of his parents, a compact Zenith radio in a leather case with a frayed handle, and an aging portable Smith Corona typewriter. The old *máquina* was maroon with flat round keys,

94 | DOUGLAS L. FIELD

had a faint green ribbon, and was set up to make the diacritical marks needed for writing in Spanish.

It occurred to David that his quarters reflected an occupant of greater efficiency and purposefulness than was the reality. This would need to change. Getting jobs done with charm and verve wouldn't cut it this time. That was the David way. But the David way was not going to get this story. He might have to practice his craft for a change. It would cost him. And he needed to figure out how not to get hurt.

Besides, he wasn't being given any choice.

He rolled out and lit out for Carabanchel. Both porteros were present. The portero was his usual taciturn and respectful self. The portera was not hers. Always before shyly effusive, today she was reticent and would not meet David's eyes.

David decided to check in with one of his most reliable sources. He found Onésimo two blocks north on Vallehermoso at the corner of Calle de Fernando el Católico—where he always was. The blind had the lottery ticket concession in Spain. This corner, by way of some unwritten law, belonged to one Onésimo.

Onésimo had a folding easel with a small tray. He pinned his strips of tickets to his easel with clothes pegs. Beyond that, he had small amounts of chewing gum, little sleeves of stale peanuts, and single cigarettes for sale. Onésimo's blindness was deceptive. Maybe he couldn't see, but he heard everything and knew everybody in the neighborhood.

"*¡Veinte tiros iguales!*" Onésimo announced his wares in an odd and resonant voice.

"Hey, Onésimo, it's me, David the Gringo. Gimme five pulls. Pick me some good ones this time. I never win lately. You're falling down on the job."

"*Hola, mi gringuito.* Here's my five best. You should buy five more. You don't play, you don't win."

As David pulled out some cash, Onésimo lowered to a whisper. David had to move closer. "Good thing you came today. You're in it

MOSCOW GOLD | 95

deep with the Cuerpo. There's a couple of new plainclothes working down here and on up toward Quevedo. They passed by three, maybe four times. They talk a lot and don't know I hear as good as I do."

"They mention me by name?"

"No, but it's you. North American. Been here a long time. Works for some newspaper. They want to find you and sweat you. At least one of them does. Sounded like, for now, they have orders to find you but not bust you—not yet anyway."

"What for?"

"Not stated. Only you were mentioned. Well, your description. No other gringos."

David faked a coolness he did not feel. "Thanks for the tip, Onésimo. Keep your ears peeled. I'll be in touch. Vigilance!"

⌇

Fernando el Católico was coming to life. David crossed to opposite Onésimo. He decided to try to spot any surveillance as he went out to Carabanchel. Only DOCICA knew about DOCICA—he hoped anyway. Nobody there had any interest in letting their secret get out. DOCICA needed to be kept on the under.

He went into the big open market on the corner and wandered among the fishmonger stalls and butchers. The market was a maze of aisles and hidden corners. No one appeared to be paying attention to him. No one loitered about. Back out on the sidewalk, he idled up the street, looking in shop windows for reflections of anyone following him or anyone dawdling. Nothing. Then he continued, brisk and with purpose.

When he was all but past the entrance to Galerías Preciados, the big department store, he ducked inside, zipped through to the Arapiles exit in the next block to the south and hailed a passing taxi. David watched the exit door until it was out of sight. No one followed him out. *So far so good.* He told the cabbie to take him to Plaza de la Moncloa. He slouched in the back seat so he could see the driver's mirrors. No cars appeared to stay with the cab. At Moncloa, he caught the *tranvía* (streetcar) for Carabanchel.

Tranvías were a public transit staple. Large and unarticulated, they sported a dark blue and cream livery. They were torpedo shaped and pointed at both ends. When you got on, the driver gave you a flimsy ticket in case a transit inspector accosted you. This was a constant threat promulgated by the transit authority that David had never experienced. There weren't any transit inspectors, he'd decided. They had a row of hard wooden seats by the windows and duckboards on the floor. They were Madrid fixtures, fast and efficient if not luxurious.

Along with the Metro, they were the only way to Carabanchel.

The main thoroughfare in Carabanchel had yet to be paved. Dusty in summer and muddy in winter, it added a kind of Wild, Wild West atmosphere to the place. Now it was unquenched dry. The odd stray dog or all-black clad widow with a string bag threaded their way through miniature vortices of wind that kicked up dirt, paper napkins from the bars, and other small bits of rubbish. The buildings, once whitewashed, were now dull beige and built of cheap ceramic block that had been faced with plaster—plaster that was spalling off with no prospect of repair ever in sight.

No one suspicious was on the streetcar. David was the single passenger to alight in Carabanchel. With Isham, Calvín, the portera, and Onésimo, David's suspicions and worries were aroused. He hurried into DOCICA. He thought he was safe—at least for now.

Ariel returned. David was at the window fiddling with the *persiana*. She didn't leave right away as she had always done before. Instead, she sat in the chair behind his desk, folded her legs under herself, and exposed just a peek of thigh.

"Too dark in here, Ariel, and that's my chair." He smiled, taking a place across his desk from her. He pronounced her name /Ah-ree-ALE/.

MOSCOW GOLD | 97

"Camarero will be up in a minute with the coffees." Smiling back, Ariel tilted her head to the side. "How long have you been in Spain? You talk like us."

"Better part of ten years. First came when I was fifteen." David enjoyed the prospect of telling Ariel about himself. "Parents enrolled me in a colegio up in Vallehermoso. Wanted me to learn what *they* call Spanish."

"They well spent their money. How did you learn?"

"El castellano has been an adventure for me. I didn't know a word when I got here. If I wanted any social contact at all, I had to learn. At first, it was lonely. I couldn't understand or talk to anybody. After a while, though, it went pretty fast. My Spanish classmates were gracious. Taught me the good words and the bad."

"But ours is a simple language," she teased. "It would have been easy for a man so intelligent as you, no?"

"More complicated than you might think—for Americans anyway. You have verbs that conjugate, nouns that have gender, two past tenses, and a subjunctive mood. For us subjunctive's like an 'ifya, couldya, wouldya' language within a language that seems to differentiate between objective and subjective reality. All stuff that confuses us. And you all can't even explain it."

"Yes. I think we don't know why we do it. We learn as babies," she admitted.

"You want to know how el castellano started for me?" David asked.

"*¡Por supuesto que sí!*"

"We were on the train, the folks and me. From Paris. Just crossed into Spain up in Irún. It came up noon. I got hungry; suggested we go to the dining car for lunch. The old man said it wouldn't be open, that you all eat much later in Spain. Not for a couple of hours or more. He gave me a handful of coins and told me to go to the bar car and get a Coke."

"And your parents, they expected the barman speaks English?"

"Dunno, but *I* figured he wouldn't. I asked them how to say, 'I want.' My mom said, 'It's, *quiero*.' So off I go. Bar car mobbed. Everybody crowding around, not lining up like we do." David gave her a wink. "So, I muscled my way up to the front, and there was my Coke sweating in the cooler. I pointed at it and announced, 'Quiero.' I held out coins. Coins were taken. Coins were returned. I had my Coke. And, Ariel, with that single word, there started for me an enduring and intimate linguistic relationship with el castellano. Been a beautiful dimension in my life."

"Did you never return to Norteamérica?"

"I did," he said, "for about four years. Did a journalism degree at University of Missouri, in Columbia. Missouri's my home state."

The waiter from the bar downstairs came in with their coffees. Two little demitasses on a tray, espresso coffees so thick and strong you could stand a fork in them, and sugar cubes, each in their individual wrappers labeled with the bar's name and address.

"*Gracias, joven,*" said David. All waiters, regardless of age it seemed, were called *joven*, young man. David handed him a few coins. He departed with a little bow. Ariel stirred a sugar into her coffee daintily. David unwrapped a cube, popped it in the front of his mouth, and drank some coffee through it—an earthy local custom that he enjoyed.

Ariel returned to their conversation. "Ah, *Missohooree*. I know of that. Not a small state; in the center of the country, no?"

"Yes, it is. How do you know about Missouri, Ariel?"

"You are not the sole one to have studied, my dear *Meestair* David," she replied amiably. "I learn here about your Mark Twain and big rivers—Huckleberry Finn and Jim floating on a raft. Why did you come back to our poor, dusty Spain?"

"Missed all the beautiful women. I was lonely."

"Now you mock me." She faked a little pout. Then she flashed the smile—straight white teeth setting off graceful cheekbones. Ariel was tall for a Spanish girl, trim and toned. "There are beautiful women in America—Kim Novak, Rita Hayworth, Audrey Hepburn. Many others."

MOSCOW GOLD | 99

"Maybe, but they didn't go to the same parties that I did," David tried to joke.

"I ask you to be serious, David. Why did you come back? America has much more to offer you than we do here, no?"

"Don't make me tell you. I might get all emotional," he tried again to be offhanded.

"This I doubt." Ariel was serious. "If it were true that you missed us Spanish women so much, I'm thinking you would take advantage of the opportunity to tell this one your history. Or am I in error?"

She pinned David with a searching look from rich dark brown eyes set in a fair freckle-sprinkled face framed by brown hair, dark brown but flecked with glints of red.

"You're persistent," David remarked. "Confident too."

He saw a little shrug of the shoulders, a lift of the eyebrows. "Go on. I listen."

"It's like this," he started. "You're born and grow up in a place. You know the lingo and the culture. You have family and friends. Life works in its old and time-honored way. You take it all for granted. That's the experience of most everyone in the world. I imagine it's been yours."

"Yes, of course. I was born in Madrid. Always I live here. Life goes on as always."

"Well, for me it hasn't been like that," David reflected. "I left what you might call the comforts of my adolescence about halfway through. Came here. You've lived in a place. Everything is regular and normal. You imagine that how it is *here* is how it is *everywhere*. When I came here, I thought life here would be just like it is in Missouri, just in a different language. But it turned out that Madrid was a profound change."

"Do go on, David. I am liking to hear you."

David obliged. "Maybe it's sentimental, but by the time I got to nineteen or twenty, this way of life, this language, this city, these

100 | DOUGLAS L. FIELD

people had made an indelible impression on me. Coming back was coming home, Ariel."

He thought a moment and then continued. "Plus, here, even under the dictatorship, I have more liberty than I would in the 'land of the free and the home of the brave.' In the States, there would be pressures. Advance in my career. Earn lots of money. Marry. Have a family. I have none of that here, and running around with a US passport, the dictatorship doesn't affect me very much. At least, it hasn't so far."

"Living in Madrid is a means for you of avoiding responsibilities, how do you call it, maturities?"

"Maturity. Ow. But, yeah, it is. Or until recently it has been. Stuff has started to change for me here in recent days—upsetting my feather bed. Maybe you'll let me tell you about it one day."

"I will. And I like you, David Fordham," Ariel commented with a wry look and a laugh.

"Do you? You're forward for a Spanish girl."

"You have known a great many Spanish girls, then, to make this comparison?" she said, still laughing.

"Well, no it's just that—"

"Not forward. A little assertive maybe." Ariel stopped him. "Someday soon, Spain will move into the twentieth century. We Spanish women here won't have to be withdrawn and cloistered always and forever. Life is to be lived."

"Taking an advance on Liberation Day, are you?" David asked.

"Thank you for telling me this story." She held his eyes for the briefest moment. Then, "I should check on Jaime's progress. You're not making any!"

"Let's talk again, Ariel."

"Yes, David. Do let's."

CHAPTER 12

Madrid: Friday, August 16, 1963

David was in the MonteAzul.

Siesta was over. He was meditating on his prospects for tomorrow night. He had arrived before the place filled up and had gotten his favorite place in the back corner. He had a smoke or two and thought over his mounting pressures—that and he wanted to take advantage of Ariel's indication that they could talk again. As to Ariel, he could hope that the plan he had made would come to fruition. It was a chancy play, fraught with potential for failure. But if he had it figured right, it was ripe with possibilities.

Then there was the gold story. He knew he was forced to move forward on it. Isham would blow up his life in Madrid if he didn't. It wasn't just a standard story either. The gold story placed him at risk in a world he did not know or understand.

He also needed a backup plan—some kind of insurance policy. If he was being leveraged, he needed to figure out how to leverage back.

He spent the morning in the *Herald*'s morgue researching the gold. He already knew most of the information in the public domain. David confirmed that Stalin had never provided acknowledgment of the gold's receipt. It was allowed, however, to circulate through "sources close to the Kremlin" that full value and more had been extended to the socialist brethren in Spain—for any monies received by Moscow.

The bastard got it, David thought. Stalin overcharged for inferior stuff and pocketed the difference. Spain got robbed. That was a fact.

Then he made a short but intense foray into the world of clandestine tradecraft. It had developed to a high state of advancement during World War II. Now, with the Cold War on in full, the profession was progressing exponentially. Safe houses, establishing and avoiding surveillance, cutouts, dead drops, honey traps, and brush pass exchanges were all the stuff of good espionage, along with codes, code breaking, disinformation ploys, propaganda, and double agents. This was a very big topic and not one to be absorbed in a single day.

David acknowledged to himself that he needed someone to teach him. But who would know about it? He would have to get lucky. He decided to start by avoiding being followed by the cops and, if he was, to losing them.

By midafternoon, he let his thoughts turn to yesterday's conversation with Ariel. It had been a pleasant vista in what had become a tense landscape of late. Through office chitchat, he had learned that he and she were sort of neighbors. She lived ten or eleven blocks away from him on Calle de Gaztambide, nearer to the university. Number 67, he thought it was. A plan to see her again began to form in his mind.

After leaving the *Herald*'s offices on Plaza de España, he headed down Calle de Bailén towards the Royal Palace and the Teatro Real. There, he picked up the first of what he needed. Back up Princesa, at a fancy stationery shop, he bought a large and expensive white envelope. Gaztambide ran out onto Princesa. On his way up to number 67, he made one more stop and was all set.

Once inside 67, David asked the portero, guardian, and protector, "La Señorita Muñiz resides in this building, does she not?"

Pursed lips and a hint of suspicion, "That is possible, *caballero*. Who is asking?"

"An acquaintance, sir, nothing more." But his look said he might *like* it to be more. He handed over a single red rose on a long stem nestled in a skinny white box with a cellophane window and the white envelope. "Perhaps you would be so kind, if you had a moment extra, to take it up?"

In a flash, the man's Latin sense of romance was piqued. He was at once won over. He smiled conspiratorially. "If it could wait five minutes, señor? But no longer, of course; the flower is delicate."

"Yes, and most grateful to you." A crisp new and folded hundred-peseta note confirmed David's gratitude. In reciprocation it earned the portero's. *Everybody happy.*

⁊❧

Up at fifth floor, right-hand door the landlady answered the portero's discreet knock. "Buenas tardes, Doña Sagrario. *¿Se encuentra la Señorita Ariel?*" (Is Miss Ariel at home?) He knew she was. It was his job to know such things, but proprieties were to be maintained

"*Claro que sí, momentito. ¡A-a-a-ri-e-e-el, te buscan!*" (Surely, just a moment. Ariel, it's for you!)

Ariel appeared.

"Ah, Señorita Ariel, I'm sorry to disturb you, but a young man asked that this be brought up." He handed her the box and note with a gentle smile.

Ariel was confused and could see no indication as to whom they were from. "Who left this for me?"

"Ah, I am sorry Señorita Ariel, but he did not tell me his name. A young man. One roughly your own age."

"When did—"

"Mere moments ago. He left as he came, in but a moment."

"Thank you, Don Hilario." She gave him a few pesetas, as was customary in the circumstances.

As the door closed, Doña Sagrario said, "What is it, Ariel? My child, that *is* a beautiful flower. Have you a secret admirer?"

"Don't know, Doña Sagra. I'm, well, quite perplexed."

"How do you know if you are perplexed, *mija*, if you haven't opened the letter. Hurry."

In the envelope was a single sheet of paper. On heavy and expensive paper, engraved, announcing:

Orchesta Nacional de España
Rafael Frühbeck de Burgos, Conducting
Alicia de Larrocha, Piano

Manuel de Falla	Noches en los Jardines de España (Nights in the Gardens of Spain)
Joaquín Rodrigo	Concierto de Aranjuez
Edvard Grieg	Concierto para Piano en La menor, Op. 19

Teatro Real de Madrid
Sábado, día 17 de agosto, 1963
A las 2100 horas

Ariel handed it to Doña Sagrario.

Sagrario had to find her glasses. When she did, "It appears, my dear, that you have been invited to the symphony for tomorrow night."

"I can't go, Sagrario. I don't even know who. It would be unseemly."

Hands on her ample hips, Sagrario gave Ariel a knowing look. "Ariel, my dear, something like this never falls out of thin air. Surely you will have some idea of who your sender is. Perhaps someone whom you have recently met? Someone whom you've not yet had the time to tell me about?"

Ariel blushed. "Sagrario, I can't possibly—"

"Let's find some water for your flower while you think it over. Of course, it *is* a big decision," Sagrario interrupted.

Then she exclaimed, *"¡Ay de mi, Ariel! ¡Pero que lindo detalle!"* (Oh my, Ariel. What a lovely touch!)

CHAPTER 13

Madrid: Saturday, August 17, 1963

The Teatro Real is sited to notable advantage on the Plaza de Oriente, a leafy French-style square straight across from the Royal Palace.

David, apprehensive, had arrived from the MonteAzul at 8:30. He had spent the earlier part of the day flopping back and forth between doubts and recriminations for not having played Ariel straight and hopes that she would assume that it was he who had sent the invitation and would be intrigued by the romance and adventure of it. He hoped he hadn't wrecked a promising friendship.

While worrying he decided to give the cops a chance to expose themselves if they were watching him. He went up to Fernando el Católico and picked up a watch he had had repaired. He walked up to and almost past the watchmaker's but, at the last instant, ducked inside. The shop had a little bay window that protruded out into the sidewalk, giving a good view of the area. It was Saturday morning busy, but he saw nothing out of the ordinary. No one rushing forward to see where he had gone. No one loitering about seeming to wait for him to come back out.

MOSCOW GOLD | 109

David had a shoeshine guy he liked. The stand stood in the entrance to the public market. He went there next. The fellow always took his time, so David had good opportunity to observe the street activity from the shadows.

"How's business, Julio?" David asked as he settled in.

"*Más o menos,* not easy making a living in Madrid these days, you know."

"Tell me about it." David acted sympathetic. "Almost everybody has to have a little something on the side. Like my portero. He moonlights out at the big abattoir in Vallecas. Leaves the portera to handle the building a lot."

After Calvín's conversation on the way to the Benidorm the other evening, David probed for indication that Julio was a government watcher.

"Friend of mine from school works over at the Ministry of Tourism. Tells me a lot of folks get a little extra from the government— serenos and porteros and the like—keeping track of people in the neighborhood, promoting the public safety and good order. Something like that might work out for you, Julio. You have a lot of customers, and you're here all day long. You talk to people. You see what goes on."

Julio had, by now, brushed the polish off David's shoes and was ready for the shining rag. He now applied the rag assiduously without looking up—affecting intense concentration. "I would know nothing of such things, señor."

David thought his reaction and response were a clear admission that he, in fact, did know much of such things. David decided to leave a small bit of disinformation with the man.

"I'd love to get something extra," he said disingenuously. "My paper pays well enough, but I could do with more. I'm out of luck though. Regulations are that us foreigners aren't supposed to be working in Spain. Don't want us taking jobs from you all, I guess. So, I can't do it."

The normally talkative Julio finished the shine without comment. David hopped down and paid him with just a little extra tip.

110 | DOUGLAS L. FIELD

"Don't suppose the government would make an exception in my case," David said with an ironic look, trying to find Julio's eyes and failing. "I am a reporter after all."

Julio was bent over neatening up his tins of polish and brushes.

David crossed the street and went up to Onésimo and his lottery easel. "Hey, blindman."

"Got your shoes shined, huh?" Onésimo looked unseeing in David's direction.

"How would you know that? Do they have a different squeak?"

"Nah, I can smell the polish."

David marveled and shook his head. "I'm wondering how old Julio over there manages to make a living. Polishing shoes at a *duro* a pop doesn't seem like it would cut it—even with tips. I've heard that a lot of people around the neighborhood are getting a little extra for keeping track of the rest of us and reporting to the authorities."

"A lot of people are, yeah. This a surprise to you?"

"What about Julio?"

"Him too."

"Thought so. You told me yesterday that the Cuerpo are on my case. Truth is, they think *I'm* working illegally. I just told him I'd like to get a side job, but I can't 'cause it's illegal. I'm hoping he'll report that. Put them off the scent a little."

"He will. Maybe already has. Network's pretty tight. But you don't have a side job anyway, do you? So, there are no worries, sí," Onésimo said mockingly.

"No. Of course not." David responded in kind.

"No. You wouldn't. It would be against the law."

"Hey, Onésimo, speaking of my legal job, my editor's making me do a story on the Moscow Gold. You know what that is?" David changed the subject.

"Never heard of it. What is it? Like some kind of Russian cigarettes or something?"

MOSCOW GOLD | 111

David laughed. "No, you jerk. I wish it was that easy. Dates to the civil war. Banco de España here in Madrid sent the country's gold reserves to Soviet Russia to keep them away from Franco."

"Let me guess. We never got it back."

"Something like that. But listen, Onésimo, my name comes up over the work thing, but have you heard mention of me in connection with my doing a story on this Moscow Gold?"

"Not yet. But if the bad guys are talking about it, I will hear. I always do."

"You're a good friend. Give me twenty pulls. Can't say I'm feeling lucky with all that's going on. Maybe though."

And so it had gone throughout the day. David engaging in various quotidian activities. Not trying to hide anything. Keeping it simple in case they were keeping track of him. Hoping he could catch them. He didn't.

In the afternoon, he went several blocks up Vallehermoso to a shop on Avenida de la Reina Victoria where they repaired and rented bikes. He hired one for an hour and took it across the street to a large park. He sat on a bench for several minutes—enough time to let any minders rent their own bikes. Then he took off riding. No one appeared to follow. He circled around the park and doubled back several times on his own track. If anyone was on to him, he never detected it. It took up waiting time till the Teatro anyway.

Now. Finally. At the Teatro it was coming up 8:50.

No Ariel. David was starting to get nervous. It had seemed a good idea when he had first thought of it but now not so much. The plaza in front of the theater entrance had filled with people. There was a crowd lined up to get in. He stood where he could see the Ópera Métro exit as well as the circular drive where the taxis dropped off theatergoers.

No Ariel.

The crowd surging to get in began to have its way. It started to thin out, perceptibly. Back and forth from Métro to taxis. Still no Ariel.

There she came! Up the steps. Out of the Métro. She looked cool, collected, purposeful, and very dignified on a warm evening. She wore a white sleeveless blouse with a high collar and tailored in an understated way to compliment her figure with a straight dark gray skirt and a stylish maroon purse.

She looked around and got a couple of *piropos*, the gratuitous and unsolicited compliments Madrid men are unable to keep from shouting out to attractive women walking alone. She ignored them and headed for the theater entrance.

David slipped up beside her and put his arm in hers. "Ariel, you came. I was afraid you wouldn't."

She turned towards him, smiled and gave him a light kiss on both cheeks. A hint of *L'Air du Temps*. "To be truthful, at first I was hesitant. I wanted to, but I had some doubts. I worked through them. You came up with a memorable way of asking me." The voice low and smooth.

"Did you know it was me?"

"I became confident." Ariel smiled. "I went down later and interrogated Don Hilario. He gave me a pretty good description. Good-looking guy, speaks well, but not a Spaniard, he thought. The evidence added up."

He moved half a step away and took her in. "You look nice. I like *your* description. It's good to see you. Let's go in. We'll just make it." He had the tickets, purchased yesterday afternoon, already in hand.

"Who's the girl?" asked Monge. He and Zapatero were loitering by the taxi stands in front of the theater. They were well melted into the large crowd.

"Dunno. Think she's a Spaniard?" Zapatero responded.

"Looks like it to me. She's attractive."

Zapatero nodded.

Monge said, "I want to hurt this punk. Aren't there American girls enough that he doesn't need to come over here and poach on us? Jackass."

"Be patient. We'll get him. Go and call Chema. Fill him in. Symphony will take a couple hours, maybe more. We can go and get a beer. It's on you."

⁓

Orchestra seats. Back some but near the center. "Rafael Frühbeck de Burgos. That's an odd name. Is he part German?" David asked when they'd been seated.

Ariel knew the answer. "No, he's as pure Spanish as I am. Frühbeck's his true last name but he added the 'de Burgos' later as a stage name. Burgos is his hometown. Provincial city up in Old Castile. He went to the *conservatorio* there. Then studied in Munich, I think it was. Wanted to give himself a little extra distinction I guess."

"Aren't you well informed!" David commented.

"Do you think so, Mr. Journalist from Missouri, USA?" Pronouncing it *Ooh Ese Ah,* she said good-naturedly. "We Spaniards have to keep track of each other."

"Do you know him? Met him?"

"No, no. By reputation only. That and what you can read in the papers. How is it that you come to like this kind of music? Not Bobby Darin and the Brothers Everly?"

"Well, long story short, through a roommate at university. He had a trust fund. Spent most of it on classical recordings," David explained.

Then the lights went down.

"We listened while we played dominoes and bridge instead of studying," he whispered in her ear.

The conductor and the orchestra acquitted themselves with aplomb. The little pianist from Barcelona produced fire and verve for the piano concerto and the ensemble soul and tenderness for the indigenous pieces.

After the intermission and not long after the program had started again, Ariel put her hand in her lap. Lovely long and well-proportioned fingers, nails freshly varnished dark red for the occasion. David reached out and held it. Ariel made a low, almost inaudible sigh. She leaned in slightly, closer to his shoulder.

Madrid nights in the summer are almost always exquisite, inviting, comfortably warm, usually windless—ideal for being outside. But in this twenty-fifth year of the Franco regime, madrileños were restless. So yearning were they for freedom that every evening they enjoyed the summer with a palpable urgency, as if they sensed life to be leaving them a bit behind. The tempo of nightlife pounded and throbbed. Madrid was unwilling to risk the loss of even a single moment.

Every now and then, however, there took place a providential confluence of elements, perfect temperature, a whiff of jasmine on the barely perceptible breeze, some calming and ethereal spirit afoot that caused the city to pause and draw its breath. Pressure and compulsion fleeted away. The people lived a blissful and carefree evening. As such things will happen, this August Saturday was one of those nights. And David and Ariel got contentedly and irredeemably caught up in it.

After the performance, they followed the crowds out into the plaza and headed up toward the action on Princesa. They found an outside table on the sidewalk under a large red-and-white Cinzano umbrella. It was busy. People were passing by, and waiters scurried in all directions but less frenetically than usual. They decided on Cuba libres that came in due course as they talked.

David was an inveterate sloucher. He slid down in his chair, crossing his legs at the ankles. Casual affectations aside, he watched Ariel with intense interest. She sat straight and poised, listened, smiled, and laughed often. When she talked, her voice came as a deep, creamy, and mellifluous alto. She made the faint and fetching whistling of her esses like only Spanish girls seem to be able to do.

Ariel had been born in 1940, David learned, right after the end of the civil war. Her mother, whose own mother had been part Irish, had died young. Mamá had been distant and aloof, leaving Ariel, for the most part, to her own devices. "Almost as if she had me, gave me an exotic name, and then forgot about me," Ariel said.

Her Papá was, in essence, inept and ineffectual. Not outgoing, he kept to himself. He owned a little cap and beret shop. "He's on the Calle Mayor, headed up to the plaza from Puerta del Sol, right there where the street narrows."

"I know that shop. Has an old style, black-and-gold sign. Gorras y Boinas Muñiz. I've been in there," David remembered.

"That's Daddy. 'Since 1913, by special appointment to King Alfonso XIII,' and all that folderol, but Daddy hasn't been there that long," Ariel recounted.

"I didn't buy anything. Never thought berets are that much my style."

"You should. Daddy needs the money. I don't see him at all often. I think at best he ekes by. Lives at the back of the shop."

The Hunger Years had been difficult for Ariel's family, as they had been for everyone. Too little to eat and too little fuel in the winter. "In those years Spain's only friend was Juan Perón of all people. In Argentina," she said without resentment.

"Franco's repaid him the favor. He's in exile here in Madrid. I tried to interview him. Couldn't get access," David put in.

Ariel ignored that and continued. It had seemed to be in vogue to punish Spain for Franco's alliances with Germany and Italy. Perhaps an understandable sentiment but, she thought, unfair to the Spanish *people*, as it had been the *government*, not they who had made those decisions. "Americans have the idea that it is a simple matter to throw off a socialist or fascist dictator. They hold it against people who don't. But it isn't easy. I pray you in the United States never have to learn this firsthand."

Well, her family, such as it was, and the country, had persevered. By the late '50s, there was improvement. There had been sufficient resources to afford her education. For that, she was grateful to her father. After finishing school, she had first worked in a *gestoría*, a type of glorified escrow company very prevalent in Spain. When he was starting up DOCICA, Jaime Castellón had enticed her away and out to Carabanchel. For some years, she had lived at the Gaztambide flat. Her landlady, Doña Sagrario, acted toward Ariel like a doting aunt. Ariel felt she had every reason for contentment.

David took in her story and more her manner of telling it. Not even in the difficult or unpleasant parts did her expression lose its warmth and openness. She was not the least resentful or embittered. David was fascinated.

"Don't you have *some* ill feelings out of all of that?" he asked.

"It's easy to be Spanish, bitter, and cynical. I can't do much about being Spanish." She smiled. "But I've committed not to be either of the other two."

"You've had commendable success, I'd say."

What a delightful person, David thought. *A beautiful woman with a beautiful soul.*

"There's no benefit to me in moping over past adversity. But growing up as I did has made me wary of taking risks. That's the one thing. Stability and regular order. Careful and cautious. That's Ariel. Nothing unpredictable. So far I've managed."

"You're an optimist on top of everything else," he grinned.

"God is good and so is life. For certain this night, no?" Ariel replied.

After a time, they decided to move on and found another sidewalk café to their liking. The conversation was a little lighter now. Ariel flirted, tossed her hair, and seemed to enjoy herself to the full. She leaned into David's conversation, brushed his hand or arm on occasion. The brown eyes flashed, now passionate, now exquisitely tender. They talked of anything and everything, politics, office gossip, the weather in Missouri. David was enchanted.

When they talked about the office, David mentioned the attention he had been getting from the cops. "I'm not supposed to be working out at Carabanchel. I think the cops suspect that I am."

MOSCOW GOLD | 117

"You ought to talk to Ignacio." she remarked. Pronounced /Eegnahtheeoh/, the name was very common in the Hispanic world.

"Who's Ignacio?"

"Jaime's technical guy. Runs the machinery. You've seen him. Middle-aged. Ruddy complexion. He fought in the war. Quite bravely, I think. *Cosas clandestinas. ¿Qué sé yo?* I'm sure you've met him."

"I *guess* so." David was unsure.

"Surely you have. Ignacio. Ignacio Arjona. Nickname's Nacho."

❧

Time came to go. They made a reluctant but long and agreeable walk up Gaztambide from Princesa.

About halfway along, Ariel pointed and whispered, "David, look, look!"

On the far side of the street an elderly couple were walking in the same direction. They were stooped and moved slowly. Then David heard it. *Tap, tap,* and *tap.* They both were blind. They walked arm in arm, the wife on the building side, the husband on the curb. Each had a white cane. She tapped their way along the buildings' edges and he along the sidewalks'.

Ariel was moved. "¡Ay! *¡Qué preciosos son!* What a beautiful picture of marriage." She hooked his arm in hers and held it tightly. "I wonder who they are and where they live. I've never seen them in the neighborhood before."

David saw that she searched David's face for his reaction. "How does it go?" he said, looking back at her. "'And the two shall become as one flesh.'"

They caught up to and then passed the older people. "Just like us," David murmured into her ear, "they couldn't resist being out on such a beautiful evening."

She gripped his arm even tighter. If that were possible.

Though late, the night *was* still a perfection. Not long now before the street sweepers would be coming out.

118 | DOUGLAS L. FIELD

Then at number 67, Ariel said, "I should go in. It was a beautiful evening. Thank you for inviting me."

David gazed at her. "I'm sad it's over." He clapped twice. In seconds, the sereno.

"A pleasant evening, isn't it, Don Genaro?" Ariel said.

"Oh yes, Miss Ariel, conspicuously." Affecting to be the soul of discretion, Genaro concentrated on finding the correct key and turned for the portal door.

"Let's talk again, Ariel."

She grabbed him around the neck, one foot on tiptoe, the other raised behind her and gave him a quick kiss on the mouth.

"Oh, David, do let's!" Then she ran inside—without looking back.

၈

The lights burned late at the Comisaría San Bernardo. Monge and Zapatero had headed in when their subjects left Princesa. Chema Jaso was waiting for them.

"What do you make of it?" Chema asked.

"Looked like a couple of young *novios* out for the evening," replied Zapatero.

"Are they getting along? Any tension we can exploit?"

"Looked pretty mutual to me," said Zapatero. "I'd say they were having a good time."

"Agree. Nothing suspicious tonight as far as Room 11 is concerned." Monge tried for a measure of objectivity that he did not feel.

"Who's the girl?" demanded Chema.

'Don't know yet. We'll get that in the morning. No sweat though. She's not avoiding or anything like that," promised Monge.

"Get it. We may need the connection. Some leverage even. Use her to squeeze him if we have to. We're done for tonight." Chema dismissed them.

၈

MOSCOW GOLD | 119

Lights were, as well, burning late in the Office of the Cultural Attaché at the embassy of the United States of America.

"They're a couple of Dago rubes, Jackie; of course they didn't make me."

"I've told you, Nick, don't call me that. Keep it up and you're fired," snarled Isham.

"You're not going to fire me. I'm the best you've got, and I'm way better than them two," Nick Barnickle replied.

"Well, then, how about I put one of my size-13 boots up your ass and teach you a lesson right here, right tonight? I don't like you. I don't like being called that. And I don't like being here this late. We're going to do this may way, *Nickie*. You got any questions?"

"OK, *Jack*. I was just being friendly."

Disagreeable a human being though he was, Jack Isham had to agree that, at what he did, Nick Barnickle was the best. Career CIA. Specialty in tradecraft. Subspecialty in surveillance. He'd been in and out of the hot spots—East Berlin, Hungary, Gdansk, Prague. Never burned. Always good for excellent product.

"This was a walk in the park tonight, Jack. The two Dagos followed the subject to the Royal Theater. He never saw them, and they never saw me. Then the Dago chick showed. Her and the subject went to the theater. The surveillance took a couple of hours off and then picked them up when they came out. They kept an eye on them while they went for a couple of drinks, and he took her home. A cinch."

"You're sure they weren't aware of you? And what's with all this 'Dago' crap?"

"Yes, I'm sure they weren't aware of me. Who do you think you're talking to here? I'm a professional. Have faith. The Brits, they call the Spanish Dagos, like they call the French Frogs. Dates back to the days of the Royal Navy or something like that. Kind of cute, don't you think?" Nick twittered.

"What I think, Nick, is that it's kind of crass. Be careful, or I'll send you to charm school—at your own expense. Get out of here, keep me

120 | DOUGLAS L. FIELD

advised, and don't get caught. The *Spanish* police are smarter and more capable than you give them credit for."

David walked home to Calle de Vallehermoso and to bed but, in the event, not to sleep. He had a lot to sort out and now the girl on top of the rest.

CHAPTER 14

Madrid: (Later on) Sunday, November 8, 1936

After leaving Cóndor at the Pintor Rosales flat, Aníbal made his way into the heart of the city and east toward Paseo de la Castellana.

Day having dawned, he decided to chance hiding in plain sight. Nervy, Nacho stuck to the main boulevards. He relied on the innocuousness of his bakery cover to avoid coming to any adverse attention. It might work. It might not.

The heat of summer had dissipated. It had turned gray and cold. Low gray sky brooded over gray buildings, gray streets, and gray sidewalks; mimicking what the Parisians call the *grisaille,* it is *la grisalla* as they have it in Spanish—pervasive grayness. The cold air hastened and then scattered the fall of leaves. Madrileños accustomed to scorching summer heat were making sluggish adaptation to the sudden change.

Mood reflects weather. Cold fear, together with cold wind, infused Nacho as he worked his way toward the big boulevard.

Fear also infused everybody else in the capital. No one with right-wing or Catholic sympathies dared to venture forth. Professionals of

MOSCOW GOLD | 123

all disciplines either offered formal and vocal declaration for the Left or went into hiding. All out the Calles de Alberto Aguilera, Carranza, and Génova, Nacho saw the doors and windows of residential buildings were shuttered tight. People were in hiding, reduced to sending loyal servants out to lay hold of what limited food and supplies were available.

At the Glorieta de San Bernardo, Nacho stood aside to allow passage of a speeding French embassy Citroën Traction-avant. The big black car was complete with large flags flying from the front fenders and painted on the doors. Not much car traffic other than the diplomats now.

Mono-clad militias and checas were unhindered and uninhibited. No government or police presence was evident or effective. There was good reason to be afraid. If not the order of the day, summary executions on mere suspicion of rightist inclinations were the order of the night.

As Nacho approached La Castellana, vague shapes bundled and muffled to the point of anonymity against the cold were hefting corpses from the street onto a horse-drawn cart. Madrid was under siege—from without and within.

His destination on La Castellana was the War Ministry. Nacho, to his appreciable peril, was spying on the Loyalist government. For Aníbal, the Ministry had become a major source of actionable intelligence. Lord's Day or not, there was a crush of business there today. Nacho needed to work his sources.

The defense of Madrid had been placed in the hands of a *Junta de Defensa* (Council of Defense). It was of hurried creation. Supposed to be an equitable representation of the various Popular Front factions, the council consisted exclusively of young men, including one Santiago Portillo, a communist who would soon rise to leadership.

Cabildo Morelos worked in the War Ministry. He was the anarchist observer at the ministry and served on the Junta de Defensa. As such he was privy to the proceedings, strategy sessions, and policy decisions of both the junta and the ministry.

Cabildo, the anarchist, and Aníbal, the *panadero*, had become friends.

Aníbal found a bench in the parkway opposite the War Ministry. He settled himself and his makeshift transporter in to observe operations. They were chaotic this morning—comings and goings, messengers on motorcycles, and bicycles tearing in and out of the porte cochere; solemn military officers arrived in a hurry and left again soon after.

Before long, Cabildo made his way out of the ministry. He came over to Nacho's bench. Nacho would break or otherwise "damage" one or two of his loaves for convenient "sharing out" of goods thus rendered unsalable with his contact. Cabildo knew he was in for a spot of *almuerzo*.

Nacho's meeting with Cabildo today represented the culmination of weeks and months of careful cultivation dating back to July—to just after the rising had started.

"Buenas, camarada," Cabildo said as he sidled up to Nacho's bench. "Not the best of days to be hanging around here, Aníbal. Security's tight. The guards are nervous. Franquista spies everywhere. Lots of suspicion." Cabildo looked back toward the building at an approaching figure.

One of the militia thugs who putatively guarded the War Ministry slouched over—dirty blue mono, black-and-red anarchist armband. *"¿Y este desgraciado?"* (And this miserable loser?)

"A fellow worker," Cabildo answered for Aníbal. "Delivers bread. I'll vouch for him. Any of that left, camarada?"

Nacho fished out a chunk for Cabildo and one for the mono.

"You carry bread in that contraption?" Mono asked.

"Ahumada's Bakery. Use it for home deliveries, camarada. Just a little rest here in the shade. We panaderos start our day early," Nacho prevaricated.

MOSCOW GOLD | 125

"Bad place to rest. What's your name? That's the War Ministry over there."

"Then I'd better move on. I'm called Aníbal." Nacho looked under his tent. He produced a couple of chunks of pistola, one end already broken off. "Before I start off again, will you camaradas join me for a bite?"

"Very kind, Aníbal. Appreciate your generosity. I need to get back across the street," the anarchist said, stuffing the bread in his mouth. "Careful or you'll have the whole mob over here." He shrugged as he moved off.

"The proletariat is family, camarada."

Cabildo Morelos was in his early thirties. He was a true believer but an insecure one. His insecurities resulted in a certain loquaciousness, as if he were talking through his beliefs to build his confidence in them. He was also a man under stress—a guy who needed a sympathetic listener friend. Nacho obliged.

Nacho kept to his legend, to the cover story that he was a simple rustic, lucky to have a job in the city delivering bread. He listened and was scrupulous about not asking any questions. He got what he got. He let his source's information trickle out as it would. The contact was lulled into a sense of security. Aníbal was rarely disappointed.

Morelos was dark complexioned, with thick black hair and heavy eyebrows in effect grown together. He needed to shave twice a day and always had a stubble of beard. The man needed a cryptonym. Nacho thought he looked Egyptian, so he called him Faraón, Pharaoh.

Today, Faraón had information well worth Aníbal's risk and effort. Faraón described intense activity at the ministry and before the junta. His news was all bad. Faraón's bad news not only trickled but also gushed forth.

Faraón was just one of the sources Aníbal had recruited and developed. There was also Maria de los Ángeles Sandoval. She was a maid in the home of Colonel Vicente Rojo, one of the Republic's most capable officers and second in command to General Miajas.

126 | DOUGLAS L. FIELD

Maria de los Ángeles enjoyed the good favor of the Rojo family because, among other reasons, she was a very devout young woman and, thus, felt to be trustworthy. What was unknown to the colonel and his wife was that Maria de los Ángeles's younger brother Julián, also a devout young man, had been a novitiate at the seminary in Alcalá de Henares and had been tortured and executed by a gang of leftists who had sacked the parish church in that town at the very outset of the war.

Since then, Maria de los Ángeles had harbored a smoldering hatred for the godless Republic. She was a regular bread customer of Aníbal's. She bought for the Rojo family. Through apparent idle chitchat, Aníbal learned of her brother's fate and of the identity of her employer. After that, he plied her with some gentle questions about what intelligence might be overheard at home. She had been low-hanging fruit.

As Agent Isidora, she began to provide high-grade product in the very natural context of making normal grocery purchases for her employer family.

Isidora the Devout had continued to cultivate the trust and confidence of her family. She took care to attend to their needs—a little extra wine or small cognac for the Colonel after the children were off to bed, offering the tender ear of a confidante to la Señora de Rojo when she was troubled. Continuous and valuable snippets relating to the colonel's work came to her.

After seeing Faraón, Nacho moved along to Isidora's street. She appeared in due course for her daily bread buy. For her and the Rojos, there remained but a lonely pistola and a couple of individual loaves called *barritas*. Isidora's news had been no better than Faraón's.

So, chilled by the advancing autumn weather, Nacho serviced his contacts Faraón and Isidora. Having collected their information, Aníbal returned to his own place to evaluate and summarize the take. Then he created and encoded his message. He started on page 119 of Clarín's masterwork.

The message would be delivered tomorrow.

CHAPTER 15

Madrid: Monday, November 9, 1936

Someone was at the door of the Pintor Rosales flat, the morning "bread" delivery.

Cóndor opened to Aníbal. Aníbal set the pistola on a sideboard.

"Do you bring good news, Aníbal?"

"The opposite, Cóndor. The Reds are holding. A great misfortune that our battle plan became known to the enemy," Aníbal lamented.

"We did what we could, Aníbal. Good job the *chequistas* didn't tap you on the spot yesterday morning."

"The militia patrols are everywhere. It becomes worse each day that passes. Cóndor, you must continue to remain inside. We will provide you with food and supplies. Conditions in the city are hideous. Looting, terror, and murder all night. Then all day collecting the dead."

"Maybe today it ends. I had thought, hoped, it would be yesterday," Cóndor said.

"Maybe, maybe not, Cóndor. The latest intelligence is hidden in the bread. There are more problems."

MOSCOW GOLD | 129

The sixth-floor *piso* enjoyed advantageous views over the Casa de Campo. Nacho and Cóndor kept well back, lest the merest flash or glint from inside be observed.

Cóndor held up a pair of binoculars. "I watched the battle flow yesterday—and then ebb. Today I hope to see it flow decisively," Cóndor announced.

"Consider it doubtful at this point, Cóndor," Aníbal admonished.

Cóndor looked out at the Casa de Campo. The ancient royal hunting preserve had now become a huge seven-square-mile city park spanning rolling hills and the Manzanares River west of town.

"Our forces were concealed out there yesterday morning," Cóndor said wistfully. "Their attack came out of the low trees and scrub. They have concrete bunkers hidden in the foliage."

Nacho said nothing before Cóndor went on. "The plan was a good one. It should have worked. They were to occupy University City and the Plaza de España. The tactical position would have been ideal— artillery with a clear field of fire up the Gran Vía and into the interior of Madrid. Menacing yet avoiding excessive damage to buildings and monuments in the Centro."

"The Reds defending the city got hold of the plan. I reported that yesterday," Nacho said.

"I got your warning into their hands," Cóndor went on. "It was so close. The international press already has us as winners. I saw headlines—'The Last Hours of Madrid' and 'The Death of a Capital.' Radio Lisbon described General Franco triumphantly entering the city on a white horse. Fanciful balderdash that. I doubt the Caudillo has a white horse."

"They held us off," Nacho lamented. "The Reds transferred thousands of troops from Carabanchel to the Casa de Campo here. *Carabinieros,* regular soldiers, militias, and even a battalion of women."

"Women! Will the Red bastards stop at nothing?"

"Less than half of these fighters had any previous experience of combat," said Nacho. "But it worked. Faraón claims that Varela was beaten back. His moors fought their way into University City. They occupied several *facultades*. Story is that some of the savages found the laboratory animals—cooked and ate them. Got sick and died."

"Idiots," Cóndor growled.

"In this sector, our troops were stopped on this side of the river—down there where it's steep," Nacho pointed.

"The Generalísimo should have been more aggressive and driven harder towards the city center," Cóndor observed.

"He wanted to minimize collateral damage downtown, or so I heard," Nacho replied. "Preserve the national heritage and all that."

"Might be a worthwhile sacrifice—if it ends the war."

"Maybe, but according to Faraón, the real setback was the arrival at the front of about two thousand foreign fighters—in some sort of international brigade. They were soldiers from all over Europe. Faraón says our gold reserves in Moscow are being used to pay the foreign fighters."

"I had heard that. Using our money to pay extranjeros to fight against their own people."

"The stupid madrileños thought they were Soviets," Nacho went on. "Morons were cheering, 'Vivan los rusos,' all along the Gran Vía. Trouble is they are steady soldiers. Not like the militias. Our guys stalled out. The defenders of the city are celebrating a great and emotional victory."

Cóndor went to the sideboard where Nacho had placed the pistola. He got himself and Nacho a sherry. As he poured, he said, "Since the troop movements have already started, I am able to tell you that Varela's switching the thrust of his attack back down to the southwest—back toward Carabanchel."

"That might not be wise, Cóndor. Isidora says Mrs. Rojo intimated that the anarchist Durruti and a column of his followers will be arriving late today. It is being deployed, at Durruti's specific insistence, to University City. That's another three thousand guys."

MOSCOW GOLD | 131

Cóndor nodded at the sideboard. "Your message will get where it needs to go. There still may be hope. You are a very brave man, Aníbal. Spain is grateful. You will be rewarded. Be sure of that." Cóndor raised his glass.

CHAPTER 16

Leganés: Monday, November 23, 1936

Less than ten miles southwest of Madrid, in the small town of Leganés, Generalísimo Francisco Franco convened a roundtable of his advisors and subordinates.

His expression was explosive. "What is our precise status? The short version?"

Franco had addressed no one specifically. His counselors of war looked at each other and then their gaze fell collectively on the intelligence chief.

The man summoned his courage. "For the present, Caudillo, Madrid city has been saved for the Republic."

"And by what means have we been denied our objective?"

"The arrival on the eighth of the XI International Brigade and, a day later, the XII International Brigade, sir, as well as Buenaventura Durruti and his anarchists from the Aragón front."

"And how did those *incapazes*, those *ineptos* manage this tactical feat?" Franco demanded.

MOSCOW GOLD | 133

"We believe with the connivance and support of the Soviet government in Moscow. Financed by the Banco de España gold reserves that the Reds alienated to that location in October."

Franco quivered with rage, "It is my will that we locate, arrest, and try for treason all who have been responsible for this outrage against the Spanish nation. Get me proposals as to how we can work our diplomatic contacts to effect the return of our property. Do it now."

"Sí, Caudillo. *Inmediatemente.*"

The little generalísimo looked around the table gritting his teeth. "Today I am suspending the frontal assault on Madrid."

Then he looked at General Mola. "Mola, your reservation at the Café Molinero on the Gran Vía still stands. Unused." Sarcasm palpable.

"Yes, Caudillo." Mola tried to defend himself. "But Madrid has not become 'the Graveyard of Fascism' as the red posters have promised."

Franco continued to fume, "*Pero no pasamos.* We didn't pass. Not yet anyway."

PART III
SARDINERO BEACH

CHAPTER 17

Carabanchel: Wednesday, August 21, 1963

A Carabanchel workday.

On his way out, David found the portera alone. He decided to chat her up. "I haven't seen much of your husband lately, señora. Must be a busy time at the slaughterhouse."

"Yes, Mister David, in fact it is."

"Isn't that unusual for August? Many folks are on holiday this month, no?' David asked.

"My husband tells me that it is conditions in the provinces, on the ranches. They have created a glut. It's been a dry year. Forage is scarce, so the cattlemen are selling early."

"Then additional burden is on you to maintain the building." Understanding. Comprehending. It was a statement not a question. David acted like he understood that her husband was gone all the time and she was overworked. He tried to show her a little tenderness.

"Well …"

"I recognize the capable work that you are doing," David went on. There! A hint of the old smile.

MOSCOW GOLD | 137

He seemed to be getting somewhere. He decided to try a little flattery. "I'm also grateful to you for looking after mail and messages that come for me—as you were so kind to do a week or so ago. It was an important message from a professional colleague. I would have hated to miss it or have had it delayed. Thank you again for your diligence."

"You're most welcome, Mister David. It is a pleasure to have you in our building."

David decided to ladle it on. "In my time here in Spain, I have come to realize the importance of the institution of the portería. We do not have such a thing in my country. You and your husband contribute to the welfare of everyone who lives here. You both are very careful about our security and safety. It is good to have competent people on duty in the building all through the day."

She could not hold David's gaze. A long pause.

What's she conflicted about?

She looked up and managed a considered and slow reply. "Not only do the portero and I endeavor to look after the safety and comfort of our residents, but we also do our best to preserve their confidences— and, eh, how shall I say it, their privacy. But please understand, at times in Spain, this may not be so easy."

Now she did look him in the eye, firm and steady, plus the old smile. "You do understand me don't you, señor?"

David thought a second. Best to be blunt. "Someone has been making inquiries about me here in the portería?"

Now she held his gaze—steady. She said nothing.

"And these inquiries were official, weren't they?

Gaze still steady and still no answer

"I understand, yes. Of course, I do, señora, and *muy amable*. Have a pleasant day."

Out the door and up toward Arapiles, he looked for and checked in with Onésimo. Onésimo was in his usual place and all about his usual business. David clomped up to the blind man, telegraphing his approach.

"Hey, chief. What stinks around here?

"Ah, my favorite gringo. Did you forget to change your socks? When are you going to lose your accent? I would recognize you anywhere."

"What accent? I have a good ear, and I just copy you. Besides, I'm more Spanish than El Greco." David played along.

"El Greco was a Greek, you peon," Onésimo sniffed

"Than Velázquez then. Any buzz?"

"Yup. Good job you came by today. Couple of Cuerpo pukes from the San Bernardo Comisaría walked by here yesterday. Grousing about leaning on your porteros and not getting anywhere—at least not with Mrs. What's more, it sounds like the whole comisaría's pissed about being shorthanded because these two are out on what they called 'the reporter stakeout.' That's gotta be you."

"Yeah, that's gotta be me."

A hundred-peseta note slipped into Onésimo's shirt pocket. "*Cuídate*. Sounds like I need to make myself scarce."

David headed for la Plaza de la Moncloa, where he caught the Carabanchel tranvía.

While the tranvía meandered along toward his destination, much thought swirled around in David's head. No doubt about it, the Cuerpo was on to him. Their persistence was ominous. He wondered if he would be able to catch them in the act and if catching them would cause them to back off.

David also rehearsed in his mind some other events of recent days. Ariel's and his evening out had been most agreeable. David had hoped for a nice time, but they had gotten along and gotten acquainted well beyond what he had imagined. A girl hadn't caused him any loss of sleep since he didn't know when.

He would be seeing her again as soon as he got to Jaime's and was anxious to know if she shared his sentiments—or if she even would let on.

Research on where the gold went after the Krelmin had borne a little fruit, as the *Trib's* morgue had a smattering of *Paris-soirs*. Looking

MOSCOW GOLD | 139

at them, he ascertained that Paris's precious metals had experienced minor diminution in prices late in 1936 and in 1937. He found a few vague references to subtle increases of street crime in Paris and the activities of Soviet "diplomatic" personnel.

He could get more in the *Paris-soir* morgue. They would have a full set of old editions. Paris was where the known eyewitnesses were. David knew he would be making a trip to Paris. With Ariel now in the mix, he would rather stay in Madrid. It was one more decision to make.

David snapped back from his reverie about three miles before his destination. At the fringes of his awareness, he noticed a youngish man with no briefcase or portfolio get off the tranvía. At the same stop, another of similar profile got on.

The Carabanchel tranvía was a milk run line populated by middle-aged and older persons, lower class, people laden heavy with packages or merchandise, schoolchildren, nannies, and maids. David himself was something of an anomaly. Unusual for one empty-handed young city boy to be riding out here, much less three.

Uncrystallized disquiet gathered inside David's head. First the portera and then Onésimo. They were looking for him, and their interest would not be friendly.

The second young rider was just sitting there doing nothing. No newspaper, no book. In a fog, he stared into space. He was a typical-looking man—dark hair, dark pants, short-sleeved blue shirt open at the collar, one of umpteen gazillion Spaniards just like him.

David's stop was coming up. If they were following him, they would connect him with DOCICA. That must not happen—not now, not ever.

How to lose this guy? David remembered something he had done with his pals from school. Madrid tranvías had doors on the right side at the very front and very back. The fronts and rears of the cars also angled inward toward the long axis, making a blunt point at both the front and back ends. When the doors were closed there still was a partial step outside the vehicle. There were exterior stanchions for ease of embarking and alighting. When the back door was closed there was, even so, just enough room for an enterprising adolescent who wanted to fare evade to hop aboard the outside half step, hold on, and ride unseen by the motorman.

David watched for another tranvía approaching in the oncoming direction. One did. David's streetcar stopped just as the other was pulling up close to it. At the last second, he ran out the rear door, hurried around the back of his tranvía, in front of the oncoming one and down its right side to the rear door, where, as in days of old, he got up on the narrow step and crouched down out of everyone's sight, including that of the other rider on the old tranvía and the driver of the new one.

The two tranvías hastened away from each other on their opposite paths. David rode two stops, hopped off, and bolted into a bar. No one followed. He then took a circuitous and, he believed, unobserved route back toward the DOCICA office.

❧

"Jaso. *Háblame*" (Talk to me).

"Chema, it's me, Monge."

"Ah, my loyal Monge. How is your day today? Most pleasant, I hope. *Inútiles*, you and Zapatero. Whole San Bernardo Battalion's griping about overload with you two goldbrickers on stakeout. What have you been up to, may I ask?"

"Keeping Spain safe for fascism, what else?" Monge said.

"Don't get political funny man. It can backfire. What's he been doing?" Jaso demanded.

Monge told him and then added, "This afternoon he got on the tranvía toward Carabanchel. Zapatero and I double-teamed him. I got off at Empalme, and Zapatero got on. Subject hopped off right before Carabanchel. That's where we lost him."

"Has he made you?" Chema inquired.

"Maybe. Zapatero says he jumped off and disappeared."

MOSCOW GOLD | 141

"Not good. He may go into hiding. Room 11 wants eyes on him. What about the girl?"

Monge was ready for the question. "She's Spanish—like we thought. Ariel Mercedes Muñiz Morales. Born in May '40. Works for one Jaime Castellón, good Falangist credentials. He's prosperous *and* connected, Chema. In the cinema business. Translates foreign movies, American mostly."

"Where's this Castellón guy located?"

"Offices uptown. Nice area. Salamanca somewhere. They do the real work in Carabanchel. Sixteen, eighteen people."

"Does the girl work in Carabanchel?"

"Don't know yet."

"Well shit, Monje, what do you think? The American's riding on the Carabanchel tranvía; he's hooked up with a girl that works for Castellón. Castellón translates movies made in English. The American's working off the books for Castellón. Has to be. Him and the girl are friends from work. We just got him."

"Makes sense, Chema."

"Of course, it makes sense. How come it took me to figure it out?"

Monje avoided answering, "We bring him in? Sweat him? Get the truth out of him? Suit me fine to deport his ass."

"Not so fast. It's complicated. If Castellón's connected and with Room 11 involved, I need to check."

"Señor Sáenz? Room 11? Inspector Jaso here."

"How are you, Inspector? What is the news?"

"We have all the principal individuals under active surveillance. It does appear that the subject has become aware of our interest in him."

"That was not intended to be the case, Inspector."

Jaso had no choice but to play it straight. "Correct. But he's smart, and he's suspicious. He may be getting some help."

"Is he pursuing the matter that we are interested in?"

"Not confirmed. It may become harder to maintain contact. I expect he will now try to evade. We are close to confirming that he's working off the books for a cinema dubbing operation in Carabanchel. That point of contact may be our hook."

"Is that distracting him from his investigation?"

"Unknown. We can bring him in for questioning. The only way to find out."

"Not yet, please. That may be an alternative. Later. Not just now. Room 11 are not the only ones interested. Other interested parties' goals are different than ours. Room 11 is managing the conflict. Please reestablish contact. I'll be in touch."

❦

Inside DOCICA and undetected, David felt he could relax. His room was quiet and empty. He went into the main office and found several people talking, including Ariel. She looked up smiling already, perhaps at some bon mot, and acted a little surprised to see him.

She putting on here?

"Hello, everyone." David greeted the group. Idle chatting continued, so he went back to his office. After a discreet time, as he had hoped she would, Ariel followed.

"The enchanting Miss Muñiz, what a pleasure to see you!" David said using the formal form of address. He knew that Spanish people who are on familiar terms with one another will sometimes, in exaggerated fashion, use the formal form of address to imply friendship.

"And you as well, Mr. Fordham!" She responded in kind. "I've been excited to see you all week. Did you arrive home without incident Saturday night? Well, no, it would have been Sunday morning?"

In the local fashion and with a perfunctory hug, Ariel brush kissed him on each cheek—left then right, just a little longer on the right.

Today she had the look. Graceful and poised, she wore a summer print dress with a swishy skirt. Maybe a little extra makeup.

MOSCOW GOLD | 143

"It *was* late. Time I found a taxi, I was near enough to Vallehermoso, so I just walked the rest of the way."

"That's a bit of a hike, but then I imagine you slept well." Faint irony, eyebrows raised for the briefest moment, the head tilted a little. Smart. Understated. Understanding.

"Like a baby," David fibbed. "You're looking *muy de moda*, today, Ariel."

"Oh, I've had this little frock forever."

"You should be on the cover of *Elle*."

"And you should stop exaggerating." Ariel's smile was a genuine one, affectionate. A fetching blush, and then she said, "I ought to get back to work."

"Well, then let's talk again soon." David was not ready for her to leave.

"Oh, yes. Do let's!" It was becoming a happy little personal ritual for them. Insider code.

"How about supper tonight?" David took a chance.

"I know for sure who's asking."

"I can send you a flower."

"I've saved the first one."

"Look for you at nine?"

Ariel raised her eyes to the ceiling and affected to think it over a longish moment. *"'Busca y hallarás"* (Seek and you shall find), she paraphrased. Then she grinned and went back into the main office.

David went to find Ignacio Arjona.

Nick Barnickle could scarcely contain his mirth.

"He did what?!"

"He ditched 'em, Jack. He flat ditched 'em. Funniest thing I ever saw." Barnickle was sprawled negligently in a chair across from Jack Isham's desk.

"Who ditched who?"

"The subject, Jack. Who else? Them two Dag ..., er, I mean Spanish cops."

"Slow down, Nick. Tell me what happened," Isham demanded.

Barnickle saw the opportunity to tweak Jack Isham's tail. He embraced it. "I tailed him this morning. Routine, innocent stuff. Then he's down at what they call Moncloa. Lotta streetcar and bus stops. I figure he's gonna take one, so I take a chance. I hop on. The number 8 streetcar. Bingo. I'm right. He gets on. I was already on, so no way he would suspect."

"What if he didn't get on. You would have lost him." Jack tried to deflate him.

"Naw." Nick was not being deterred. "My instincts are good. If he didn't get on, I would just have hopped off and hurried back to where he was standing around. Anyway, sure enough, one stop and his tail gets on too—only one of them. I call 'em Tweedledee and Tweedledum."

Now Barnickle caught his stride. "This time it's Tweedledum. Well, we hit Empalme. Dum gets off and Dee gets on. Your guy hasn't reacted at all. They all three look out of place. That's a working-class line out there. Them three are all city kids."

"You ever even heard the word *humility*, Nick?"

"So, we're almost to that dump they call Carabanchel." Nick ignored him. "Everybody still oblivious. Then there's another streetcar coming the other way. At the very last second, the subject hops off our car. He runs behind us and in front of the one coming the other way. He must've run down the far side of it, hung on somehow. When the other streetcar pulled away, you couldn't see him anywhere. Gone. Just like that."

Nick paused a second and then concluded, "A thing of beauty, Jack. A thing of beauty it was. Comical."

"He lost you too, Nick" Isham chided.

"Oh yeah, he did. He's a smart little rat. A natural spy."

"So, he's made the two Cuerpo types. That's clear. Has he made you too, Nick?"

"In your dreams," Barnickle scoffed.

"How can you be so sure?"

"I fit in. Promoted myself one of those blue monkey suits the construction workers wear—got it all grimy—and some of those stupid straw shoes, even a black beanie like they like. As I say, I fit right in. Davey boy never knew."

"OK, genius, where is he now, then?"

"Who knows? It might be a little harder for me to nail him now, but I'm your man."

"You say you're my man, Nick, but you don't know where he is? How am I supposed to think that works?"

"I'll get him, Jack. He's good but not in my league—not by a stretch."

"You'd better get him. And then you'd better keep him. The Company needs this, Nick. We need to get our hands on what he's going to turn up. And in order to get it, we need him safe and on the job," Isham thundered.

"I told you, I'll get him."

"Let me tell you why this is important. Have you ever heard of the Bay of Pigs?" Jack fumed.

"Yeah, down in Cuba. I wasn't in on that little party. I was in Bratislava. That's in Czech—"

"I know where Bratislava is, Nick, you dope. It's lucky for you that you weren't in on it. That was a screwup for the ages. JFK and that little punk brother of his sabotaged the whole op because, when it came time to pull the trigger, they didn't have the onions for it, either one of them. Then when it all came a cropper, the little weenie brother blamed the Company."

Isham worked himself up. "Dulles had told them not to do it, but they authorized it anyway. And then when push came to shove, they wimped out. Blamed us."

146 | DOUGLAS L. FIELD

Nick tried to show unfazed, but it was not indifference that he was feeling. Isham was more stoked up than usual. Nick had a nice career with the Company. Isham could hurt Nick if he decided to. Nick shrugged his shoulders. "I'm on it, Jack. Keep your shirt on."

"Too right you're on it. And I'm on you. This op here, Nick, we need it to work. I need it to work, and so you need it to work. Restore some of our lost cred with the administration. The only way it's going to work is if your friend and mine does what we want him to."

Isham clenched his jaw. "This fails, and there will be people looking for people to blame. You're good at what you're good at, Nick Barnickle; well, I am too. And you know what I'm good at? Dodging and deflecting blame when the caca goes south. You are putting two and two together here, m'boy?"

Nick got up. He left the office without saying anything. At the door, he looked back at Isham. He tried to show just the right amount of defiance. The conversation wasn't fun anymore.

David found him in a small workshop on the ground floor surrounded by numerous recording machines. It was stale in there with the smell of hot wires and old vacuum tubes.

The man had one of the machines apart. He looked to be in his early fifties. What hair he had was auburn with mustache to match but going to gray. Cheater glasses perched on the end of his nose. Not a Spanish complexion, David observed, northern more like, perhaps damaged by too much sun. His face was scarred but not by acne. It was almost like he had been a boxer in his youth with his nose maybe broken, maybe more than once. He was of average height, rawboned, and gangling.

David watched him work for a second. His movements were fluid and economical. It looked like he had lost part of a finger, maybe parts of two, on one hand, somewhere along the line.

"You Ignacio?"

"Could be. Depends who's asking?" The reply was terse, his muscles tense.

"I'm David. I work upstairs with Ariel and the others."

"¿A sí? Do you now?" He did not look up.

"Ariel suggested I look for you," David persisted feeling a little meek.

"You from here?"

"No, Norteamérica. Been here a long time though."

He looked to relax his body some. *"No me digas"* (You don't say). "It suit you here?"

"I'd say it's like a lot of stuff. You can't live with it, and you can't live without it."

"Sounds like you understand Spain. What can I do for you?"

"Trouble with the heat. I may need to disappear," David confessed.

"You can call me Nacho."

"Ariel says you might know about the police, keeping them off your back. Stuff like that."

"I might. Story?" Nacho showed less than loquacious.

"Working here to start. A couple of Cuerpo types have taken an interest in me. Over by Quevedo, they've hassled me off and on. More often now. They suspect I'm working illegal. Jaime says he has that covered. They tailed me out here today—a double team deal. I lost them," David explained.

"I can maybe help. Was undercover for a while in the civil war. You had to avoid attention. Lots of espionage in those years. You got good at it. It can be done."

"Seems like *they're* pretty good at it. I thought it was random. Didn't know they were following me till today," David said.

"Cuerpo are not all that sophisticated. Could be you just didn't know to be aware. Jaime does have the illegal job thing covered. He's connected. Cuerpo wouldn't surveil you for moonlighting out here. What else are you doing? Drugs? Politics? Sex trade?"

148 | DOUGLAS L. FIELD

"Nothing like that. I'm a journalist. Write for an American paper. Economic and money stuff. As bland as it can be."

"Gotta be something," Nacho persisted.

David explained the gold story assignment, how it wasn't voluntary and recounted a little of what he had already done.

"*That's* what's getting you the attention. We knew about that gold—in the war. We knew they shipped it. We couldn't stop them. My controller detailed me to drive part of it. Bunch of anarchists tried to steal it. Had to fight them off," Nacho blurted out, waves of memory coming over him.

"We?" David asked.

"I was a spy for Franco. To be blunt. Ran a small network. Got and carried out orders to obtain specific intelligence. Reported up the line. Ended up infiltrating a Red army unit. Wound up a refugee in France. Standard stuff." Nacho acted like it had all been routine.

"Doesn't sound standard. Sounds dangerous."

"It was, and it is. Your gold story is dangerous. It's always interested me ever since '36 when we moved it down to Cartagena. It's always been in the back of my mind how we could get it back. It's a long shot now," Nacho said, remembering.

"Seems like there's still plenty of interest."

"I don't know what the Cuerpo's interest is. That seems odd. But you're right; they won't be the only ones. You will need to be careful. The easiest thing for most of them is to catch you and kill you." Nacho did not mince words.

"Can I be blunt?" David said.

"Can I stop you?" It was not contentious. The corner of his mouth turned up.

"How did you justify working for Franco and his fascists? Nasty people, no? Killed a lot of innocent, sincere opposition, didn't they? Ones they didn't kill, they chucked into labor camps."

"No question," Nacho acknowledged. "I was enthusiastic when it all started. The situation here was hopeless. The whole leftist

MOSCOW GOLD | 149

lot—socialists, communists, anarchists, all of them—had the country so fouled up by '36 that something had to be done. What we called 'the uprising' had good prospects of making things better. We didn't know yet that Franco would surface as leader. That evolved later, but at least we were throwing off the collectivism. I thought there was opportunity for initiative and to pursue ambition."

"You got disappointed?"

"Oh, yes. Most of us that fought the war were. The Reds were worse, if you can believe it, than the franquistas. The Reds abused, enslaved, and killed more people than the fascists by orders of magnitude. That the Reds were worse killers doesn't excuse Franco and his crowd. Don't get me wrong."

Nacho stopped and thought for a second. "Look, I got it from both sides. In the end, most of us did. I was threatened with death more than once by the Reds. Barely escaped. I was betrayed and kidnapped by friends of Franco. In the end, I gave nothing and still give nothing for either of them. It came to me I just had to survive. I did. Here I am. Not political. Not anymore. Just here."

"Will you help me?" David asked.

"This is not for novices or neophytes. They're all killers. And they never give up—the Soviets most of all. You can't trust anybody."

"Should I trust *you*?" said David.

"Now you're asking some right questions. Let's start with how you lose a tail."

∽

After finishing with Nacho, David hurried back to Quevedo. He accomplished two missions.

First, he called Calvín. "Buitre, it's me, Paladín."

"Paladín, you are staying out of trouble?"

"Can you meet me at seven? In that little Plaza del Conde del Valle de Suchil, by the fountain, in front of the old Conde Duque Hotel—right over there by Arapiles."

150 | DOUGLAS L. FIELD

"Do I want to do this, David?"

"Yeah, you do. See you there."

Next, he went over to Fuencarral and down a couple of blocks toward the Glorieta de Bilbao. Joyería Maite, there it was. Would they have what he wanted? It turned out they did. A rare find in Madrid.

⁓

David was waiting by the fountain when Calvín got there. He dispensed with any small talk. "Remember when we talked over at the MonteAzul? You told me to be careful? Remember that? Well, I have been careful, and I think I've caught the cops following me."

"Who? Cuerpo? Guardia Civil? Not Spanish maybe?" Calvín wanted to know.

"No idea. Have to think they are Spanish, though."

"More than likely. You have continued looking into the gold, and you suspect that it relates to that?" Calvín's question was rhetorical.

"You got it, *machote*. What do you make of it?"

"I think whatever it is relates to the gold. There's been no mention of it, but the inside talk at my shop is that the economic situation is grim," Calvín mused.

"Locating and securing the return of the gold would relieve some of the pressure, no?" David pointed out.

"Right. What interest do Spanish authorities have in impeding you?"

"And why are they wasting their energy?" David added

"Hard to say. Who else besides Spain could be interested?"

"Isham, my editor, got the whole thing started," David reminded Calvín. "Who's pulling his strings? Nothing makes sense. You got any contacts in the security apparatus?"

"No, but I know people who do. I'll nose around," Calvín promised. "I'll have to be discreet. You will too. What precautions are you taking?"

David described his session with Nacho and some of what he had learned.

MOSCOW GOLD | 151

Calvín thought a moment. "I'd go ahead and get lost and stay lost. That's the safest move. They follow you here?"

"Wouldn't have showed if they did."

"I learn anything, how do I find you?"

David had his answer ready. "Blind guy, name of Onésimo, sells lottery tickets on Vallehermoso between Fernando el Católico and Arapiles. He'll know."

⁓

When his taxi stopped in front of Gaztambide, David saw that Ariel was already down in the lobby socializing with Don Hilario. When she saw the cab arrive, she came right out. David held the door, and she hopped in.

He slid in next to Ariel. "La Calle de Ibiza, behind Retiro," David told the cabbie. "Most of the way to Dr. Esquerdo. I'll tell you where when we get there."

"That sounds interesting, David. I don't go over there often."

David did not answer her directly, "Where's your chaperone? Just to preserve appearances." David grinned, referring to the now abandoned Spanish practice that a girl would never go out with a young man unless accompanied by some female relative or friend.

"I arranged for her to have a sudden and severe headache." Ariel acted serious.

"Aren't you crafty!"

"Oh, I'm safe with such an honorable man as you." There was a quick lift of one eyebrow and a conspiratorial smile.

They enjoyed each other's conversation while the cabbie acted like he was hurrying straight to their destination. When he turned onto Ibiza, it appeared as a pleasant boulevard containing a profusion of restaurants and cafés.

"There. On the right. La Ciudad Blanca," David directed.

"This looks nice," Ariel put in.

"Named for Arequipa, Perú, as I recall," David explained. "Owners are Peruvian, but the place is as Spanish as you and me—well, you anyway."

Ibiza the street was wide, but the traffic lanes were narrow and at the extreme edges. The entire center was a long and wide parkway, tree- and bench-lined and peppered with the outdoor tables of the corresponding eateries. Ciudad Blanca's were set on point beneath mature plane trees and under white umbrellas. They had the place's name in bright blue letters. David and Ariel settled in facing each other.

Inside at the bar, Spanish wait staff were always no-nonsense, all business. Outside, just the opposite. When the waiter came, *"Señores, qué van a tomar?"*

"David, you chose for us."

"I know it's French, but do you have Dubonnet? Plus, a little jug of water." David looked at the waiter.

"Claro, señor. Right away." Skeptical, a little condescending.

They must teach that in waiter school here.

After he moved off, "That's an interesting choice, David."

"Like sherry but different. It'll make you a little hungry." He took in her startling good looks. "That's a different necklace."

Ariel was turned out—stylish and demure. She wore a dove-gray pleated skirt and dark maroon blouse. Her nails were painted to match the shirt. She wore an elaborate necklace of beads and polished stones hanging in strands of different lengths.

"It's my fertility necklace," she replied.

"That so? Are you planning to have a baby?" David tried to make his look a little salacious. But if Ariel noticed, she didn't let on.

"I call it that to scandalize my friends," Ariel said.

"Well, you scandalized me."

"No, I didn't. *Mentiroso.*"

The drinks came.

"First time you've mentioned friends?" David stated. "No boyfriend; never had a *novio*?

"Novio? Who has time? Now and then I see one or two girlfriends from school. Most of them are married now."

David's investigator instincts made him probe. "You don't want to follow in their footsteps?"

Ariel shrank in her chair a little. She looked shy and vulnerable. "I'm thinking about taking my vows. The nuns at *cole*, my teachers, I admire them."

"Maybe you shouldn't be here with me. I'm not nun material."

"Maybe. But I am." Now not so shy.

David studied Ariel's face. It betrayed nothing. "*Mentirosa tú!* Now you're the liar!"

A very sweet smile. "No way to talk to a nun, David. Did the idea distress you?"

"To the core!"

"Good for me to stay a step or two ahead of a guy like you."

"I'm the soul of innocence and propriety. But why no novio? Beautiful girl like you. Has to be your choice," David said.

"You know Spain, David. The eternal cycle of life for us girls. Get *comprometida* to one of a million boys, one pretty much like the other, one older than us. A long engagement. Marriage. Children. Mistresses. Serial adulteries. Early widowhood. I reject it."

Ariel was serious now and went on, "There were several who would have liked to be my novio. Two or three who acted like they were, formalities aside. But I have a vote. I've always voted no."

David watched her but didn't reply.

"I'm sorry," she said. "I've turned our conversation far too serious. Forgive me."

"No, Ariel, I asked because I wanted to know. I'm pleased you told me. I imagine your Principe Azul is just around the next corner, and you will be smitten, your affections irretrievably lost."

Now she looked at David for a long time. "Wouldn't that be sweet? Hope so." Playful again.

They ordered a roast chicken—the house specialty that came golden brown, falling off the bone with a light dusting of rock salt, white asparagus spears, and creamed greens of some sort.

As they ate, David said, "Remember when we talked in the office? I said my Madrid featherbed is getting ruffled. Like to hear the story? It's progressed since then."

"Mm. Yes."

"I write economic and financial stories for my paper. Lots of it's kind of technical—not scintillating, but useful. My editor's a guy named Isham. Different than regular editors. We're not that fond of each other. Calls me over to Café Gijón. Just a week ago today."

"Why Gijón? Not the office?"

"That was my question. It was siesta too. Only him and me in the place. He tells me he wants me to do a big exposé on the Moscow Gold. You know what that is?"

"Sure," Ariel said. "Who doesn't. 'Spain's great lament.' If only we had that money, all our problems would be solved."

David explained, "I'm supposed to find out all about it, do the research. Who sent it out of the country? Where'd it go? What did Spain get for it? Is any left? What refund's owed? Obvious questions, no?"

"Obvious. Why you? Why now? Why haven't all these questions been answered long before now?" Ariel agreed.

"You're smart. They should have been. And if they haven't, it's because somebody hasn't wanted them answered—maybe a lot of somebodies."

Ariel put her hand to her throat, "David, it's not good for you to be answering questions that important people want left alone."

"I'm in a squeeze. Isham wants the story out. The people at the bank seem to be cooperating. The police may be following me. A lot doesn't add up."

MOSCOW GOLD | 155

"This sounds dangerous for you. Abandon the story. Tell your editor no," Ariel said flatly.

David shook his head. "My editor is not giving me that out. Doing the story isn't voluntary. He'll get me deported if I refuse—threatened as much. It was vague, but that's what it was. I don't want to get deported, not just now."

"There's risk. To yourself. To those who are close to you," Ariel stated.

"Are you worried about me?" He looked at her—steady and for a long time.

"Very worried," she said, not looking away.

He reached across the table and touched her forearm. Then drew his fingers down across her wrist and pressed her thumb in his hand.

"Look. I have something for you." Letting go, he pulled out of his pocket a small box wrapped in plain green paper.

"What?"

"A little token of my affection."

"David! What is it?" She tore it open. The box had a lid that popped up. "¡*Aretes*! How pretty they are!"

"It's called Krementz. They make it in the States—in New Jersey. Kind of hard to find here in Madrid. Those are their rosebuds, for pierced ears. All Spanish girls have pierced ears, no?"

"This one does. David, they're lovely!"

She put them on. Her head tilted to the side, taking off the old, putting on the new with slender, graceful fingers. "Thank you. I will always treasure them."

"I hoped you would like to have a remembrance—of an American friend."

"Not *an* American friend. *My* American friend." She stared at him. Her eyes glistened. "David, you are causing me to have to sort through my thoughts and my feelings."

"I am?" he asked.

"You are." The eyes were still bright and sparkling.

"When you're done, will you tell me?" he said gently.

"I will." The sound barely made, hardly heard.

The evening paseo was on in force, and it seemed like everyone in the barrio passed by. A few, the observant ones, noticed a handsome and happy young couple dining under the trees. The couple's conversation had waned, lost in the moment.

Ariel broke the silence. "Did you find Nacho?"

"I did. We talked for a long time. You had already left when we finished."

"Was I right about him?"

"Yeah," David confirmed. "He was hesitant at first. Then he opened up—after he was convinced that I am who I said I am, after he figured out that I understand Spain."

"Was he a spy?"

"For the Franco side. Knows all about secret intelligence, codes, agent networks. Did it all. Quite effective near as I could tell."

Ariel thought it over a second. "Would have been dangerous—at that time and in that war. I'd say he's lucky to be alive."

"Man's brave. No doubt about that. You almost wouldn't know it looking at him now. I imagine I'll find out more as I get to know him."

"You can't be persuaded to drop this story? Then you wouldn't need Nacho." Ariel was not giving up.

"I'm in a bind. I can't." David gave her a resigned look.

"Then what's your hook? I think you say that in newspapers, no? 'Hook'?"

"We do. And good question, Ariel. The Spanish Reds sent it to Moscow. After that, it's less clear. Thing is that gold doesn't just disappear. It went somewhere. Who got it? Who still has it? Where is it now? That's the hook. I get who's got it now, and the mystery unfolds."

"So, you find out who's got it, then what? What's Spain going to be able to do about it?"

David looked around to see that no one else was within earshot. "Depends on who's got it. If it's someone less popular than Franco,

MOSCOW GOLD | 157

Spain might have a shot at something. Soviets aren't giving it back. That's for sure. But they can be made to look bad—untrustworthy, thieves, immoral, all that. Franco hates them."

"Spain's an outcast because of his politics. Who knows? For now, the Caudillo suppresses all our animosities. Maybe that's good, but I don't care if he gets that money back or not. How can your story be worth the trouble at this late date?" Ariel vented her frustration.

"All part of the mystery," David agreed. "If there's nothing to be done, why such intensity? Just the intensity of interest proves something's up—shows there's something worth getting at."

"If it's something that a lot of powerful people are all worked up about, you should stay as far away as possible. That's what I think."

"And you may be right, but I'm stuck with the story, Ariel. Where the gold went is the hook. Indications are it might have gone to Paris. I'm going to need to go there and nose around very soon."

"Oh, speaking of travel"—Ariel seemed glad to change the subject—"there's some kind of a cinema event in Santander next week. Jaime's asked me to go up there."

"When do you leave?"

"Friday. Pasado mañana. Going up by train," she replied.

David mulled this information over a minute. "Do you have duties on Saturday?"

"No, not till Monday."

"Ariel, if you were the *Trib*, would you consider Santander to be on the way to Paris?" David asked with a hint of conspiracy in his voice.

Ariel caught on instantly. "Oh, yes. I can say I would—even more if there were confusion between Santander and San Sebastián. They *are* close together, and it *is* a common mistake."

"Suppose I happened to find myself up there Saturday, would you be interested in having a look around town?" David ventured.

"You know my answer!"

However supercilious, David and Ariel's waiter did not hurry them.

158 | DOUGLAS L. FIELD

"I think our fellow would let us sit here all evening," David said after a while.

"It's a fine evening."

In time, David caught the waiter's eye, raised his hand, and rubbed his thumb and forefinger together—the universal sign for, *Bring our check, please.*

"Shall we walk some before we head home?" David suggested.

"Sure. Settle our supper a little. I'd forgotten what a nice street this is. Thank you for bringing me here."

"Calle de Ibiza here runs right into el Retiro. Walk through the park? We can go by the pond," David suggested. "Since the Caudillo has suppressed all your animosities, Retiro should be one of the safest places in the world."

She jabbed him gently with her elbow. "I'd love to."

After they had walked awhile, Ariel hooked her arm in David's. They didn't hold hands and walk apart as other couples did. They leaned into each other, shoulders touching, known to each other, close enough to breathe each other in, comfortable and intimate, like longtime lovers.

"Do you forgive me for staying with the story, Ariel?"

She looked straight at him and hugged his arm tight. "No."

"You don't? Will you ever?"

"No. Never." Ariel pouted. "You say you have no choice, but I'll fix it with Jaime. You can hide out in Carabanchel. In one of those chabola things he has. Wait till things cool down. I don't want you hurt, David. I'm afraid for you. For us."

"Will you bring me *calamares* and beer sometimes? Maybe some churros in the mornings?" David tried to make light, but he did not miss that she had said "us."

"No. Not that either. You've been bad." She softened a little

They went past General Martínez Campos on his horse and up to the back of Alfonso XII's monument that looks out over Retiro's big rectangular pond. They walked up to the decorative wrought iron fence that enclosed it. Ariel stood in front of David and a bit to his right. He put his arms around her waist. She continued to look out over the water, raised her left hand, and touched the side of his face.

"Ever rent a rowboat on the pond?" David asked, his lips near her ear.

"Back when I was a girl."

"The folks and I hadn't been here too long. Back in the '50s," David recalled. "I told them one Sunday I was going to Retiro. The old man said, 'OK, but don't rent a boat. It's dangerous with the *vapor*.' Remember that little steamer that used to circle the edge? Well, of course I rented a boat and almost got run over by the vapor while I was paddling around. Got home and the old boy asks me if I'd had a good time and if I'd rented a boat. Put on my best innocent face and said no."

Now they were standing side by side and resting their forearms on the railing. "Well, of course they had followed me down and seen me. They were standing right about here, I imagine. I was busted!"

"My upbringing was very benign." Ariel was appalled at the thought. "I would never have been brave enough to defy my parents like that."

"Well, I figured that, if I didn't get caught at least once in a while, I wasn't testing their limits."

"I think you've never stopped testing limits, David," Ariel made a pointed reply. "I think you are testing them now. Are you being followed tonight?"

"I don't think so. Sniffing out a tail is one of the things Nacho wants to cover in my, uh, training." David smiled at her. "But we aren't to that lesson yet."

"Well, you should hurry up."

Still arm in arm, David and Ariel walked out of Retiro at Charles III's gate in the Puerta de Alcalá and headed up the Gran Vía. Not long and they came upon the Pastelería Sábarra, still open and well patronized.

"*¿Se te ofrece un cafecito? Te invito,*" David offered.

160 | DOUGLAS L. FIELD

"*¡Sí, cómo no!*" Ariel agreed.

David thought her worries had lifted some. She seemed pleased to prolong their time together.

The place was lit bright. The coffees came, along with a small plate of lemon-flavored madeleines. The couple faced each other on stools at the bar, knees touching, as they chattered away.

After coffee, they caught a cab back to Gaztambide.

In front of Ariel's building, "Thank you for another delightful evening, David. You're full of such pleasant surprises."

He grabbed her around the waist and held her to himself. "Let's talk again soon?"

"Do let's. On Saturday. I'm staying at the old Sardinero." Ariel snuggled in.

"I know that hotel. Went there with the parents once years ago. I'll look for you in the Casino Bar at 10:30."

"*Hasta entonces,* David" (Till then).

The sereno, now on scene, had the door open.

"And David, thank you for your beautiful gifts, all of them, but tonight for the earrings most of all." Ariel touched them.

David didn't quite yet let her go.

"*Gifts," she said. What's she mean by gifts?*

Ariel hugged him hard around the neck, broke away, and then cantered inside.

CHAPTER 18

Odessa: Tuesday, December 8, 1936

Igor Semyonovich Zytseff, captain of the Soviet merchant motor vessel *Komsomol*, reread his cargo manifest.

Iron ore for the Port of Antwerp. In heavy and odd-shaped wooden crates.

"Kharkov," he said to his first officer, "is this not the second time we have loaded large crates of 'iron ore' for Antwerp?"

"Yes, sir, a couple of months ago. They only made it as far as Cartagena," Kharkov recalled.

"Quite right. And we loaded crates in Cartagena, did we not?" Zytseff continued to ruminate.

"A great many. Tractor parts I think it was."

"Tractor parts my arse, Kharkov. We took airplanes to Spain. We brought back payment, and now we are taking them more airplanes. We're sailing into the middle of a civil war—in an unarmed ship that can't outrun a rowboat."

"Aye, aye, sir." Kharkov was discreet.

"Don't quote me, Kharkov."

MOSCOW GOLD | 163

"No, sir."

Six slow days out of Cartagena, Zysteff had anchored in open water in the Gulf of Odessa, just outside the seaport breakwater. Not allowed to dock, *Komsomol* unloaded the mysterious and heavy crates into lighters. He and his crew had waited without shore leave. They subsisted on boiled fish and cabbage.

And they waited. Waited while the ship began to stink. Waited while late-autumn storms boiled up in the Black Sea, lashing at the dumpy old *Komsomol*'s slab sides and knocking her all about.

Orders were at last flashed by Aldis lamp. Proceed to Pier 13 for refueling, revictualing, new orders. Once alongside, Captain Zytseff had hurried to the Odessa captaincy. There, an affable Commodore Gabelko had received Zytseff in Gabelko's overwarm second-floor office.

"Sorry to make you and your crew wait in the bay in all that wind and weather, Captain Zytseff. Crowded conditions here in the port, you see. How was the voyage from Spain?" Gabelko inquired.

"Uneventful, Commodore," answered Zytseff.

"The condition of the *Komsomol*, Captain? Is she seaworthy?"

"Altogether, sir," Zytseff assured the commodore.

"Good. What's her best speed again?"

"Eleven knots."

Gabelko made the mental calculations. "So, six, eight days back to Cartagena if we need you to return there."

"A close approximation, yes, sir."

"Very well," said the commodore. "Your cargo is at the pier, and the dock workers will get you loaded forthwith. You're to take on fuel and supplies for a voyage to the Belgian port of Antwerp. Good beer in the Low Countries. You would enjoy it—if you were going there. Your orders and manifest will indicate that you are carrying iron ore to that location. You will shape course and, in all respects, act as if you are doing that. Understood?"

"Yes, Commodore. You have been quite clear."

"However," Gabelko continued, "as soon as the Spanish port of Cartagena bears sixty degrees off your starboard bow, you will alter course for that port. Make your best speed—straight in. They'll be expecting you. Still understood?"

"Yes. Will these orders be in writing, sir?" Zytseff asked.

"A fair question, and no. The only orders you will have will be those relating to Antwerp."

"And after unloading at Cartagena?" *Komsomol*'s captain wanted to know.

The senior officer turned flinty. "You will be met there and given further instructions. No one on board other than you is to know anything other than that *Komsomol* is bound for Antwerp laden with iron ore. I've been quite clear on that, have I not?"

"Quite clear, sir."

"Excellent. And since you have no further questions, I bid you a pleasant voyage, Captain. It'll take you a few hours to get loaded and fitted out. You'll have to enjoy Antwerp's beer another time." Gabelko turned away.

"Aye, aye, sir," Zytseff said as he departed.

Now Zytseff was back standing on his bridge. After unburdening himself to Kharkov, he went back to observing the loading.

Large, unmarked crates. Most were quite long and thin, others rather squarish. The long ones seemed to be light, the others, heavy. The dockyard apes had dropped one of the big square ones. The crate, well and truly smashed, had sent splintered wood all over his deck. No iron ore was in evidence. Anyone who was curious could have thought it looked like an aero engine nacelle and the forward fuselage of an aircraft.

"Tug's alongside, sir. Ready to proceed to sea." Kharkov broke in to Zytseff's contemplations.

"Very, well, Mr. Kharkov, let go your bowlines. All ahead slow and give her enough starboard rudder to move away from the pier."

MOSCOW GOLD | 165

Pier 13. That was unlucky. Zytseff knew that the new Soviet man was consummately rational. He rejected all forms of religious faith, mythology, and superstition. Yes, but all sailors, Soviet or otherwise, were superstitious.

Secret cargo to Spain. Zytseff recalled it all in his head. Secret cargo back from Spain. Over a month in virtual quarantine outside Odessa. False manifest. Secret sailing orders. Docked at Pier 13! Same process repeated.

Nothing good will come of this, he said to himself, *nothing good at all*.

"Tug's signaling to let go astern, sir," Kharkov reported.

"Do it, Mr. Kharkov. As soon as the tug waves off, make revolutions for five knots, course 193 degrees. Once you have Vorontsov Light on the port beam, increase speed to eleven knots. I'll be in my sea cabin."

"Aye, Captain."

Zytseff sighed at the prospects the coming days presented—a long winter slog through the Black and Mediterranean Seas posing as an ore carrier to Antwerp and, finally, entering the Spanish blockade zone. Then he was to make a "fast" run back into Cartagena—in an eleven-knot ship. Ridiculous.

Komsomol's captain gave a wistful gaze back at the pier. Most of the stevedores and their equipment had cleared off. One lone figure in a peacoat and watch cap hurried back up it toward Odessa city.

CHAPTER 19

Berlin: Thursday, December 10, 1936

Sepp Staupitz had been awarded a month's leave after Cartagena—in recognition of superior service, the admiral had said. He was back and not yet posted to a new assignment. Sepp was in Canaris's office to provide an up-to-date briefing on the Spanish gold.

"Our man has reported from Odessa, Admiral, sir. Says that one of the Soviet freighters that carried the gold there has been reloaded and sailed."

"When?"

"Tuesday, day before yesterday, during the day."

"Do we know what she loaded, Sepp?"

"Crates of some kind. Lots of them, sir,"

"Consistent with military equipment?" the boss asked.

"Entirely."

"Are we monitoring her progress?"

"Kriegsmarine intelligence picked her up in the Bosporus early yesterday. She'll be in the Sea of Crete by now, I expect—off Naxos or

MOSCOW GOLD | 167

Santorini. Somewhere like that. She's not all that fast." Sepp checked notes he held in his hand.

"Who's the Regia Marina's attaché?" Canaris wanted to know.

"Capitano di Corvetta Zeno. An efficient officer."

"Good. Give it to him," the spy admiral ordered. "Let's see what the Italians do with it. The old Russian tub should never make port in Spain. Then Koba can decide if it's worthwhile to ship his goods in his own ships. The Spanish Reds may find it difficult to take delivery of their purchases—no Abwehr fingerprints anywhere."

"Should work, Herr Admiral."

"Oh, and Sepp, have we picked up anything on disposition of the Spanish payment?"

'Yes, Admiral. We believe the gold at the moment is still in Moscow, with indications the Russians are preparing to move it. We've picked up tentative feelers in the major bullion centers—vague and insubstantial, but they're getting ready to move it."

"Excellent as always, Sepp. Our policy going forward will be to deny the Spanish Reds the benefit of their purchases and to relieve the Russian Reds of the benefit of their money."

CHAPTER 20

**The Western Mediterranean Sea:
Monday, December 14, 1936**

Four ratings and Fire Control Officer Teniente Tomás Quiroga manned *Canarias*'s fire director control position on a large armor-protected platform high on the mainmast above B turret.

Canarias was new and fast. She was one of only a few ships in the Spanish Nationalist Navy. Built under license from Vickers, she was, for all intents and purposes, a Royal Navy County-class cruiser. She carried main armament of eight 8-inch guns and a menacing array of smaller armament. She was capable of thirty-three knots.

Canarias formed the centerpiece of the rebel effort to blockade Republican ports in the south and east of Spain. Quiroga and his crew were in operative control of her firepower.

Steaming some forty-seven nautical miles southeast of Republican Cartagena and navigating along a fifteen-mile oval northeast to southwest, *Canarias* found herself on the northeast leg. She punched through heavy quartering seas, at times making green water over her raked and handsome bows.

MOSCOW GOLD | 169

Among her many innovations was Quiroga's fire director control. Her turrets no longer aimed and shot independently. Firing was coordinated from Quiroga's sophisticated fire control position. He and his sailors were equipped with the latest state-of-the-art British range finding, training, and elevation computing devices.

General quarters had sounded just after midday meal. *Canarias* pulled off her patrol station and hied herself off to the southeast. Around midafternoon, a ship hove into sight on an approximate reciprocal course. Quiroga saw blinkering from the approaching ship and assumed she was friend not foe. He received no orders to determine her range or train his guns out on her.

She turned out to be Italian, a newer destroyer, painted bright white. A huge Regia Marina flag flew at her fantail. Long and knife-edge narrow in the beam, she hauled into hailing distance. Quiroga's sailors had their optics fixed on her.

"What ship, Gómez?" Quiroga asked.

"RM *Usodimare,* sir. Book says she's about two thousand tons and can do thirty-eight knots. Nothing bashful about her, sir. Look at that flag," Gómez replied.

The megaphone conversation between bridges was short. Quiroga could make out no details. *Usodimare* bristled and hummed and throbbed with power. Her urgent message now delivered, *Usodimare* dug her stern deep into the restless seas. With style and grace, she curved away to the east.

"Fire control, Bridge."

"Fire control, aye."

"Mister Quiroga, this is Captain Moreno. Anticipate sighting a medium-sized merchant vessel within the hour. Consider her a hostile target and maintain firing solutions on her. Pending my further order."

"Aye, aye, Captain."

Quiroga told off his ratings. "Bridge expects to sight a merchantman. Conduct all ranging and aiming evolutions on her as soon as we spot her. Keep her in your sights and your computations updated."

170 | DOUGLAS L. FIELD

Canarias had her quarry in sight in under fifty minutes. She turned out to be a medium-sized, middle-aged merchantman plowing along on a heading of about 330 degrees. She wore Soviet colors, was seen to head straight for Cartagena. Not trying to be stealthy about it. As if such a vessel could be stealthy.

Captain Moreno closed to 750 meters and ordered the Russian to stop. She continued. Time and patience were short. *Canarias's* 4.7-inch, 40-mm, and 20-mm guns were trained out. There would be no need for the big rifles. Quiroga was soon directed to lob a warning shot across her bow.

More signaling to the target and orders to Quiroga to recompute followed. The bridge ordered another warning shot. The second one worked. The target hove to, and two lifeboats were lowered.

"Fire control, Bridge."

"Fire control, aye."

"Mister Quiroga, we will allow the target's crew to take to their boats. Compute a shooting solution for the portside 4.7-inch battery on the Russian. Hit her amidships."

"Solution computed, sir. Ready to open fire."

The lifeboats loaded up and rowed lustily away.

"Open fire."

The crash of the 4.7s was deafening. Quiroga's shooting solutions and the gun captain's aim were accurate. Soon, the Russian was brightly on fire below her bridge, her fuel tanks having lit off."

"Secure from firing," ordered the bridge.

"Firing key secured," Quiroga acknowledged.

The Russian was a stout old bird. It took her well more than two hours to sink. Plenty of time to approach her boats and to take on board her crew of some thirty-six officers and men—as well as Quiroga was able to count them.

"Mister Quiroga, open fire with the 20 mms and sink those boats."

"Sink the boats. Yes, sir."

MOSCOW GOLD | 171

That done, *Canarias* made revolutions for thirty-one knots and headed west for Cádiz, leaving all evidence of the existence of the Soviet motor vessel *Komsomol* and her cargo well on their way to the bottom.

CHAPTER 21

Moscow: Friday, December 18, 1936

"How far did she get?"

"Just past where she would have altered course for Cartagena, Comrade Chairman." Commander Letchkov stood to attention.

"Was this result not to have been expected?"

"I believe, Comrade Chairman, the thinking was the Spanish rebel navy would never dare to provoke the Soviet Union in this fashion," Letchkov said neutrally.

"That kind of 'thinking' falls far short of the mark, Yuri. How did they learn about her?"

"We think the Italians spotted her and advised the Spanish rebels."

"Fascism is a great evil, Yuri, and it spreads like a cancer. We shall need to increase our vigilance," Stalin fumed.

"Yes, Comrade Chairman."

"You are dismissed, Yuri, but please know that I am disappointed."

"Yes, comrade." Letchkov made an about-face to leave.

"Oh, and, Yuri, henceforth let us not risk anymore Soviet vessels in the matter of delivery of matériel or supplies to Spain—not ever.

Let it be their responsibility to collect what they have bought. Is that understood?"

"Perfectly, Comrade Chairman."

"The Spanish gold is in payment for supplies, not Soviet ships."

"Of course, comrade."

"Good. And by the way, who is the captain of our poor *Komsomol*?"

"Igor Semyonovich Zytseff."

"Where is he now?' Stalin asked softly.

"In a fascist internment facility, I imagine, comrade."

"Yes, well, in the event that Igor Semyonovich survives his internment, I think it will be a good idea for him to come here to Moscow. I would like for him to have a short debrief with Lavrentiy Pavlovich."

CHAPTER 22

Madrid: Tuesday, December 22, 1936

The red, yellow, and purple for now had halted the red, yellow, and red, Aníbal lamented to himself.

Attired in a blue-black suit and a well-pressed but, from too many launderings, a no longer pure white shirt, and an unimaginative tie, he headed up to Plaza Mayor from Puerta de Toledo.

Today was dead drop day.

In La Latina, he passed a bread line. Some union women were distributing. They had stacks of round loaves piled high on a trestle table. The women were dressed in civvies. Each wore the *gorra* of the Republican army, pointed at each end, darkish olive-gray green with a tassel that hung down from the front peak and bounced off the nose.

That's a lot of bread to find in one place these days, Nacho thought. *I ought to know.*

For anything, you had to have a ration card. The lines were long mothers with children, old people, and men like Nacho in business suits and ties. Here was Madrid's population in miniature. All were

MOSCOW GOLD | 175

hungry, none were patient, and all were having trouble queuing up and maintaining order.

Further up in the northeast corner of Mayor, la esquina de los Austriacos had been hit by a rebel artillery shell. It was pockmarked and blackened.

A *patrulla* stopped him as he exited to head down to Sol. "Where are you headed, camarada?" demanded their corporal.

He resisted strong temptation to tell them that he was a franquista spy headed to service his dead drop over on La Castellana. "Going to work."

"What work? You look like a capitalist."

"*Arquitecto.*"

"Documents," was the response. More of a statement than a request.

Nacho produced them including his *pase*. The corporal gave it scrutiny.

As the grim autumn of 1936 had turned into numbing winter, the stresses weighing upon Madrid were compounded by inadequate food supplies. Evidence the bread line. Ahumada was having trouble getting flour. Aníbal's baker's assistant cover was tending toward unworkable and obsolete.

Nacho had developed a second "legend." This one more exalted. Except when he serviced Faraón and Isidora, he posed as a senior architect in the putative Madrid design firm of Robles Ulloa with offices on the Paseo del Prado.

Arjona knew little of architecture. No matter. He donned his business suit and carried a large portfolio with elevations and plans for a proposed insurance building, just up Recoletos near the National Library. For good measure, he threw in a sketchbook and a few drafting implements. He knew more about architecture than these bumpkins.

The others crowded in and had a look at Nacho's pass over their corporal's shoulder.

176 | DOUGLAS L. FIELD

The glory of the architect legend was Nacho's pase. A perfect forgery, it purported to have been issued by the Republican Ministry of Public Works. It identified Nacho in detail as an architect and attested to his socialist bona fides. It ordered that all interested parties accord him every courtesy and ease him on his way. The pass was decorated with official stamps affixed in dark blue stamp pad ink and endorsements added in red handwriting—all in keeping with well-engrained Spanish custom of the time.

Many of the chequistas who guarded the city for the Revolution were fresh from the countryside. They either lacked education or had none at all. Such was the case this morning. Nacho noted with cautious amusement that the patrol leader "read" the document upside down. His subordinates were as unlearned as he; either that or they dared not embarrass him. At least none was overt in noting the error.

The corporal returned the pass, not quite finished. "That's a big briefcase. What's in there?"

Nacho had had enough of cowering. Communist Madrid was not yet totally classless Madrid. A touch of arrogance was dangerous, but it could still work on some of these *peones*.

"You read my pass. The Ministry of Public Works requires you to expedite my movements. Please do so."

Nacho and the corporal locked eyes.

"Clear off, camarada," the man ordered.

The best thing for the patrol to see at this moment was the back of Nacho's coat. Affecting insouciance, he moved away down Calle Mayor toward Sol. Once out of sight, he increased speed and doubled to the right back up Calle de Preciados. Then he headed to San Bernardo, where he turned north for Quevedo.

Madrid was a mess. It was not "besieged" as the international reporting maintained. Just the western and southern edges were under direct threat. The assault on the capital had devolved into a standoff. The Parque del Oeste up against Argüelles and the buildings of University City were static, dug-in front line areas. On occasion, the standoff burst into blatant, sanguinary contention and, on others, lapsed into begrudging, temporary truce.

Nationalist artillery was situated on advantageous ground out on the Toledo and Coruña roads and on Garabitas Hill. It dueled with Republican batteries dug in on good, elevated ground north of the city. Everyone remaining in Madrid lived in a crucible, doubly stoked by the fire and the noise generated by the belligerents.

Against these conditions and the persistent and biting cold of winter, Nacho soldiered on.

Cóndor had assigned Nacho a contact code name Alois. Alois was informally known to Aníbal and Cóndor as the Dutchman. A strange name, the Dutchman. Alois was neither tall nor blond nor blue-eyed. He spoke excellent but somewhat accented Spanish. After their initial meeting, contact was maintained through a dead drop.

The Church of Saint Teresa of God is in Chamberí up Calle de Eloy Gonzalo from Quevedo on the Plaza Pintor Sorolla. There was an unused wooden door in the crumbling stucco wall that surrounds the church grounds. That door had a large rusty hinge that had come loose from the wall but was still affixed to the door. Each week Nacho's obligation was to walk by and check the hinge. If it was closed back against the door, he was signaled to service the actual dead drop at another location. If it remained open and flat against the wall, there was no news.

The dead drop itself was a round recess at just above eye level in a chestnut tree on the Plaza Emilio Castelar. The pocket had been formed around the stump of a moderate-sized branch that, in years past, had been pruned away. The size of a tennis ball, the recess tended to collect odd bits of paper, junk, and cigarette butts. When he would close the signal hinge, Alois would also leave for Aníbal at the drop an encoded and wadded-up message.

Aníbal worked his way towards Saint Teresa's with refined purpose. There it was. Hinge all the way closed. Alois had something for him. He set his big portfolio down and bent over to tie his shoe. By the most natural of actions, he flicked the hinge back full open. Ready for next time.

Now he went without detour to the dead drop. Two blocks before arriving, he lit another cigarette. At the drop, he stubbed out the smoke against the bark of the tree and both "disposed of" his butt into the recess and retrieved Alois's message—all in a single unobtrusive move.

It had been in the papers that a rebel warship had sunk a "neutral" Soviet freighter "in an act of piracy on the high seas." It had carried, they said, some innocent cargo for up on the North Sea somewhere. The communist organs were trumpeting the latest fascist outrage in a state of quavering high dudgeon. The rebel press maintained that the offending ship had been laden with military supplies and equipment destined for the port of Cartagena.

Back at his room, Nacho's decode revealed Alois's take that the sunken ship was suspected of carrying replacement aircraft to the Reds. Further, the Soviets had ended use of their ships for delivery of additional arms and supplies. Strict cash and carry. Buyer to make his own arrangements to haul it off.

Nacho got out *La Regenta*. After forwarding Alois's advice, he encoded his own observations. The sunken cargo was not benign after all. The rebel blockade was working. The Reds would face increasing difficulty replenishing lost aircraft, immediate opportunity to win the air war. Redoubled effort was needed to destroy aircraft already in Spain.

Nacho refrained himself from adding editorial comment on the expenditure of all that gold and how it looked like socialist solidarity and brotherhood had their limits.

CHAPTER 23

Madrid: Thursday, August 22, 1963

David met Nacho after siesta at the Cuatro Caminos Metro.

Everything was opening back up. There were good crowds on the streets. They would increase as the workday ended and the paseo got started. The plan was to get street craft practice working from the big glorieta down Calle de Bravo Murillo toward Quevedo.

Once up on the street, they found a *terraza*, and Nacho gave David a thumbnail lesson in the basics of getting and staying undetected in a big city. "You create an illusion. All it has to be is small things. Change the way you part your hair. Grow a mustache. Get fake glasses. You create a look that fits in where you are. You make people see what they want to see so they don't think about you."

"Seems too easy," David said.

"That's the beauty of it. It's called 'hiding in plain sight.' You fit in. Anything radical, out of the ordinary would call attention. It needs to be expected, natural, predictable, comfortable. Do that, and they'll look at you but never see you."

MOSCOW GOLD | 181

"Sounds like there's bravado to it. Element of surprise. I like that." David was catching on.

"That's it. Brazen it out. And you never engage in a straight-out fight. You wouldn't win. There's always more of them than you. But you can use that to your advantage. A group always reacts slower than an individual. You get in and get out. Hit and leave. You were never there."

"What about spotting and losing a tail?" David sked.

"Come on. I'll show you."

They moved off down Bravo Murillo toward Quevedo.

"There's a whole procedure to it. You might not think so, but watchers have lots of vulnerabilities. You take advantage. You look for guys who you see more than once or guys who look out of place, suspicious—ones who move when you move and stop when you stop."

"Seems pretty obvious."

"There's more to it." Nacho seemed enthusiastic. "You set up a 'street detection route.' You look innocent, but it flushes the bad guys out. You find open places or an empty park where they have no cover or where they will look out of place. Then your tail has to move in close on you or risk losing you. Nobody else around prevents them from blending in among a crowd. You look around you for traffic as you cross a street. Or you change your pace and then your tail has to too. That's how you catch them."

They dodged in and out of businesses and alleyways as they went. Nacho pointed out advantages and disadvantages of the different locations. David got good practice. He was catching on.

"It's a lonely game," Nacho expounded. "That, plus they can make mistakes all day long, but you have to be perfect. You make one tiny one, and they have you."

"Have you detected anybody on to us this afternoon?" David asked as they got toward Quevedo.

"No. I imagine they haven't picked you back up since you last lost them. They won't rest till they find you though."

"I'm going up to Santander tomorrow. On to Paris from there," David indicated.

"Your challenge in the next couple of days is to stay a day or so ahead of them. Out of Spain, you may get a little breathing room. When you come back, it'll be different. Then you'll need a long-term cover. Can you get back in without being seen? I had to do that once," Nacho reminisced.

"I still have to work that out."

"Do it. And be careful. They know most of the tricks. You'll need fake documents. Good ones."

"I had thought of that. Might find some in France."

"You can find anything France, or so they say."

"Thanks, Nacho. I'm stuck with this gold story. This had been a real experience. It will help me get what I need and then get clear."

"Maybe. I was dubious a first. This activity isn't for everybody. It takes courage, confidence, stealth, and guile. I can see now that you've got what it takes. Do you have people telling you to trash the story and avoid the risk and trouble?"

David nodded.

"You and I know you can't do that. They don't, but you and I do. You'd never get out from under it if you did. But be careful. You're no good dead—not to yourself or anybody else."

"You're a good teacher, Nacho," David said, and they parted.

MOSCOW GOLD | 183

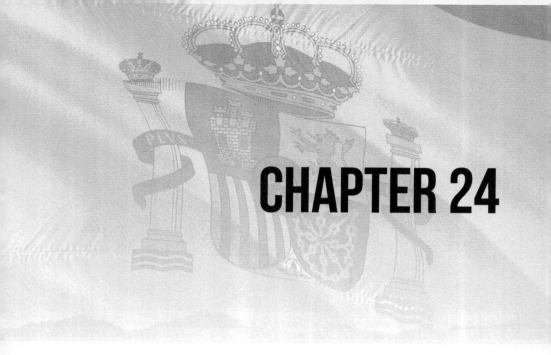

CHAPTER 24

Santander: Friday, August 23, 1963

David arrived in Santander by train.

He went to the station bar. "A *jarra* of Mahou," he ordered. "Thirsty trip. All the way from Pamplona today." David figured if the cops came around asking questions the barkeep wouldn't associate him with coming up from Madrid. Maybe Pamplona would throw them off.

The tap was expertly made. David took a deep pull and then fished in his pocket for some coins. He put down twice the normal price and slid it forward. The barman saw.

In due time, he set several glasses in front of David and made show of polishing them.

"Looking for a place to sleep. Off the register," David muttered.

The barman wandered away without answering, busy with his usual. After a while, he returned, collected David's money, and left a folded sheet of paper in its place.

David finished his Mahou and left. There were two addresses under the fold.

All Spanish hotels and lodgments, by law, collected and reported to the Guardia Civil the identities of their guests. This take was collected by the local branches at midmorning every day for the previous night. These practices were known to David, and he determined to frustrate them.

Like everywhere, Santanderos often needed a little extra. If you knew how to find them, there were flat owners with the space who would give you a room and a washbasin. A couple of hundred pesetas up front, no identity card, no passport, no questions. Just a key to the apartment door and *muy buenas noches*.

The first address did have room and asked for his *documento*. He looked in his grip, acted apologetic, and said, "Give me a minute. I must have left it in the car."

They must have gone and got licensed, David decided

The second attempt worked. He paid for two nights, collected his key, left his stuff in his room, and went back out.

CHAPTER 25

Santander: Saturday, August 24, 1963

David arrived at the Sardinero in a pale green rented SEAT 800.

SEAT is the Spanish sister company to Italy's FIAT. Nowhere as numerous but a little larger and more powerful than its proliferative little brother, the 600, the 800 looked like an inverted bathtub on wheels. David parked under the grand portico in front. He gave a handsome tip to the bellman just in case Ariel made him wait.

The morning crowd at the Casino Bar was limited. He found a table and ordered coffee. The Sardinero was a large square edifice painted pure white. It sat out on a point jutting into the Cantabrian Sea. Those few who were up had put on bathing costumes. They appeared headed for the beach. The weather prospects were favorable—light breeze; clear skies; mild temperature; and blue, blue water. It was just a little cold this far north, even at late summer.

"Meestair Fordham, Meestair Fordham?" Another bellhop, this one diminutive in forest green livery with a pillbox hat.

"I'm David Fordham."

"Yes, of course, Señor Fordham, a message from la Señorita Muñiz." The little man presented an envelope on hotel stationery lying on a small silver tray.

A few pesetas. "Thank you."

"Will there be a reply, Señor?"

David held up a hand and popped open the envelope. "David, I'm delayed just a little. Can you wait for me a few minutes? A."

It looked like she *was* making him wait. That ratcheted up the intrigue for David. A few more pesetas. "Say to her, 'All morning.' Got that? 'All morning,'" David directed, and then he pocketed her note.

"Sí, señor. *Claro que sí.*" And he scurried off.

As advertised, Ariel did in time appear in light blue Capri pants and a yellow short-sleeved shirt, collar turned up, and a dark blue and red scarf loose at her neck. Big sunglasses were perched on her hair and her bangs were coifed to perfection. David saw she was wearing his earrings.

"Ariel! Over here!"

"I'm sorry to be delayed, David." She feigned coyness and gave a conspiratorial laugh.

David took an unhurried look at her. "Worth the wait. Can I get you anything?"

"No. I've had breakfast. Shall we go? Beautiful Santander awaits." Ariel was happy and animated.

"I have a car. Parked out front. Thought you might like to take a drive outside of town. I picked up some things for a picnic in case we get hungry."

"*¡Pues entonces, adelante!*"

David took the A-67 west toward Santillana del Mar. Even in August, Santander was green. It was hilly here. Dark hedgerows inscribed irregular patterns across the lighter green swales and slopes. Little white villages and haciendas appeared in randomly ordered profusion. Santander was Old Castile, but it was different—northern, fresh, clear, clean, and green, a relief from Madrid.

"This is an idyllic place, David. What made you think to take a drive outside of the city?"

"Don't know. Maybe we can look around town this afternoon. There's something out here that I thought you might like."

When they reached the road junction that, to the right, led to Santillana, David instead turned left. It was a paved but hilly and curvy one-lane road. His driving was brisk. The tires squealed as he drifted through a couple of longer turns.

"That was fun. Turn around. Let's do it again."

"You got it."

And they shot them again with much exhilaration.

After a very few miles they came, at the top of a gentle rise, to a small and unmarked gravel turnoff. David drove up to what appeared to be the entrance to a cave. It was guarded by an, at the moment, unmanned hut.

"What is this place, David?"

"The Cave of Altamira. Looks like nobody's here. Come on. Let's go in. You'll be amazed."

The cave was long, maybe a quarter of a mile. It varied from six to thirty feet in height. There wasn't much light and that artificial. Numerous colorful drawings adorned the rock walls. Some were of various sorts of animals and others of human hands.

"How do you know about this?" Ariel marveled.

"They talked about it in school. I've always wanted to have a look. It's a Spanish national treasure. I guess they argue over how old they are, but they are old. On the order of fifteen thousand or thirty thousand years. Discovered around eighty years ago. A rock fall, so they say, covered the entrance for several thousand years. Then a tree fell over, knocked the rocks away. The entrance was again exposed."

They were standing in a main chamber not far from the cave mouth. There was a large mural depicting a herd of bison, some horses, and a deer. The paintings were completed in clever shadings of black,

MOSCOW GOLD | 189

brown, and red. They made cunning use of the natural contours in the cave walls to create a three-dimensional effect.

It was cool and a little damp in the cave. David put his arm around Ariel's waist. He held her. Loose. She didn't recoil. Then she put her arm around him.

After a time, David commented, "Pretty good work for a bunch of *primitivos*, yeah?

"Do you think the paintings are that old?" Ariel asked. She seemed distracted.

"Who can say? The dating opinions change all the time."

They wandered through the cave and looked at more of the paintings. Ariel shivered.

David hugged her close. "Are you cold?"

"No."

"What then?"

She turned and faced David, wriggled in closer, "*Preocupada*. Worried about you. About your being followed. About the police harassing you and your editor pressuring you."

"Don't spoil our day worrying. Let's have a good time."

"Don't spoil our friendship by getting yourself thrown out of Spain, David. Or worse. Have they followed us up here? I'm involved now too."

"Ow, you mean it." David could see her concern, even in the low light.

"I do. I have to decide if you're worth the risk."

David was unable to answer. "I don't think they followed us out here. Good job you had us turn around back there. I didn't see anything when we went back. We'll know if they come in here after us. Only one way in."

"They're not so stupid as to follow us in here, you *golfo*. You're never serious, David, except when you're serious; and then it's about the wrong things."

190 | DOUGLAS L. FIELD

"OK. This could be a good place for me to hide out. Would you bring me stuff to eat?"

"No." She sulked.

"Come on. It's getting hot in here. Let's go to Santillana. I'll check the parking lot for bad guys before we leave the cave."

"¡Cretino!"

They headed outside.

"Nobody's messed with the car. No one else has been up here." David made a show of inspecting the car and of looking for tire tracks in the dirt parking area. There were none other than from the SEAT.

The town wasn't far. On the way, David told Ariel that Nacho had taught him about how to detect if he had a "tail." "Let's try it when we get to Santillana. Could be fun."

Ariel rolled her eyes.

David described some of what he had learned.

"Seems pretty obvious, David."

"Worth a try, no?"

"What are we going to do if we spot someone?" Ariel asked, unconvinced.

"Dunno. We haven't had a chance to talk about that yet. Play it by ear."

Ariel seemed to relax some. As they drove into the little town, David tried to keep it light and playful. "Why do they call it Santillana del *Mar*?" he asked. "It's not by the sea."

"It's not *llana*, either. There are hills everywhere," Ariel joined in.

"Cute, Ariel. And no santos running around."

Ariel let him hold her hand as they walked around.

"Let's go in the Colegiata," David suggested. "It's just the place. It has a big cloister with an arcade running all around."

It was a quiet morning at the twelfth-century Romanesque church grounds. David and Ariel weaved in and out of the arches, showed themselves, ducked into alcoves, walked slow and then fast. There was nothing.

It did not take long before it became a game of hide-and-seek that got them laughing and not thinking about surveillance anymore.

"Looks like we're in the clear," David announced after a while.

"*Tonto*. How would you know? We've more been having fun than being spies."

"Does it have to be either-or?"

After Santillana they drove back into the city.

⁓

David arranged for a big parasol. He set up a picnic. They found a secluded spot in the shadow of one of several rocky outcroppings. Of fine light beige sand contrasting with deep azure water, Sardinero Beach was the pride of Santander. It is wide and flat with the old hotel anchoring its back. David had brought bread, *chorizo, queso holandés*, and a couple of beers. They ate desultorily and watched the water.

David studied Ariel. The sun and the wind made the variegated browns and reds of her hair their personal playground. They ruffled the collar of her shirt and fluttered the ends of her scarf. He tried to be surreptitious, but he was enjoying looking at her. Once or twice, she caught him. She smiled, taking neither note nor offense.

The afternoon warmed with occasional breaths of wind off the sea. David got hot and took off his shirt. Ariel undid her scarf. Then she untucked her blouse. As she chattered away, she undid a top button. A little later, the bottom one. Still a little while longer and David watched with undisguised interest and surprise as she unbuttoned the rest of it and took it off. He tried hard, but without much success, to appear unruffled.

Underneath she wore a bright turquoise and chartreuse polka dot bikini.

"Do you like my bikini?" It was perfect affectation of detachment and innocence.

"I do."

I like looking at you and you know it, now, don't you?

"Jaime's wife got it for me last year when they went to Cannes. They're not available here—the morality police and all."

"She did good," David affirmed.

"Do you like the colors she picked?" Ariel asked, still the innocent.

David let her question hang in the air for a moment. "Am I being honest? I was more enjoying how well it fits." He tilted his head right as a piece of uneaten sandwich flew past his left ear.

"No gentleman would notice such things."

"I'm no gentleman."

Across a couple of intervening feet, Ariel catapulted herself at him. In an explosion of light brown sand, she tackled him and tried to get him in a headlock. They wrestled and feinted and fought. Sand flew everywhere.

After they settled back into what was left of their picnic, David waited a little while and then deadpanned, "You should take your shirt off more often." It started all over again.

In the end, Ariel asked, "Can we be serious for a minute?"

"Uh-oh. You know me and serious."

"I want to know who you are and how much this gold story is to you."

"First part's easy. Me? I'm a poor kid from Middle America. Got dumped in Madrid a few years ago. Then I found a beautiful Spanish girl to take to the beach. Everybody out here's jealous of me, you know."

"Serious, David."

"That's too hard for me."

"No, it isn't. Talk."

"Is there another beer?" David deflected.

"Talk."

"You're gonna be disappointed."

"David."

"OK. Serious," David began. "Me is easy. The gold story's complicated."

"I think I will be able to understand."

MOSCOW GOLD | 193

"You know the word *indolente*? I'm indolent. I love to get everything all done with minimum effort and then bask in the sweet-do-nothings of indolence, idleness, and freedom. Just like we're doing now. Ariel, this is paradise for me."

"But you work hard on your stories," Ariel objected.

"Not so much, but this story is different. It's going to tax me whether I like it or not. This gold story is going to drag me out of my indolence."

"Then just don't do it."

"Not an alternative, Ariel. Don't you see? I'm being forced into the gold story. Isham can make me pay prices I don't want to pay. And he won't hesitate to do it."

"You have skills, training. Find another paper," Ariel reasoned.

"Won't work. He can get me thrown out of Spain. Maybe after he gets me thrown in jail for a while. I lose Spain, I lose it all."

"You're exaggerating, David. You have to be."

"I don't know yet what the gold story is. But all my instincts tell me that it's a story worth getting. Somebody's hiding something. I don't have any choice but to find out who and what. I won't be free till I do."

"How can getting a story make you free?" Ariel wondered.

"This is what Isham hasn't thought of," David explained. "Right now, he has me leveraged. But if I go about it right, if I do my investigation right, if I handle the finished story right, then I leverage Isham. Then my leverage buys me back my freedom."

"But you know it's risky. It's not fair—all that risk."

"Fairness and risk are irrelevant, Ariel. I must get the story. Life is a series of battles. Battles have risk. Most go how they should. But then you win some you should lose, and you lose some you should win. Just hope you have more wins at 'game over.'"

"That's a pessimistic outlook," she thought.

"Pessimistic? Not so much. Realistic maybe. But I'll tell you this; battles interrupt my sweet idleness. I prefer lolling here on the beach with you. But I'm stuck with this one. I just have to finesse the gold story to my advantage."

"Thank you for telling me. That's another beautiful gift from you to me," Ariel murmured.

They were quiet for a while.

"Ariel?"

"Mmm."

"Who are you? I had to tell. Now you do."

"Oh, no one interesting at all," Ariel acted demure.

"I'll throw you in the ocean."

"Not you and an entire army!"

"That's the North Atlantic out there, Ariel. It's cold," David assured her.

"My life is well set, stable. I'm content—I think because I don't take many risks. I think you like risk. I don't. But I'm sensing more risk. My own little private harmony is being upset."

"What are you going to do about it?"

"I don't know yet, David, but I'm excited to see. I think sometimes that you find what it is that you want most while looking hard for something else."

⁊

The day began to die. They picked up and headed for the Sardinero.

"*Las arenas de Santander.* ¡Ay! ¡Ay! ¡Ay!" Ariel muttered.

"'The Sands of Santander.' Sounds like a cinema epic that Jaime would have us translating—Christians and Moors battling to the death before the city gates." Then he saw she was walking gingerly.

"Oh, I get it. Sands of Santander in your shoes." David observed.

"Sand everywhere."

"Everywhere?"

"Everywhere," Ariel admitted.

"You started it," David pointed out.

"And I finished it."

"Baloney. You want me to brush you off? I'm very thorough," David said.

"Yes, but if we start that, we could get in trouble."

"I love trouble," David persisted.

They were, by now, walking up to the big entryway doors.

"Well, we're here. So, it looks like we are safe. For now, anyway. David, take me to supper tonight?"

"Here. In the lobby. Nine on the dot!"

༄

Nick Barnickle fished in his pocket for a token. He was having a beer at the Café Bodeguita. The phone was located at the end of the bar. He dialed. Automatic collect call from anywhere in Europe, he'd been told.

"Isham."

Ha! It works.

"He's up in Santander, Jack. So am I. He came up on the train yesterday. Alone. Didn't meet or see anybody on the way."

"Why's he in Santander, then?" Isham demanded.

"He met the girl after he got here—this morning at her hotel. She must have already been here," Barnickle explained.

"What's she doing there?" Isham was surprised.

"Not sure."

"I don't pay you not to be sure, Nick." Isham got testy again.

"Good guess this is just a stop for him. You said he might go to Paris. On the way if he goes through Irún," Nick theorized.

"Spanish police?"

"Haven't seen 'em, but they know they're here. Hotels will report them to the Guardia Civil. You said Room 11 is friendly in this. Why would they tail him?"

"Room 11 says they want the story. They act like they're cooperating. But something in my gut tells me Room 11' s questionable. Anybody else on to him?" Isham dodged the question.

196 | DOUGLAS L. FIELD

"Anybody like who?" Nick persisted.

"Like anybody. How the hell should I know?" Isham was getting impatient.

"Nobody. I'd know it if they were."

"I need him to get this story, Nick," Isham growled. "And when he does, I need to control it. I don't like sharing. Not with Room 11. Not with State. Just the Company. That means you need to be on him and tell me if anybody else is. Then I can figure out what to do to protect what's mine. Stay on him, Nick. Lucky for you, you found him again."

"Not luck, Jack. I say he heads for Paree. Tomorrow or Monday." Nick stood his ground.

"Stick with him, Nick. He lost you once already. Boy's not stupid."

❧

David supposed that he had left Ariel with the impression that he was headed back to his lodgings. He wasn't.

He retrieved the SEAT and drove around Santander till he found a public restroom where he could wash his face and comb his hair. All that he had brought north was in the car. He had left his key in his room this morning. He would waste tonight's lodging.

❧

This time Ariel was prompt. She showed in the lobby on time.

"Did you resolve your sand problem? I wish you would have let me help." David greeted her.

"¡Canalla!" Faux outrage. Flirtatious look.

"Let's see if we can get into Mistral. Its close," David suggested. "Ever been there?"

Ariel shook her head.

"Mistral's different. Half on the boardwalk and half on the beach sand. You sit where you can find room. It's a seafood joint. Waiters

MOSCOW GOLD | 197

carry around big platters of today's catch. They yell, 'I have prawns!' Or, 'I have mussels!'"

"Mmm. Sounds fun!"

"You wave to the guy who has what you want. He dishes you some up. You pile up all the shells and bones. Then there's a last waiter shouting, 'I'm collecting!' When you're ready, he looks at your garbage and adds up your bill."

There was still light in the August sky. Mistral was wide open and noisy, loudspeakers blaring American rock and roll. It was only open in the high summer season. It was always packed—not the place for an intimate dinner, but perfect if you wanted not to be overheard.

David found them open seats across from each other at the end of one of the tables. They ordered various of Mistral's offerings and dug in. Being out in the sun and wind had left them hungry and thirsty. David ordered a couple of jarras of Águila.

"What's that song? I hear it everywhere," Ariel asked after they were seated.

"'I Will Follow Him.'"

"She has a good voice."

"Name's Little Peggy March. I think she's only about fifteen," David said.

"Do you like popular music?" Ariel wanted to know.

"How could I not? It's America's primary contribution to Western culture."

The song changed. "What's this one?" Ariel asked. "It's hard to understand."

"It's called 'If You Wanna Be Happy.'" David was laughing. "The lyric says that, if you want to be happy, you should never marry a pretty woman."

Ariel looked confused. David went on. "It says, 'So from my personal point of view / Get an ugly girl to marry you.' In English, it rhymes."

She still looked unsure. He explained, "Look at it this way. In that song if I married you, I could never be happy."

"But why?"

"Because, Ariel, you're very, very beautiful."

"You Americans are strange sometimes."

"I'll explain it to you later." David was bemused at her continuing discomfiture. He changed the subject. "I need to go to Paris tomorrow."

"Can't you avoid it? You know it's dangerous, don't you? I do."

"It's like I said on the beach. Isham has me cornered. Only way I get out is to get the story and then somehow turn it on him. I have some ideas."

"How long will you be gone?"

"I figure I can be back in Madrid by the end of the month," David answered. "There are people in Paris who were involved in person with sending the gold to Moscow. Some are in exile from here. I suspect that they will be able to lead me to others who are also still alive who have vital information."

"What information, David? Can't you get it here in Spain?"

"I need to pin down where the gold went. We think we know, but it's not nailed down. Then I need to show what happened to it after it got there—what they did with it. After that, the last piece is to establish where it is now. Those are the elements of the story that aren't known. They're the elements that get me free."

"David, possession of that kind of information is a terrible exposure for you? *Más que nada*, I'm worried about your safety." Ariel pressed him to abandon the trip.

"No one knows my plans. I can stay a few steps ahead of anybody who wants to hurt me."

"There it is. 'People who might want to hurt you.'"

"Isham doesn't know where I am. At least I don't think he does. When I leave Spain, the Cuerpo loses jurisdiction. The French aren't involved. What do they care? Nacho's taught me about avoiding trouble. I should be good."

MOSCOW GOLD | 199

'There has to be a way out of this, David. If you put as much energy into getting out of this awful gold story as you are getting into it, you could be safe."

"I've thought it through a hundred times. There's no way out—not without going for the story. I do that, and there's a chance."

Ariel saw there was no more discussion. She said nothing.

"There's one more thing. I need you to help me. When I get back to Spain, I may be on the run. I may have items I need safeguarded."

"David, you're not serious!"

"Ariel, can you meet me two weeks from today in Segovia on the parapet that overlooks the short end of the aqueduct? At the top where the steps go up. You know where I mean?"

"I do know where you mean, but I can't. I'm afraid. You're involving me in this, David."

"You're already involved, Ariel. The cops have to know about you and me. They must. I'm sorry. I hope you can forgive me. I didn't know the trap they were putting me in. For your safety, you only know that I'm doing the story. If they ask you, I'm in France. You can be truthful that you know no other details. Your exposure is minimal."

"No, David. I'm not like you and Nacho. This is scary."

"Please think about it, Ariel. Don't say no. Not yet. Segovia. Two Saturdays from now. September 7. Meet me there at noon. Figure out somewhere that I can keep some items safe. Is it clear? Will you remember?"

"I'll remember, but—"

"If you come and I don't, tell Nacho. He will know what to do. And Jaime. He has connections. But don't worry. I'll show up."

"David, it seems as if you are trusting me with your life. It's frightening."

"Don't be frightened. Let me trust you," David urged her. "And you trust me, sí? Just think about it. Think about getting there. To Segovia. To the *acueducto*."

Ariel sat motionless. She said nothing.

200 | DOUGLAS L. FIELD

After an additional time, they left Mistral and walked up toward the entrance to the Sardinero. It was late now, dark out. To the side of the entrance, there was a shadowed area under a copse of trees.

Ariel stopped there in the dark. She turned and faced David. "May I ask you a question before we go in?"

"So formal. Is it a hard one?"

"I think it is," Ariel admitted.

'*Tú dirás*" (Say on).

"David, do you remember our conversation on the beach this afternoon?"

"Of course." He started to make light of it and smiled.

"Behave and answer me. I want to know if there is anything, anything at all, that you would work hard, work with a will not to lose, David? You are fighting not to lose the gold story. Do you have more to lose, more than the story?" Ariel appeared serious.

David nodded, holding her eyes.

"*Bien sabes que sí y que eres tú*" (You know very well that I do, and that it's you).

Her gaze was fixed back on him, intense.

He put his arms around her waist. "Ariel, I've upset your harmony, made you feel at risk. I don't want to lose you."

The look never wavered, her eyes liquid and glittery, with an almost imperceptible nod.

David traced the line of her jaw with the backs of his fingers. He held her close and kissed her on the mouth. For a second or two, it felt to him as if he carried part of her weight. After a long moment, she pulled back a little. She affected mild annoyance, smiled, and said, "You take that back." Then she kissed him.

There in the shadows, in front of the Sardinero, they embraced and kissed each other again and talked a little and kissed some more.

"Meet me in Segovia, Ariel."

Then she went in.

MOSCOW GOLD | 201

PART IV
OPERATION MARKGRAF

CHAPTER 26

Madrid: Thursday, February 11, 1937

Once the Siege of Madrid settled into the Standoff of Madrid, Nacho suffered.

The city staggered under the weight of impasse. Nacho had been stopped and interrogated five times since Christmas. In January, a communist patrol had stopped him in Lavapiés. This time his pase had failed to satisfy. They'd arrested him and were frog-marching him to the local tribunal for further investigation when their captain had shown up and detailed them to reinforce against an anticipated rebel attack up by Argüelles. Nacho had slipped away into the back streets, but it was a close-run thing.

There was little or no food or fuel. Merely existing was high risk. Ladies with buckets and string bags braved artillery fusillades and aerial bombings waiting on long and dangerous out-in-the-open queues. The shelling was round-the-clock. Night after night, its coruscations lit the western, southern, and eastern skies, creating over Madrid a perverse and bellicose aurora borealis.

MOSCOW GOLD | 205

Nacho showed up this morning at the Pintor Roslales flat in suit and tie with his portfolio in tow.

"They all but had me, Cóndor. I was frightened this time. Pure luck I got away."

Cóndor was forced to act.

"Madrid's become too dangerous for you, Aníbal," he stated at the flat. "They're picking people up on any scintilla of suspicion. Their different factions are even arresting each other. The Revolution is eating itself. Lost contact with Agent Augusta last week. We try to find her; we share her fate."

"I've considered some possible new legends. I'm done as el arquitecto."

"That and we better get you out for a while. Let your trail cool."

"Servicing my agents?"

"Difficult with Faraón. I'll give him to Ahumada. Tell him who you are and then blackmail him. Isidora's easier. Ahumada can handle her too."

"Faraón might not survive the shock. He's delicate."

"Civil war is not for the delicate." Cóndor shrugged.

"No."

"I'm sending you to Agent Clotilde, in Ciempozuelos. She'll be expecting you."

Cóndor handed Nacho an envelope. "Go now. Details in the envelope. Don't even return to your rooms. You're going on a hydrological survey down there."

CHAPTER 27

Ciempozuelos: Thursday, February 11, 1937

Nacho hiked the half mile up Avenida San Juan de Dios from the train station to Ciempozuelos's central plaza.

The buildings alongside the wide avenue formed a venturi such that he had to lean into an arctic headwind the whole way. Agent Clotilde's house was located north of the center at the edge of town.

Nacho arrived windblown and cold. Clotilde herself admitted him without fanfare and offered tea. Clotilde or Dolores Torres de Rubalcava, known in the locality as "Lola," was a widow of indeterminate but by no means advanced age.

Lola supported herself by making fans with matte silk lace webbing for the expensive ladies of Madrid, Aranjuez, Chinchón, and Alcalá de Henares. She lived with her nephew Roberto, "Beto," a teenager of some moderate speech disability.

The advantage of Agent Clotilde's house at Calle Azucena 16 was its camouflaged attachment to a small cave in the low hillside next to which it was built. The place was historical. In former days, it had included an outdoor privy. In later times a modern, indoor-plumbed

MOSCOW GOLD | 207

toilet had been added. The new loo was near the front of the house, with the old now enclosed within the structure at the back.

Known only to Lola, Beto, and a very few trustworthy confederates, the stool in the old privy was hinged. It could be raised to allow access, not to the indignity of its former utilization but to the cave behind the house. This unsavory manner of ingress had always discouraged even the slightest inclination by authority toward investigation of any potential access to the grotto.

The cave not only provided secure storage for all manner of contraband, but also connected to a network of similar caves in the area. Should anyone find themselves a fugitive from the people's justice in Ciempozuelos, successful evasion and escape was facilitated.

In keeping with his new legend, the notional hydrologist Ignacio Arjona was in Ciempozuelos to scout possible sites for a groundwater-pumping complex his Madrid firm had been contracted to design. Ciempozuelos means, after all, "One Hundred Little Wells," and the Republican authorities in the capital were preserving the gigantic fiction that life was proceeding as normal.

Nacho discovered that Lola and her household were cool and somewhat distant but as amiable and comfortable as current events allowed. Not long after Nacho settled in, Beto appeared and was introduced. He had a small packet for Clotilde.

Nacho watched Lola look for and find a book, sit at her dining table, and begin to make notes.

"*La Regenta*?" Nacho asked with a lift of his eyebrows.

"No. His other one." She looked at the book cover. "*Fortunata y Jacinta.*"

"Page 211?"

She nodded.

"They ought to get a little more creative," Nacho muttered.

It was not long before Clotilde looked up.

"Done already? You're faster at that than me."

"Cóndor's got it that an attack will be coming through this area. We're trying to take the Valencia Road. Cut off Madrid from the south. There's the Pindoque Bridge, over the Jarama. They think that when the Reds figure out what's coming, they'll blow it. You're to see what you can do."

"See what I can do? "Nacho expressed his exasperation. "Am I an explosives expert? I thought Cóndor was sending me for a rest. You think Beto could help?"

Lola thought he could.

Nacho soon comprehended that Beto's impediment was to his speech only. His talking was loud, squawky, and indistinct, but he was otherwise of quite normal, if not superior, intelligence.

Beto was thought of as something of a village idiot, wrong though the notion was. He was both condescended to and tolerated by the locals. They were accustomed to his moving around the Ciempozuelos area at odd times and on odd missions of his own fantasy. Little did anyone expect that he was an acute and incisive observer. When accorded sufficient patience and attention, Beto could describe his observations in detail. More, he had a profound knowledge of the ground around Ciempozuelos and its languorous and viridescent Jarama River.

Beto shared Lola's secret rebel sympathies and he, too, was a good spy. And he knew it. He had a very effective cover and unfettered access to the entire region south of Madrid. He was above, or as it was in the minds of some of Ciempozuelos's more pretentious, below suspicion. Nacho code-dubbed him Dámaso and was soon forwarding valuable Dámaso product through Clotilde to Cóndor.

"You know this Pindoque Bridge, Beto?" Nacho asked.

"Ouayo quayeee," Beto replied. Of course, he did. He went on by way of his squawks, screeches, and scratches to add that a unit called the 18th Peoples' Solidarity Brigade were defending it.

"We go have a look tonight?" proposed Nacho.

Beto agreed they could.

"Let's get some black clothes, boots, and some wire cutters. If they've set charges to blow the bridge, maybe we can do some damage."

Beto nodded and then explained that, on occasion, he hung around the bridge. He was known to the defenders and not considered a threat. The Loyalist soldiers had talked freely in his presence—unsuspecting. He had overheard that the bridge was, in fact, wired for destruction—just in case.

Beto's primary means of locomotion was what appeared to be a decrepit bicycle. It was one, however, that he capably kept serviceable and in good repair. Beto said he could arrange a bike for Nacho too.

After dark and from the erstwhile jake, the two made use of the interconnected caves to surface again outside of town and over a quarter mile from Lola's house.

After traveling many miles in the mud and dark, they arrived in the vicinity of the bridge. Without Beto, Nacho would never have found it.

They ditched their bikes in some high foliage and proceeded on foot. Pindoque turned out to be a two-section truss rail bridge with concrete anchorages on both ends and in the middle. Planks had been laid between the ties so vehicles could pass. The terminus anchorages were guarded, but there was no patrol on the roadbed.

"We have to get past the guards," Nacho said unnecessarily. "We'll go downriver a couple of hundred meters and then come back along the water's edge."

Beto nodded.

Nacho led the way down river. The Jarama at Pindoque was shallow and sluggish. The banks rose at a shallow angle from the river, and there was little vegetation on the water's edge, so there was no cover. And it was muddy.

They crouched low and sneaked through mud that wanted to pull their boots off and threatened to make loud sucking sounds with each step. As they approached the anchorage, they heard the voices of the sentries—quiet but animated conversation. One lit a smoke. Awake but not alert.

Once under the bridge, they hauled themselves up to the underneath side of the roadbed. Darker there in the shadow. Harder to see. The steel latticework of the underside provided space for them to crawl across. Nacho thought this would be where the Loyalist sappers would put their demolition charges.

Once up on the under supports, Nacho signaled to Beto that they should crawl out on opposite sides. He pointed to his eyes and then to the steel girders. He took out his wire cutters and made a cutting motion. *Find the charges and cut the wires.* Beto moved out.

The sappers had staggered the charges at twenty-meter intervals. Nacho found their first one. Beto saw him cut the two wires and secure the leads so that the cut ends did not dangle and give away their sabotage. Beto found a charge and followed suit.

They got into their rhythm. They went faster as they moved along. The steel structure went through the concrete at the center anchorage. They could not crawl through. It would have to be up and over.

Beto was light and lithe. He pulled himself to the outside and up onto the roadbed. Nacho's boots were wet and muddy. He threaded his body through an opening in the steel lattice and started to climb. His right foot slipped, and he swung into space. He managed to hold on with one hand and flopped back against the steel. He scrambled back to the steel understructure.

Before he could start climbing again, Beto slithered back down. He made a walking motion with two fingers. Someone had decided to walk the bridge. Nothing to do but hold on and hold still. The sentry crunched past. They couldn't tell if he was looking over the edge. They hid their faces. After an eternity, it was again quiet. Nacho nodded his head up and down once. *Go up and look.*

Beto went back up on the roadbed and verified they were clear. He lay down and reached over to help Nacho up. They were across the concrete and back down on the steel. They moved across the second section. No charges. They looked at each other and shrugged. They kept on to the far anchorage. They found no more charges.

Nacho led them down off the bridge under the far anchorage and to the river's edge. When he felt they were safely away, he made swimming motions. Beto shrugged, and they swam across.

Back at the bikes Nacho said, "I nearly fell. What a cock-up. The lazy bastards only wired half the bridge. I guess they figure one section down makes the whole unusable."

It began to get light.

Beto led them home, wet and muddy. Lola appeared to make no reaction. Nacho thought she might be a little amused at their plight, but he couldn't be sure. She went to find her book.

"I'll encode a message. Beto can pass it on after he cleans up."

CHAPTER 28

Ciempozuelos: Friday, February 12, 1937

At midmorning, Beto came roaring back into the Azucena house with news of the not unexpected Nationalist attack in force westward headed for Ciempozuelos.

Five brigades of *regulares* and foreign legionnaires were driving across the Jarama and hard toward the Madrid-Valencia highway. It was an all-out effort to isolate and reduce Madrid once and for all.

The Azucena residents took counsel and decided that the Moorish Nationalist troops were unpredictable. They might not believe proclaimed Nationalist sympathies. It was preferable to preserve cover in case the fortunes of battle changed.

By afternoon, the fighting moved past. Beto went out on a reconnaissance. It appeared that the Republicans had been surprised. 18th Peoples' Solidarity Brigade had been routed. There was no news on the bridge.

"We have to go back tonight, Beto," Nacho ordered. "Just for a look. We won't come back wet and muddy this time."

Beto shrugged. Lola's expression remained impassive as always.

⁓

Their second slog to the bridge found it to be intact and unguarded. With no one around, they were able to make close inspection. The rains had stopped, and the skies had cleared to reveal a partial moon. Still, the bridge was difficult to evaluate in the dark.

The bridge itself seemed undamaged. The roadbed, ballast, and rails at both anchorages were twisted and torn up, but the structure itself seemed solid, resting on its concrete abutments. There appeared to be blast and burn marks on the steel superstructure but little else to indicate significant damage.

They hung around the area in a quandary until dawn. Upon querying some early-rising locals, they had the answer. The Republican sappers had wired the bridge for destruction in the event it might be overrun. When the worst had indeed occurred, they had blown it. Witnesses reported that the explosives on either end had ignited in a huge fireball. The entire bridge had been lifted intact several feet straight into the air. It had then, just as intact, fallen, in precise and perfect fashion, back into its original location.

Beto got it figured first. His sounds and gestures indicated that Nacho and he had cleared the bridge span of explosives but that there must have been others on the anchorages that they missed.

"The stupid bridge flew up into the air and fell right back down. If we hadn't cut the middle charges, it would have been blown all apart," Nacho agreed.

Beto pointed out that, since it blew, no sabotage would be suspected. "We're in the clear," Beto noted.

Back at Azucena, Nacho filled Lola in. "This is crucial intelligence," he said.

Lola agreed. "Message something like 'Pindoque Bridge blown but passable. At least to vehicles?'"

"*Exactamente*. I guess we leave out that it's passable both for further attack and for counterattack," Nacho said and looked at Beto.

They both started laughing.

"Cóndor should be able to figure that one out on his own," Lola contributed, adding a rare smile.

CHAPTER 29

Ciempozuelos: Saturday, February 13, 1937

Cóndor replied by return message.

There was no comment on the Pindoque incident. "Verify existence of Loyalist airfield Arganda. Advise hardware and personnel present."

Agent Dámaso already knew of it. It was located south of Arganda del Rey, east of the Azucena house. He squawked that he liked airplanes and already had a couple of blinds at the site.

"I can watch," he seemed to say. "Tight but you'll fit."

"Have to be a daytime op, Dámaso. We'll need a cover."

Beto went into the cave. He returned with berets, very worn flannel shirts, and a pair of shepherd's crooks.

"We can use our boots from the bridge, Beto," Nacho added. "Muddy will be good—expected."

They had to hike. It was three miles over open country. No good for the bikes. Beto led to an abandoned stone structure very close to the perimeter wire. One wall was tumbled. The hut's contents had been looted long ago. There was an alcove with small windows that faced the airfield.

MOSCOW GOLD | 217

They squeezed in. Beto had piled up stones so they could sit. They settled in for a long watch.

Nacho approved. "You're good at this, Dámaso."

Not long, and Beto cocked his head. Then Nacho heard it. An approaching aero engine. No, two. The planes materialized and flew downwind over them. Nacho got a good look. They were stout-looking biplanes with short fuselages and squarish engine nacelles. They banked deftly onto final and landed in formation. The pilots hopped out and appeared to congratulate each other.

"Must have been a successful sortie," Nacho whispered.

The pilots spoke to each other in a foreign language. The wind was blowing just right for Nacho and Beto to hear. Beto pointed to his ears, shrugged his shoulders. and raised his eyebrows.

"Russian, Beto. They're speaking Russian. I don't know any Russian."

A trio of Republican Air Force ground pounders ran up. The group switched to Spanish. The Russians claimed an Italian Savoia-Marchetti bomber had been shot down and another damaged.

Then the Russians' tone changed. They said the air war was changing. Opposition aircraft sent up used to be second-rate. Now there was an advanced German type, the Something-or-Other 109.

Not only that but the fascist enemy had acquired German 88-mm antiaircraft guns—dead-on accurate and effective. Republican aircraft not shot up aloft by the new fascist aircraft were being shot full of holes from the ground. One of the Russians pointed to the proof—holes in his wings and horizontal stabilizer.

The pilots walked off toward their mess, and the ground crew turned to the repair of the planes.

Beto had a name for this plane. But at first Nacho could not understand it. After a while he got it—Chato.

"So that's what the Spanish troops call it? Chato? Snub nose? It's the Polikarpov I-15—a Soviet aircraft, Beto. Do you know how many there are?"

Beto held up the fingers of both hands plus one more hand.

"Fifteen. An entire squadron."

Beto explained further. Fifteen planes had been delivered in November. There had been loses, however. Additional deliveries had been expected, but there was delay. Shipping issues.

On the way back to Ciempozuelos, Nacho then recounted to Beto how, in October, the government in Madrid had sent Spain's gold reserves to Moscow, in exchange, it was presumed, for this very sort of aerial war matériel.

"Those Chatos and a lot of stuff like them is what the Republicans have gotten in exchange for all that gold. You have to wonder whether it was worth it. Sounds like we're getting better stuff from the Germans and Italians than Madrid is from the Soviets."

Beto wondered why Moscow.

"Madrid scuttlebutt had it that the finance minister, a guy named Negrín, saw Soviet Russia as a lesser threat to Spain. Huge miscalculation," Nacho told him.

"¿Ansiah? ¿Iguaerah?"

"¿*Francia o Inglaterra*? Good question, Beto. About one quarter of the gold *was* sent to France. They have it in a repository there. The British? Not trustworthy. They would find a way to steal it."

"¡Aahronay!" muttered Beto, which Nacho had by now learned was, "¡*Cabrones*!"

Beto added, "We should go and steal it back—you and me." He pounded his chest.

"Yeah. We should. We're a team. I'll ask Clotilde to tell Cóndor!"

MOSCOW GOLD | 219

CHAPTER 30

Ciempozuelos: Sunday, February 14, 1937

The team got a short rest.

Cóndor's answer to Clotilde's report on the airfield and the aircraft and personnel present came in after siesta.

"Air raid Arganda. 0615/15/02. Observe and provide damage assessment."

Nacho said, "We gotta go back out there, Beto. Tomorrow at dawn. We'll get today free."

Beto said nothing and left. Beto was Beto—doing Beto things.

The day off allowed Nacho to observe Agent Clotilde. She was neither tall nor short, neither thin nor plump. She had a pleasant longish face with lips darker than average that needed, and got, no extra color. She displayed an attractive smile and had the arched and rounded eyebrows common among Spanish women.

Attire ordinary, serviceable, and modest, her figure showed neither full nor spare, ample, satisfyingly mature. In Nacho's presence, Lola was matter of fact, laconic, reticent—uncommon among the voluble Spanish.

Lola used the day off to work on her fans. Nacho got used to the *thrrreeep, thrrreeep, thrrreeep* of their furling and unfurling. Nacho had heard it said that the Italians talk with their hands and the French with their faces. He didn't know any Italians or French but thought Spaniards talked with their hands *and* faces. Spanish women added their fans—wrist up, wrist down, the number and rapidity of beats all in their separate and distinct ways, indicating derision, joy, contempt, or delight and a spectrum of other emotions. Lola was no different. As it was with most Spanish women, Lola's fan seasoned and added depth to such conversation as she made.

Lola maintained rigorous regularity and order in her house. *La comida* was always at two thirty in the afternoon. After dinner, Lola cleared up and put away in neat order. Being a man of his times and culture, Nacho would never have offered help. Had he done, his offer would have been tartly rejected. Nacho contented himself with watching.

After cleaning up, Lola routinely repaired to her bedroom and had her siesta.

CHAPTER 31

Arganda del Rey: Monday, February 15, 1937

Aníbal and Dámaso slipped into the cave at 02:30.

They fetched up wet, tired, and dirty at the stone hut well before sunrise. After they settled in, Beto produced a hip flask.

"This'll do," said Nacho. It was *anís*—raw and ragged but warming in the winter cold.

Beto made no response. This was his place. He was in his element. He would provide.

What they could see of the airfield was eerily quiet. Sentries breathed clouds of vapor and made regular rounds. Planes were scattered about in sandbag revetments.

"They're not on high alert, Beto."

"There's no antiaircraft guns," said Beto's sounds and noises.

"I don't see any slit trenches. They'll have no cover. Bombers at all accurate, and they get creamed," Nacho whispered. Sound carried here at night, even more than in the day.

"Need to kill pilots and planes. Planes no good without pilots."

"You're a bloodthirsty bastard, Beto." Nacho smiled.

MOSCOW GOLD | 223

"A few dead Russians, who cares? They stole our gold."

"Yeah, who cares?"

They were silent for a time. This time, Nacho heard it first—a faint hum. They couldn't place it at first. Then it grew. Out of the northwest. The sound grew fast. Nacho and Beto searched the sky for aircraft and found none. The airfield was waking up. Running figures could be seen in the morning gloom.

Beto saw them first. The noise rose to a roar. No need to be quiet. Beto was shouting and pointing. Around a dozen three-engine bombers approached, stately and sedate, in tight vees of three, height staggered. Tiny black dots streamed down as the planes arrived overhead.

Explosions began. North of the field it seemed. Nacho thought the bomb aimers had missed. Then the explosions walked over the north perimeter fence and into the planes and structures. Towers of dirt, debris, and dust prevented them from seeing the damage. Beto was jumping up and down and yelling. Nacho was trying to pull him down when a great orange fireball erupted and did it for him. It was the fuel dump. Fire poured out across the field, sluicing into the revetments and setting alight damaged and undamaged aircraft alike.

The bombs moved past the airfield. One hit a few dozen meters from the stone hut. The wall protecting Nacho and Beto disintegrated in a shower of rocks and mortar. Nacho was down—buried, bent, and twisted. Sand and grit filled his mouth and eyes. He was blind and struggled to breathe. His left leg screamed. He couldn't get his hands to his face. Panic rose. He pushed off some rocks and tried to wipe away the grime from his mouth. Some choking breaths and he got more debris off. Nacho was still not able to stand.

He looked for Beto. Saw him rise to all fours, debris cascading off. Beto stood and brushed himself off, looking for Nacho. Beto struggled over and took Nacho by the coat and one arm, pulled him out. Their cover was destroyed, but it didn't matter. No attention from the airfield was directed their way.

Yet they had to stay down. Now about half a dozen biplane fighters swooped in low and strafed the field—wrecking and killing all that was left. By now, the burning petrol was forming billowing black clouds that began to lift on the slight morning breeze. Figures moved among the destruction, attending to other figures. Some responded. Most did not. The drone of aero engines faded off to the southwest.

"We need to get out of here," Nacho croaked. He tried to stand but slumped back. He could see Beto talking but couldn't hear. Beto must be asking what was wrong.

"My ankle. Broken. Sprained. Don't know," he said but could not hear himself.

Both were hawking up dirt. Beto grabbed Nacho under the arms and helped him up. Nacho pointed to his left leg. There seemed to be no blood. Nacho put his left arm around Beto's shoulders, and they tried to hobble away.

Beto got them to a copse of trees where they could get out of sight but still have a view of the airfield.

Beto was exultant. "Blew them all to shit!" he seemed to say.

Nacho had to smile. "Just keep out of sight. We don't want them to catch us now. Let me rest a minute. See if I can walk."

They waited and observed for about half an hour. There was a fire brigade on the airfield—of sorts. It did what it could, but it was clear that tents, sheds, and many aircraft were wrecked. A wagon pulled by a tractor came out and collected numerous recumbent forms.

Nacho was able to limp away. Beto found him a dead branch that served as a walking stick, and they were able to move well enough.

They arrived back at Azucena before noon. They were filthy. Lola appeared to suppress a chuckle at their plight, but Nacho couldn't tell for sure.

They drafted a report to Cóndor. Lola began to encode. "Raid successful. Most squadron Chatos killed. Heavy casualties personnel."

MOSCOW GOLD | 225

"Got any more of that anís, Beto? We saw demolished a fair bit of what the Reds have gotten for our gold. If we could just figure how to get back the rest."

Beto did have more.

Lola gave a little shake of her head. Then she wrapped Nacho's ankle tight. "Good job you're back," she said looking at him. "I think you'll live."

⁓

The excitement abated. Stability and order seemed to settle in as Lola took up her regular afternoon routine. This afternoon after all the excitement of his and Beto's return from Arganda, after helping them clean themselves up, after nursing Nacho's injury, and after dinner and cleanup, Lola had gone in for siesta. But today she had not closed her bedroom door all the way. It had been left some two inches ajar.

Beto had gone out again. With little else to occupy Nacho, this occurrence set his mind to work. Had this been regular routine? He had not noticed. Was it an unintended oversight? Was his imagination overactive after the bombing raid? Or could it be a sign? A clue? A hint? A deliberate act by the habitually intentional Lola?

He decided to take the chance. He tapped Lola's door twice. Hearing nothing, he pushed it. Slow. Silent. Open.

From the semidarkness, "I perceive that you are a spy, Señor Aníbal—one with acute powers of observation. I hoped I would not be disillusioned."

Nacho's vision accommodated to the relative gloom. Lola lying on her bed. Wearing nothing but a cameo on a black ribbon close around her neck. She was propped up on some pillows, her hands behind her head. "I am, Señorita Clotilde—a spy sent to uncover the hidden secrets of Ciempozuelos."

Thrrreeep. The right hand found one of her fans. It dropped open. A mild fluttering, coy and demure, provided artificial and temporary décolletage.

Nacho regarded her. "You look right out of Goya, Lola."

Lola cocked her head, pursed her lips a little, and then with a rare and ironic smile, said, "We've lost our minds in this insane war, Nacho, not our culture."

She raised the sheet, an unspoken invitation. "Beto won't be home till after dark. You won't need your ankle."

On that one day and in that way was siesta liberally and pleasurably prolonged.

CHAPTER 32

Moscow: Wednesday, February 17, 1937

Commander Letchkov surveyed Saint Basil's Cathedral and the rest of Red Square from his chief's large office windows.

The entire vista was white, solid, frozen white. "A severe winter, Comrade Chairman."

"Nature's great blessing to the Rodina. Cold, ice, and snow. They have frustrated would-be invaders and conquerors often in the past. And they will again, I think. Threats from the outside are the lesser of our problems. Always our greatest danger lurks within. Besides, it's better now this way than in March and April when it becomes all sooty and slushy. Won't you agree, Commander?"

"Yes, of course, Comrade Chairman."

"How are our comrades in Valencia doing in the matter of arranging transport of their purchases? I recall that there would be no further utilization of Soviet sealift for those purposes," Stalin inquired.

"It has not been easy for them. The French pay serious lip service to the interdiction of all war matériel to Spain. In practice they turn, if not a blind eye, a myopic one to the subject. Some is passing through

MOSCOW GOLD | 229

to Barcelona—ammunition, light arms, machine guns." Letchkov had the essential facts at his fingertips.

"What about the heavy stuff? Tanks? Planes?"

"Much more difficult, comrade. You will recall the latest shipment of Polikarpovs was, uh, impeded. Since then, nothing." Letchkov trod with care.

"Hmm. Regrettable."

"We are advised by our people on the ground that the fascists managed to locate and bomb an airfield south of Madrid. Destroyed the better part of a squadron of fighters. Killed several pilots and ground crew, Soviets among them."

"Were steps not taken to conceal the existence of this airfield?"

"They were, Comrade Stalin. There are enemy networks active in and around Madrid. It is believed that a fascist spy located the place and called in the bombing raid."

"As I said, Letchkov, the danger comes always from within. Are these traitors Spaniards?"

"Doubtlessly, sir.

"They shall have to be dealt with. But let us switch for a moment to another topic. Did you count the payment, or I should say the deposit, as I instructed?"

"Yes, Comrade Stalin, 7,800 cases. We learned they sent 2,200 cases to France."

"Hedged their bets, did they? Well, we would have done the same, no?" The Russian leader was not surprised.

'The Spanish in many matters have been inept, Comrade Chairman, but in that, yes, it appears they spread the wealth around."

"Refresh me, Letchkov. Who is the senior Soviet trade envoy in Spain?" Stalin dissembled.

"Stachevski, Comrade Chairman."

"Yes. Arthur Andreivich, isn't it? Do you know what some are calling the Spanish shipment?" Stalin stroked his mustache.

"I'm not sure what the chairman—"

"Letchkov, do not weasel."

"'The Stachevski Shipment,' Comrade Chairman, or so I think I may have heard," Letchkov answered submissively.

"The time has come to convert the Spanish gold to hard currency." Stalin moved on. "I want to do it through Paris. For the moment, I need a stable France as a counterbalance to Germany. A delicate operation I imagine. Hard to keep secret. Pilferage. Outright theft. Any suggestions as to who we might entrust with this task?"

"The aforementioned Comrade Stachevski himself has already a level of familiarity with the situation," the commander suggested, knowing that Stalin's intentions were already fixed.

"That precise thought had occurred to me as well, Letchkov. Good thinking. And it's 'his' shipment anyway, isn't it? See to it, Comrade Commander. As always strict and accurate records will be kept of all transactions—full documentation, receipts, everything in proper order. Nothing must go amiss, Yuri, nothing."

"Of course not, Comrade Stalin."

"Oh and, Letchkov, have Stachevski locate and eliminate the fascist spies you mentioned. The deaths of our comrade pilots are not to go unavenged."

CHAPTER 33

Berlin: Tuesday, March 9, 1937

The late winter weather in the German capital was better than it was in Moscow, but it was poor enough.

Admiral Canaris had no intention of going outside until it was time to return home late this afternoon. He turned his attentions with alacrity to several of the primary "irons in the fire" that the Abwehr had in and around Europe.

The admiral gave a stout tug on the bell pull that hung near his desk, and his aide popped his head in.

"Ah, Heinz. Fetch Sepp, will you?"

Once Staupitz arrived, "What do you have for me, Sepp, on the Spanish, well, I suppose one might say, the 'Moscow' gold?"

"We're getting little whiffs on the breeze, Admiral, that Stalin's started to sell it for hard currency—or at least that he intends to start doing so very soon."

"Good. This is what we've been waiting for. 'Selling' the gold is far too generous a term. 'Fencing' it would be more accurate since he, in practical effect, has stolen it, hasn't he?"

MOSCOW GOLD | 233

"Yes, sir, quite accurate," Sepp confirmed.

"Well, no time for parsing, I suppose. What recommendations do you have for me?"

"Our sources have it, Admiral," Sepp began, "that the Soviets intend to launder it in small to medium amounts through gold dealers in Paris. We need to influence the process. There are no potential buyers whose possession of that gold would favor our interests."

"Well reasoned. Go on."

"The Abwehr needs to buy that gold, sir."

"It's a lot of money—a very lot. Your thoughts on that?"

"Germany's principal potential enemies over the medium to long term are Russia, England, and America. Our mission regarding the gold should be to destabilize all three, while, at the same time, furthering our own interests."

"I doubt that the Reichsbank will issue a draft, Sepp."

"No. And we don't want them involved," Sepp agreed. "My idea is that we buy the gold with counterfeit American and British currency. Russia is then deceived and loses the value of assets it misappropriated anyway, and the American and British economies are destabilized through the devaluation of their currency."

"Brilliant, Sepp. Truly brilliant. You must have got wind of what we've got going down at Sachsenhausen."

"Yes, sir, I have. Some Viennese counterfeiter working down there. Quite a good one, or so it seems. He's printing up British pound and US dollar notes. The British ones are beautifully authentic; I hear, even the Bank of England has fallen for them. US currency is more difficult. Hard to match the paper I gather."

"The story is," Canaris explained, "that, for some time now, the Abwehr has been monitoring a certain SS Major Bruno Uppmann. The major's named his effort after himself. Calls it Operation Bruno. Uppmann's a cheeky little shit, but the Abwehr have infiltrated his operation. I have assets laying hold of significant quantities of his, shall I say, 'product.' Uppmann is paying protection money, counterfeit though it may be, to the Abwehr."

"The irony is delicious, Admiral, sir."

"Isn't it? Your orders, Sepp, are to buy up as much of that gold as you can using as much falsified British and American money as comes available. To make it work, you will need some of the real stuff too. I think I can arrange that for you."

"Use the Paris embassy as needed, sir?"

"So ordered."

"Just one more matter, sir. The plan needs a little extra— something to keep the Russians off balance, distracted. Deflect their attention from the 'bad bills' and from looking too much into whom their buyers are."

"Every operation needs a diversionary tactic or two. What are you thinking?"

"They will expect and plan to defend against forcible assaults on their transfers. We should attack some of the shipments but use surrogates. Ensure that no Abwehr fingerprints are on any of it. Use contacts from out east. Spread some financial largess to Bucharest, Sofia, Belgrade, or Budapest. Let them steal small amounts of the gold and keep it for themselves as long as they don't get caught."

"Distract the Russians' attention with the expected, and they don't have time to discover the unexpected. Excellent. Enjoy Paris, Korvettenkapitän Staupitz."

CHAPTER 34

Madrid: Thursday, April 8, 1937

Cóndor recalled Nacho to Madrid.

Nacho went to the Pintor Rosales flat on the Ahumada delivery bike but without bread. There wasn't any to be had. Once upstairs, Cóndor greeted him.

"Pindoque was remarkable, Aníbal. Straight up into the air and straight back down, was it?"

"So the witnesses said. We missed the charges on the anchorages. We're lucky the bridge is not in the Jarama. I'm sorry."

"Nothing to be sorry for, Aníbal. The bridge is unusable for rail traffic, and we hear the Reds are fearful even for lighter stuff. Plus, many of their troops are uneducated peasants and superstitious. They won't even cross on foot. The operation did not fail. When the history of the war is written, the 'Pindoque Incident' will be one of its mysteries."

"No names being known or mentioned?" Nacho asked.

"None. Likewise, as to the intelligence sources for the Arganda raid. It was very much a success, Aníbal. Nine aircraft destroyed, along

MOSCOW GOLD | 237

with repair facilities and the petrol dump. An additional aircraft or two will require extensive repair. Arganda has been put out of action. How's your ankle by the way?"

"Recovered nicely, thank you."

"Relative to keeping our intelligence sources protected, we have learned that the Republicans' Soviet advisors are not pleased that Arganda is out of commission. Orders have gone out to locate and eliminate the persons responsible for alerting the Italians. Protection will be required. That includes for you and me."

"It should include Dámaso as well."

"It will. Dámaso is easier than you. Our judgment is that you need to get out. Way out. I'm sending you to Paris for a short stint there."

"Paris?"

"You remember the shipment of gold that you were a part of? German intelligence let it slip that Moscow intends to dispose of it through Paris somehow. We've indicated interest. They seemed reluctant but agreed to cooperate."

"The German guy in the Kremlin must be good."

"Don't ask, Aníbal The spy business is more intertwined than you might imagine. They know. We know. You're to contact Agent Alois. You'll remember him. Your assignment is to ascertain who acquires our money and where it goes from Paris."

CHAPTER 35

Paris: Monday, April 12, 1937

It took a while before Staupitz got to enjoy Paris.

He called his plan to acquire the Moscow gold Operation Markgraf. The fewer individuals involved in any operation, the better. He preferred working alone, but Markgraf would need help. Admiral Canaris detailed his own assistant, Major Hans Grebe, to the project.

Staupitz set up headquarters in a small suite at the Hotel Alsina at 39 avenue Junot up on Montmartre. The location was well away from the embassy. It was down by the river on the rue de Lille. The embassy was accessible but a level of anonymity could also be hoped for up on the hill.

Winter had lingered in Paris, and Grebe arrived amid a days-long rainstorm. He had been briefed by the Abwehr admiral himself, who swore him to secrecy under penalty of "extreme prejudice."

"Weather's awful, Grebe, but we'll get started on our project. Distract us from the rain and gloom," Sepp said after they exchanged formal military salutes.

MOSCOW GOLD | 239

"Just as well, sir. I have the information you asked me to look into when you are ready for it."

"Some underworld sources I've got up on Place Pigalle have it that some 'Russians' are making business contacts here," Staupitz began. "There are bullion dealers in the Bourse and numismatists in the rues Vivienne and Richelieu. They tend to keep to their own. Paris coin dealers are fussy, don't like to buy from foreign visitors. Pigalle has it that their scruples have somehow been assuaged—Soviet heavy-handedness no doubt. But it's confirmed the stuff is coming. Craven swine will *sell* to anybody."

"They're in the business of taking in other people's money, sir. I imagine we will become good friends," Grebe commented.

"Here's our cover. Two Swiss brothers," Sepp went on. "Wealthy but frugal. We desire to diversify a significant portion of our holdings into hard assets in view of the political and economic heavy weather boiling up over Europe. The Alsina is suited to the notion that we are well-heeled yet colorless Swiss endeavoring to maintain a level of anonymity during a delicate financial sojourn in the French capital."

"Very plausible," agreed Grebe. He had completed some preparatory work requested by Staupitz. "You inquired about holding companies. To hold title to the coins once we, eh, 'purchase' them."

"What do we have on that?"

"We undertook the legal work to set up several entities. We tried to be creative with the names. Holdings Levant, Ltd., Gestoría Andaluz, Almacenes San Lorenzo, SA, the Shiloh Corporation, along those lines. All are duly formed, constituted, and funded. They are resident in various jurisdictions, including the United States, the United Kingdom, the Netherlands Antilles, and Lichtenstein. Appropriate board resolutions were filed designating yourself as attorney-in-fact."

"Very good, Grebe. Did the admiral have comment on the names?"

"You know he did, sir. He was quite the enthusiast. Offered several ideas."

"And then the matter of the Gibraltarian banks?" Sepp asked.

"These span a broad continuum from Gibraltarian iterations of the largest British and European banks to small family-run concerns. The admiral preferred, and so we opened, accounts and safe deposit facilities at medium-sized institutions. They have odd enough names too. As I recall the Bank Jacob Joffre, Alicante Offshore, and Southwick and Esterborough Building Society are some of them. Oh, and the family-owned ones, Ruggiero Brothers and Banco Coligaray."

"Perfect, Hans. I expected no less. Let's dispense with the military formality unless there's brass around. I'm Sepp. Let's go down and find a café. I need a coffee."

Once they were out on the street, the day continued blustery and cold. It was much too windy for umbrellas. They buttoned their coats and held onto their hats. Sepp wondered if they would stand out among the French as German, but no one gave them even passing notice. They found a warm and busy place on the rue Gabrielle.

"May I ask why Gibraltar?" Grebe said as they settled in. "It is an *English* colony."

"Gibraltar is the key to the whole operation, Hans," Sepp said as he gestured to the barman for a pair of coffees.

"The Abwehr is certain general war is coming after the Spanish conflict is concluded. If the gold is placed there, it will be subject to confiscation by the British," Grebe protested. "We and they will doubtless wind up on opposite sides."

"It's nuanced," Staupitz explained. "Our side in Spain will win. Then they owe us with no convenient way to repay. In the broader war, we and the Spanish will be allied. Gibraltar is a part of the Spanish landmass. It controls the entrance to the Mediterranean. Our mutual interest is to eject the British. Spain gets their land back. We control the Strait."

Their coffees came, and Staupitz told the waiter to bring them a couple of Pernods when he got the chance. "Help with the warming up, eh?"

MOSCOW GOLD | 241

Then he went on, "The Gibraltarians are more British than Spanish, but they are even more Gibraltarian than British. Once they feel threat from us and Spain, they'll look first to their selfish interests. Our deposits will be leverage in dealing with their new masters. Little chance they allow confiscation of our deposits."

"In the event that Gibraltar is not returned to Spain?"

Sepp looked around the café, which was bustling and animated on a stormy afternoon. Everyone else was French.

He leaned close to Grebe and whispered in a collegial tone, "An impertinent, if not treasonous question, Major Grebe. In that far-fetched eventuality, our holdings will be in your nominee companies—not identifiable with the Abwehr. Gibraltar's serious about its banks. Gibraltar's unique. It's the one place in Europe where these assets will be safe and secure for the Abwehr, regardless of how the war plays out."

Grebe's expression remained impassive. "It appears that Markgraf's infrastructure is in place. Operational execution can begin."

⟋⟍⟍

Later back in their hotel suite, Staupitz read Grebe in on his idea that they should steal some of the gold in addition to buying it.

Grebe was not convinced. "We want the Soviets and the gold dealers comfortable with the regularity of our purchases. Robberies will elevate suspicions and distrust. The Soviets might be tempted to take a closer look at us."

"On the other hand," countered Sepp, "they will figure on attempts on their shipments. Without any, there will be suspicion. The Soviets are distrustful. Clear sailing would be ominous to them."

"So, we lay on a limited series of attacks," Grebe continued. "Some are designed to succeed. Others we will intend to fail. Just frequent enough to keep them from becoming either very comfortable or very concerned."

Sepp continued the thought. "Ivan will then concentrate on his procedures for protecting his shipments. It will be the more beguiling

242 | DOUGLAS L. FIELD

to him if his 'successes' outnumber his 'failures.' He is less inclined and has less time to expend energy discovering where the gold is going after he gets his 'money.'"

"So, our question becomes," Grebe completed the circle, "what operatives do we have who will succeed both at succeeding and failing and with no connection to the Abwehr?"

"I have that covered," Staupitz said.

Then after a pause he added, "Our Spanish friends are sending support and assistance. Agent Aníbal. I know him from Madrid. This is not assistance that we want or need, Hans. I will be arranging for it to be eliminated."

CHAPTER 36

Paris: Monday, May 3, 1937

Winter had lingered in Paris.

But in the time it took Nacho to get there from Spain, it had given way. Pent-up demand for spring, for longer and warmer days, for the color and mildness of pre-summer had now been satisfied. Paris flourished under shimmering skies that even turned the river clean-looking and blue. Summer dresses and shirtsleeves were out in force on the boulevards and in the parks among the primroses, camellias, and rhododendrons.

"Agent Aníbal! Welcome to Paris." Alois feigned warmth as he took a seat across from Nacho at a small outside table at the Café Truffaut on the Place Clichy. "How's been your war?"

Nacho bridled at the flippancy of the question but remained impassive, "Hungry. You look the same as before."

"The worst is yet to come I fear, Aníbal. Significant discomfort is coming for us all. The trip to Paris?"

Nacho raised an eyebrow, questioning the wisdom of discussing sensitive information in an open location.

MOSCOW GOLD | 245

"Not idle curiosity, Aníbal. It's information that is useful to us," Alois reassured.

"Cóndor found me an old FIAT coupe and a third of a tank of gasoline. Left it for me in the town square in Ciempozuelos. That area is in contention. I started driving down toward Fuenlabrada. Didn't see anything. Circled back up toward Móstoles, and a Royalist patrol stopped me. Confiscated the car and took me to Franco's HQ in Leganés."

"Simplicity is the soul of a good operation. I imagine they put a little more gas in and infiltrated the car back into Republican territory," Alois supposed. "How was their security?"

"Adequate. They were expecting me. Cóndor had it wired. They took me to Franco's security people. Cóndor had given me a set of code phrases. They were exchanged, and I was passed on. Even saw the great man himself."

"Were you introduced?"

"No. Saw him standing in a group of advisors. He appeared to be giving orders."

"What's he like?" Alois pressed.

"Little guy. Much shorter than I expected. Energetic. Serious. Has a high-pitched voice. Seemed capable and competent. Who can say?" Nacho shrugged.

"The trip on to Paris?"

"Two ways into France from Spain. Either end of the Pyrenees. Through the mountains and you're walking—Irún or Port Bou. The rebels control Irún, and the Reds have Port Bou. Car ride to Burgos and the train to Irún. All out in the open. French border security was lax. After that, an all-night train ride here. Simple."

"I expect getting back into Spain, either end, will be tougher?" Alois mused.

"That's probable."

"Well, it's good you're here," Alois lied. "We'll need to set up means of contact. I don't want to know where you are staying and won't tell

246 | DOUGLAS L. FIELD

you where I am. You'll come here to the Truffaut every day. But vary the time. Tomorrow's Tuesday, the third day of the week. So come at three. Stay only fifteen minutes. Then Thursday at four, Friday at five, and so on. Go back to one on Sunday. Either I or someone will make contact. Code word 'Aranjuez,' like the summer palace."

Nacho then watched Alois get up and leave without pleasantries.

CHAPTER 37

Paris: Wednesday, May 5, 1937

Not only was Paris in full bloom, but so also was Operation Markgraf.

Staupitz and Grebe had decided to double-team the coin dealers. Together they developed contact, if not relationships, with such establishments as Jules Pinchon Numismatique, Numismium, and the Filigrane d'Or.

"Hans, the coin dealers know there's going to be a glut on the market, but they are keeping supply and provenance information very close. Limited to their own small cabal," Staupitz announced.

"Excess supply drives down prices. They're smart enough to know that." Grebe followed the thought. "This new 'inventory' is rare and of enduring value. They can hold it indefinitely. All they need is capital to fund their continuing purchases."

"This is something we can help them with," said Staupitz. "Considering our intended manner of payment."

MOSCOW GOLD | 249

"Of all of them, the least disagreeable is Vokárny," Grebe went on. "Agreed. We'll go by and have a chat later today."

⁓

The two Germans appeared after lunch at Monnaies Vokárny, *établi* 1912, Henri Vokárny, *propriétaire*, 79 rue Vivienne. Vokárny, was an immigrant from Hungary and a veteran of the French Foreign Legion. Now, in his late fifties, he had made himself into a respectable Parisian *homme d'affiares*. Of all the denizens of Vivienne and Richelieu, Vokárny maintained the best supply behind the counter. He was on occasion cordial. He was even willing to negotiate within a small range if the spirit moved.

"Henri, mon vieux, comment vont les affaires aujourd'hui?" Staupitz was known to Vokárny as Rainer Korbus from Zug. He spoke stilted but fluent German-accented French. The shop was long and narrow with a plank floor prone to audible crepitus as its occupants moved around. It sported a long, polished mahogany counter. There were cabinets, shelves, drawers, and other storage places behind to match. The entry door was always locked. One knocked with force, got the man's attention, and hoped he let you in.

Vokárny went back behind his counter, leaned against an old stool, and regarded his customers. "Looking up now that the 'Karamazov Brothers' are here!" he rumbled. A smoldering Gauloises Caporal drooped from his lips, three-quarters of an inch of ash on the very precipice of falling.

"Rainer, Rupert, how may this impoverished Frenchman be of service to your honors today?" Vokárny's laugh was indistinguishable from a coughing spasm, distinguishment being complicated by the frequency of his doing both. In what he thought was cultured banter, the man delighted in invoking the memory of Dostoyevsky's characters.

"They're Russian, Henri. We're Swiss," corrected Rainer as Vokárny knew he would.

"You'll forgive me, kind sirs. From our standpoint here in Paris, east is east. But let us not bore ourselves with politics and geography. I have several fine new specimens for your consideration today."

The man turned toward a back room and raised his voice at an adolescent boy who was working there, "Raoul, go across the street and get coffees for Messrs. Kobus."

The youngster scuttled off by a rear door.

"You continue to acquire new inventory, Henri. How is this?" Grebe, in the role of Rupert Korbus, asked.

"Ah, Monsieur Rupert"—pronounced /Roopear/—"The coins are guaranteed genuine. They are from the most impeccable source. Please place your complete trust in me. Beyond that, well, I'm sure that you can understand the preservation of discretion will ensure uninterrupted deliveries, yes?"

"Henri, you are a scoundrel. A charming one, but a scoundrel nonetheless," offered Rainer.

Vokárny ignored the compliment and said, "Ours is a felicitous relationship is it not, *meine Herren*? Better not to burden it with excessive technicality, *non*? Let us have a look at, how shall I say it, what the cat dragged in."

Whereupon there were produced a stunning assortment of British gold sovereigns and American double eagles. "The double eagles are most desirable, gentlemen," Vokárny pointed out. "The socialist Roosevelt has, back in '33, required surrender by all Americans of gold currency. Most Americans have complied. Vast numbers of US gold coins have been melted down and formed into ingots."

"And this renders the double eagles quite the rarer," commented Rupert pedantically.

After much badinage and posturing, which all parties knew to be theater, another deal was made, and the exchange completed.

MOSCOW GOLD | 251

Rainer then turned abrasively serious. "What is this, Henri? Our fifth, no, sixth transaction with you? Tell me, do you ever encounter your numismatic colleagues, say socially? Over a *kir* or a cognac."

"*Mais non,* Monsieur Rainer." Vokárny's eyes narrowed to slits. "Mine is not a friendship business."

"You never get together to tell war stories, brag a little?"

"Never."

"Never? Not even to share small tidbits of gossip about a favorite competitor or a client or two?" Rainer persisted.

"Never, monsieur. Not ever. Of course not."

Rupert took over. "Henri, you have insisted on keeping your sources a secret. We want to confirm with you, Rainer and I do, that there is an implied and corresponding covenant of silence, of total confidentiality, in all our transactions. Nothing, not the most insignificant detail of anything that has occurred between you and us, will ever be shared outside the group of us three. This is understood?"

"I would do nothing to imperil—"

"Of course, you wouldn't, Henri," Rainer interrupted. "We know that."

Rupert added, "Besides, if you ever did, we would find it out, and there would be repercussions, ultimate repercussions. But I needn't remind us of that now then, need I?"

"Non," the Frenchman replied. Succinct. Sullenness undisguised.

"In that case, Henri, it is, as always, a pleasure to do business with you. And we will look forward perhaps to seeing you in a few days. *Á bientôt.* See you soon."

Back on the street, the "Karamazov Brothers" switched to German. "A beautiful shipment, especially the Saint-Gaudens," commented Grebe.

"Glorious. American coins are gorgeous." Staupitz recalled their weight and elegant design. "Do you think Henri's keeping his own counsel?"

252 | DOUGLAS L. FIELD

Grebe reflected. "He's a craven old wheeze and no fool. He will do nothing to damage our little arrangement. He's screwing us on his commissions. We know it, and he knows we know it. He apprehends that there is reason for our complacency. He understands we have contacts. He'll preserve confidentiality at all costs."

"Very good then, Hans. On with them to Gibraltar, *nicht wahr?*"

CHAPTER 38

Paris: Friday May 7, 1937

Sepp Staupitz kept busy managing both ends of his operation.

He and Grebe did the buying and needed a dirty work team to handle interfering with the Soviets getting their product to market. In the end, he went to Bulgaria for the interference piece.

At Sepp's orders, the Abwehr chief of station in Sofia had gotten the Bulgarian team on the Simplon Orient Express for Paris. Today, he would make contact.

He found Bogdan Dobruja, aka "the Butcher of Svitsov," sitting on the sidewalk at the Café du Palais Royale on the rue de Beaujolais, nursing a glass of the dry, fruity red Burgundy wine that had lent its name to the street.

Known to Alois only as Vratska, Dobruja was whippet thin. Despite having dark hair and an olive complexion, he was sallow and seemed unhealthy. Cachectic though he looked, Vratska's movements were efficient and lightning fast. One imagined that he was expert with knife and garrote. And who knew what else.

"Vratska?"

MOSCOW GOLD | 255

"Alois?"

"The same. Welcome." Sepp sensed social niceties could be dispensed with.

"Our assignment?"

"Soviet NKVD is laundering gold coin and bullion through legitimate dealers here in Paris. Product is coming into France in their diplomatic bag. Has to be transported from their embassy to the dealers. Hit several of the shipments and relieve them of their gold. Some hits are to succeed; some are to fail."

"Some are to fail?" Vratska repeated. "Planning to fail is more involved than planning to succeed."

"Succeeding and failing are both critical. And no one dies," Staupitz confirmed.

"Strange," mused Vratska.

"One further matter," Sepp added. "There's a Spaniard; Agent Aníbal he's called. He's to be taken out of circulation for the duration. Do with him whatever you want but don't eliminate."

"This was to be robbery," Vratska said, slow and cold. "Kidnapping is more. One-third."

"Twenty-five percent, and your team can keep the take from two of your successful hits," Sepp replied, equally cold.

"Agreed."

"Café Truffaut on Place Clichy, six o'clock today. Seven o'clock tomorrow, etc. Code word 'Aranjuez'."

❧

Dobruja returned in the afternoon with Zahn, his junior operative, in tow. They went back to the rue de Beaujolais café.

"Good spot, boss." Zahn wanted to appear keen. "Street covers whole block between Vivienne and Richelieu. Any Russians going to dealers pass right by."

"Just try to look like you fit in, Zahn," Vratska growled. "Any Russians going to the dealers will be alert for anything looking out of place. They're good at it."

Todor and Auloy arrived from different directions. They took seats close to one another but facing in different directions—close enough to hear Vratska even if he spoke in a stage whisper.

"These Russians are controlled," Dobruja muttered, "even down to their expenses. I figure they'll run their operation on the cheap if they can. Easiest way over here from their embassy is the Métro."

Auloy fished out a map. "A straight shot from Invalides to Opéra, boss. Then change for one stop. Get off at Pyramides. Should pass right by us."

"Todor," Vratska rasped, "you be ready to establish a tail if we pick one of them up. I want to know which dealer they use."

"Yes, boss." Todor shook his head.

Another forty-five minutes went by. Vratska studied a copy of *Le Figaro*. He was challenged to make it look realistic, as he knew little to no French. Auloy continued to examine his map. Despite his chief's earlier admonition about fitting in, Zahn ogled any girls who happened by.

"There. Headed past Richelieu, going into Vivienne," Vratska hissed. "Look alive, losers. The one with the briefcase."

A heavy and fit-looking man in his early thirties walked with evident purpose toward them. Dressed in an ill-fitting and baggy suit with a careworn flat cap, he carried a medium-sized leather briefcase. His gait evoked the simian, hunched forward, leading with his shoulders.

"A Russian peasant if I ever saw one," remarked Todor. "And look, the briefcase is heavy. More than papers in there. It's just hanging straight down. Doesn't swing like a normal case. Looks like it weighs a dozen kilos."

"Todor, you're the peasant. Stop staring at him. You might as well walk over and introduce yourself. Find out where he goes and don't get caught. Once you've done that, return to the safe house."

"Auloy, stay here and see if you can catch him on the way back. Observe what he's carrying and mark down how long he was gone. Then tail him back. Let's verify that it's the Soviet embassy. You can report at dinner."

Auloy shook his head and settled in to wait.

Vratska looked at Zahn. "Zahn you're the new man. Chance to prove yourself. Go to the Café Truffaut that the Kraut told us about. Collect the Spanish package and take him to the safe house. Boyko and Petar will meet on the way there. Do you remember the code word?"

"Aranjuez. Weird word."

"Go and collect him, Zahn. You know the drill."

❧

From his visit to the rue Vivienne, NKVD goon Gennady Orlov walked to the Soviet embassy. It was in an old mansion behind a walled garden on the rue de Grenelle. Orlov was a street craft newbie, and he decided to try out some surveillance detection techniques on the way back. Nothing. Or so he thought.

Access was through a dark archway. The NKVD itself guarded the embassy. As Orlov was NKVD, he was passed without formalities. Once inside, he went up to the Trade Ministry's offices. Arthur Stachevski, trade envoy to the Spanish Republic, fresh in from Barcelona, was waiting for him, along with two aides.

"Ah, Gennady, just talking about you. Took you longer than I expected. Thought you might have run off to Deauville with the 'shipment' and the comely French girl of your dreams!"

There was stilted, almost macabre laughter all around.

Discomfited, Orlov tried not to show it. He got to the point. "Without incident, Comrade Stachevski. The Frenchman Pinchon handled the transaction himself. Everything proceeded as briefed."

258 | DOUGLAS L. FIELD

Orlov lifted his now lightened briefcase onto a table and removed the bundles of currency. "May I count it, comrade? Follow all protocols?"

"Of course, Comrade Orlov. Vasha," Stachevski tilted his head towards one of his aides. "You do the honors for Comrade Orlov. Here in his presence, naturally. And, Orlov, while the counting is being done, what took so long?"

"I hope not to presume, comrade, but I took some time to evaluate the method of delivery of shipments. I tried to observe any surveillance."

Orlov, looked like a brute, but there was real intelligence inside that pointy head, Stachevski thought.

"And your conclusions, Comrade Orlov?"

"A single courier is not good. I detected no surveillance, but there is danger on the street and on public transport. Especially the Métro."

"Your proposed alternatives?"

"Provide an embassy car. Or use taxis. A group of couriers or at minimum a one-man backup."

"The money is correct," announced Vasha. "All in English pounds and American dollars. Large denominations. As agreed."

"Give Comrade Orlov a receipt. Get the money in the bag to Moscow." The former trade envoy cocked his head toward the door as if to indicate that it should be done forthwith.

The parsimonious dolts in Moscow are managing everything down to the last farthing, Stachevski said seditiously to himself.

"Your thinking is well reasoned, Orlov. But Moscow Center concludes that the best defense of the shipments is innocuousness. Use of an embassy car would draw attention. The opposition recognizes them. Parisian taxi drivers are connected with organized crime. If we use taxis, there could be talk. Talk is always trouble."

"I see. Still, should we not send an extra courier?"

"Not yet. Yours is not the first effort that we have made and will not be the last. No difficulties so far. Let us see whether that happy situation continues."

Orlov headed for the door.

"All right. Ulanov will make a solo run on the Métro tomorrow morning. Then we'll do another tomorrow afternoon. Let's assign it to Timoshenko the Ferret. Igor, you'll tail him. Then Orlov. The three can switch off. With Igor as extra security."

Stachevski stared out the window at the garden below. The French gardener the embassy employed to keep it up, was pottering away.

"What of the Spanish spy, Igor?" Stachevski asked.

"Madrid station reports he is not thought to be in that city. Our deep cover asset in Franco's headquarters observed one fitting his description there. Vague talk he might be sent to Paris. Bit of luck that, if true."

"We'll still need help to find him. Needle in a haystack," Stachevski said. "Igor, Vasha, the gold operation is a recipe for disaster. Impossible to keep it secret. The coin dealers talk. The French mob knows everything. The British and the Germans watch us all the time. One misstep, and it's a hanging party for all hands. One kopek of that money disappears, and we'll all be on a slow train to the Lubyanka—in third class, no doubt."

Igor and Vasha just looked at him.

"And finding this Spaniard—hopeless. You both may leave me now."

~❧~

Zahn did know the drill and did not like it. But he was new and needed to show himself willing. He trotted up and out of the Place Clichy Métro and looked around for Truffaut and the Spanish package.

"It's Friday. Should be here at six," Zahn muttered to himself. He looked at his watch and saw he was early. He started to dawdle around the place. A little over halfway around, and he passed the café. There were only ladies and an old man at the outside tables.

260 | DOUGLAS L. FIELD

Zahn decided not to take a seat. Better to hover out of sight. Let the Spaniard wait and wonder a little. Unsettle him. Boyko and Petar knew to remain at the meet in the Marais.

He found a shadowed doorway with a good view of Truffaut. His wait was short. A plain and undistinguished man moved into the sidewalk café and took a seat where there was no obstruction to his bolting for the Métro entrance. His movements were quick and fluid. Zahn noticed he was fair-haired. He had a newspaper that he set about reading. He must have signaled the waiter, as a coffee soon came.

There was a table open where Zahn could sit close but with the man behind him. Zahn moved to the table. Some minutes elapsed. No one was close. Zahn turned and stared. The other man lowered his paper and looked back.

"Aranjuez?" Zahn said precisely. Vratska had drilled him on the pronunciation. The /z/ had to sound like /th/.

It worked. "Sí," came the response.

"I hail cab," Zahn said in French. "Follow over."

Once they were inside the car, Zahn asked, "You Spaniard?"

"Yeah, code name Aníbal."

"I'm Zahn. Code name Zahn, I guess." Zahn snickered. "Don't have code name."

"Where are we going?"

"Place de la République," Zahn said. Then to the driver, *"Allez vite!"*

"Where's Alois?"

"There," Zahn said, not wanting to talk too much.

It didn't work. Aníbal was already suspicious, on edge.

"You German? 'Zahn,' is it?" he asked.

"No," Zahn admitted. "Close. Work together."

Zahn tried to keep it amicable, ingratiating. "Alois was Spain. Now Paris." Zahn smiled. "You Spain?"

Aníbal nodded. "Yeah. I met Alois there. Looking forward to seeing him again."

MOSCOW GOLD | 261

Zahn kept smiling. "We going Alois now."

They were arriving at République.

"Turn. Into Boulevard de Magenta there," Zahn instructed.

As they got out, Zahn turned to head up Magenta and said, "You follow, Aníbal, please."

Zahn moved purposefully up the wide street. It was populated with heavy Friday afternoon pedestrian and vehicular traffic. Aníbal's tension dissipated. He relaxed his shoulders and his arms hung looser by his side. Zahn then held back a little, so they walked abreast. The younger man chattered away amiably about one banality or the other as Aníbal observed the street, habitually alert for danger.

After two long blocks, they drew up next to a fruit market that was winding up for the day. Aníbal saw vendors moving product off the street and out to the roadway to waiting carts and trucks.

"Alois this way," Zahn said as he bumped Aníbal to their right and into the disassembling market. Aníbal took vague notice of two vendors wearing aprons and berets and seeming to load a vegetable cart. He sensed nothing unusual.

As Zahn and Aníbal passed the cart, one of the vendors leapt at Aníbal and threw a burlap sack over his head and arms. Aníbal had no time to react before his arms were tied and he was thrown up on the cart and his feet tied as well.

"Not to make much noise, Aníbal. Not want to hurt," Zahn said as Aníbal struggled, and the cart moved briskly off.

"Shut up, Zahn, you idiot," Boyko snarled. "You'll call attention to us."

The figure on the cart continued thrashing about and making muffled sounds. Petar picked a short length of stout dowel off the cart and clubbed Aníbal right about where he thought his right ear would be. Aníbal then lay quiet.

❧

The safe house was in a handsome *emmueble de rapport* at 16 rue des Vinaigriers just off Magenta. Zahn and the team had a flat on the second floor, which was already cluttered and untidy, with their kit left scattered about.

Vratska produced several bottles of wine and called a council of war. He first reviewed the afternoon's developments up to the time of the appearance of the Russian.

"Todor, what happened after the man passed by our vantage point in the café?"

"He walked straight to a coin dealer in the rue Vivienne. Name of Jules Pinchon Numismatique. He had to knock on the door. He was admitted. I left the location as directed."

"Auloy?"

"He was gone for thirteen minutes almost on the dot. A good guess would be that he had his business set up in advance. I imagine his was not the first time for a run like this. Anyway, he came back by my location from the direction that he had gone. When he returned, he was still carrying the same briefcase. Could be my imagination, but it looked lighter in weight."

"Where did he go?"

"Back to the Soviet embassy on Grenelle. Didn't take the Métro. He walked. Checked for a tail. Like he had just had a class in street craft. I reversed my jacket and pulled out a cap I was carrying—just to throw him off. But it wasn't necessary. He's not very accomplished, not yet anyway."

"You followed him all the way to the embassy?"

"Close enough to see that that's where he went off the street," Auloy confirmed.

"And did he suspect you were tailing him?"

"I am Auloy. You don't make Auloy."

Vratska nodded and then he said. *"Ne, ne"* (no, no), "Auloy, you're conceited is what you are."

"Zahn, what happened at Place Clichy?"

MOSCOW GOLD | 263

"Spaniard show. As expect. Accept call sign. Come to fruit market," Zahn filled in the details. "Seem like OK guy. Boyko and Petar put cart. Struggled some. Petar hit with stick. Then didn't."

"Shit, Zahn, you act like you're in love with him. He was making noise. Could have given us away."

"Alois said not kill. You almost kill."

"Enough!" Vratska commanded. "He'll live. I checked. Zahn, since you're so fond of him, you'll be his minder."

"They should share, boss," Zahn whined.

"Shut up, Zahn, you're low man," said Boyko.

"You *all* shut up," ordered Vratska. "I want to hit some shipments. I'm thinking one on the Métro and one in the street. Here's the plan." He had their full attention.

"And one more thing," Vratska concluded. "We need a contact inside that embassy. Auloy, take your big ego over there. Have a look around. See what you can come up with."

⁓

Nacho's face was on fire. He regained consciousness to discover that he still wore the burlap hood and was professionally chained and cuffed to a creaky bed frame. He thought it was dark, and he was cold. He could remember the sack being thrown over his head and trying to struggle as he was lifted and thrown flat. Then the searing pain to the side of his head, and everything had gone black.

"Who's there?" He decided to see if he was alone.

"Only me." It sounded like the guy who'd picked him up at Clichy.

"Where am I? What time is it?"

"No question."

"Take off the sack," Nacho demanded. He felt a jab in his side for his trouble.

"You act nice? I take off sack. Not nice, again you get stick."

"Nice. OK. Nice."

After some fiddling, the sack was jerked off. Nacho's right eye was swollen shut, but he could see that he was in some sort of subterranean room. Only a little natural light came down a stairway. He could make Zahn out vaguely. Zahn was armed with what looked like a length of closet rail.

What they hit me with, Nacho figured.

"Where's Alois, asshole? I want to see Alois. You were bringing me to see Alois."

"Alois change mind. Not want to see now. You with Zahn. Nice time in Paris. Eat good. Pretty girls." Zahn thought he was funny.

"You're making a big mistake. My agency has contacts with Alois's. I don't report in, they'll come looking for Alois. Anything happens to me, they'll kill him. They know where to find him."

"Not find Alois. Very sly. You with Zahn now. Behave. Relax. Everything OK. I get food later. You need, you use bucket. Chain loose for bucket."

Zahn was slapping his stick into the palm of his right hand. Nacho's good eye was adjusting to the low light. He now could feel that his restraints were loose. He was chained to the bed and the floor—like a dog on a leash. He felt around. There was a bucket under the bed.

"You've made a terrible mistake, Zahn, if that's your name. I will get out of here. I will find you. I will squash you like the cockroach that you are. Then I will find Alois and squash him."

Zahn got up and crossed to the stairs. He started up. "You rest now," he said as he closed and locked a heavy door.

"Squash! Like bugs!" Nacho screamed at the darkness.

MOSCOW GOLD | 265

CHAPTER 39

Paris: Saturday, May 8, 1937

Zahn made a morning visit to Nacho's dungeon.

He tried to be conciliatory. "Bring food. Nice breakfast. You lie on bed. I bring close. Then not trouble. Make nice."

"I'm not going to make nice, you idiot. My face burned and throbbed all night. My eye is bad. Look at my eye. You animals have probably blinded me," Nacho hissed.

Zahn peered at Nacho through the dark. He opened the stairway door wide.

"Dark here. Eye look bad. I bring medicine later. You rest," Zahn said, trying to soothe.

Nacho sat up feigning stiffness and pain. Then fast as lightning, he lurched at his captor. Zahn's reflexes were fast too. Zahn jumped back. Nacho was caught forcibly short by his chains and recoiled back onto the bed. He had kicked over his breakfast.

"You step food. Not good. You need eat. Very bad," Zahn said nodding his head. "Angry not help. Zahn not bad. Alois bad. Cause all trouble."

"Then let me out of here, and I'll find him."

"Not good you escape. Alois kill. Kill Zahn too."

"Let me out, Zahn. I'll find the son of a bitch and kill him first. You won't have to worry," Nacho replied.

Zahn started for the stairs and began shutting the door.

"Alois many friends. Kill you. Kill Zahn. You big danger. You stay. Rest. Zahn come back later," he said before locking Nacho in.

❧

Nacho settled back on to his bed. He began exploring his surroundings. His chains were lightweight but very strong. They appeared to be of prison-grade strength. He discovered that they were threaded through a steel eyebolt anchored to the cement floor. There was just enough slack to allow minor freedom of movement.

He tested the extent of his ability to move. He could sit up fully and stand partially—just enough to use his bucket. The chains snaked through the frame of the bed, but he noted that, if once broken at any point, the entirety would unthread, and he would be free. The chain was secured to common locking cuffs attached to his hands and feet.

The weak link was the chain itself. Hardened steel, it would resist being severed. But if he could somehow do it, his arms and legs would be free, and he could move around. Maybe even get past the locked door and out.

How to slice the chain? He looked for a rock to smash it with but found nothing. The bed frame might offer a possibility. Most of it was of softer metal, but springs and screws were harder. He found a screw that protruded above its recess hole. He could saw across that. He would need strength.

He stuck out a foot and raked the scattered remains of Zahn's breakfast towards himself.

❧

268 | DOUGLAS L. FIELD

"The simpler the plan, the greater the likelihood of success," Zahn had heard Vratska say more than once. Today's street plan had the elegance of simplicity, if not of straight-up brutality.

"The Métro hit went smooth enough," Zahn muttered to himself.

Now he and the rest of the team had located a short alley halfway up Vivienne from Beaujolais. It was dark, even at high noon, dank and populated with refuse bins and other large piles of junk. Petar would be unseen but have an adequate view down Vivienne. He could observe the courier's approach.

"Further reconnaissance" had revealed that, in addition to "Métroman," were two more couriers in use on alternate runs— "Bullethead," whom they had seen on the first day, and a smaller man with very angular and sharp facial features that they named "Mongoose." In later runs, the Russians had started using a follower. The shadow was always the same individual. He lacked distinguishing characteristics. They called him "Charlie." For the courier, always a briefcase—always secured to the wrist by a handcuff and chain.

"No problem," Zahn had proclaimed at Vratska's briefing. "Not affect smash. Just make grab harder."

No one replied.

Auloy had, in the event, developed a source inside the embassy.

He let Zahn get some practice and make the contact. The Soviets employed a French gardener to tend the embassy grounds. Zahn appeared at the gardener's favorite watering hole.

"Buy bit of refreshment, *mon ami*?" Zahn had said.

The gardener knew he should be wary, but a free drink was a free drink. "Calvados."

One calvados led to another, and they learned a good deal about each other. Making the deal was easy.

"When you think courier run, you leave yellow-handle broom outside gate, *oui*?

"*Oui. Très facile.*"

"I pay Calvados to bartender?" Zahn nodded toward the bar.

MOSCOW GOLD | 269

"D'accord."

This morning the yellow-handled broom, this afternoon Mongoose with Charlie in tow. Standard operating procedure.

Zahn picked them up coming out of the Métro He signaled the others.

Petar took his place in the alley. Boyko and Todor, turned out in high-quality business suits, waited at the head of Vivienne. Mongoose came around the corner, briefcase in hand. Boyko and Todor headed toward him making animated conversation. The staging of their little routine was perfect. They and Mongoose arrived at the opening to the alley at the same moment.

As they were about to pass, Todor fell a step or two behind, as if to let Mongoose by. At the instant Mongoose passed him, Boyko spun around. Both he and Todor shouldered hard into Mongoose and knocked him stunned into the alley, where Petar coolly coldcocked him and then flipped a pair of small bolt cutters out of his hip packet. In one smooth motion, he sliced the chain.

Boyko grabbed the briefcase, and all three ran fast back up Vivienne toward the Bourse and out of sight. Charlie was surprised by the suddenness of the attack. He lost a step on the attackers. He moved to give chase but saw that it was hopeless. He was outnumbered.

Zahn was saved the necessity of waylaying Charlie. Zahn turned around and walked back the way he had come.

Auloy had been parked in an unremarkable Simca a short way up Vivienne. He saw his confederates make off. He started up and moved sedately away.

Simple and brutal.

⌒♦⌒

Nacho heard someone approaching. He quit sawing. He had, by now, amassed a small pile of filings. They were from the bed and the screw, he knew, but he had made minor progress with the chain.

He blew on the filings to scatter them and stretched out with his back to the door. He tried to lie still. Like he was sleeping.

⌘

Zahn clomped down the basement stairs. He unlocked the door and let it stand wide open. His prisoner appeared to be asleep.

"You sleep. This good. Bring lunch. You behave. Not like breakfast."

Zahn had some bread, cheese, and a dried-up pear on a tin plate. He had brought a broomstick this time. He set Nacho's lunch on the floor and used the stick to push it over to the bed.

"Let me out, Zahn," Nacho tried to sound groggy. "I promise I won't hurt you. I'm only going to hurt Alois."

'Today happy, Aníbal." Zahn dissembled.

"Today not happy, Zahn. I'm stuck in this cold and stinking hole. I want out, and you're going to let me."

'Today yes happy. Team do Alois operations. All good. Happy."

"What team, Zahn? What operation?" Nacho demanded.

"Team from home. Alois hires. Do operations. Done soon. Then you go," Zahn replied.

"Hold on. You and some team are doing operations for Alois, and you're almost done with them. Then you are going to let me go?"

"Yes, yes. Good, no?"

"What kind of operations, Zahn? Team from where? What are you doing for Alois?"

"Secret operations. No talk. No worry. Operations done; team go home. You go home too."

"You're telling me that, as soon as you finish some operations for Alois, you're going to just let me walk out of here? No, Zahn, it's going to cost much more than that."

"Yes, yes. Zahn friend of Aníbal. You see. Today good day. You eat. Rest. Chains off soon."

⌘

MOSCOW GOLD | 271

Igor found Timoshenko in the alley. He was crumpled in a heap and out cold. The briefcase was gone. Igor slapped Timoshenko's face and rubbed his hands. The unconscious man began to come around, rubbing the back of his head.

"Come on, Timo, wake up. We have to get back to the embassy. Don't want to alert the police."

Timoshenko faded back out. Igor pulled him deeper into the alley and roughed up both of their clothes—made them look disheveled.

"Somebody comes by, they'll think we're drunk," he said to his inert partner. It was a challenge getting Timoshenko on his feet. He managed to get them both down into the rush hour Métro

Back at the embassy, Stachevski appeared calm as he took the news.

"Descriptions?"

"Average Parisians. About our age. Who knows? It happened lightning fast." Igor spoke first.

"Timoshenko?"

"I was almost there, comrade. Two guys in business suits. Knocked me into the alley, bashed me on the back of the head. Igor trying to wake me up. That's all I've got." Timoshenko was still rubbing a spot behind his right ear, handcuff and partial chain still dangling from his wrist.

"This was inevitable. First the Métro, now you. Can't run a high-value operation like this on the cheap. Full written reports. On my desk by morning. Timoshenko, go and get the sawbones to look at your head."

Vasha stuck his head in.

"You going to make my afternoon even worse, Vasha?"

"Afraid so, sir. Nothing on the Spaniard. We're scouring the city. Not a whisper."

"That was to be expected too," he muttered.

❧

Alois cited Vratska to a meet at the Café Truffaut. Place Clichy was teeming on this Saturday afternoon.

"Everybody's out to enjoy the weather," Vratska commented as he sat down. "Little chance we'll be made in this crowd."

"Nobody to make us anyway," said Alois. "Our operation is known to my service and to your team. No one else except the Spanish rebels."

"We picked up their agent, by the way. He's locked down and secure at the safe house. One of my young agents is looking after him. Not happy but he'll get over it," Vratska advised.

"Operation's going well so far, Vratska," Alois went on.

"Team is good." Vratska shook his head.

Alois departed the café. He headed east toward the gare de l'Est.

CHAPTER 40

Paris: Sunday, May 9, 1937

Arthur Stachevski could not believe his luck.

He had information from a shop steward in the boiler cleaning room at Gare de l'Est. Vague, but just enough.

"Somebody's running a sweet little intelligence network here in Paris. I wonder if the opposition knows half as much about us as we do about them. Probably not. Doubt they have the labor movement penetrated like we do," Stachevski said to an empty office.

"Vasha," he shouted.

Vasha came running.

"Assemble the wet ops team. Who's their commander?"

"Konavalov, sir Gregoriy Petrovich, I think."

"Get him in here."

Konavalov appeared in under five minutes. Stachevski saw he was fit and ramrod straight.

"Ah, Gregoriy Petrovich, thank you for coming so promptly. An assignment for your group."

"Say on, comrade."

MOSCOW GOLD | 275

"Moscow Center is interested in a certain Spaniard. Thought to have betrayed some of our Soviet pilots assisting our socialist brothers in the struggle there. He's in the custody of some Bulgarian operatives over near the Canal Saint-Martin—a street with an odd name. Vasha has it."

"That's a familiar area, comrade."

"Good. Make whatever reconnaissance you need. Liberate him from his current hosts. Administer justice," Stachevski directed.

"Yes, comrade. I expect we can mount and carry out an operation today."

"I imagined no less, Gregoriy Petrovich. I'm sure I do not need to emphasize that there will be no connection back to us."

"None, comrade, of course not."

 ❧

It was going on toward two full days in captivity. It seemed to be midday or not long after. No one had ventured into the basement except Zahn. Zahn had continued to bring food and to take the opportunity of talking. Zahn seemed young to Nacho. New to the undercover game. He was too talkative by half but had not given away any details of his team or their mission.

Nacho had confirmed only that Zahn knew Alois and that Zahn somehow had remorse over Nacho's kidnapping and confinement. In his own way, he had tried to be helpful.

"No matter, Zahn," Nacho muttered to himself as he worked. "You're on the wrong side of this, and you're going to pay. No good deed goes unpunished. Never. Not ever. Your case is no different."

Nacho's hands were raw and sore from sawing. He had already ground two screws down so far that they threatened no longer to hold the bed together. But he was close to his goal. The chain had lost a lot of metal. Nacho thought he was on the point of breaking it.

He sawed for what seemed an eternity on a new screw. It was time to try. He wound slack around both hands and wriggled around so he could break it over the bed rail. He gave it a mighty smash. It didn't break but gouged his hands.

He moved it a bit and smashed again. The rusty bed shrieked with the blow. The chain parted. Nacho checked his hands. At least they were not bleeding.

The reverberations Nacho had created just seemed to die down, and he heard fumbling with the lock at the stairway door. He lay back and tried to conceal the break in the chain.

❧

"All is well? Zahn bring lunch." He had a wrapped plate of food and some wine.

Zahn had found a stool and had set it between his prisoner and the door. He would sit on it when he tried to engage in conversation. He followed the same pattern today. Close enough to be congenial but not so close that he was within reach.

"You rest? Good. Calm, happy, yes?" he asked.

"No, I'm not calm and happy. And when I can get my hands on you, I'm going to kill you—slowly. Give you time to repent of your sins. Then I'm going to kill Alois. I have a special and very painful plan for him."

"Ha, ha. Please not joke about killing. Zahn is friend. Team finish soon."

Shadows appeared on the on the stairs. Figures descending. Silent.

"Zahn help. Agent Aníbal escape. Clean. You see."

Black clad figures, at least four, fanned out behind Zhan. Outside of his peripheral vision.

"You eat. Yes." Zahn smiled.

One figure whipped a garotte over Zahn's head and strangled. Zahn struggled and kicked over his stool. It was no use. The strangler's grip was brutal. Zahn was quickly dead.

❧

MOSCOW GOLD | 277

Nacho's mind was racing as he watched the attack unfold. As Zahn was dying, two others rushed Nacho. The chains on his feet were cut and he was stood up. Nacho tried to keep it concealed that his arms were now free. He crumpled to the floor holding his hands to his chest.

Two of them grabbed him—under his armpits and by his feet. They started trundling him up the stairs.

As Zahn lived his fleeting last seconds, Nacho muttered in Spanish, "No good deed goes unpunished, Zahn. Never. Not ever."

One of the attackers hissed a word at him and cuffed him hard on the right ear—where he had been hit before. He almost passed out. No need to fake weakness now. His face and eye were again in flames.

There was more hissing in his ear. Broken Spanish. Heavy accents. Something about how now Nacho would learn the fate of those who betrayed Soviet comrades to the fascists. He knew they were Russian. He knew they were accomplished. He knew they were very dangerous.

Nacho had only seconds. He was to be the next to die. He wondered why they hadn't killed him in the basement too. Didn't want his body identified, he guessed.

Now they were in the lobby of the building and headed into the street. After two days in the dark, the light was dazzling. They put him back on his feet. He wavered. More hissing in his ear. Telling him to walk, he guessed. He continued to conceal that his arms were free.

Out of the building and into the street, the attack team surrounded Nacho and moved toward an intersection ahead, bearing him along. It looked like a wide street. Nacho stumbled a few times to keep the team off balance.

Now he could see. They were headed toward a broad street that ran alongside some river or canal. The attackers mumbled among themselves. Nacho wondered what was wrong. Maybe their transport hadn't arrived.

They got to the intersection. Nacho slumped down to his knees and started moaning. Two of them bent to pick him up. With all his force he struck out with both arms. He hit one in the face and the other in the groin. His handcuffs were still on. He did damage.

The two loosened their grip on him for a split second.

As they did, he sprang up and away. He hit full speed in three strides and headed for the water. The attack team followed. They were fast and strong, but Nacho was a couple of steps ahead. He ran straight at the water without breaking stride and went over the edge, arms and legs windmilling.

It was ten feet down to the water, and he went in with a huge splash. He forced himself down as far as he could and swam underwater until his lungs screamed. He felt for the surface. He would have to breathe, quick and quiet.

He forced himself to inch to the surface, head back, nose and mouth only out. Two breaths and he went back under. He couldn't tell if any of them had followed him in. Again, he swam underwater as far as he could. Two more breaths. No shouting or splashing.

Nacho began to have hope. He continued staying underwater as long as possible. After what he thought must be several minutes, he popped his head out for a fast look. No other swimmers and some small boats tied up along the embankment. He made for the boats.

Nacho hid in the water among the boats until nightfall. The boats were abandoned. He detected no one searching from the bank.

While he waited for the right time to get out of the water, he wondered why they had not followed him into the water. They were a wet ops team. Russian. He concluded that they needed not to call the attention of the French police to themselves.

Once it was dark, Nacho got back on dry land.

That bastard Alois got Zahn and his pals to kidnap me and then he betrayed me to the Russians, he told himself as he climbed out of the water.

Now all he had to do was get back into Spain.

MOSCOW GOLD | 279

CHAPTER 41

Paris: Wednesday, June 30, 1937

Vratska made his report to Alois.

"We have run a total of twenty-one assaults on the Russian shipments, nine successful and the remainder failed. We hit them on the Métro. A couple of smash-and-grabs. The Soviets tightened up their operation. They tried using taxis. We ran one into a stone wall over by l'Étoile. Our car doors were jammed. Courier got away before we could lay hands on him."

"Good work. You justified my faith in you." Alois was pleased.

"Only we lost the Spaniard."

"He's disappeared. No worries there. Payment has been made, and you've kept the proceeds of two hits so far," Alois stated rather than asked.

"Yes," Vratska replied.

"Good. Do one more raid and keep the proceeds. Then get out. You were never here."

And so it had gone. Vratska gathered his troops, less Zahn, and put them back on the Orient Express. They went home to Sofia.

CHAPTER 42

Berlin: Friday, July 2, 1937

A respectful knock interrupted Admiral Canaris's late-morning coffee.

Out of regular routine, he got up himself and went to the door to open. "Ah, it *is* you, Sepp. I heard you were back. Come in. Come in. Have a seat. Coffee? Joachim just made fresh. How was Paris? Delightful no doubt."

"Lovely. At least after the weather got better."

"Good. I'm glad you enjoyed it. You were due for a good, long, and carefree holiday." Canaris's expression was ironic, mouth turned down, a single eyebrow lifted high.

Staupitz decided to play it safe and not take the bait. "Very grateful to you, sir."

"And our little activity there? Operation Markgraf you called it. Operation Marquis in French. Did it come off nobly?" The admiral chuckled at his own pun.

"A complete success. The Soviets have now laundered all the gold. Used a gaggle of established coin dealers. We have a relationship with each. No objection to the, ah, manner of payment was ever made.

MOSCOW GOLD | 283

The Bulgarians ran just under twenty attacks. Just under half were 'successful.' By my design, more were unsuccessful than successful. The attacks distracted the Soviets from investigating either the end purchasers or their manner of payment."

"Brilliant plan. From conception to execution, *ja*? What's the current status?"

"We've read in a couple of trustworthy Abwehr operatives. Moscow has disposed of most of the stuff. Operation's winding down."

"*Ausgezeichnet*! Where's Grebe?" Canaris asked.

"In Gibraltar. With our banks there. Handling the final details of securing our deposits of the gold. In Abwehr accounts."

"Perfect. You should both be promoted as soon as it's convenient."

CHAPTER 43

Moscow: Tuesday, July 6, 1937

Letchkov's slow treads ascended the ornate grand staircase in the Kremlin.

Guards in full dress uniform were stationed at every third step. When he got to the top, the guard at the door opened it and said, "Comrade Chairman is expecting you, Commander, you may go in."

"Good afternoon, Commander. What do you have for me?"

"The full and final report on the gold sales, Comrade Stalin."

"Give me your three-sentence summary."

"Significant quantities of the gold, virtually all of it, have been disposed of through legitimate dealers in Paris. There so far have been three hundred eighty-seven separate transactions, of which twenty-one were attacked; ten attacks succeeded."

"So, we lost a little more than two-tenths percent to theft?"

"An approximation, yes, Comrade Stalin."

"Any other pilferage?"

"No."

MOSCOW GOLD | 285

"Any hint the successful attacks were inside jobs?" Stalin was digging.

"None, Comrade Chairman. The full reports on all the attacks, including both those that succeeded and those that failed, are included with the report."

"Who did this to us?" The Russian dictator's temper was only just under control.

"Unknown, Comrade. The matter remains under intense investigation by the Paris embassy. Since the shipments have been completed, the individual cases are going cold. Suspicion has fallen on reactionary elements from somewhere in the Balkans. Maybe Turkey or Serbia, perhaps Bulgaria."

"Not the British or Germans?"

"It is thought not."

"The disposition of the proceeds?"

"Duly deposited in Gosbank," Letchkov said, "in hard currency accounts. Dollars and pounds for the most part. Mostly pounds. The receipts are attached."

"Very well, Commander, dismissed."

'There are, ah, two more matters, Comrade Chairman." Letchkov was tentative.

"Tell me," Stalin snapped.

"The American Federal Reserve has rejected some of the banknotes that we received as counterfeit."

"How many?"

"On the order of 10 to 15 percent."

"Are the notes fake, or are we being played by the capitalist imperialists?" Stalin's ire rose again.

"Fake, sir. Superior ones, but fakes, nonetheless. The capitalists don't fool around when it comes to money. The British notes may be counterfeit as well. Pound notes are easier to falsify. There so far has been no objection from the Bank of England."

286 | DOUGLAS L. FIELD

The little Georgian swore. Crass. After giving the matter some thought, he spluttered, "Well, we can hardly complain to the French authorities now, can we?"

"The falsified notes are mixed in with genuine bills. Very cunning, I'm told."

Stalin cursed again even more vulgarly. "Leave no stone unturned in determining who it is that has cheated us, Letchkov. Discontinue the deposit in banks of notes we receive in payment for the gold. Set up operations in all appropriate localities to move them into general circulation."

"Immediately, Comrade Chairman."

"And the second matter, Letchkov?"

"We were tipped off to the Spaniard's whereabouts. Our wet ops team picked him up, but he escaped. Jumped into the Canal Saint-Martin. They did not follow him in for fear of stirring up the French."

"Escaped?!? Who *are* these incompetents? Let's have Stachevski come home for, how shall we call it, consultations."

CHAPTER 44

Paris: Friday, July 9, 1937

High summer in Paris. Night fell after a long and balmy evening—not until almost 10 o'clock.

Should have been a perfect start to the weekend. Now it was dark.

Stachevski sat in his unlit office. The decoded telex dangled flimsily at his side from between his fingers.

> 14091 Stach F
> 19370907
> Return capital forthwith stop Express rail via Berlin and Warsaw stop Do not repeat not await arrival replacement trade envoy stop
> Letchkov

CHAPTER 45

Madrid: Thursday, September 16, 1937

"Kidnapped?" Cóndor exploded.

"I sent you to Paris to be safe. Who did this? How have we been penetrated?"

"I don't think we're penetrated, Cóndor. I think we were betrayed. By Agent Alois. I think we can no longer trust him or his service."

"How so?" asked Cóndor.

"Alois set up a meet at a café in a busy part of Paris. He came alone. He told me to go the café every day but at a different time. There was a schedule. All standard stuff. But I never saw him again." Nacho told him the full story up to diving into the Canal Saint-Martin.

"So, you think the Abwehr was working with this 'team' and had them waylay you, and then Alois betrayed you to the Soviets?" Cóndor summarized.

"Best guess," affirmed Nacho, "is that the Germans or the Abwehr somehow found out about and got involved with the gold. Bought, stole who knows? They didn't want us knowing what they were doing so they had me kidnapped and then turned me over to the Russians as

MOSCOW GOLD | 291

the agent who called in the attack on Arganda. No more Aníbal was the intention."

"It's a treacherous business. You were gone two months?"

"When I got out of the canal, all I had were my wet clothes. I had to eat and get some money. Found a job with a baker. He let me sleep in the back room. Built up a little money. Middle of the night one night, I lifted all the money he had in his till and left. Feel bad about that. Made my way home."

"Where are you now?" Cóndor wanted to know.

"My old place. Finessed it with the landlady."

"Madrid's still dangerous, Aníbal." Cóndor started to vent. "The Caudillo's making progress on all fronts but it's too slow. The Red revolution is eating itself. There is open conflict between the communists and anarchists. Their attention is on each other. There's a little more freedom of movement. We hear there are upwards of twenty thousand political prisoners in numerous labor camps."

Nacho had noticed changes himself. "I see that Calle de Alfonso XIII is now Agrarian Reform Street."

"The *estúpidos* changed María de Molina to Rights of the Child Street. And when that wasn't enough, it was changed again to United Socialist Youth Militias of the Home Front Street," Cóndor said. "It's laughable but you have to be careful. You're married, but you don't call your wife your *mujer*; she's your *compañera*. Get it wrong, and you're for the gulag. The fatuousness of the new moral order increases in inverse proportion to their declining success on the battlefield."

Nacho said, "I was on Calle de Rodríguez San Pedro earlier this morning. Passed a drug store. Entire front was covered in sandbags piled up like bricks, only there's a narrow passage to the inside. Nice-looking salesgirl standing outside. All decked out. Having a smoke. They had painted false windows on the sandbags. Put advertisements and displays for various cosmetics, specials, and sales in the 'windows.' Surreal. Life goes on."

"We must end this, Aníbal. ¡*Cuanto antes!* Let's talk about your future. While you were in Paris, the Reds tried to retake Brunete."

"It was in the papers there. I can read a little French. Couldn't understand all the details."

"They thought, if they retook the crossroads there, it would relieve the Siege of Madrid. Ahumada did your thing with the bread bike. He got a lot of information from the Republican troops at their staging areas. The Reds were profligate in devoting resources to the effort. They got Brunete back at first. Our intelligence through Ahumada and others was that the operation was bleeding the Reds. Our troops regrouped and kept up the pressure. By the end of the month, we had Brunete back."

"So, it was all a waste. Has Red morale suffered?" Nacho replied.

"Significantly. Which leads me to your next assignment. It's the least well-kept secret in Spain that the Reds are going to try to take Teruel from us. They think that conquering a provincial capital will play well in the international press and improve their bargaining position for a negotiated peace," Cóndor explained.

"You want me in Teruel then?"

"Yes. But not on our side. We hold the town, but we are surrounded to the west, south, and east. The Reds are hungry for manpower. They have extended conscription to the classes of 1925 to '26 and 1940 to '41. You fit into the former. Infiltrate a Popular Army formation down there. Learn and report what you can. Try the Campesinos."

CHAPTER 46

Teruel: Thursday, December 16, 1937

As Loyalist-controlled territory surrounded the little provincial capital, Nacho, through circuitous routing, got to the front near the city without crossing into rebel territory.

The crush to move men and resources to the Teruel front had left strict military order in low priority. As directed, Nacho attached himself to a battalion headed by one Valentín González, a thirty-five-year-old communist and former miner from Badajoz. González was a talented field commander. He had, by the time of Teruel, participated in every major battle of the war. González was brave and tough. He never conceded that everything was lost. Even if it were, he would contrive a way to fight his way out. His men knew González as "El Campesino."

Nacho became a Campesino without bothersome questions. His way was eased by his representation of himself as a practitioner of the all-important military avocation of scrounger. As a scrounger, neither his movements nor his occasional absences were noted. If he

MOSCOW GOLD | **295**

showed back up with the goods, he was safe. Nacho had contacts and clandestine experience. He was in.

This would be the second day of the battle. At El Campesino's direction, Sergeant Mariano López gathered his troops. "Listen up, Campesinos! It snowed yesterday. This is as you know. It's snowing today. This is as you can see. It's cold. It will be cold. Teruel has the lowest average winter temperatures in the country. According to the geniuses at headquarters, we are looking at the coldest winter in Spain in twenty years. Enemy bullets and artillery are a threat to you. This cold is a threat to you. The Revolution may lose you to fascist bullets and shells. Do not let it lose you to the cold. Do not expose your skin to the air. Take all necessary precautions to avoid frostbite and chilblains. Wear your greatcoats. Wrap your boots. Wear your gloves. They are cumbersome. Too bad. They are also warm. Do not get wet. Liquid water turns to ice. Ice is cold. Are there any questions."

There were none.

"You fought well yesterday. The 16th and 34th Brigades met up north of the city. The franquista rats in Teruel are surrounded."

A ragged cheer went up.

"Save your energy. See that flat hill to the northwest there? It's called Teruel's Tooth. Somebody thinks it looks like a molar. The enemy is up there. They have prepared trenches and strung wire. To get into the city, we need to remove them from that hill. That is our mission today. We will be attacking from the south, 34th Brigade from the north."

There was sporadic groaning and grousing.

"Form up. We're moving out. You'll get further orders from your platoon commanders. ¡Vámonos!"

It was an hour's slog to the bottom of the Tooth. The Campesinos spread out and began probing upward. It looked to Nacho to be about five hundred feet to the top. The enemy were dug in high. He saw no trenches or wire on the way up.

It was not long. Small arms fire started popping off. No machine guns yet. The fascists were holding fire, conserving ammunition. The sides of the Tooth were scored with gullies and fissures. There was good cover.

The Campesinos worked their way up. Wary. Nearing midmorning and just over halfway up, they began to take fire. They were challenged to locate the enemy shooters, whose fire was accurate and disciplined. Putting your head up would get you killed.

Corporal Porras arranged his beret on the point of his bayonet and eased it out into the open. He was rewarded with an 8-mm Mauser bullet hole in the cap. He donned it proudly.

The terrain was too steep to mount a coordinated frontal attack on the crest, and the Campesinos had to content themselves with a day of probing for weaknesses and undefended sectors in the defenses.

It continued to snow. It was bitter cold. Huge bundles of blankets were brought up. Nacho and his mates spent an uncomfortable night in the open huddled together around a small fire that they shielded from enemy view.

CHAPTER 47

Teruel: Christmas Day 1937

The battle for the Tooth was ferocious.

The defenders fought all the way. After days of concentrated effort, the Campesinos and other Loyalist units gained the crest of the plateau. More days of vicious fighting were required to dislodge the defenders from the top of the Tooth.

"Looks like today we kick them off this hill. What do you know, Arjona?" Porras muttered. The platoon was huddled around a smokey oil fire burning in a metal barrel.

Nacho was shivering. "I was over at the quartermaster's. Intelligence has it that they are conceding the Tooth. It's a mop up operation today."

"Merry Christmas! May we be truly grateful for our many and bountiful gifts," said Private Ambriz through thick layers of hat, hood, and scarves.

"Intelligence has it that the rebels are withdrawing into the city," Nacho added. "They are waiting on a relief column from Franco that has not arrived due to the bad weather. The rebel commander is a guy

MOSCOW GOLD | 299

named Domingo Rey d'Harcourt. Total Franco Loyalist. Franco's urging him to fight to the death, and we think he'll do it. There are about four thousand of them, and they are holing up in the Civil Governor's Building, the Bank of Spain, the Convent of Santa Clara, and the seminary."

"So, our Christmas present will be to go in there and dig them out. Floor by floor," Porras surmised.

'That's the way it's playing up." Nacho nodded.

CHAPTER 48

Teruel: New Year's Day 1938

"The rebels in the convent are all dead. We have taken the building—what's left of it anyway. Our mission today is to dig them out of the seminary," Sergeant López announced.

There was no reaction from the platoon. They were beyond exhaustion and incapable of reaction.

From the Tooth, they had fought their way down into the town. They had to contend with cold, hunger, and desperate exhaustion to gain every inch of ground. Casualties were horrific. The Campesinos were reduced to half strength, and that was by killed in action and only the most severely injured. The walking wounded fought on.

"Tactical procedure will be the usual," López continued. "Artillery and some tanks from 57th Brigade will shell the building without mercy. Campesinos will then move in with bayonets. It is not anticipated that we will be taking prisoners."

"After we take the building, maybe we can bivouac inside. Might be a little warmer," Ambriz said.

MOSCOW GOLD | 301

"Have that as your motivation for fighting today, Ambriz. You'll need it," López responded.

⌥

The Campesinos jumped off at at 1100 hours. The seminary had been subjected for ninety minutes to an intense bombardment. The shelling was so pervasive and thorough that entire sections of the big building were reduced to ruins. Before it was over, the falling ordinance was, in many places, merely redistributing the rubble and generating clouds of dust.

The attackers surrounded the building amid significant sniper fire from within the structure. There were five entrances, and the troops hit them simultaneously.

Fighting on the first floor was hand to hand.

"Arjona, secure the bottom of the main staircase," López shouted as he was hit in the chest and toppled bleeding to the floor.

Nacho kicked open a door leading to the space under the stairs and rushed in headlong. He met a rebel and his rifle pointing at him. His momentum carried him across the intervening distance, and he stabbed his enemy in the throat as the man vainly pulled the trigger. Out of ammunition.

The Campesinos rallied after the first floor was cleared. There were rebel troops above. Nacho and his mates began shooting up through the floor, pausing each time to listen for the sound of a rebel falling.

Porras took over from López. He set up the attack on the second floor. Most of the rebel soldiers were dead or gravely wounded—but not all. Those remaining fought like cornered rats. They knew there was no point in surrendering. They died fighting.

They cleared the third and fourth floors in similar and bloody fashion. No quarter was given by either side.

Only the fifth and last floor remained. Nacho arrived there uninjured. He worked his way through three rooms that had exposure

302 | DOUGLAS L. FIELD

to the outside and found no one. He kicked the door to a fourth room open and charged in. He saw a rebel soldier aiming his rifle out at the street below. Nacho raised his weapon. He shouted at the man. He was loathe to shoot him in the back. There was no reaction. The soldier had died at his post.

All firing had now ceased. They had taken the seminary. Nacho leaned against a wall and slid to the floor. Night came to Teruel. The Campesinos collapsed and slept where they were.

CHAPTER 49

Teruel: Thursday, January 27, 1938

The Campesinos and their comrades in the other Republican units had taken Teruel.

It had been at terrible cost for both sides. Nacho's platoon moved to consolidate their positions. The worst winter in twenty years continued unabated. They dug, barricaded, piled rubble, and excavated gun emplacements in appallingly frigid conditions.

Nacho found himself falling into periods of catatonic unawareness of his surroundings, locked inside his own head. All his life he had hated cold. Add to that, he learned somewhere in his school days that the Nordic conception of perdition contemplated a place not of burning heat, but of unending, searing, and all-pervasive cold. He now reckoned he had been consigned to Viking hell—unremitting, unrelenting, unrepentant, unmerciful cold.

Nacho's pain and punishment at Teruel were augmented by near total attenuation of his senses. There was no color. All was white—white darkness, utter white darkness. Snow and ice covered every foot of ground, every animate and every inanimate object. The odd

MOSCOW GOLD | 305

sluggish, huddled human form that moved about the whitescape was itself conformed to colorlessness. The weighted and thick cold air impeded transmission of sound. A heavy hush settled on the icy indistinctness such that even the reports of small arms fire and the boom of artillery were dampened. Dwellers of this netherworld were, of basic survival necessity, so hatted and coated, swaddled in gloves and boots, that sensation of touch was hopeless. As they relied on the movement and volatility of submicroscopic particles, which were frostily repressed, taste and smell were but fond memory.

His reverie was interrupted by shouting and cursing. It was Porras, who, upon the death of López, had been made up to sergeant.

"Pay attention, Campesinos. The fascists have broken through north of town. Worse, they have taken back the Tooth. They will start raining artillery down on us at any time."

There was no energy to react.

"Be ready to move up in an hour. We'll be supporting the 8th Brigade."

They shuffled forward. Toward the muffled sound of skirmish fire. They had a bit of good fortune.

"Look around this area," Porras ordered. "This sector has been fought over back and forth. There are foxholes and banked-up dirt that we can take advantage of. Save us some work. Get dug in."

Nacho fell into a vacant foxhole, set his weapon on the lip, and settled in to wait.

To their eternal credit the 8th held out against the rebel attack.

Around midafternoon, Porras came around again.

"Fall back to the center of the city, he ordered. "The 8th has held, and the rebels have withdrawn. Fighting's over—for today anyway."

CHAPTER 50

Teruel: Wednesday, February 23, 1938

The weather had cleared and warmed late in January.

Hefty resupply for the rebels got through. They began to advance. Nacho participated in daily counterattacks, but it was futile. The rebels, by February, had erased all Loyalists gains and had reoccupied Teruel. The Loyalist forces who could retreated south, but thousands were left behind enemy lines.

The colorful El Campesino and his troops were among those who became surrounded.

They were holed up in the very center of town on the Plaza del Torico in the former Corsetería Minerva. Minerva's stock in trade was long gone. All that remained of her fixtures was a battered female mannequin, naked and missing a leg. The irony of their current position was not lost on El Campesino's troops. Even in their forlorn circumstances, there was ribald and salacious jesting.

The ground floor in which the *corsetería* was located was set back from the street with a colonnaded sidewalk in front. The upper floors of the building were supported by fat and now pockmarked columns.

MOSCOW GOLD | 307

The windows above looked out with good fields of fire on the plaza. At street level, the columns provided adequate cover when needed. The entire plaza had been subjected to intense shelling over the course of the battle. There were braided rivers of white ice where bombs and shelling had fractured subterranean water service. Huge piles of rubble developed, which, if nothing else, were good for building barricades and defenses.

The Campesinos now numbered just under fifty. They were, for the immediate moment, safe, but Nationalist mop-up operations were proceeding apace. It would not be long before the stranded group was located, surrounded, and captured. Capture did not bear contemplation. El Campesino was exercising his maximum powers of wile and guile to extricate them and return to friendly lines. He had little raw material with which to work. They would have to brazen it out.

During the midafternoon, El Campesino stood at a third-floor window observing the movements and tactics of Nationalist patrols moving about the city. "Gather around, comrades. I have a plan. The battle here has been fierce. There has been no time to clean up. Many dead, ours and theirs, lie where they fell. Sergeant Porras is to organize several groups to collect from the Nationalist dead overcoats, caps, scarves, gloves, and rags they used to wrap their boots. Bring what you find back. We will see what we can make of what you gather."

Porras said, "Arjona, you're the scrounger. What do you recommend?"

"The key to scrounging is confidence, Sergeant. Act like you know what you are doing and are supposed to be doing it and keep moving," Nacho advised.

"All right," Porras ordered, "you know your groups. Back in an hour."

The carnage was monstrous. The Campesinos had no trouble laying hands on sufficient items to accommodate them all.

El Campesino moved his men out at dusk. He figured they would appear to be the last rebel patrol of the day. They were all fitted out in their purloined uniform overcoats and caps.

"Assume the fascist patrol formation," El Campesino ordered, "one lead man on point with two more backing him up, the main body of the detachment following. Three lag behind as a rear guard."

The plan was well conceived. It was dark enough that genuine Nationalist troops would have difficulty spotting anything amiss with the Campesinos. Yet it was not so dark that the movement of a large number of soldiers as an organized detachment would arouse suspicion.

They fell in outside Minerva's and moved straight down the plaza past the Torico Fountain and out of the city center. As they went past the Torre Mudéjar del Salvador and down La Escalinata, they passed another patrol lounging on the latter's steps.

El Campesino marched up to their lieutenant.

"These men are a disgrace, Lieutenant—slovenly and lounging about. You are on report. I am Major González. Report to my command tomorrow at 0700 hours to explain your behavior and that of your men."

The lieutenant snapped off a crisp salute, and El Campesino returned it. He then looked at his own formation and shouted, "You men there! Dress up your lines! You look scarcely better than this rabble."

The ruse worked. The Campesinos were soon out of town and on a three-mile forced march to the tiny village of Castralvo, where the front line had stabilized.

Even so, Nacho was not yet finished with the cold of Teruel.

"We will wait here until I deem it safe to cross into our territory," their leader announced.

The little formation waited in plunging temperatures until after midnight, when El Campesino sensed it was safe to cross the lines.

CHAPTER 51

Irún: Sunday, August 25, 1963

David drove all night from Santander.

It was to his advantage that he would make his border crossing into France early on a Sunday morning. He parked the little SEAT at the railroad station hotel and sent a letter to the rental agency advising where they could pick it up.

It was a decade since David had been in Irún. It had been his family's port of entry into Spain on the way down from Paris to first take up residence in Madrid. As he made ready to cross in the opposite direction, memories of that watershed day flooded back.

On the Spanish side, the Guardia Civil were as ever turned out in implausible green uniforms. They wore the strangest hats David had ever seen—shiny, black patent leather, like a French *kêpi* on backwards but with the corners of their great long bills at the back folded upward at right angles.

David desired that his entry into France go unnoticed. Recalling that the Guardia Civil were constitutionally taciturn, accustomed to intimidating and to receiving extreme deference, David obliged. He

MOSCOW GOLD | 311

approached diffidently. When asked, he showed his passport, and he moved right on when beckoned to do so.

The French border post was neat and tidy; swept; and, being so near the Pyrenees, alpine. Across the line, Spain was dry and gritty. While not crumbling, the buildings were tired and dusty. The French side appeared fresh and clean. The border police this morning were convivial and congenial. He was traveling light, with just a medium-sized grip. His papers received a cursory glance, and his belongings were ignored. On your way then. And a pleasant journey, *notre ami américain*.

He was confident that he had entered France with the bare minimum of fuss and that, if there were questions later, the event was altogether unlikely to be remembered by either side. Only Ariel knew he was in France. As a refreshing side benefit, he was now out from under the Cuerpo.

The next train to Paris on this Sunday was not until midafternoon. It would fetch him up into Paris early the next morning.

David devoted the train journey north to refining his plans for the Paris investigation. He catalogued all that he had thus far developed relative to the gold, its provenance, and its disposition. He rehearsed all that he knew about Jack Isham and did serious and lengthy reflection on the genesis and purpose of this current assignment.

As the miles clattered on beneath the trucks of his first-class carriage, David's conviction that Isham's reasons for putting the hurt on him with the gold story were more than what Isham said they were grew. The gold story was interesting, maybe even big, but not worth all but blackmailing a reporter. The thought that he might be a game piece in a matter much larger nagged at him. The more it nagged, the more it annoyed.

He salved his irritations with more pleasant but, in their own way, also vexing reflections on the day at the beach in Santander and all the events that had led up to it. His friendship with Ariel Muñiz had moved far beyond friendship and was reaching at once agreeable and arresting critical mass.

This was a surprise to him. He had wondered with what sort of woman he might ever have a permanent relationship. Ariel markedly failed to fit the profile of his erstwhile musings. Beautiful, elegant, a little exotic, generous, tender and steady, she was a girl of warmth, tenderness, and contentment from among the dour and saturnine Spanish.

¡Imposible!

He was putting it together that Ariel had been interested in and aware of him well before he had any inkling. Demure of constitution, she had, with dignity, held it close to herself. When he had first met her, she'd acted indifferent and uninterested. But then their acquaintanceship had grown into romance in a natural and unpressured way.

Now he had to worry whether it had been too much of a risk to trust her with his plans. And was it an unfair risk to her to be involved with him? Risk he was willing to embrace, but what about her? Would she show in Segovia? How best to protect her?

He wondered if Ariel was missing him and whether he had botched the whole thing. She could be angry with him. Hard to know whether she would show in Segovia. Maybe it was even doubtful.

MOSCOW GOLD | 313

CHAPTER 52

Paris: Monday, August 26, 1963

David's train chuffed haughtily into the Gare d'Austerlitz.

It was a mere three hours and forty minutes late from the Spanish frontier. There was something regal about the French railway. Delays, discomforts, and difficulties, notwithstanding, the locomotive smugged into the station. The engine driver, conductor, and additional rail crew held heads proud and high.

"Perhaps we didn't keep to the strict timetable, Monsieur, but what of it?" they seemed to say. "Through our efforts, you have fetched up intact into Paris. Paris, mind you. And for that, you owe us an enduring debt of gratitude, non?"

The train arrived a minute or so before eleven o'clock in the morning. David decided to save a couple of francs. He hoofed it from the station. Besides, he had an errand on this warmish and humid day with thunderheads roiled up over Montmartre.

The Seine glided by, mercurial and thick. It was five bridges down the river along the Quais de Saint-Bernard, Tournelle, and Montebello.

MOSCOW GOLD | 315

On the last, he found a *tabac*. He bought and wrote out a postcard of the Eiffel Tower lit up at night. It was unoriginal.

He wrote, "Paris hot and sweaty but charming as always. Back in Spain by the end of next month. Love, David."

They might be watching her mail. Maybe this would throw them off a little. He posted it to the Gaztambide address.

Moving farther along the quai, he turned left into the rue Saint-Jacques. He made a quick right into rue Saint-Séverin and then left into the rue des Prêtres-Saint-Séverin. Kitty-corner across from the Église Saint-Séverin was the rue de la Parcheminerie and L'Hotel Parc Saint-Séverin.

Rue de la Parcheminerie was the perfect street for this trip. Pure Latin Quarter, near the Sorbonne, just a block south of the Seine and a block or two east of the Boulevard Saint-Michel, it was about the length of a football field. It was flat and narrow. No motor vehicles were allowed. And it was old—about as old as the Sorbonne itself. Historic home to writers, students, and the makers of parchments, it was thus given its name. Rue de la Parcheminerie was the ideal location for an investigative journalist on a mission to Paris.

With half a dozen stories of plain whitish facade relieved a little by green-and-white-striped awnings, the Parc Saint-Séverin presented as architecturally minimalist among the medieval buildings and Gothic churches. David tried to check in and was not surprised to find that it was too early. He left his bag with the concierge and headed up to the rue de la Harpe.

What started as a sunny day had turned overcast. It seemed like rain. Taking a chance on being just a little ahead of the weather, he scuttered across the Pont Saint-Michel, in front of the busy steps of the Palais de la Justice and into the Cité Métro. He was headed for the 16th Arrondissement in pure uptown Paris.

The 16th was bookended by the Palais de Chaillot and the Arc de Triomphe. It was home to old Paris money, inbred high society, and the secrets of centuries of French wealth and power. It wasn't easy to get

316 | DOUGLAS L. FIELD

into the 16th, much less to be taken in and accepted. He was curious how those at his first stop had managed to do it.

That first stop was on the toney avenue Henri-Martin. Coming out of the Métro at street level, it was now raining. The well-heeled Passy district seemed just a little sad. Henri-Martin was what he expected—stately buildings with mansard roofs; high-end shops on the street level; expensive flats above, very expensive flats. He went west past the 16th's Mairie.

There it was. Number 78 *bis* presented as a handsome building—ecru, neoclassical, landscaping groomed and coifed, wrought-iron portal with gold-painted accents. These quarters were not attained on the salary of the average Spanish civil servant. On the marquee at 78 bis, each name was printed in the same font, neat and permanent, installed next to its owner's doorbell.

David ran his eyes down the list of occupants. There she was—María Frankman y Buendía, third floor, left. He played the button with what he thought would be an urgent long-short-short-long-long pattern. He was surprised to be buzzed in. The lobby kept with the building's persona. Two gilded empire chairs greeted him, along with a Persian rug of some sort, plus the faint aroma of linseed oil.

The elevator added to the cachet. Ancient and wheezy, its fat electrical connections cord was affixed to the top, rather like a long leash. At David's call the lift soughed down to the lobby. Double mahogany and glass doors opened into the mirrored cabin. He pressed the actuator bar, no mere black button here. The old apparatus seemed to sigh in resignation. It started up again. David could have walked up twice as fast but would have foregone a pleasant experience.

The landing was silent and decorated with several charcoal drawings. David knocked on three, left. Not long and a statuesque woman opened. She was in her late sixties at least, tall, straight, and vigorous looking with intelligent if sad brown eyes. No jewelry evident, but she was patrician and, this being a late summer's day, had a fan folded and hanging from a dainty little cord on her left wrist.

MOSCOW GOLD | 317

It's her! She must be Spanish! David told himself. "Good afternoon, Mrs. Negrín."

"And you, young man, would be just who?" she said in French.

David flashed his credentials from the paper. "David Fordham, *International Herald Tribune.* I'd like to talk to you about your late husband." He answered her in Castilian.

"Ah. My dear departed husband. And what interest would the mighty *Herald Tribune* have in him?" She acceded to Spanish.

"I'm looking into the 'Moscow Gold.' I know you are aware of it. May I come in?"

She regarded him skeptically for a long moment. "You're rather pushy, aren't you? *Pero, sí, pásate.*" She used the informal manner of address—like one would to a kid. David needed to seize the initiative here.

She offered him a large stuffed *sillón* in a salon of tasteful decor. She took a straight-backed and armless chair across from a heavy coffee table.

"Monique! Bring the young gentleman a coffee, will you? And for me."

"There's no reference to Dr. Negrín on the marquee. I wasn't sure I had the right flat." He thought it wouldn't hurt to lay a little guilt on her.

"Does there need to be? Didn't you see the commemorative plaque?"

David realized he should have been more observant. So much for seizing the initiative. "No, I missed that."

"During the war and in his hour of greatest need," she said, "the French Left could not bestir itself to help my husband. After the fact, after all was lost, only then did he become their darling. When he died, they adorned our building with that unprepossessing little plaque. They recognize this as the last residence of his life. They love that sort of thing here, you know. Especially *my* neighbors. Brings distinction to the building and all that."

318 | DOUGLAS L. FIELD

"In Madrid too. They're all over there."

"Foof. Madrid! That's just us mimicking French culture. We're fond of doing that."

He noticed that she said "us" and knew that she still considered herself a Spaniard. Monique brought the coffees. Silver service. Milk and wrapped sugars.

"What is your interest in the Spanish gold reserves, Mr. Fordham?"

"I write stories on the Spanish economy. Determination of the full details of events surrounding those assets from the time they left Spain until now might inure to the benefit of the Spanish people. Beautiful place you have here. Wow!"

She was not intimidated and gave him a little disdainful look. "You put before me a very great dilemma. To assist Francisco Franco and his fascist cronies, I would lift not a finger. The people of Spain, Juan's and my people, they are a different matter."

"Franco can't live forever. When he's gone, those gold reserves—"

"Alas, he's lived far too long already." She flipped open her fan, one or two strokes accentuating her abhorrence of the man. "As for my countrymen, I fear I can help them very little."

"If I may be candid, Mrs. Negrín, your circumstances seem to be better than those of most of them."

"You may be. My wealth is legitimate. My husband had the benefit of not a single *céntimo* of that money, if that's what you're insinuating, I've lived for decades now with that kind of thinking. I am accustomed," she said unfazed and evidently unoffended.

"You'll forgive me, but it's an obvious thought." David backpedaled.

"Obvious, yes. Everyone seems to be able to think of it. Try to understand this. In October and November 1936, we all feared that the franquistas would overrun Madrid. Don Juan felt it essential to place the gold into safekeeping out of their reach. He knew there were risks. He exuded outward calm and confidence, but this was an agonizing decision for him. Few are those who can accept this, but I knew it."

MOSCOW GOLD | 319

"But why the Soviet Union?" David asked. "Was it naive to trust Stalin?"

"With the benefit of hindsight, perhaps. In 1936, the Russian Revolution was still young. Its excesses were not yet fathomed. My husband was a socialist and believed to the marrow in socialist brotherhood and solidarity. The fascists were getting all manner of military supplies, gratis mind you, from Germany and Italy. Purchases from abroad were the exclusive choice for keeping the Republic supplied. As the Soviets were the natural enemies of our enemies, his choice was all but dictated to him, no?"

David thought she looked like she loved him despite all his faults. "Was the gold ever accounted for?"

"An incisive question, young, eh, David, is it? But since they involve Joseph Stalin and his minions, are they not themselves quite 'naive,' as you say?"

"The Nazis kept detailed records on their activities even when nefarious. Why not the Soviets?" David argued.

"Oh, records I am confident—in fact, I know—they kept. It's just that to expect anything much to turn up at this late date, this is not reasonable."

"Is there documentation that specifies how and for what it was used?"

"Of that I am unaware, but I doubt it."

"At the end, was there any balance in favor of Spain? Was, or even better, is there a refund owing?"

"It would be delightful if there were, but I do not know. Moreover, I have no idea how to find out," she said with a sad expression.

At this point she stood and walked toward the interior of the apartment. "Monique, let Manolo in, would you?"

She came back to her seat. "I have someone I would like you to meet."

Just then, a large and stately liver and white Dalmatian dog nosed into the room. "Come, Manolo, meet Mr. Fordham, a visitor from

320 | DOUGLAS L. FIELD

home." She looked at David with a wry look. "At least so he most adroitly pretends to be. He may succeed in hoodwinking many, Manolo, but not us. No. No, he's North American, I think. *Puro yanqui.*" Now she smiled with affection at David.

The dog came over to David and sniffed at him amiably. He ruffled the animal's ears. "As they say over there in the States, 'You can take the kid out of the country, but you can't take the country out of the kid.' Nice dog."

"Oh, we Parisians love our pets. Don't we, Manolo?" David and Manolo were making friends. This seemed to please Mrs. Negrín. She now turned serious again.

"Manolo, Mr. Fordham is asking about Papi's gold." Then to David, "Unlike Azaña, my husband remained in Spain until the final collapse of the Republican front and his expulsion from office in March 1939. He by then was prime minister. He then came here and organized the SERE—the Servicio de Evacuación de Refugiados Españoles—to help our exiles. He had to close it up in 1940. Pressure from the wretched franquistas along with the German invasion of France, you know. Juan carried on under a different name, but I do not know the details. He felt it was the least he could do."

"I would like to have known him," David said, hoping to encourage her to keep talking.

"My husband was by no means perfect, but he was a charming, vibrant, and optimistic man, out of character for a Spaniard. You would have admired him."

She now rose again and, hands on her hips, regarded David and Manolo, who, by now had laid himself down at David's feet.

"Manolo seems to like you. So do I. Although I assure you, I was reluctant to at first." She gave a hint of a smile.

She seemed to reflect for a moment and then appeared to decide, "My husband entrusted me with something that will interest you. He left its disposition to my discretion. I'm seventy-one years old. Time

MOSCOW GOLD | 321

may have come for me to act. Will you and Manolo play nicely while I go and look for it?"

Without waiting for reply, she disappeared into the interior of the flat.

David got up and looked around the room. To his left was an ornate credenza with a gallery of framed photographs on top. He studied them. From the clothing, he could determine that most had been taken in the '30s. Many had backgrounds in Madrid. One caught his eye—three men, one short, one tall, one medium.

After ten minutes, Mrs. Negrín reappeared. "Ah, my photos. Recognize anyone?"

"Who are these three, may I ask," David replied.

"My husband, of course; Méndez Aspe, his deputy; and the Russian."

"Which Russian?" David probed.

"Difficult name. Stav something or other. Their trade envoy or some such bunkum. The one with whom Juan arranged the shipment."

She went on, "Back to the business at hand. I thought I knew where this was, but it took me a minute to find it."

She then produced a worn and old buff-colored file folder that she handed to David. "This may have relevance to your research."

David looked at her—inquiring.

"Please read. Let it speak for itself," she directed.

Eight pages. Formal. Typewritten. On a manual machine, before there were electrics. All in French. Signed, rubricated, and sealed on the last page with great flourish by the Soviet finance and foreign ministers and the Spanish ambassador.

It was dated February 5, 1937. The text of the document began, "Certificate of the receipt of the deposit in gold sent by the government of the Spanish Republic to the State Depository of Precious Metals of the People's Commissariat of Finance of the USSR at Moscow."

David was stunned. "It's Stalin's receipt for the gold!"

322 | DOUGLAS L. FIELD

"This is a small exception to my comment a moment ago about written records. There may be many questions about this gold, young man, but one issue is settled. It was sent to and received by the Russians in Moscow. As to what happened to it thereafter, I cannot be of much help. But it did get there."

David handed the folder back to her.

"No, Mr. David Fordham, American journalist who acts so much like a madrileño, you keep it. I entrust it to you. It is of no value to me at this point. Consider it a deposit, a down payment on your very complete, honest, and honorable report on this delicate matter."

"This should be with Spanish authorities. It belongs to Spain." David was amazed.

"It should be with *legitimate* Spanish authorities. I could not bear to turn it over to the current rabble in Madrid. I may not live long enough to see Franco's demise. Exercise your wisdom and conscience as to its fate."

David again tried to protest but she said, "No, joven, my decision is made. The document is yours. You should take it. But if you do, be very careful. The subject matter of your investigations is touchy—in the extreme. Do you understand me? There are numerous interested parties with multiple and competing agendas. Possession of this document could place you in significant danger from those who may not want it to surface."

She held out her hand. David took it and then kissed her on the cheek, "Thank you, Mrs. Negrín, I—"

"No. Now none of that. I'm sure you are anxious to be on your way. You must have before you a great deal to occupy your attentions here in Paris. I wish you Godspeed."

"You are a very gracious lady. It has been an honor to meet you. One last question, if I may. Well, perhaps two?" David delayed departing just a moment.

"Of course."

"Méndez Aspe?"

A raised eyebrow. "Another good question. You have done your homework. He's here in Paris, although I think he plans soon to move to England. But for now, rue du Temple, over in the 3rd, number 48, I think it is."

"And Santiago Portillo?"

"Also, here. Your good fortune is holding. He's back from his 'sojourns' in the Soviet Union and its colonies in Eastern Europe. How wrong we were about the Russians! Communist Party of Spain headquarters up on Montmartre, rue de Rennes I think it is. He's always there. Craven young skunk, he'll talk to you. Lives for the notoriety. Aspe may be a whole different matter. *Ve con Diós, mijo!*"

David reached for the door.

"Speaking of Méndez Aspe." She turned and went to the credenza. She picked up the frame they had discussed and took the photo out. "Here take this too. It doesn't represent a happy memory for me. You have it as a souvenir of our visit. It will help you identify him—if you can even find him."

"No. I—"

"Put it in your folder, David."

Once back out on the street, it had stopped raining. The afternoon was muggy with sunlight that dazzled, bouncing off the puddles, shining the gutters and wet streets. David hurried down toward Trocadero and the river. He hoped to get over to Santé before they closed.

He was elated. He now had in hand the first piece of the gold story puzzle and a good start on leveraging back his freedom.

Bearing in mind Mrs. Negrín's admonition, he checked cursorily for someone following him. He picked up nothing. Nobody but Ariel knew he was in Paris. It was half a dozen Métro stops to Denfert-Rochereau.

David came out again into bright sunlight that hurt his eyes. He made straight for the Boulevard Saint-Jacques. The offices and publishing facilities of France-Soir are located in that street across from the La Santé Prison. La Santé—Health. *What a name for a prison, he thought. Who says the French don't have a sense of humor?*

La Santé had been a favorite lockup of the Gestapo in occupation times. Even now, it was still very much in business. *France-Soir* was the direct descendent of *Paris-Soir*, and *Paris-Soir* was a leading newspaper in prewar Paris.

A stylish and flirty girl at the front desk confirmed that the *Paris-Soir* archives were indeed at this location. With solicitous promptitude, she had him shown by an aging custodian to the basement where they were housed. The old fellow left him on his own and unsupervised to sort out the cataloguing system and to complete his research.

$$\infty\!\sim\!\!\circ$$

By the time he made it back onto the Métro, the workday was staggering to its end. Once up on Montmarte, David hurried out onto the rue de Rennes and ran right into number 24.

El Tejón Rojo—the Red Badger—was in his office. He was always in his office. Staff was long gone home for the day, but the indefatigable Portillo toiled on. The door was unlocked, and David walked right in. Portillo heard him come in and called him to the inner sanctum.

In what seemed to be equal magnitude, stacks of books and piles of cigarette butts surrounded Santiago Jacinto Portillo Salas, General Secretary of the Communist Party of Spain. Close to fifty, Portillo chain-smoked. He was never without a lighted smoke, either between his nicotine-yellowed thumb and forefingers or hanging from his lips. Not even the several large ashtrays that dotted his office withstood his capacity to fill them.

Beyond the perpetual butt, he was a smallish but stout man, square-faced with luxuriant dark and curly hair that had receded to a line of demarcation extending straight over the top of his skull from one ear to the other. He wore very thick tortoise shell, '30s-style round glasses. From behind his ever smoke-fogged glasses, there peered what would

MOSCOW GOLD | 325

have been beady eyes, were they not magnified by the heavy lenses. A pointy nose and a mouth that was a mere slit in his face rounded out the visage of a serious, dedicated, and doctrinaire person of remarkable ruthlessness, perseverance, and single-mindedness.

"What can I do for you, young man?" he growled through wisps of smoke.

"David Fordham, *International Herald Tribune*." The credentials were proffered. "Conducting some research on events that occurred in Madrid in 1936. I think you were there then."

"Your newspaper is a capitalist rag. It has never been either kind or fair to me." Portillo acted irascible, but his remark was not hostile.

David supposed he was used to it. That or maybe the coverage had not been as bad as it could have been. He doubtlessly he liked notoriety—good or bad.

"Maybe we can change that this afternoon." David offered his most engaging look. "I'm looking into a number of issues relating to what is known as the Moscow Gold. You're familiar with the Moscow Gold, aren't you?"

"I, young newspaperman, have dedicated my life to strengthening the Communist Party's position among the proletariat and intelligentsia. My efforts have survived opposition from Marxist-Leninist, Trotskyite, Stalinist, and other social democratic factions— opposition that has been intense and perilous to my health and well-being." He fixed a disdainful, if-only-you-could-hope-to-achieve-such-sacrifice stare on David.

"And the gold, you *are* familiar with the gold. Madrid, 1936. You were there, Mr. Chairman." These were statements from David, not questions.

"After the outbreak of the fascist rebellion, I joined the Communist Party. It was November. It was already cold that year."

David began to wonder whether the man had hard worked himself into a state of mental disintegration. It appeared as if he might have talked himself into a trance.

Portillo went on. "I was very pro-Soviet in those days. It was November 7, 1936. I was twenty-one. They elected me councilor for public order of the Defense Council of Madrid. We were young and committed. Hardly out of our teenage years, we were."

"Juan Negrín. Did you know Dr. Negrín? He arranged for the gold to be shipped to Comrade Stalin in Moscow. He did that between October 20 and 28, 1936. Were you aware at the time that the gold had been moved, Comrade Chairman?"

"We, I, was given supreme power to defend Madrid. But with what guns? With what ammunition? By which soldiers? We had nothing. But out of nothing, we did mount a defense of the city. They stood to the barricades and front lines, the women and the men, even the youth. We stopped the fascist rats. Then we held. We held Madrid. For twenty-nine glorious, progressive, collectivist months, we held the city. It was one of the most heroic acts of all human history. That is the record. That record, my record is clear." He sank a little deeper into his reverie.

David was becoming a little impatient and exasperated. He thought that, if he annoyed the man, it might shake him loose. "Under your leadership, during your term, several thousand military and civilian prisoners, including many women and children, were killed by communist-affiliated groups. In Paracuellos del Jarama and in Torrejón de Ardoz and maybe other towns and villages, not to mention Madrid itself, no?"

"I had nothing to do with that event. Paracuellos. If it even ever occurred. Nothing," Portillo snapped.

"It occurred, comrade. You well know that it did. The fact of its occurrence is well documented. It represented the biggest mass killing by your side during the war." David picked at a troubling memory.

"I was not involved. The fascists, they were the killers."

"Maybe not pulling the trigger, but it occurred on your watch, by your authority. You were aware, you approved," David challenged Portillo further.

"Absolute slander, a disgraceful smear on my legacy. I am innocent of that blood." Portillo was no longer enjoying David's interview.

It was obvious to David that Portillo was not forthcoming. He did not deny that the massacre occurred, only his personal involvement. He had to have known about it. If he admitted anything about the gold, it would undercut his denial of the killings.

"Well, then the gold, what about the gold?" David demanded.

Portillo seemed to come out of his trance. "I have been accused of involvement with that alleged event as well. I deny participation in what is, in any event, a filthy franquista myth."

"Do you deny that the gold ever existed?" David persevered.

"I do not know that. You can imagine I was not in those days included among the list of those who were invited to visit the vaults of the Bank of Spain."

"Do you deny that Moscow received the gold?"

"I was privileged to have an interview with Comrade Stalin in '48, about seven years before he died. Since this reproach, this obloquy has hung heavy on me and has been a discredit to the PCE, I hazarded to ask him about this so-called 'Moscow Gold.' He denied that it was ever received at the Kremlin. That is all I can say on the subject."

"So then, no Spanish gold in Moscow?" It was a surprise that Portillo was still talking to him.

"None."

"How long have you been here in France?"

"Since '44. Nineteen years? So what?"

'Then you speak and read French?" David prepared to snap the trap.

"Claro."

David extracted the receipt Mrs. Negrín had given him. Stoking a little drama, he perused it, flipping the pages one at a time. "Your French good enough to read this, comrade?"

Portillo took it and read. It took him a while. When he was finished, he handed it back. No comment. He would not look David in the eye.

David pounced. "Stalin lied to you. Either that, or you are lying

328 | DOUGLAS L. FIELD

to me. What happened to the gold? Who has it now? How much of it is left? You're a communist, but you're also a Spaniard. Franco will be gone someday. You may have the opportunity to go home. If you do, there will be questions. You won't be able to dodge them."

Portillo lit a new cigarette off the one he already had going. "You better be on your way. Thanks for the interview." His look was serene, but beneath the surface, he was livid.

"You haven't answered my questions. You're a man who's concerned about how history will remember him. Give me something good to write about you."

"I told you. You need to go now." The communist leader thrust his chin towards the door. Portillo's countenance menaced.

"What are you going to do? Have me killed too?" David probed recklessly. "Let me give you some names. Gabriel León Trilla. Jesús Monzón. Joan Comorera." David went all in.

"Go," Portillo hissed.

"Trilla and Monzón. Fellow communists, but you ordered them executed, didn't you? You had them both killed. But Comorera, he was smarter than you. He saw you coming and took precautions. Beat you at your own game."

Portillo nudged David out the door and closed it. Just before it shut, David heard him mutter, *"Yo he tenido que eliminar a alguna persona"* (I have had to eliminate some person). The sentence was awkward, stated in the singular, yet it implied more.

David had enjoyed going toe-to-toe with the Red Bastard. Forget Badger. But the threat was real enough. Nacho and Mrs. Negrín might be right. He could be entering dangerous territory. And with the Portillo interview, he had no advancement of the story to show for his trouble.

That evening and back in the Latin Quarter, David made a brief local reconnaissance, with the result that he settled on one Chez Roland for supper. It had seven tables, black-and-white-checkered floor, paint peeling here and there from the walls and ceiling, a wobbling coatrack, and little rivers of condensation sliding down the windows. None other than Roland himself carried off the entire operation, from waiting tables to cooking to acting as sommelier.

The plat du jour was described in great and only partially understood detail. David ordered it on the theory that Roland's culinary heart would be in it. Thus, it should be good. He hoped it was not kidney or sweetbreads. He ordered an expensive Bordeaux and settled in to await the results of Roland's exertions—and to reflect.

The day had been a mixed bag—huge success with Mrs. Negrín, a total bust with Portillo. There was time, moreover, to mull over what he had found at *Paris-Soir*, which was nothing new or helpful. David had solid confirmation that the gold had gone to Moscow. Next question, what had Moscow done with it?

Economics were David's bailiwick. He had looked at precious metals price information. Gold in mild decline late in 1936 when there were vague rumors of some Spanish reserves coming on the market. Recovery and stability until spring 1937 and then a slight but enduring decline that lasted into the late summer. Other precious metal commodities remained unchanged during the time.

Paris-Soir had been France's premiere newspaper in the '30s leading up to the German invasion in June 1940. It could claim to have been the great city's newspaper of record for the time. The archives were very complete. David had concentrated on late 1936 and the first half of 1937. Reportage on local developments in the neighborhoods and the police blotters revealed nothing meaningful, other than a few witnesses reported odd assaults and altercations and some incidents involving different types of motor vehicles.

It was proof of nothing but consistent with the results of his research at their morgue in Madrid and with efforts to sell off the gold in Paris. David continued to see Paris as the most convenient place for the Soviets to move the gold. It would have all been on the under. The Soviets would have avoided tainting the free market that they didn't believe in by disguising any glut on it.

Méndez Aspe would have to be the next step.

His dinner arrived. It looked like medallions of beef, not an organ dish after all. And it was a delight—almost an emotional experience.

After the plates were cleared away, "Perhaps a small dessert, monsieur? *Île flotante avec crème anglais? Pain perdu?*"

"*Pain perdu,* yes, Roland, just the thing."

Pain perdu. "*Lost bread*" thought David. *Goes with lost gold. Lost gold that may be found again. From clues here in Paris.*

❧

There was a pay phone in a poorly patronized Alsatian restaurant on the Boulevard Saint-Michel. Ideal, thought Barnickle, for calling in his report.

"He's just running around all over Paris," Nick began without preamble.

"You make him sound purposeless. Our boy's not like that. He's very intentional. *Where* is he going and *what* is he doing?"

Barnickle provided details. "Slipped over the border quiet as a mouse."

"Doesn't want anybody to know he's left Spain. When he comes back in, he'll sneak in. No one will know he's back. When he's not seen around Madrid, people are going to think he's left for good. That's my guess anyway. Room 11 is not gonna be happy. What else?" Isham demanded.

"He went out to the high-rent district—what they call Passy." Barnickle made exaggerated emphasis on the last syllable—/Pa*seee*./ "They oughta call it 'Pan*seee*' if you ask me, what with all these limp-wrists here."

"Nick, the Company could feature you in an 'Ugly American' training film—how *not* to act while abroad. What happened next?"

"He was in a ritzy building over there for quite a while. Interesting, he went in empty-handed but came out with some kind of a large folder or an envelope maybe."

"Ah, the widow Negrín. That's good. And?" Isham blurted out.

"The widow who?"

"The Widow Nobody-to-you, Nick. Need to know, buddy. What else did he do?"

"Spent some time in a building on rue de Rennes. I looked at the tenant board. Looks like the Spanish Communist Party's office is in there," Nick said.

"He found that butcher Portillo. Pinko blackguard that one."

"Black what?"

"Blackguard, Nick. Fancy word for a contemptible scoundrel. Portillo's the leader of the Spanish Communist Party in exile."

"Yeah, there's commies all over around here. I can smell 'em—even more than I can the rest of these Frogs," Barnickle agreed.

Isham sighed. "You'll never learn. What else?"

"Spent the afternoon in a newspaper over near Montparnasse. Then he went and ate alone at some dive here in the Latin Quarter. Keeping faithful to his little Spanish chickpea, looks to me like."

"It's *chickadee*. A chickadee is a cute little bird. A chickpea is a garbanzo bean. Shit, Nick, where did you go to school?"

"California. Oakland, to be exact. Public schools all the way. So what?"

"So, *what* I'm trying to do is account for your ignorance. You're such a rube. And why are you always talking about the girl. You in love with her too?"

"Uh, no." Nick got defensive.

"'Uh, no?' Well then, leave her out of it. She may be useful to us sometime. Anybody on to him?"

332 | DOUGLAS L. FIELD

"No, Jack, he's clean. At least so far."

"It won't last," Jack advised. "We don't have anything here yet either that anybody's on to him, but he's starting to tweak tails there. People are going to begin to wake up."

"Nobody interested in him yet."

"He's going to draw attention. You are to make sure that no one gets to him before he gets my story. Clear?"

"I'm *on* it."

"You'd better be. Go and have a Cinzano. On the Company. But stay awake."

∞

"Room 11."

"Federico? Jack Isham here."

"Yes, Jack. Nice to hear from you. What news do you have on our 'Project'?"

"He's in Paris. As we expected. Making the contacts we expected," Jack replied.

"Good then. Everything is going according to our plan." Sáenz seemed satisfied.

"So far, but I expect him to pick up trouble. He will need protection soon enough. The resources you have committed may need to be deployed." Isham accorded unaccustomed deference.

"Very well. You and the inspector are in contact?" Sáenz accepted it.

"Yes."

"Then all will be well," Sáenz stated.

"Should be. If the Project survives. He is in danger of awakening what, from extensive experience, I know to be practiced and deadly actors. Assuming he does survive, I expect him to try to disappear and infiltrate himself back into Spain unnoticed." Jack maneuvered for a little wiggle room.

"His survival is nonnegotiable. We have made that clear. What is the level of danger that we lose him? The man you have on him, he is competent?"

"Completely, but there are no guarantees, Federico."

"Room 11 has full faith in you, Jack. I hope that extends to your man." Sáenz hung up, dispensing with the usual formalities.

CHAPTER 53

Paris: Wednesday, August 28, 1963

It cost David some time to locate Méndez Aspe.

Unlike María Frankman, he did not advertise his presence at 48 rue du Temple. The concierge in that building was a tomb.

"Good morning, Monsieur." David offered his most ingratiating smile. "I'm looking for a gentleman by the name of Méndez Aspe. A mutual acquaintance tells me he lives in this building. May I know which flat?"

"I do not know this name," came the terse reply.

"Surely you do. A Spanish fellow, tall, approximately seventy."

A vacuous expression.

"I see on your marquee that there are several flats with no occupant listed. Which is his, Monsieur?"

'The residents of this building are responsible for maintaining their marquee. If this person whom you seek does not appear, then I think the conclusion is plain. He does not live here. Good day to you, sir."

David reached in his pocket for some paper money while holding the concierge's eyes. He peeled off and offered a 500-franc note. The conflict that registered in the man's face confirmed Méndez Aspe's residence in the building, but David's offer remained unaccepted.

"He lives here, sir." David gave him a little sneer. "Thank you for your cooperation. I'll tell him when I see him."

There was a sidewalk café across Temple from number 48's portal. There David had a convenient and natural vantage point from which to await and observe his quarry's appearance.

When Méndez failed to appear during the first morning of David's stakeout, David needed a new plan. He investigated the refugee organization that María Frankman had told him her husband and Méndez had founded. Its latest iteration had high-end offices on the rue Marignan off the Avenue des Champs-Élysées. David went there.

At the far end of the second floor, its space was behind a polished wood door with a large, frosted-glass insert, the name calligraphed in both French and Spanish. The waiting room was appointed with posh furniture and expensive carpets. There was money coming in from somewhere—lots of it.

"Mr. Fordham to see Monsieur Méndez Aspe," David said in Castilian to the French receptionist who sat behind a substantial counter.

She shrugged and said in French that she did not understand him. He suspected that her inability with Spanish was freshly discovered.

David switched to French.

"Monsieur is not in, I'm sorry," she said flatly.

"When will he return? I'll wait."

"Impossible. It will be some time. He has gone abroad."

"How long? Please make me an appointment."

"Monsieur keeps his own calendar."

"Abroad? When does he return?"

A shrug.

336 | DOUGLAS L. FIELD

"May I speak to his assistant, his secretary?" David clicked up the urgency.

"Ah, but he has none."

As he stood talking to the receptionist, he could see into what appeared to be individuals' rooms deeper into the office. They looked to be occupied, messy, and in daily use—not tidied up for a lengthy time away.

"Have you a brochure that describes the society's activities—should I wish to avail myself of its services?"

"Aucune."

"Can you provide me with audit reports submitted to your directors, government agencies?"

A slight shake of her head. She didn't even look up.

The conversation was not a total loss. It confirmed Méndez Aspe worked there. David did not believe the man was abroad. That he was on a fundraising tour for destitute Spanish refugees from twenty-five years ago David thought implausible.

David remained confident that Méndez Aspe was in Paris. It was obvious he would not be cooperative. David prepared himself that the man would have to be confronted—bluntly. David sifted through his memory. What was it one contemporary observer had said? "His health was always something very serious. He was a very nervous man." Hadn't Manuel Azaña in later years described him as incompetent and a morphine addict? Not an unbiased witness, Azaña, but if it was true, Negrín might have been writing the scrip.

David went back to his café observation post on rue du Temple thinking he had some good stuff if he could just catch the man.

During the afternoon, he must have observed the comings and goings of every single resident of the building—except one, the one. Into the late afternoon there was no joy.

He occupied part of his time writing a letter to Ariel. It was short and terser than he liked. He intended it to be opened by the Cuerpo. It said he was safe and working along well on his project, but that completion would be delayed. Ariel would know that was not so. He mentioned planning to visit Roman ruins in France. He knew that she would read that as confirmation of the Segovian aqueduct date.

He had bought the airmail postage earlier in the day and addressed the letter, adding his name and return address on Vallehermoso. As a finishing touch, he affixed a large and colorful "Par Avion" sticker, hoping the watchers would not miss it. He then wrote a series of ten more letters to Ariel, all of them reporting to her notional activities of his in and around Paris—all of which would be posted at various intervals going forward.

෪

Not long after dark, David spotted a lanky and stooped figure coming down Temple from République. David jumped to his feet and maneuvered fast to get close enough to confirm it was Méndez.

David managed to fall into step next to and slightly behind the man. The Spanish exile appeared much older than in Mrs. Negrín's photo, but it had been twenty-five years. Bald now, the long, narrow, and burdened face had grown thicker. He wore rimless glasses with octagonal lenses. But the skepticism, the raised eyebrows, the perennially pursed lips, and the pointed chin were still evident. The living and breathing embodiment of a seventeenth-century Spanish grandee, Méndez was unmistakable.

"*Monsieur le Directeur Général*, or should I say *Señor Director General*? How are you this evening?"

After trying hard to ignore David failed, "Who are *you*?"

"A friend of Don Juan Negrín."

"He's dead." Méndez regarded David as he might dirt on one of his shoes. "Besides, you're too young."

338 | DOUGLAS L. FIELD

"Not for his legacy. How do you think I found out all about you? Learned your address?"

"María! ¡*Zorra!* Bitch!" Méndez pulled his key from a front pocket, "A pleasant evening to you, young sir."

"Not so fast, Francisco. I've had you under surveillance for two days. I know everything you've been doing." David exaggerated. "Let's go across the street and have a cognac. My observations have raised a few questions. They won't take long."

"I have no answers for you. There would be no point."

It was time to bully him. "I think you do. I know who you are. I know where you sleep. I know where you work. I've seen with my own eyes that your circumstances are anything but impoverished. Where's the money coming from, Francisco? I know about SERE and the new agency too. I was over there just today. Nice place."

Méndez's face remained passive, but David thought he saw a tinge of concern in the eyes. David went for broke.

"How are you feeling, Francisco? How's your health? How are the nerves? Stomach holding up? OK? Azaña thought you had a questionable relationship with certain, shall I say, medications? Is that so? Who's writing the prescriptions for you now, Francisco? I can find out. Come on across the street."

David took him by the arm. He jerked away. Their eyes locked. Méndez waivered. More fear in the eyes. The man's fear prevailed. He followed David.

They went into the café. David walked up to the zinc bar. "A couple of Remys," he said to the barman.

They came. "My treat," David said. Snide. "I'm interested in the gold, Francisco."

"So's everybody. So what? And who are you that I should discuss that topic in the impossible event that I had any information about it?"

David produced his credentials. They were received with the withering and unspoken combination of disdain, derision, and dismissal that is achievable only by a Spaniard of one of the upper classes.

Then he flipped out María Frankman's photo. "Look. Here you are with Dr. Negrín and the Russian. I'm looking into the disposition of the gold, Francisco. You were in on it. You know about it. It's a lot of money. The Spanish people deserve to know. You know where it went, and you're going to tell me."

"The Spanish people, who tolerate the current regime, deserve nothing—nothing from me. In any event, I know no more than what can be read in any of the many histories of the time. Some of it came here. The rest went, under the direction of Negrín and Largo Caballero, to Moscow for safe keeping and to pay for military equipment and supplies."

"Not good enough. What accounting was there? Is Spain owed any refund? Where is the physical gold located now?"

"These are questions that have been asked over the years since the end of the war. They are questions that have never been answered. I'm afraid I cannot help you."

"I think you can help me. And as we discussed just now in the street, you have much incentive to do so."

"*¿Y me quisieras chantajear?* (And you would seek to blackmail me?) Go ahead. I have nothing to tell you. Nothing to lose." Familiar form of address. Condescending. Hubris now outweighed fear. Hubris calculated to put David down.

And so it went for twenty minutes. David brought up the refugee agency again. "I know you are connected there. It's the wellspring from which all blessings flow for you. Consider the potential consequences of an exposé in my paper of you and it and your activities. You bagged out at the end of the war and fetched up here in Paris. Been living in the lap of luxury ever since. How would the French government react?"

"I have no fear of that," Méndez spat back.

"Bullshit you don't. You can't afford to lose that gig. Then there's the matter of how you not only gathered up the gold and sent it out of

340 | DOUGLAS L. FIELD

Spain but also raided all the vault boxes of your fellow citizens. You seized their gold holdings and jewelry and valuables. Lots of those people are still around. They remember. They'd love to have a piece of your ass, Francisco. Tell me what I want to know!"

Méndez's face darkened, filled with malevolence, but he said nothing.

David pressed on. "It's even worse, Francisco. I've seen the Soviets' formal receipt. They got 7,800 cases. Witnesses say there were 7,900 cases; 100 cases are unaccounted for. That's about seven thousand kilos of gold, some nine million francs worth. It's the money, Francisco. It's your soft lifestyle here in Paris. You haven't been back to Spain. Nobody in Madrid's living like you are. You stole their stuff. It's your, how shall I call them, predilections. It's the move to England. How do you think British immigration—"

Méndez stood up. He had had enough. "I'm leaving. You do what you must." He favored David with a look of pure hatred. "I give you one word—one word only. The word is *moscardeaux*." And he was gone.

❧

The agent at the Spanish desk at Moscow Center was having a quiet night. Just after 23:50, the encrypted phone rang.

He picked up. "Spain desk."

"Paris embassy."

"Ready. Say on."

"We have reliable reports of contacts by an American journalist with at least two Spanish *prominentes* here—individuals in the post-civil war refugee community."

"Reliability level?" asked the agent in Moscow.

"High. Phoned in direct by a Spaniard called Portillo. Chairman-in-exile of the Spanish party. Not the first time we've had contact with him," Paris said.

"I'll kick it up the line."

"Tell them Portillo asks for elimination."

"Got it. In the interim, place this individual under immediate surveillance. Ascertain identity and intentions. Further instructions will follow."

CHAPTER 54

Paris: Thursday, August 29, 1963

David was awake early.

He went up to the Parc Saint-Séverin's little rooftop café for croissants and a fine morning view of the rooftops of the Latin Quarter.

Moscardeaux had occupied the rest of his previous evening. Nothing had come up in any of the Paris telephone directories, maps, dictionaries, business guides, or other sources he'd accessed. Was this a person? Place? Thing? Appellation? By morning, moscardeaux remained a mystery.

Now he sought to organize his prospective research for the day. The discussion with Méndez had centered on the gold. David reasoned those persons, places and locations involving precious metals and gems should have priority.

He started with a couple of swanky jewelry shops in the Place Vendôme, first Jaubalet and then Boucherone. No one knew moscardeaux or could associate it with anyone or anything. Perhaps monsieur should check with the Prefecture of police. David did not want to do that yet. It would draw all kinds of bad attention. He would leave that as a last resort.

He tried Delfine Pariente. His discussion with the very efficient and terse manager there yielded the same fruitless result as before. He noticed a young woman, an underling, standing by the side at a display counter, attempting to be unobtrusive but also to overhear his conversation.

David turned to leave the shop. The officious manager bustled into the rear. On David's way out, the front door the girl gave him a fetching smile and said aloud, "Bon jour, monsieur." Then at a volume intended for him only to hear, "Try the rue Vivienne."

David thanked her and hurried out to find a Métro. He went down. A big map of the city hung in the ticket hall. He found it over by the Palais Royale. He could walk just as fast.

Once there, the reason for the girl's gratuitous tip was obvious. Numerous coin dealers and numismatists. He rebuked himself for not having recalled sooner that much of the Spanish gold had been in coin.

He decided to pick a shop and start. The door was locked. He could see someone inside. His knock was greeted by a dismissive wave. Go away. He tried several more locations. The response was always hostile—or uncomprehending, or both. Among those he could get to talk to him, no one recognized "moscardeaux." It became clear to David that this was a district where you needed to be known to do business, much less get a hearing. Here, he was painfully unknown.

When it became evident to one shopkeeper who did open to him that David was not a buyer, the man started to shut the door in his face. David was at the point of losing patience and hope. He gave a pleading look. "What is moscardeaux?"

A low and reluctant growl in reply, "Vokárny." The door then shut tight in his face.

David felt deflated. One mystery had led to another. Now what was "Vokárny?" An odd word. A name?

344 | DOUGLAS L. FIELD

He walked up toward the Bourse and decided to sit down and have a beer. Both the sun and the humidity were high. The sky had turned white. It was what he called Missouri weather. He asked the patrons near him if they knew Vokárny. None did.

The waiter bustled up sweating. "Oui, Monsieur?"

"*Bière pression*," the waiter started off. "Oh," David said loudly toward his back, "do you know a Vokárny in this area?"

The waiter turned and pointed up the street.

"Cancel the beer." David said as he stood. He left a couple of small bills.

It was a typical Parisian shop, across the street from the café—wood facade, gold letters over hunter green. "Monnaies Vokárny."

The shop was dark, the door locked. He knocked once. No response. Then insistent rapping. A smallish man of around forty in a gray smock answered.

"Are you Vokárny?"

"Alas, no. He is deceased." The little man's countenance saddened for a second. "Six years it is now."

David's disappointment was palpable. "Did you know him? Does he have family?"

"May I know the reason for your inquiry, sir?"

David explained, succinctly and quickly. He concluded by describing the "moscardeaux" clue.

A look of puzzlement came over the little man's face. "'Moscardeaux is neither a place nor a thing, my dear sir. *I* am Moscardeaux—Raoul Moscardeaux. I have taken over this shop after Henri's, that is Monsieur Vokárny's, death."

David extended his hand. "I'm very happy to have found you. It has been something of a search."

Moscardeaux's handshake was European. The palm was soft and damp, no return grip, more of a quick touching.

"Are you aware of the Spanish gold?

"*Évidemment,*" said the little man raising his eyes toward the store's sign.

"Is there any way of knowing whether Mr. Vokárny was aware of it?"

Another customer came up and glided past them and into the interior. He was male, wearing unremarkable clothing, maybe not Parisian.

Moscardeaux said after him, "*Un instant, Monsieur.*"

Moscardeaux turned away from the door, leaned out past David, and peered into the street.

"I may have a small amount of information for you, but not here. Not now," he whispered almost in David's ear. "If you would be willing to meet me for supper?" He seemed nervous and furtive.

"Of course, of course," David blurted out. He regretted being overanxious, but he couldn't help it. "Where? What time?"

"Over in Saint-Germain des Prés. Aux Charpentiers, on the rue Mabillon. You know it?"

"I'll find it."

"*Bon.* Nine o'clock this evening. It's Friday. There will be a crowd. That's good for our purposes. I'll get us in."

"Perfect."

"Until later then. It may not be wise for you to be seen here. You should leave now."

CHAPTER 55

Moscow: Thursday August 29, 1963

It was by now late Friday night in the Russian capital.

They were working overtime in the Lubyanka Building at Dzerzhinsky Square. Formerly known as NKVD and then MVD, KGB, the Committee for State Security was this night, as always, on high alert. At the direct authorization of KGB Chairman Vladimir Yefimovich Semichastny, Colonel Boris Vucetitch had convened a working group to address the intelligence coming in from Paris.

"Who is it, Pavel Leonidovich, that is keeping us here after hours? What is he doing?" Vucetitch asked his chief of staff.

"An American. One David Langston Fordham, associated with the *International Herald Tribune* newspaper. Looks like a freelancer. He is a longtime resident of Spain. No known connection with the Primary Opposition. We think he's looking into the question of the Spanish gold reserves that were sent here in 1936 as payment for the material assistance that the Soviet Union afforded the duly constituted Spanish Republican government in its struggle against the forces of fascism.

MOSCOW GOLD | 347

The fascist Francisco Franco needs the money. Thinks its removal from Madrid was wrongful. Wants it back."

"Why is this a problem?"

"Probably isn't. This issue has been raised from time to time ever since the capitulation of the legitimate Spanish government in early 1939. It is typical for there just to be talk. Then the controversy boils down after a while. We don't particularly care."

"Then why are we being kept here late?"

"The amount in question is substantial to say the least. Roughly $20 *billion* US at current rates of exchange. While we would countenance no claims whatever relative to it, it is thought best to head inquiry off—avoid scandalous allegations, sensational media reporting."

"And what has our Mr. Fordham to do with any of this?"

"He is an investigative journalist. He has contacted the widow of the last Spanish Republican Prime Minister, Juan Negrín; one Francisco Méndez Aspe, Negrín's finance minister; Santiago Portillo, chairman of the Spanish Party; and several of the French coin dealers through whom we sold the gold, which it turns out was almost all in coin."

"How close is he to discovering details that could be prejudicial to the Rodina?"

"We do not know that. He seems to have gotten rather further along in his investigations than those who have gone before him."

"Does anyone else have any comment?" Vucetitch addressed this question to the entire group.

Silence.

"Has Gospodin Fordham any associates, collaborators in his investigations?"

"None that we have identified."

"Well, let's get to the point, comrades. Am I wrong that our most convenient and efficient course of action is to arrange for this gentleman to have an unfortunate accident?"

Again silence.

348 | DOUGLAS L. FIELD

"I hear your vote to be unanimous in favor then. Pavel Leonidovich, you are authorized to advise Paris. Thank you, gentlemen, for staying late. Have a restful weekend. Our comrades in France will not."

Polite but restrained laughter accompanied the gathering of their things and their departure from the conference room.

CHAPTER 56

Pullach: Friday, August 30, 1963

At five foot four and one hundred forty-nine pounds, the sixtyish German gentleman would not have been thought by any definition to be imposing.

He wore an expensive Savile Row suit, a very Teutonic homburg, and heavy spectacles with the darkened lenses de rigueur those days in Europe. Without the hat and glasses, he had a very high forehead and a close-cropped mustache. His hair was straight, thinning, and combed straight back, insufficient to offset his quite prominent ears.

Yet this unassuming little man stood at the epicenter of postwar West German power and prominence. Reinhard Gehlen was president of the BND, the Bundesnachrichtendienst, or Federal Intelligence Service. The BND was the direct descendent of the German eastern military intelligence agency, which agency then Wehrmacht Major General Reinhard Gehlen had headed. At the end of World War II, Gehlen had contrived to be taken into custody by the US Army. He'd demonstrated his value as an intelligence professional, was spirited into the United States under the alias "Hans Holbein," and was debriefed at length.

In 1946 and with the consent and assistance of what would very soon become the Central Intelligence Agency, he set up the Gehlen Organization, or "the Org." Therewith, he became the CIA's principal eyes and ears in the Eastern Bloc. Gehlen and the Org recruited from the former German security services, including many operatives of Admiral Wilhelm Canaris's counterintelligence agency, the Abwehr. In 1956, the CIA loosened its control over the Org. It became the BND. Gehlen was still at the helm.

The BND's headquarters were established in the south Bavarian village of Pullach, hard by the Austrian frontier. Pullach is a pretty town of wide, treelined streets with pale yellow buildings and terra cotta tile roofs. There are numerous churches with high white steeples or copper clad *Zwiebeltürme*. As he walked back to his office late on this summer's evening, Reinhard Gehlen found Pullach and the rest of his current circumstances acceptable and agreeable.

Before he had gone to dinner, preliminary reports were coming in from his sources inside the KGB that it was on to and concerned about an American nosing around Paris into the old Moscow Gold controversy. He went into his office and placed the Homburg crown down on his side table.

Gehlen's aide-de-camp was alert to his chief's return and came in right away with an update.

Before the young man could speak, Gehlen said, "Nothing like a good hat, Johann. Never pinch the crown. Always handle by the brim *and* always set a good hat down on its crown. *Was hast du für mich?*"

'The Soviets are moving forward, *mein General*. They don't want any more details on the gold surfacing. They've ordered a wet operation on the American. Priority soonest."

"Very well, Johann. Alert the Americans. And find Sepp."

Gehlen settled in to review a stack of cables and reports. Soon, there was a hearty knock at his door. Josef Staupitz, the late Agent Alois

352 | DOUGLAS L. FIELD

and now deputy director of Intelligence-Western Europe in the BND, appeared with a sly smile. Staupitz was still fit and trim. He looked very little different than he had during the war. The dark hair was flecked with gray. That was all.

Gehlen looked up, a hint of conspiracy, "*Komm herein*, Alois. How goes the battle?"

"Swimmingly as our English brethren would say, Herr Holbein, swimmingly. KGB's a bit of an ogre, but I think I've got it worried!" They enjoyed a chuckle. Both gloried in using their old code names and reliving their wartime exploits.

Gehlen explained the Paris situation in detail. Then he gave his orders. "Sepp, I have tipped off the CIA. Had to. They have KGB penetrated and may already know. To maintain trust, CIA must hear from us too. Protecting *our* interests in the gold is not changed. Those accounts and deposit boxes are *German*—bought and paid for by the Abwehr, as you, of all people, know." One eyebrow lifted in irony.

Gehlen continued. "KGB may eliminate this American. Regardless, we will be vigilant as to *our* interests. Put your best people on it. You go if needed. That gold belongs to *us*—the security services. We have always preserved and defended it, with complete success so far. We, you and I and many others like us, may someday need it. We will continue that tradition, *nicht wahr?*"

"Absolutely, General. Consider it done."

CHAPTER 57

Paris: Friday evening, August 30, 1963

"Jack? You there? This is Nick."

"Nick, good job you called. Quick. What have you got?"

"The game just changed—lightning quick."

"What changed?"

"It's the Ivans," Barnickle said, breathing fast. "They're on to him now. All of a sudden. They have a whole operation going. It came up in the blink of an eye. They're consistent in their operational tactics. This is more than surveillance. Looks like a black op."

"Has he tumbled to it?"

"Not yet. He won't. They're real good at it. They don't fool around, Jack. We're out numbered here."

"Good work, Nick. I'm picking up the same information from the Germans. What's he doing?"

"He went over to the area of town where all the coin dealers are. He visited several, but it was short each time—like he wasn't getting what he wanted. Anyway, he talked for a brief time to one last shopkeeper

MOSCOW GOLD | **355**

and then left. Now he's over in Saint-Germain des Prés. Looking for some address, I think."

"OK. Nick, this just got serious, real serious. We agree that the Russkies are looking at extreme prejudice here. Stay in touch. I'll send the cavalry."

"Hurry."

"We need to get to him first, Nick. We need what he has. It's a race now."

⁓

The rue Mabillon doesn't run into the Boulevard Saint-Germain. It's close, but you need to take a short jog on the rue du Four. Mabillon's hard to find. Add to that that Aux Charpentiers's outdoor sign is understated. David was having a little difficulty locating the restaurant.

But he did find it in due time. Understated or not on the outside, inside, it was crazy busy. Moscardeaux had been right. It was Friday night. It seemed like most of the 6th Arrondissement was in the place.

Raoul, good to his word, had arranged a table and was waiting for David. "You found it. And me. *Splendide*. How about a kir?"

"Perfect choice, yes."

Moscardeaux signaled the waiter. David looked around the dining room. It was packed to the gunwales with patrons. There were polished wood tables and red leather upholstered chairs, a big fireplace on one wall, several large inlaid pieces of intricate marquetry furniture set around to juice up the *ambiance*. Aux Charpentiers. The Carpenters. That should have been obvious.

David's drink came. "I chose this place," said Moscardeaux, "because, while I cannot guarantee that we will not be seen here, I can guarantee that we will not be heard. The subject matter is delicate, as I indicated earlier. What is your investigation all about?"

David responded in detail. Moscardeaux listened without any interruptions or questions.

356 | DOUGLAS L. FIELD

"What is the motivation of your editor in instructing you to look into this topic at this particular time?"

"He thinks the Franco government has money problems. Believes that, if they could get a line on the gold, it would lift their prospects on the world markets, so to speak. He says that, after the big rapprochement between Spain and the United States in the fifties, Spain is a friend. He would like her to succeed more and better. That's what he tells me anyway."

Moscardeaux took off his glasses. He surreptitiously removed a handkerchief from his pocket. He daubed his eyes, turned away for a second. Then he polished his glasses.

"Contributing to the advancement of Spain and the Spanish people is something that I, too, am interested in—intensely. I appreciate, no, share your editor's sentiments. May I recount to you a story?"

"Of course. I'm a newspaperman. I live for stories."

"Well then. To begin, my precise given name is not Raoul Moscardeaux. I have changed it to facilitate my life here in Paris. My true name is Raúl Moscardó. I am Spanish."

He switched languages, "Castilian is better for the telling of the story, no? I was born in Madrid in 1922. My father was General José Moscardó."

David was stunned. "I know the story. Everyone in Spain does. Then Colonel José Moscardó e Ituarte, holed up for seventy days in el Alcázar, the Citadel in Toledo. Right after the civil war started. Had, what, 1,600 people with him? They suffered immense privation. Waiting for Franco to relieve the siege. When he wouldn't surrender, they arrested his son—your brother, of course."

"My brother Luis," Moscardó confirmed and continued the story. "He was sixteen. My father asked to speak to Luis. They let him. Father told him, 'Commend your soul to God and die like a patriot, shouting, "Long live Christ the King" and, "Long live Spain."' It is thought that my brother was executed that day. We learned later that his death was not accomplished until about a month later."

MOSCOW GOLD | 357

"Franco redirected his assault on Madrid to relieve the Alcázar. Your father became a hero, was made general. But that would have been small comfort," David commented.

"It was a double tragedy," Moscardó said. "Later military analysis has agreed that the distraction of relieving the siege in Toledo in July, August, and September 1936 allowed Santiago Portillo and the Junta de Defensa time to reinforce Madrid. The Caudillo's attack on the capital in November was blunted. The opportunity that we had for a short war was lost."

Raúl's telling of the story was enthralling. David asked, "So you were in the Alcázar during the siege?"

"No. My other brother Roberto, also older, and I went with our mother to Burgos, where we were more secure. Then after the siege, my father sent me here to Paris, where, it was hoped, I would continue to be safe. I became apprenticed to Henri Vokárny late in 1936 and was with him until his death."

"Why have you never returned to Spain?"

"I became settled in Paris. The adolescent years are impressionable. The life of France was indelibly stamped on me at a tender age. My life is here. I have never felt the desire to leave."

"I sympathize." David understood. "I went from Missouri to Madrid at the age of fifteen. Madrid's branded on my whole nature. Can't imagine that ever changing."

"Thank you for allowing me to tell the story. I don't often get the opportunity."

"Will it offend you if I ask a couple of questions about the gold?"

"On the contrary, I am in full support of your editor's sentiment that additional information about it can only help Spain, anti-communist Spain. That I am disposed to do. I'm sure you comprehend," Raúl said.

"I assume Vokárny bought gold from the Soviets?"

"Yes. We and the several other coin dealers in the rue Vivienne and the rue de Richelieu bought up the Russians' stock. It took a period of months—in the spring and early summer of 1937."

358 | DOUGLAS L. FIELD

"What happened to the gold after the coin dealers acquired it?"

"There were buyers. For example, there were two brothers. They pretended to be Swiss. They had an inexhaustible supply of funds. Bought most all the coins we could get from the Russians. I was in the shop at times they came in. Henri would detail me to run various errands. I was just a fifteen-year-old kid. I did know enough to know that they were very serious men. Their demeanor was one of veiled threat. They would ask incisive and probing questions. Henri found himself at pains to dissemble." Moscardó could see by David's expression that this was critical information.

"Did they patronize other dealers?"

"I imagine that they did. My personal suspicion was that they were not Swiss but German. Henri thought so too. Secret service types we thought. Distasteful perhaps, but we were in business. We had stock; they had money. What were we to do?" Moscardó shrugged.

"Was it ever determined what they did with the gold once they took possession?"

"Not clear. They never took possession in their individual names. They said they owned several companies. But they were reticent. For their part, the 'brothers' were curious about our sources for the gold. Henri equivocated on that. I recall that they, in response, discouraged him from concerning himself with the gold's ultimate destiny."

"Do you have more details as to whom else they patronized and what they did with their purchases?"

Raúl nodded. "Give me a day. As you may have apprehended when we talked at the shop, this matter is still sensitive and dangerous. After all these years. I get ominous inquiries, little attempts to intimidate."

"Like the guy who walked in when we were talking in the street?"

"He wanted to make some vague talk about American double eagles and British sovereigns. I had none on hand. He left."

"The very coins that comprised the majority of the Spanish holdings."

"You've done your research. Meet me again tomorrow afternoon at five. There's a small orangery in the Jardin du Luxembourg, in front of the Petit Luxembourg. Not the Musée de l'Orangerie. That's in the Tuileries. Luxembourg, do you know where I mean?"

"I'll be there. No one will know but us."

"Well then, enough of reminiscing! Let's order our supper?" He beckoned over their waiter.

CHAPTER 58

Saint-Cyprien: Sunday, March 12, 1939

Nacho was one of some 450,000 Republican refugees who crossed into France this month and last.

The French were unprepared for the onslaught. First, there were the women, the children, the elderly, and the infirm. Then there were the men of military age.

Nacho was unable to avoid captivity. He could not simply claim to be a Nationalist spy. He was surrounded by angry and defeated Reds. They would have killed him on the spot. Fear, hatred, and paranoia ran so high among the Nationalists that, even if he got back into Spain, the chances of his proving his claim before he was shot were slim. The French were not sympathetic to anybody's claims about anything.

He would have to suck it up and bide his time.

Detainee No. A-62541-01 sat on his haunches by the wire and watched the camp awaken. There was little routine here. Even less on a Sunday. A warm and humid sun was rising over the Mediterranean. With it came the antipodal prospects of some drying and the hatching of hordes of mosquitoes and sand fleas.

"How many?" A prisoner sitting on the sand next to Nacho posed the question.

"Same as always. Got to be. It never changes. Around a hundred. So says Laurent, anyway. I never counted."

The second man was small and wiry. If he had to, he could move lightning fast. He was good at getting in and out of small places. At Saint-Cyprien this could often be desirable. He was known as Nipi "el Gallego." His name may well have been Junipero as he claimed, but no one knew or cared.

"One day I think I'll count. Just for the record," Junipero said to Nacho as they looked out over the camp toward the sea.

Their conversation referenced the number of dead detainees overnight. There was dysentery and typhus. Detainees slept in groups of half a dozen or so out in the open but sleeping on the sand could kill. No matter the number of greatcoats and blankets prisoners slept on and under, they got wet from moisture below the surface. There was no turning to one side or the other. The cold wind would freeze the damp material. There were no huts, ramadas, or shelters. Pneumonia ran rampant.

This was the time of the morning during which patrols of Senegalese troops who guarded the camp went through it and collected the unfortunates who had not survived the night.

"What's the point, Nipi? It won't change anything."

The boredom was excruciating. All they had was talk.

Nipi changed the subject. "You at Teruel, Nacho?"

"Yeah. Campesinos."

"Me, too, with the 8th," said Nipi. "What happened to you after?"

"They sent me back to Madrid. Got my fingers and face fixed up. Frostbite." Nacho left it out that Cóndor decided, since the center of gravity of the war had moved east, Nacho should return to the Campesinos and continue to provide intelligence from within their ranks.

"Then the Ebro and then the retreat and then here?"

362 | DOUGLAS L. FIELD

Nacho nodded.

"Where'd you cross?" Nipi's reference was to the battle of the Ebro. After Teruel, the Nationalists had reached the Mediterranean. The Republic was cut in two. The Reds' last throw was an attack across the River Ebro to cut off the Nationalists east of Zaragoza, relieve Valencia, and sue for peace.

"Miravet. We had to ford. It was a holocaust. Sniper fire and artillery cut us to ribbons. We managed half a dozen miles south of the river and then were driven back. Had to swim back across. At night. Neary drowned. A waste."

"I missed the Ebro," Nipi said. "I was at Lérida. Fought that butcher Yagüe. We lost. After that, we were driven into retreat. Barcelona, Gerona, Figueras."

"Us too." Nacho shook his head. "We couldn't stop them."

"We fought all the way. I crossed at Port Bou. On February first. It was pitiful. There were miles and miles of us. Not only soldiers either."

"Tragic. Never forget it. Were you at Areglès-sur-Mer?" Nacho asked, not interested. Conversation was better than silence—for now, anyway.

"Nope. Always Saint-Cyprien. How was Areglès?"

"Not as bad as here. Wetland divided into big sections surrounded by barbed wire. Dryer than here. Food and water bad. Toilets primeval. Guards would come around and spray us with oil—for the lice and scabies. But here in St.-Cyp we got ninety thousand guys crammed into a mile and a half long by half a mile wide. We're between the sea and swamp. The wet is killer."

Nipi decided he had had enough conversation. "I have to go to Daladier."

"Don't fall in. I'll be here when you get back."

The camp had a latrine—of sorts. It was a long log suspended on poles under which the cleansing Mediterranean tide flowed in and out. About a year ago, the socialist prime minister of France, Léon Blum, had been succeeded in his post by Édouard Daladier. In mock

MOSCOW GOLD | 363

gratitude for the amenities provided by their French hosts and still resentful over the inability of the French government to have mustered any meaningful support for them during the war, the Spanish prisoners had dubbed their latrine "Boulevard Daladier."

After Nipi left, Nacho turned to refining the plan he was working on. He had to get out of Saint-Cyprien. One reason was Nipi. The other was that his life was in danger and not from the horrific conditions. The entire camp was defeated Reds. They knew there had been spies that had infiltrated their units. Spies were blamed for the unending losses. Vengeance was in the air.

Nipi's questions just now were innocent enough. Knowing Nipi. But others asked questions too. Nacho figured his cover was good for only so long. There were rumors of secret and summary courts-martial in the camp. A lot of people died every night. An extra one or two would never be noticed. It was time to go.

As to Nipi, Nacho had, in a manner of speaking, adopted the little Gallego. The camp was divided into large square corrals. Specified groups of prisoners were assigned to each. Nacho and Nipi had been in the same corral since the outset. They messed together, such as it was; slept in the same general vicinity; and wiled away the stultifying days in one another's company.

In recent weeks Nacho had detected what he thought was deterioration of Nipi's mental state. Nacho feared Nipi was becoming "wire happy." If so, there was danger he might do something rash to escape—something like charging the barbed-wire enclosure fence in broad daylight. It *had* happened. When it did, at best, the prisoner received brutal punishment. At worst, he was shot.

By the time Nipi got back, the mosquitoes were already swarming. "We make our move today, Nipi. We have to get out of this cesspool. I didn't survive the war to die in this French pesthole."

"If we get caught?"

"Good possibility of that, Nipi. Consider it well. My calculation is that, if we get caught and after they knock us about a bit, they'll shovel

364 | DOUGLAS L. FIELD

us off to Vernet-les-Bains. I've heard that Vernet is bad but not that much worse than here. It's worth the risk to me. I'm going."

"What's the plan, jefe?"

"Don't worry yourself about that. Just trust me. I've cleared it with Carmona. Be ready to move immediately that I say."

As Nacho had anticipated, Nipi didn't need to think it over much. "De acuerdo."

Nipi was crestfallen that he was not taken into Nacho's confidence, but he cared more about getting out of Saint-Cyprien than he cared about his ego, so he stuffed it. Nacho knew all about "need to know." At this point Nipi didn't need to know any details. Time would come soon enough for that.

There was an escape committee in the camp—if you could call it that. It was very loosely constituted. There were few resources that could be offered to would-be escapers. Carmona was the president of the committee. Nacho had told Carmona his plan details. Carmona offered two items of assistance. He agreed to lay on a diversion at the precise moment Nacho and Nipi needed it. And he gave Nacho a name—the name of a man in Perpignan. It was the best Carmona could do.

Over the course of the civil war, Nacho had acquired several skills. Some of them might be thought of as odd. Some were soon to be forgotten now that hostilities were over. Some of them had fierce practicality. By far the most useful avocation Nacho had developed was that of picklock.

Nacho's lock-picking mentor, with delicious and elegant irony, had been a quartermaster in the Popular Army. The two had spent hours of hurry-up-and-wait military idleness practicing this craft. As a result, Nacho had attained the highest degree of competency. The initial subject on his course syllabus was the design and mechanics of the most common locks in Spain. These were divided into dead bolt types that were typical on doors and cabinets and into padlocks. Most locks being used in Spain were of French design and manufacture.

MOSCOW GOLD | 365

The French devices were all vulnerable to frustration by a simple implement that was little more than an artfully bent wire. After understanding the construction and operation of common locks, Nacho had, under his teacher's close tutelage fashioned himself a set of picks. He took half a foot or so of eighth-inch thick wire, bent just under an inch on one end to close to a right angle but not quite. After that, he formed the opposite end into a triangular shape, like that of a common key supplied to open a tin of anchovies.

Hammering the business end flat and tempering it by heating to red-hot with immediate immersion in water finished the process. If absolute perfection was desired, a few grains of sugar could be sprinkled on the burning end. In that way, makeshift carbon steel was created. If necessary, some careful and judicious filing dressed up the finished product.

Before he was through, Nacho had a set of about half a dozen picks of various sizes and shapes. These were easy to conceal. Nacho always kept them with him and at hand. The hems and seams of clothing and even the folds of a forage cap were all ideal places for concealment. He even made one with a short shaft that, if he made a soft fist, nestled hidden inside the palm of his hand.

Nacho contrived never to be without his picks.

After understanding the operation of common locks and fabricating his tools, it was necessary to attain thorough proficiency in defeating any lock that he might encounter. This Nacho rehearsed, first at his leisure and then, as he got the feel of it, under self-imposed time pressure. When the practice of his new competence counted, he would need to perform under intense stress.

Nacho had put his training to profitable use during his time with the Campesinos. He'd developed a cool facility and built up for himself invaluable experience in varying conditions. His reputation and value to them as their scrounger had been enhanced by his display of his lock-picking skill—an added confirmation to a cemented and perfected cover.

As a refugee in France, he'd managed to keep his lock picks and preserve ready access to them.

The Senegalese guards operating under the direction of French officers at Saint-Cyprien were armed with machine guns to protect the wire and discourage unauthorized departure. Refugee camp duty was dirty and undesirable. No native French-enlisted troops were assigned to it. The African troops who were thus assigned resented it. They thought it discriminatory. In these conditions, it was no curiosity that, to a man, the Senegalese were subject to bribery and corruption.

Cigarettes were the currency of choice. An unopened packet of American Chesterfields was the equivalent of cash money—lots of it. Due in no small measure to his talents and experience, Nacho was, in camp terms, quite prosperous. He was able to trade for and acquire valuable quantities of smokes in excess of his own personal needs. On this day, he had expended some considerable capital among the Senegalese.

Saint-Cyprien was a slap-dash affair. It had been installed in a rush by an overwhelmed and overburdened French government. It was much improvised, including the security arrangements. The installation was oriented north to south in conformity with the run of the coast in that area. So far, there were no permanent buildings. At the north end, the French Army had set up a large administration tent. Behind it were tent barracks for the guard troops. The officers and other supervisory personnel were billeted a short distance away in the little coastal town that gave the camp its name.

The main gate was constructed of wooden poles at the north end of the prisoners' enclosure. For somewhat more security, the administrative tent was situated in the area between the main gate and an access road that led to the town and, thence, to the coast road to Perpignan. Anyone leaving the confinement area had first to pass through the main gate and then the administrative area and finally through a postern that gave out onto the access road. The administrative area functioned, in effect, as a large and elaborate sally port.

MOSCOW GOLD | 367

There were among the refugees a cadre of trusties who coordinated between the French administration and the inmates. It was accepted that, from time to time, trusty prisoners would be present in the administration tent. Of this phenomenon, Nacho had every intention to take advantage.

As it was Sunday, vigilance was down. Nacho made surreptitious preparations during the afternoon. There was a mammoth Senegalese sergeant known to everyone as le Géant with whom Nacho now made contact and who, as a result, palmed two unopened packs of American cigarettes. Nacho then told Nipi to gather his kit and to be near the main gate as soon as night had fallen. Until then, he was not to be seen with or have contact with Nacho.

The day wore wearily and mindlessly on—just like every other. It was the warmest day so far of Nacho's confinement. The insects made existence unbearable. Nipi stayed away as instructed. The sun got lower in the western sky and fell behind low trees and scrub that lined the swamp behind the camp. Dusk turned to night. Nacho sidled over near the main gate. Nipi approached as well. Nacho kept his attention directed toward the camp and away from the gate, although he inched nearer to it. He was gratified to see that Nipi was following his lead and was not looking at the gate.

As they watched, some loud and abrupt words were exchanged between two of the prisoners. Then there was overt shouting followed by shoving. Punches were thrown. Many prisoners moved closer to watch the fun. Fighting was prohibited. It could result in the loss of privileges. A number of prisoners stepped in to break the scuffle up. Their attempts did not have the intended result. The original antagonists turned their anger on the ones trying to separate them. General mêlée resulted. Carmona had been good to his word.

The guards on duty, cudgels and shillelaghs drawn, entered the fray. At the height of the brawl, Nacho beckoned Nipi to the gate where le Géant had stationed himself.

The huge man muttered to the gatekeeper, "They're trusties. Let them pass."

The gatekeeper was skeptical but knew better than to defy le Géant.

Nacho and Nipi were out of the main camp and into the administrative tent. Nacho, without running so as not to arouse suspicion but with great purpose, moved to the postern gate that led the rest of the way out of the camp.

"Nipi, watch our back. Le Géant is supposed to have this fixed for us, but he could guarantee at best a few seconds."

This was the critical moment. Nacho wiped sweating hands on his greatcoat. His favorite pick materialized. He would now need to exercise all his skill under sharp pressure. He threaded the pick into the keyhole. Locks were picked by feel. He closed his eyes. He could feel the force of the interior spring. He thought he had good contact with the dead bolt. Ever so carefully, he lifted the spring. *Don't drop it now, Nacho.* It dropped.

Nacho swore and wiped his forehead. He tried to dry his pick.

"The coast is clear, jefe, but hurry. They've almost got the fight cleared up."

Nacho started again. Again, the spring. He held his mouth just right. Lifting, lifting. Then, gently he rotated his pick. There it was! A soft click more felt than heard. The lock was defeated. He pressed down on the handle. They were through.

Nipi closed the gate, and they made off down the access road to the west. Within fifty yards, they disappeared into the darkness of the scrub line. Nacho began to have faint hope that they might make it.

"Where'd you learn to do that?" Nipi hissed as they moved along.

"It's a long story. I'll tell you later. I should have locked the door behind us. No time though. Figure that it'll be the gatekeeper himself who discovers it's unlocked. He'll just relock it. He raises any alarm, he just gets himself in trouble."

MOSCOW GOLD | 369

"Where are we going now?"

"Perpignan. I have the name of someone—on the marina. About five miles. If we have to, can you walk that far?"

Nipi looked at Nacho. "Pffft. Five miles. In my sleep."

CHAPTER 59

Perpignan: Monday, March 13, 1939

The two escapers melted into the darkness.

They arrived without delay at the coast road. Their escape from Saint-Cyprien had not been noticed. No alarm was sounded. No searchlights came on. The access road was a winding dirt track lined with thick vegetation. Hiding was never necessary. They slunk through the village and arrived, undetected, at the coast road.

Now a critical decision. Should they try to hitch a ride into Perpignan, or should they walk? Each alternative had its advantages and disadvantages. Catching a ride would be fast. They might have a benefactor drop them in the city very near their ultimate destination. They would minimize their time out in the open, along with their risk that some curious flic might take unwanted interest in them.

The camps that had been set up along the southeast French coast were controversial. So were the refugees themselves. Passions ran high in some circles in favor of and against both. It was a crapshoot whether whoever stopped for them would be sympathetic or hostile. Hitching

MOSCOW GOLD | 371

a ride would be an all-or-nothing proposition. Either they would be driven to where they needed to go or to the nearest gendarmerie.

Walking was anonymous. It avoided direct exposure to any locals. But it wasn't totally anonymous. Two scruffy men hiking toward Perpignan in the vicinity of the camps would be conspicuous. If they walked, every time they encountered a vehicle, a bicycle, or even another pedestrian, they would have to avoid being seen. And then they could do so only if they saw whoever they might come across in time—and then only if there was a place to hide.

The odds that they would encounter curious locals were high. Their time of exposure while walking would be long and worrisome. Many who they encountered would be indifferent or unaware, but it was probable that there would be numerous encounters, each one presenting potential risk.

Nacho explained their considerations and alternatives as they stood in the shadows on the verge. The coast road was an all-weather, two-lane highway over which, even on a Sunday night, the occasional vehicle passed.

"What's your poison, Nipi?"

"You know the old army saying, 'Never stand when you can sit, never run when you can walk, and never walk when you can ride.' Why walk if we can ride?"

Nacho had reached the same conclusion but based on what he hoped were more empirical justifications. "All right. You look a little less scary than I do. You'll step out and try to thumb a ride. Make sure it's big enough for both of us. If they stop, I'll step out. If they don't want to take us both, I guess they'll drive off."

"Sounds good, jefe."

Some time went by. It got cold. This was good. It explained the wearing of their heavy coats. The first car that passed was a two-seater Talbot. It went by at speed without stopping. *No doubt the local Comte. Drunk and headed home to the grande château from the arms of his paramour.*

372 | DOUGLAS L. FIELD

Next was a Citroën four-door, which also did not stop or even slow.

Another half hour passed. Nacho began to reevaluate. If they had to walk, they would need to get going.

Then rose the glow of headlights—not bright, but yellowish, an old car. Or one with a weak generator. When it appeared, it was not a car at all but an old Renault stake bed farm truck, narrow tires, coffin hood with no grille and an open cab. The backlite was small, about the size of a sheet of paper. Nacho had an idea.

"If he stops, Nipi, you get in and tell him you're going to the Perpignan marina. He's going slow. The engine is noisy. After he starts up again, I'll sneak out and hop into the bed. He won't notice, and I can keep an eye on him. I'll make sure he behaves."

Nipi nodded and looked at Nacho. His typical bravado was gone. Now there was fear in his eyes.

The old Renault came *poppity, poppity, pop, pop, pop* to a painful stop some way ahead of where Nipi was standing. He ran up to the cab. The driver was fiftyish. He wore a tweed jacket, heavy striped pants, and a sweat-stained broad-brimmed hat.

"You're out late, mon ami. Where you headed?"

As Nacho had instructed, Nipi hopped in without specific bidding. The driver goaded the flivver back into motion. Nacho padded after the moving truck. He grabbed hold of the tailgate at the left rear and swung aboard—slick and silent. He moved forward and crouched out of sight behind the driver.

"Boat dock. Perpignan."

"You didn't learn to talk around here. Where you from?"

Nacho had been afraid of this very kind of thing, but Nipi had an inspiration. "Portugais." Nipi's native Gallego was a language related and like Portuguese. That might explain his accented French.

"Long way from home, non?"

"Oui."

"Don't see too many Portuguese around here. Been here all my life. You must be the first one. Lots of Spaniards, though—with the

MOSCOW GOLD | 373

end of the war and all." He skewered Nipi with a fixed gaze that was penetrating even in the dark.

"Mmm."

After that, they rode along in silence for a couple of miles. Perpignan was inland from the coast. The driver soon turned off the coast road and headed west along the south bank of a long inlet called la Tét. Their destination was coming into view. The city was built around a prominent hill, atop which was a stone fort. Nacho could see the fort lit dim in light reflected from the city. *Almost there.* Nipi was not talking, which was unlike him. Nacho could see Nipi through the backlite but not the driver.

Now they were driving along the water. Nacho saw the masts of small boats in the harbor.

"And what, *jeune homme,* will you be doing at the yacht basin in the middle of the night."

"Meeting a guy."

"A guy? Who? I know most everybody around here."

"A guy with a boat." Nipi's answer lacked conviction.

"There's lots of guys with boats. Who?"

"Uh, name's Lucien," Nipi faked.

They were drawing up abreast of the boat harbor. It was lighted bright by the streetlamps and the boats themselves. Except for the racket of the old truck, though, it was quiet. There was no one about. It was well-lit but deserted.

"Lucien is it then? What are you and 'Lucien' up to tonight?"

"Going fishing."

"Fishing, my fat arse," said the driver. Just then, the pistol appeared—lightning fast—in the driver's left hand. Held very steady, it was leveled at Nipi's head. "You're no more Portuguese than I am."

Nipi was military. He knew all the common firearms. This was an FN GP 35—Belgian, Browning, black, and basic. A semiautomatic, it was small but with high power for its size and easy to operate.

Nipi tried to dissemble, distract. "Nice gun. A Browning, isn't it?"

"Yes, it is," sneered the driver, "and just how would you, Monsieur Hayseed from Portugal know that? You're Spanish Army is what you are. You're fresh out of one of the camps. Which one? Areglès? Saint-Cyprien? Saint-Cyprien, I'd guess. That's where I picked you up."

They were now starting to pass the boat harbor. "Let's just go around to the Hôtel de Ville. Poste de police over there. Then we'll get some ans—"

Bam! Bam! Bam!

Nacho battered the top of the cab. The noise reverberated and frightened. At the sudden sound, Nipi bailed out to the right. Driver got off one shot. Nacho jumped off the left side of the truck bed and punched the driver with all his power. He hit him hard on the left temple. Nacho felt the crunch of bone. Driver crumpled. Nacho scooped up the Browning. Then he lit out after Nipi, who had run back to the right, down towards the boats.

Nacho had lost sight of Nipi. Nipi would go for the waterfront. Nacho saw masts down a side street. He ran into it. He knew in an instant this was right. There were large splats of blood on the cobblestones, one about every ten feet. Nipi was hit and bleeding—a lot. Nacho caught up to him in a shadowed alley that ran off the quay.

"¡*Gilipollas*! The asshole shot me, jefe. I'm bleeding all over the place."

And he was. It was running down his left sleeve and now making a puddle on the ground.

"Get your coat off. Let me see." He had been shot clean through his lower left shoulder. "The bullet went clear through. That's good. We gotta stop the bleeding. Can you move your arm?"

Nipi raised it, grimacing, to about parallel with the floor. "That's good too. Maybe missed the bones."

Nacho ripped Nipi's shirtsleeve off and tried to pack some of it in the exit hole, the exit being the more severe. He wrapped it tight around Nipi's shoulder and armpit.

MOSCOW GOLD | 375

"Get your coat back on. Maybe it'll keep some pressure on the bandage. We have to find someplace to hide."

They moved down the quay. At least Nipi wasn't marking their trail any longer. After about three blocks, Nacho saw the sign. P. Guenard, Fournisseur d'Articles Navales. A ship chandlery. This was the showroom. There had to be a warehouse nearby. They went around the next corner. About half a block up was a weathered and dirty wooden door. It was big, like you could back a truck up to it. And it was protected by a stolid and impenetrable-looking hasp and lock.

Nacho's pick was out. He worked it as fast as he could. This device looked different, more impenetrable than the usual. But they were all the same. It had to work like all the others—had to. In the end, it did. Its size and appearance tried to disguise the fact that it operated, and was vulnerable, just like any other.

The old door slid rather than swung. There was the strong odor of hemp, tar, and mineral spirits. Their eyes adjusted. They were welcomed by large stacks of cordage, barrels, and cans. Shelves bent low under the weight of heavy merchandise.

'This is going to have to do for the moment, Nipi." Nacho slid the door closed. "How's the bleeding?"

Nipi shrugged his coat off. The makeshift bandage was saturated bloody. Nacho thought it was, nonetheless, slowing down a little. At least it was no longer dripping on the floor. Nipi said nothing. He was brave but in visible pain.

"What about the driver, jefe? He'll have got the cops. They'll be searching for us."

"Maybe not. Just as he shot at you, I kayoed him. Hit him as hard as I could. Right by his ear. Look at my hand." It was barked and swelling. "He was no longer conscious. I took the pistol." Nacho produced it out of his left greatcoat pocket. "There was a bad sound when I hit him. Something cracked. Don't know if it was him or me." Nacho regarded his right fist and opened it with difficulty. "May take him a long time to wake up. May even be dead for all I know."

Nacho thought it over for a minute. "If we're lucky, somebody will find him still out cold. No one will know to look for us until he comes around—if he ever does. By then, we're long gone."

Nacho had an idea. "They have medical kits on boats, right?" He found a light switch. Even with it on, the place was storeroom dim. He tried to determine the logic that had gone into organizing the warehouse. Before he got it figured, he found the medical kits with the signal flags and nautical charts. French logic! Nacho filched one.

Nipi started looking ashy. When Nacho poured disinfectant into the wound, the injured man convulsed, but never cried out. There were gauze pads and athletic tape. Nacho packed both ends of the wound and bound Nipi up tight. The remains of the kit, plus that of another, went into both of their deep coat pockets.

They arranged coils of rope into chairs of a sort. Both were able to sit and rest. Nacho killed the light. For the moment, he felt they were passably safe. His two looming unknowns were when the chandlery people would come to work and how he and Nipi would get out of Perpignan. He imagined they had three, three and a half hours.

Nipi had fallen asleep, and Nacho even dozed a little, but Nipi's stirrings and the throbbing of Nacho's hand kept him alert. Soon enough, he could see the beginnings of daylight through the warehouse's filthy windows.

"Nipi, wake up. How bad are you bleeding?" Nacho had a look. The bandages were wet, but pinkish. At least it wasn't bright red. "Let's leave it alone for now, sí? If we take it apart, we might start it up again. Soon as we find our ride, I'll redo it."

"Who's our ride?"

"Name's José. Has a fishing boat."

"Trust him?" Nipi's voice cracked. His mouth was very dry.

"What choice? Carmona does. That's all I got."

"When do we go?"

"Soon now. Can you walk? Gotta get out of here before any of the workers arrive."

MOSCOW GOLD | 377

Nacho got them back out on the quay. He relocked the slider. They went west under a bridge that appeared to carry a heavy volume of traffic across la Tét. Passing a café, Nacho went weak in his knees smelling the coffee. They needed something, but they had no money.

Past the bridge was a large city park that fronted on the inlet. It was out in the open, but there were not many alternatives. This would need everything Nacho knew about hiding in plain sight. They acted like a like a couple of old pals out for an early walk. At least it was cold enough to have their coats on.

The best Nacho could do was a pair of makeshift walking sticks that he harvested out of the thick foliage between the park and the water. Nipi sat on a bench with his stick held between his knees, while Nacho made expansive conversation doing broad gestures with his stick. From time to time, Nacho would do some mild stretching exercises.

Their everyday theatricals may have been persuasive from a distance, but all was far from well. Nipi continued to look very pale, even shading to gray. He was struggling to stay upright.

It developed into a quiet Monday morning. Those few who were out seemed to be occupied and intent on their own business. No one appeared to have disposable leisure time. No one noticed Nipi's distress.

But Nacho knew. Fear welled up in his chest. "This isn't going to work. We need to get you to a doctor. You are getting weaker."

"I'm fine. Go to the doctor, go to jail, Nacho."

"You've lost too much blood. You may get infected. I'll be blunt. You look like you're going to die."

'Then let me die. If we go to a doctor, we'll end up back in a camp. *No puedo más, jefe.* No more. I *will* die if I go back. I only *might* die here. I like my chances." Nipi was committed seeing their escape through.

"I'm not going to stand around and watch you croak."

"Jefe, promise me you won't let me go back."

There was a long silence.

378 | DOUGLAS L. FIELD

"¿Jefe? ¡*Júrame!*" (Swear to me!) Nipi pleaded.

Nacho groaned and stared at Nipi for a long time. "We're going to have to go. Every minute goes by, chances are Driver wakes up and the cops are on us." Nacho got Nipi up, and they moved slowly off.

❧

Nacho eased them over to the fishing fleet dock. Progress was slow and painful. Nacho feared exertion would make Nipi bleed again. They inched along. It was still early, but there were a few people about.

Nacho hailed someone on board the *Yvette*. "Capitán José Larrañaga?"

The answer was a thumb pointed farther down the dock. "*La Sirena.*"

Nacho helped Nipi move forward.

La Sirena. The Siren. A beautiful sea nymph, part woman and part bird that lures sailors to their destruction on the rocks and shoals by means of her seductive singing. The name was a stretch. *La Sirena*'s nymphean beauty consisted of a broad beam and flat bottom. She was very wet in any kind of a sea. What form and style she might ever have dreamed of was offset by a blunt bow, a plain and square wheelhouse, and awkward-looking fishing derricks gracing her unshapely flanks.

La Sirena was a working girl. Once she'd had a pretty white paint job with bright green rail and bumper strake. But that was all, by now, a sun-faded memory. The only song that came out of *La Sirena* was the rhythmic *thunk, thunk, thunk* of her tired old diesel.

Through *La Sirena*'s salt spray-abraded and cloudy windows, Nacho could see someone in the wheelhouse. As he and Nipi approached, the man went outside and stood by the rail.

"Looking for José," Nacho said almost under his breath.

"*Who's* looking for José?"

"Carmona," came the answer.

"St.-Cyp?" Larrañaga also whispered.

Nod.

MOSCOW GOLD | 379

Larrañaga looked around. Nobody else in evidence.

"Come aboard," ordered Larrañaga. He opened a door that led to a small cabin below the wheelhouse.

Once down below, he asked, "How much trouble you in?" He looked at Nipi, who was at the end of his string.

"My pal has a gunshot wound. Bleeding a lot. He needs a doctor. I hit the guy that shot him. Left him out cold in his truck up on the main street. I took the gun." Nacho pulled it out of his pocket.

"You're safe for the moment. Doctor's a problem. Too dangerous to take him to the doctor. Even if he comes here, can't guarantee he keeps quiet."

"Forget the doctor. I'm fine," wheezed Nipi.

"He's not fine," commented Larrañaga.

"No," agreed Nacho. "I tried to bandage him up. I think I slowed the bleeding."

There was an upholstered bench next to the bulkhead. Larrañaga found a life jacket. "He needs to lie down. He can use this as a pillow."

Nipi was soon asleep. Larrañaga and Nacho went up to the wheelhouse.

"I can take you to Spain tonight. Port Bou. Is that what you want?"

"That's what Carmona said," Nacho confirmed.

"Port Bou's best.," the captain explained. "It's just inside Spain but small, better than Palamós or San Feliu. Barcelona? No way. Port Bou was loyal to the very end. Lots of resistance still there. Most of the Republican armaments and supplies went in through Port Bou. All sorts of people there who know who's who, what's what, and how to act. Plus, it's nearest. What's with your friend here?"

"He insists on talking his chances." Nacho gave a rueful look. "Says he won't go back to the camps. Says, if he dies, he dies. Thinks he'll die anyway if he goes back."

"Trouble is, we can't leave till tonight." Larrañaga lamented. "Fleet never goes out during the day. Patrols would pick us up right away. May pick us up anyway. Then I have to get you down there and get myself back to reenter port with the rest of the fleet at dawn. If *La Sirena*'s not here, her absence will be noted and investigated."

"Why do you do this?" Nacho wondered.

"I'm Basque. I am looking for an independent Euskal Herria (Basque Country). This will never be realized unless Spain is wealthy and prosperous. Even then, it's a very complex matter. Even then, it may not happen. If Spain is war-torn and impoverished, she will never relinquish las Vascongadas. That much is sure. So, I do all that I can to promote Spain's recovery and prosperity. If that includes delivering able-bodied men back into Spain, well so be it. Besides, I get paid."

"You get paid? Who pays you?"

"Not sure. People connected with Juan Negrín and some of the others. Paris people. Some refugee society they set up. It's all very discreet—code names, all transactions in cash. If I get caught, there's no paper and no one for me to give up."

⁓

Larrañaga went ashore midafternoon. He told Nacho to keep himself and Nipi out of sight and to ignore anyone who might hail the boat or come on board. He gave them some food—his lunch that had been packed for him at home it looked like—and a couple of warm beers that he scratched up from someplace.

"Let's have a look at your wound," Nacho said after Larrañaga was gone.

Nipi moaned and tried to sit up. He needed help. He was pallid and clammy. The bullet wound looked bad. Nipi was not bleeding red blood anymore, but the wound continued to weep, and the ragged edges were angry and inflamed. Nacho bandaged him up again and sat back to wait.

"Hurts like hell, jefe."

"Yeah, you still need a doctor."

"We discussed that. Where's the captain?"

"Went ashore. Don't know where."

Hours went by. The sun settled low over the farmland behind Perpignan. Nipi slept in fits and starts. Larrañaga came back. He had another man in tow.

"This is Christophe, my deckhand. We sail. How's the patient?"

"Maybe the same. Maybe worse."

"Worse, looking at him. I promoted some pain pills for him from a tame doctor I have in town. Better get him started on them now."

Nacho took the proffered vial.

"Oh, and you two have called some attention to yourselves. Farmer from several miles south of here was found this morning knocked out in his truck. Has a skull fracture. Came around this afternoon. Says he picked up a suspected escapee down by St.-Cyp. Was taking him in when some other guy clocked him from behind. He guesses they both got away. I didn't hear anything about a pistol or anybody getting shot. I imagine the gun's not authorized, so the farmer hasn't mentioned it."

Nacho gave Nipi a couple of pain pills. His skin seemed warmer now, but he was very weak.

"Christophe, go and cast off." Larrañaga went up to the wheelhouse. After a series of strange whines, thumps, and grinds—her beating heart—*La Sirena's* redoubtable if superannuated diesel was urged to life. They motored out into la Têt. *La Sirena* did a sedate glide down the inlet. Other boats joined them in the stream.

Christophe came below. "There are controls at the three-mile limit. We are often boarded and inspected. I will need to squirrel you away for safekeeping."

He went to the fore part of the cabin and banged hard on the polished wood paneling. It came away and revealed a small compartment between the paneling and the outer bulkhead. The two fugitives sat inside, closeted by the reinstallation of the paneling. It was pitch-dark. The little space was without handholds.

"You'll be in here about an hour, maybe an hour and a half. We'll let you out as soon as it's safe. Enjoy your cruise, gentlemen." Christophe fancied himself something of a humorist. Nacho inferred that the immediate future would not be pleasant.

It wasn't.

At first, *La Sirena* rode easy on calm waters. After about twenty minutes she started to roll and soon hove to. Her engine stopped. She began wallowing. Nacho heard talking. Someone had come aboard. Larrañaga's voice was identifiable. There were two or three others, speaking French fast and colloquial. Nacho could understand only snippets. It sounded amiable. The sound moved around the boat—up in the wheelhouse, on the deck, and then in the cabin.

Once the voices were in the cabin, Nacho could hear better. There were sounds that suggested searching the cabin. Cabinet and compartment doors were opened and slammed. Nipi was getting worse, muttering and talking in his sleep. Nacho woke him. He was unable to respond. Nacho held his breath when one of the newcomers made a comment about what was hidden in the walls of the cabin.

Larrañaga pressed on unfazed. If the man only knew. In fact, *La Sirena* had just been down to Barcelona. She had picked up a limited supply of Spanish delicacies—for her crew's personal use of course. Would the gentlemen care for a sherry? In fact, there were an unopened bottle or two that needed a good home. More laughter, some tapping on the cabin interior walls, even more laughter, and mutual congratulations over the thoroughness with which the cabin had been checked. The conversation moved outside. Then it ended. *La Sirena* got under lumbering way again.

Christophe came to let the escapers out of their hidden compartment. In the light, Nipi was much worse. Ashen before, his skin was now florid, and he was sweating. He was hot. Had a high fever.

Now their discomfort began in earnest. They were well away from land and in the open sea. Larrañaga had turned them south southeast. Moderate quartering swells were butting *La Sirena* about. Flat bottomed as she was, her rolling was sickening. Not only that, but she was pitching as well. After cresting a wave, she would slide down its

MOSCOW GOLD | **383**

backside and bury her bow in the next trough, causing her to shudder and stagger.

No sailor was Nacho. He was bilious.

Nonchalant, Christophe came below.

"Are these conditions typical, Christophe?" Nacho knew that despite its beauty from the shore, the sparkling and transcendent Mediterranean had a reputation for consuming both men and vessels.

'Typical? Well, they're not unusual. It's a nice night out there. Skies are clear, gibbous moon, great visibility, and freshening wind. We should raise Port Bou in a couple of hours."

Nacho groaned at the thought of two more hours. "Who were our visitors?"

"French customs. A bit of bad luck that they picked us out for inspection tonight—what with you two on board. It's almost always perfunctory on the way out. They are much more thorough when we're coming back in. Captain's got 'em pretty well bought anyway. How's your pal?"

Nipi's fever was worsening. His breathing was very fast and shallow. The motion of the boat aggravated him. Nipi was again lying on his bench, but Nacho had to prevent him from falling off. As they stood there talking, Nipi began to talk in his sleep and cry out. He had become delirious.

"He wouldn't go to the doctor. The best we can do now is get him to shore."

Christophe avoided looking at Nipi. "Captain's on it."

Nipi was in a bad way. The action of the seas on *La Sirena* had worsened the further south she went. She continued to pitch and roll. Nacho was alarmed. They tried to tie him to his bench, as he was unable to support himself. The boat's motion had pounded his limp body without pity. Worse, his movement reopened his wound, and he started bleeding again. Nacho had endeavored to restrain him but with little success.

Now as they came into land, he was fire hot to the touch, pouring sweat and babbling.

They did not go straight into Port Bou. The Spanish coast at the extreme northeast corner of the country was rough and rocky with palisades, *rías*, and narrow inlets in abundance. *La Sirena* nosed into the calm black waters of one of the inlets. She found a small jetty, and Christophe tied her fast. Waiting was a battered American Dodge Brothers pickup with Jaén license plates.

They had to carry Nipi off the boat. They propped him in the pickup bed. He was, by now, insensible. Larrañaga tilted his head toward the driver of the Dodge. "This is Puig. He knows what to do. You can trust him."

Then he reached into the inside breast pocket of his pea coat. He handed Nacho a wad of banknotes.

"What's this?"

"A little something for the continuation of your trip in Spain. I think there's 15,000 pesetas there. Should get you well along your way. Compliments of our mutual pals in Paris. Idiots hashed up the war. It's the least they can do."

Then came a short and sharp exchange in Catalán. Nacho could understand some of it. Puig was to get Nipi to a certain Dr. Companys in Port Bou. After that, the regular routine.

CHAPTER 60

Port Bou: Tuesday, March 4, 1939

As directed, Puig took Nacho and Nipi to Dr. Companys.

The little physician had a bare-bones surgery on a back street in Port Bou. Nipi was in extremis, his breathing very fast and shallow. His delirium had subsided because, Nacho supposed, his body had exhausted itself. Nipi was comatose and unresponsive.

"He should have had medical attention long before now!" inveighed Dr. Companys, fluttering his tiny hands in anxiety and frustration. "How am I to save his life at this point? This is not possible. Not possible."

The man was rotund, around sixty, and bald, with fluffy white wings above his ears. He was dressed in a black suit and waistcoat and dark bow tie—prim, proper, and professional.

Nacho, himself bone weary, tried to calm the doctor. "You are correct, Doctor. I urged him to seek care in France, as did Captain Larrañaga, but he refused. He refused many times—each time we asked him. He feared being re-interned. If he dies, it will be the result of his own decision. No fault whatever would attach to you. Please

MOSCOW GOLD | 387

make your best effort to save him. That's all I ask. That's all he would ask if he could speak."

"It's in God's hands, God's hands. I will do what I can, but I fear it will not be enough."

CHAPTER 61

Port Bou: Friday, March 7, 1939

The issue hung in the balance for three days.

Dr. Companys cleaned and sutured Nipi's wound. Both he and Nacho expended considerable effort in inducing Nipi to take liquids. Dr. Companys's limited facilities and resources and the unavailability of medications, much less any blood for transfusions, compounded the gravity of Nipi's condition. Nacho despaired of his survival.

Nipi had almost died, but in the end he didn't. The much-beleaguered Dr. Companys remonstrated and tut-tutted for days, but neither his nor Nacho's vigilance faltered. The worst was in the middle of the night. Several times, they thought Nipi was going.

After several days, Nipi appeared to improve. His normal color returned, and the fever broke. Then one morning he was able to speak. Very weak, almost unintelligible, it was speech, nonetheless. After that, his recovery was steady and rapid, if not complete. He had functional limitations in his shoulder and still wore a sling.

MOSCOW GOLD | 389

CHAPTER 62

Barcelona: Friday, March 21, 1939

As soon as Nipi was ambulatory, Nacho began their preparations for their return to Madrid.

Their return may have been by the regular routine, as Larrañaga had called it. But it had been, by no means, easy. Puig drove them in the beat-up Dodge to Barcelona. The roads were impassable, bomb damaged, and cratered. Spring rains had turned many stretches into large gooey mud hazards that required the three of them to get out and free the truck from their clutches.

When they got to Barcelona, the effects of the war were everywhere evident. Most of the buildings along La Rambla were scarred, blackened, and pockmarked from bomb and artillery blasts and small-arms fire. One building of residential flats had a collapsed exterior wall. The interiors of the apartments were exposed. Passersby saw inside the rooms with their wallpaper, picture frames, beds, stuffed animals, and furnishings all untouched and undamaged in their places.

"Looks like a big dollhouse," commented Nipi.

"The bombings were brutal here. They went to great lengths to punish Barcelona." Puig had said as he drove around piles of rubble, twisted tram tracks, and erupted sewer and water lines.

"I wonder if it's this bad in Madrid," Nacho mused. "What's the next step in getting there?" he muttered to no one in particular.

CHAPTER 63

Madrid: Tuesday, April 11, 1939

The next step had been a long trek back across the country.

For the most part, they hitchhiked. They caught rides in the few commercial trucks that had loads for movement westward—Lérida, Zaragoza, Calatayud, Sigüenza, Guadalajara, and Alcalá de Henares. Their itinerary was slow and tedious. As they got west from Barcelona, they entered arid country where the irritation was dust, rather than mud. Add to that the inability, due to wretched road conditions, to travel very far during the day or at all at night. Fuel supplies were spotty. They were often delayed waiting for petrol deliveries.

In the countryside, the new government was not yet well organized. There was less danger of reprisal or arrest for those who had fought for the Republic than there was in the big cities. In this respect, Nipi had much to hide. He and Nacho were often secreted deep inside truck cargos behind, boxes, bales, and carboys. Now and then, they pilfered tins of sardines, jars of olives, and bottles of wine. So, they alleviated their discomfort—a little anyway.

After many days, many bad roads, and many dry and dusty towns, they were dropped in Vallecas. There they caught a tranvía into the Plaza de Cibeles.

"Look at the balconies, Nacho." Nipi pointed upward. "The flags of the Republic are all gone. Only the 'Old Spain' ones now."

"I suppose that was to be expected," Nacho replied. "What we need to be careful of are these Falangist gangs running around all over. A pair of Republican soldiers aren't that popular right now." They had watched as bands of Falangists roamed the streets. With their right arms raised in salute and shouting Nationalist slogans, they went about smashing portraits of Republican leaders and ripping down posters.

"To the victor go the spoils, as they say," Nacho muttered.

"What's going on in the fountain?" Nipi asked.

Shovels in hand, gangs of madrileños were climbing up on the statuary in the Cibeles fountain.

"They're digging the figures out from the bricks and earth that were used to bury them, protect them from the artillery and gunfire. It worked. They're in pretty good shape. Neptune's next, I'd guess," Nacho observed.

"Whole place has changed since the siege." Nipi commented as they walked along.

And it had. The numerous streets whose names had been changed reverted to their original names or, in some cases, to still new ones inspired by the now fascist political order. They saw that priests and nuns reappeared in public, bestowing as many blessings as might be requested. The Guardia Civil were out in their traditional uniforms, capes and caps. Even the language regressed. People again could say, "Buenos días," rather than "¡Salud!"

"Gone back to the way it was. That's Franco's whole point. What a crushing waste!" Nacho lamented. "Let's get off the street. It's dangerous."

394 | DOUGLAS L. FIELD

CHAPTER 64

Madrid: Saturday, August 31, 1963

Ariel was up early and on her way to Carabanchel.

DOCICA worked half a day on Saturdays. She took the stairs down rather than the elevator. It promised to be a clear, hot, dry day. She had not even grabbed a sweater on her way out the door.

The portero was already in his place. "Muy buenos días, Señorita Ariel. Are you well this morning?"

"Quite well, Don Hilario. You?"

"I'm very well. You have mail." He handed her both a letter and a postcard. "From France it seems." He gave her a circumspect smile.

"A nice day made even better by letters from abroad, Hilario. Thank you." She tried to act pleased. Her correspondence was from David. She had been both anticipating and dreading it. His missives placed back before her the conundrum she had been wrestling with since Santander.

She slid her mail into her purse and headed down Gaztambide. She had decided, since it was a pleasant morning, to take the streetcar to Carabanchel. *A nice day to stay above ground*, she thought. One was

MOSCOW GOLD | 395

CHAPTER 65

Paris: Saturday, August 31, 1963

David, too, was up early.

If Raúl Moscardó delivered this afternoon as David hoped he would, David's work in Paris would be nearing an end. He needed now to give attention to getting back into Spain undetected and staying undetected once he got there. He would need a false persona.

He took the Métro down to Porte d'Italie. Saturday was flea market day. He wanted to arrive before the good stuff was gone. The flea market was held in a large open lot of several acres. It was dense with sellers' tables and booths. Many even displayed their wares on the ground.

The market appeared random and disorganized, yet sellers with similar stock were grouped together. It took David a while to locate his section of interest. Even after he found it, what he wanted was still elusive.

"It must be of that particular issue? If not, I have several of very high quality, monsieur."

"Quality is important, mon ami, but the source even more so," David stated.

"In that case I am unable to accommodate you. It may not be so easy. Sorry."

He shopped without success through several more locations. He located what looked like a military tent and went in. The proprietor was anything but military. Rumpled and sporting at least ten days of beard, he sat in a corner of his tent at a small deal table. On the table reposed a cutoff artillery shell brimming with Gitane butts. The shell's latest prospective occupant dangled from his lips and waggled up and down when he spoke.

"It has to be Spanish *Republican*?" asked the man.

"Yes. Republican," David confirmed.

"Let's see. These are rare nowadays. That war has been over for a quarter century. In years past, there were a number in circulation as their refugees wore them over the border in winter '39. They were soon compelled to sell them off for food." He rattled through his stock.

"Ah, yes, monsieur. Fortune has smiled on you." He produced an army greatcoat. It was medium brown and had large lapels and dark buttons embossed "RE." It extended to calf length. "It is a large one, perhaps too large for you."

"No. It looks perfect. Let me try it on." It *was* too big but not to excess. "I need it a little large," said David. "This one will serve my purposes. Now, do you have any caps?"

"That is a little easier." He produced a selection of caps, and David chose a brown beret that even had its insignia still attached. He was also tempted by a forage cap that had the traditional Spanish tassel hung from the front peak. In the end, he took both.

"What about a blanket? To complete the *suite*, non?"

"No need. It's hot where I'm going." The young American paid and left.

⌒⌇

People living in Spain had to show identification frequently. The cover he was working up did not go with a US passport. He had asked Raúl and the concierge at his hotel, and both agreed that the flea market was also the place to find fake documents. Raúl even knew where a suitable individual had his stall.

Next to a far corner of the market, David located the prim little man all turned out in suit and tie sheltering from the sun under the canvas awning of his booth.

"Carte d'identité? Espagnole?" David tried his limited French.

"Oui. Do you require current or past?"

"Current. It needs to be up to date and faultless."

"The precise name is el Documento Nacional de Identidad," advised the dapper little guy, "known by its millions of bearers as the 'DNI.' Madrid has changed them little since the mid-'40s. Won't be at all difficult."

He rummaged through a box that looked like a four-by-six-inch card catalogue and pulled out a blank document. Basic blue and white, it bore elaborate engraving and a watermark.

"Come. Come. I will need your finger and thumbprints. Do you have a photo?" the little forger asked.

David had anticipated this question. He produced a small picture of himself that he had acquired in Madrid at a shop that specialized in passport and identity card photos.

"Perfect. Who shall you be and what address?"

David mulled this for a long moment. "Diego Campos Lázaro, San Justo 27, Madrid. Do I need a birth date?"

"No, the card has reference numbers that refer back to the individual's 'registry' information. Your registry numbers, of course, will be false. Understand that the card will not survive any detailed scrutiny. Give me half an hour—to affix the photo and laminate it the way the Spanish like to do. I will have it ready."

"I have other items to locate. I will be back." David headed over to the medical supplies and implements section. He made a quick and uncomplicated purchase there.

After that and after he had picked up his new identity, he went looking for a *parfumerie*.

Since David's plans involved posing as a beggar, to succeed, he thought he needed to learn some of the more conducive tactics and techniques. He doubted that anyone had ever written about means and methods for mendicants, so he thought about where he could affect a meaningful reconnaissance. Where to find persuasive examples of open anonymity, authenticity, and genuine ability to be looked at and not seen? He decided on venerable Montmartre.

The day had developed with pleasant grace. Gargantuan cumulonimbus castles built up over the city all morning and early afternoon, setting themselves against vivid robin-egg-blue skies that hinted at the end of summer. The temperature was comfortable and perfect for shirtsleeves.

David was through at the flea market by midmorning. He returned his acquisitions to his lodgings and headed out to the butte. He got off the Métro and hiked up rue de Clingnancourt to the foot of the butte. It was about three hundred steps up the rue Foyatier to the plaza in front of the basilica. Or, for the price of a Métro ride, one could take the *funiculaire*.

David decided to take the stairs. At the top, he came out winded on the broad pavement apron of the Basilica that afforded a nice view of Paris to the east and south. Ornate wrought-iron fencing with 1890s style streetlamps bordered it. He spent a few moments catching his breath, looking at the view and back down the steps he had just come up.

On the stairs coming up, separately and on opposite sides of the steps, he saw two men about his age. They were plainly dressed in casual pants and green shirts of similar shade. Both were fit and not challenged by the stairs. His neophyte street craft instincts were alerted. The men seemed out of place. They got to the top of the stairs one ahead of the other. Both turned left and entered the confusion of souvenir shops and stalls selling religious artifacts. He lost them out of sight.

He returned his attentions to the object of his trip. Leaning against the fence with his back to the view, he studied the details of life at the foot of the basilica. Because, he presumed, the proximity of the big church put people in charitable frames of mind, the blind, the disabled, and all manner of beggars gathered there, along with the ubiquitous street performers, caricature painters, and general riffraff.

David observed them all. He evaluated their strategies and tactics for separating people from their small change. He assessed which methods were the more productive and innocuous. He observed whether it was more profitable to speak to passersby or remain silent and woeful looking and whether it helped to have a child, a dog, a crude sign summarizing your sad story, or just your beret with a few coins in it, no explanation offered. He noted, too, that people avoided eye contact. Even those moved to donate interacted more with the mendicant's hat or box for collecting coin rather than with the supplicant himself. *Perfect!*

Among the most successful was a blind accordion player who had an advantageous spot next to the steps that went up to the entrance to the church. It was beyond trite, but even phlegmatic David was moved at the rendition of "La Vie en Rose." It earned the man a few of David's francs. He took it all in. Then he recorded his observations and conclusions in his memory.

Once finished, he went inside the basilica to have a look at the mosaics; before heading back down toward the river.

David was unsettled by the two guys who'd followed him up the stairs. They fit the profile of everything Nacho had told him about spotting followers. It was good that he had chosen to take the stairs. If they were surveillance, it had forced them out into the open. In anticipation of seeing Raúl Moscardó again and desiring that their meeting be kept to the two of them, David decided to act like a spy and to spend part of this pleasant afternoon in Paris engaged in some amateur street craft.

He left the basilica. Rather than going back down the way he'd come, he circled around the church. He stayed high on the butte until he descended to the rue des Abesses and the Abesses Métro. He had figured this for a quiet station. He was not disappointed.

Once down on the platform, he loitered about reading posters advertising cultural events and public notices regarding the Métro and its various services. He waited through the passage of three trains. It appeared, from time to time, that he was the only person on the platform. As he lingered, he measured the time between arrival and departure of the trains. A fourth train came. With his back still to the tunnel as the train came in, he continued to "study" the notices. Then at the last second, he whipped around. He barged onto the red first-class car in the middle of the train just as its doors were closing. Hardly anybody ever paid the extra required for first class on the Métro, so he and one very chic and solitary woman were the sole red car's occupants. David was the last one to board. The platform was empty as the train pulled away.

He rode past Place de Clichy, a very busy station and got off at Liège, which was quiet like Abesses. At Liège, he waited until he heard a train coming on the other side. As soon as he did, he bolted to the opposite platform, timed it just right, and rode all the way to Carrefour Pleyel. Nothing. He traveled down to Concorde and came out of the Métro on the rue de Rivoli.

There were plenty of people on the street. The Rivoli sidewalk was covered and comprised a long inside arcade inside of which there were numerous expensive shops. David got some good practice. He varied

404 | DOUGLAS L. FIELD

his pace, stopped and started. He went in out of different stores. The crowd on the street was not homogeneous. It was split about equally between tourists and Parisians. The tourists' dress was distinct from the locals'. The former were portlier than the more delicate French and talked at higher volume. The locals were purposeful and hurried about their business. The visitors lollygagged, even more so the women.

Nacho had taught him to identify anyone who looked out of place and individuals he might see more than once. David worked his way east on Rivoli, in and out of different types of establishments. At one point, he spotted a thickset young man in very plain clothes—black pants a little too large, rumpled light blue shirt with sleeves rolled up above the elbows, belt too long and wrapped over itself to take up the excess. He didn't look either local or tourist. Not one from the stairs, but close enough.

Soon enough, he got to La Samaritaine and went in. He shopped through the cosmetics and women's wear sections without incident. David was the only one out of place in there. Then he went up to the toy section at a far end of the fourth floor. There he found a lavishly stocked area of plastic and wooden airplane and ship models, paints, glues, and accessories. He opened a few boxes, making as if to be a serious shopper. All the while, he was checking for incongruities. There! In the neighboring section. Cookware. Another youngish plain-dressed man. No reason for him to be buying pots and pans. At the second David saw him, the man disappeared into another part of the store.

David was confident now that he was being followed. He decided to trail his skirts over in the Tuileries. He hustled back down the Quai du Louvre, nicked through the Place du Carrousel in front of the main entrance to the museum, and moved into the wide-open and expansive Jardin des Tuileries. Rivoli and La Samaritaine had been crowded. The Tuileries were deserted by comparison. He went up to the Terrasse des Feuillants that parallels Rivoli, where he ducked in and out of several high hedgerows and a *pissiore*.

MOSCOW GOLD | 405

Then he moved out into the open. He crossed at a brisk walk the decomposed granite trail to the large pond at the Concorde end of the garden. He took a seat in one of the chairs that lined the pond. The chair he chose was located next to one already occupied by a middle-aged gentleman. The man was reading his morning paper. David greeted him without looking at him. The pond was large. It offered an excellent vantage point for making note of whomever else was around. He exchanged a few more words with his new neighbor.

Another single man, this one in a plain beige shirt, approached to within thirty yards or so and took another empty seat. David asked his companion if he might have a brief look at his paper. Another man joined beige shirt and sat next to him—too far away to make out any details. David caught a break. His neighbor said he was through with the paper. David could keep it.

Now. On his feet. With the paper under his arm, he headed for the Terrasse du Bord de l'Eau and the river. He stopped by a trash receptacle. He put his shoe up as if to tie it. Bent over and looking back, he saw the other two were on the move. He dumped the paper in the trash bin and headed out of the park. Once at the street, he made a quick glance over his shoulder as if to check for traffic. One of his tails had fished the paper out of the trash. The other was nowhere to be seen.

An ugly dose of realization set in. David felt real apprehension. Until now, he hadn't thought he would come under surveillance. But he had.

He headed fast to the east and went back into La Samaritaine. He tried working the elevators in a fashion like what he had done in the Métro. It appeared to David that he had shaken his followers. He popped out of the big department store on the rue du Pont Neuf and jumped into a waiting cab. He had himself delivered to the Gare de l'Est. He hoped if they were still with him that they would think he was leaving Paris.

He ran more street detection routes around the *gare*, picked up nothing, and then caught the Métro to Odéon. He would be ahead of time for his meet with Moscardó. There would be time to spot and elude the opposition.

⁓

The young KGB operative caught up with Major Myshnov on the Pont Neuf.

"He's on to us, Major. He worked the rue de Rivoli and then went into La Samaritaine. He made Dmitri in the store. Then he went over to the Tuileries and tried to elude us there. He appears to have made a contact. Medvedev and Krinsky had him under observation by that big pond. He left. Abruptly. Medvedev followed, and Krinsky is checking out the contact."

"What did he do next?"

"He went back into La Samaritaine. We picked him up going in, but he manipulated the elevators, and we lost him. We saw him headed out the door where he hailed a cab. We were too late to keep up," the younger man said.

"Which exit?"

"Rue du Pont Neuf. Just up the street there." The young man pointed toward the north end of the bridge. "The cab took him north—at least as far as we could see."

"Up towards the Gare de l'Est. He wants us to think he's finished his business and is leaving Paris," Myshnov surmised.

"I'm sorry we lost him, comrade. We—"

"Don't trouble yourself or me with apologies, Feodor. KGB does not 'lose' its subjects." Myshnov leveled a withering look. Then he relented a little. "It's no matter. He's not leaving town. Not yet anyway. Get his hotel back under surveillance. Make it tight but be invisible. We'll pick him up again there. Trust me in this. Now get on it. Try to redeem yourselves."

⁓

David came out of the Métro and feinted around to the west. He slipped past Saint-Sulpice. He went into the Luxemburg Garden at the northwest corner close to the palace. He was early. The place was wide open. He found a bench in the heavy shadows of some thick ornamental bushes off the main footpath. It was perfect. The day was very bright. David, sitting in the shadows, was invisible to those whose eyes were adjusted to the bright sun. He was able, in comfort and at leisure, to observe activities. His erstwhile followers did not appear.

Moscardó arrived on the stroke of five o'clock. The palace made an interior corner at the bottom of the garden in which were placed numerous fruit trees in large wooden boxes on little casters. *The Orangery, of course.* Interspersed among the trees were park benches that faced away from each other and shared a common back. Moscardó took a seat in the sun, and David slipped in opposite him.

"Raúl! Thanks for coming."

They each turned a little sideways one toward the other. They could talk but appeared from a distance not to be together.

"Were you followed?" asked Raúl.

"Earlier. I shook them off in La Samaritaine. I've been here a while. We're clean."

Moscardó was reassured and proceeded to tell David, "I dug around the coin shop. Vokárny kept handwritten records of all the gold transactions that we did. Looks like he was quite careful about it. Not alone either. I talked to some of the others that I'm on terms with. The previous generation in their shops did the same thing. I imagine the old guys got together and had an informal agreement on the sly to document what happened—just in case or if the authorities got to asking questions."

"How much?

"A very great deal, David. Almost all in coins. Both the others and us. The totals will take your breath away."

"Any indication where it went?"

"The buyers kept those details close," Raúl explained. "Just like with us, at the other shops, it was two Swiss brothers. I mentioned before, I thought they were not Swiss. Had to be German secret service types. They kept the destination of the gold to themselves; told us it was none of our business. They implied in their heavy way that, if we knew what was good for us, we would not concern ourselves. My colleagues say they treated them the same way. We all knew where our interests lay, and we went along. Well, the old guys did anyway."

"Are there any details at all as to the ultimate disposition?"

"Most times, the buyers didn't take possession in their individual names. It was some nominee company or other—organized in various places all over the world. You'll see. It's kind of a time capsule, I expect. You can research the nominees."

"I'll see?" David was confused.

Moscardó looked around the area. He saw no one paying any attention to him and David. He slid a packet wrapped in colored paper from Galeries Lafayette out of his shoulder bag. An innocent looking package, it was a nice ruse. "These are Henri's contemporaneous records, plus those of several of the competition."

David was shocked at the trove of information. "I'm very grateful, Raúl. These are important original documents—incredibly valuable. Exactly what I need. May I ask a delicate question? Well, two?"

Moscardó raised no objection. David pressed forward. "Why would Méndez Aspe give me the clue to find you?"

"I can only guess. The Spanish community in Paris is small. We're on opposite sides but are aware of each other for years. He must have known some of the gold passed through the shop where I worked. I don't like him, but in his perverse way, he seeks the best interests of Spain. On that level, we are bedfellows. I imagine he thought he could help Spain *and* get you off his back. Besides, he likely feels as ripped off by the Soviet communists as the rest of us."

"Second and more important, why trust me with this? Why now?"

Moscardó looked away, stared at the ground.

MOSCOW GOLD | 409

"Raúl, tell me why."

He gathered himself. "Not easy to say."

David let him think. It seemed he would not answer, and David was prepared to leave it at that.

Then the little man sighed. "A form of survivor guilt I imagine. We made a lot of money—a lot of money off Spanish gold. The occupation in Paris was hideous. The *schleuh* took everything. People froze and starved. Not us. We coin dealers managed better. We knew how to stash assets. No one ever knew."

"There are many elements to righting a wrong. These papers are important. I'll give them back when I'm through."

"No. Keep them. At the end of the day, it's better for me that we do not have them around."

The day was starting to wane. More people were about—nannies and their charges, the occasional dog. There was a long silence.

It was Moscardó who, in the end, spoke again. "You've asked about where the gold went from here. I've told you I can't be of much help on that. One thing, though. I have some distant relatives involved with banking down in Gibraltar. There was family lore that gold stocks may have been deposited there. Carlos Ituarte, a cousin somewhat removed, lives or at least lived in Madrid. That's all I have."

"Gibraltar? I wonder why Gibraltar?" David blurted out.

"Gibraltar's a very convoluted issue. It's not just that the UK's got it and Spain wants it. And it was vastly more complicated in the prewar years."

"What's the abbreviated version?"

Raul explained, "It was the crown jewel of military installations in Western Europe. Whoever had it would win the war. Hyperbole? Maybe, but it controlled access to the Mediterranean. The British needed to keep it. The Germans and Italians needed to get it. Franco angled for it to be returned to Spain. He was willing to leverage both sides. And he's slick. Never forget that. Then there were the Gibraltarians. They played all sides to foster their own interests."

410 | DOUGLAS L. FIELD

"It has been stated to me by a party on the periphery of all this that there are 'multiple agendas' involved," David recalled.

"Whoever said that is right—not only respecting the gold but also Gibraltar. It would be quite poetic if the two intricacies were, in fact, intertwined, wouldn't it?"

"Raúl, you've helped me, more than you know."

"David, I think I know you. I trust you. I've done what I can for you. Do one thing for me. Let your investigations and reporting be done for the best benefit of Spain and the Spanish people. Will you do that, David?"

David looked at Moscardó for a very long time and then said slowly and very precisely, "That I can do."

Moscardó blanched and caught his breath. "My brother's last words to my father—that awful day in the Alcázar!"

"I know the story, Raúl."

Moscardó stood up, blinking back tears. "We should not leave the park together. Give me ten minutes. And David. ¡*Cuidado*!" He embraced David for the briefest moment. Then he was gone.

While he waited the ten minutes, David realized that he now had two major pieces to the gold puzzle—Maria Frankman's receipt and Raúl Moscardó's chits. One more piece to go. Then he could square accounts with Isham. Now he had to get himself and his documents back into Spain.

The KGB major gathered his troops. "We go on the American tonight. Five-man team plus me. All black clothing. We'll wait for him to return to his hotel. It's narrow and dark over there by Saint-Séverin. We'll grab him, tie his hands, and invite him to come with us for a look at Notre Dame over on the Pont au Double. As soon as we're there, we do him and over the rail he goes. Then we split up. Meet at the embassy, and we leave Paris without delay."

It was a simple and straightforward hit. They did this kind of thing all the time. No one had any questions.

❧

Nick Barnickle met the Spaniards at the Spanish embassy. Additional information had come from Isham. Nick had a description of José María Jaso, the team leader.

"Anybody speak English?" Nick asked.

"A leetle. *Un poquito*," said Jaso.

"No translator?" Nick was aghast.

"No, el Señor Isham believes that you have some Spanish. *¿No es verdad?*"

Barnickle shrugged. "We'll have to do our best. I'll talk slow. Inspector Jaso please translate as you can."

Nick explained the situation. David Fordham was aware that he was being surveilled by a team of Soviets. It was a surprise to Nick, but he had been adept at evading them.

"He may not appreciate that they want to kill him, however. Our challenge is that Señor Isham's operation, and our mutual interests, Room 11's and the Company's, needs to play itself all the way out before the Soviets may be allowed to succeed. The subject may have already obtained some of what we need but not all of it."

Nick looked around to see if he was being understood. He couldn't tell.

"The point is the subject needs to get finished before he gets dead. We are to ensure that he gets finished. The Russians will be running a team of about half a dozen. They will pick the subject back up sometime this afternoon or tonight and intend to move on him. This is always how they work. They act lightning fast if they need to. We will be at an advantage as the Russians will be concentrating on their target and won't anticipate our presence."

Jaso then briefed his troops. There were five in addition to him. They would not be outnumbered, but then, neither would the KGB. The Madrid team were all dressed in dark clothing with rubber-soled shoes. Everyone had a black balaclava. Jaso was disinclined to fool around with knives, garrotes, and the like. Each team member had a silenced Sig Sauer M11-A1 9-mm pistol that he carried in a black holster under his left arm.

Nick proposed and Jaso agreed that their best move was to stake out the KGB staking out David.

"Just to confirm, Chema, the use of ultimate force is authorized?" This was Monge.

"Confirmed. Authorized. By Room 11."

"On French soil, Chema? The Frenchies won't like it." Now Zapatero.

"The *Frenchies* are never gonna to know. It will be as if we were never here. Señor Barnickle, are you ready to move?"

"Uh, yeah. Uh, sí. Ready to move."

MOSCOW GOLD | 413

CHAPTER 66

Madrid: Saturday, August 31, 1963

Ariel was enjoying the paseo with the Doña Sagrario, her landlady, and another woman who lived in the same house.

They had strolled down to Quevedo on Fernando el Católico from Gaztambide and were enjoying a refreshment at a terrace half a block down Fuencarral from the glorieta.

"It's time for the summer heat to go," said Sagrario after they had ordered.

"A long and mild autumn before the rains would be quite agreeable, Sagra," the other lady acknowledged.

Ariel smiled as both others fluttered their fans. "I hear that the Ayuntamiento is building a large swimming pool complex out by University City. The authorities have authorized the pools and surrounding areas to be coeducational. We three should go. It would be an adventure."

Sagrario had the vapors, her fan beating furiously. "Ariel how can you imagine such a thing as an adventure, much less speak it aloud?"

MOSCOW GOLD | 415

Their companion smiled. "Sagra, keep an open mind. I agree with Ari—"

Before she could finish, a pair of men approached their table. One seized Ariel by the left arm and lifted her from her chair. The other flashed some sort of credentials and kicked the chair out of the way and took her other arm.

"You are Ariel Muñiz?"

Ariel nodded.

"You will come with us."

They moved her to an unmarked car that was waiting at the curb a short distance off, assisted her into the back, and drove off.

Sagrario and her friend were speechless and terrified.

"Oh, my heavens, Ariel. What have you done? Where are they taking you? Why?" Sagrario whimpered.

Both women started to cry as others around them offered comfort.

ᴄᴡ

Ariel was driven to the San Bernardo Comisaría and hustled inside. She was escorted through an entry door into a small chamber. The entry door was then locked noisily, and a door that opened into the main part of the interior of the building was unlocked and opened.

She was placed in the custody of a matron who moved her brusquely to a plain room with a table, a cheap lamp, and three chairs.

"You will sit there," ordered the matron. "You will be attended in due course."

Ariel sat. She looked around the room. There was no decoration or other furnishing. One door only provided access. The matron made sure Ariel heard it lock. There were no windows.

She waited. The room was silent. She could hear no other activity in the building.

After what seemed like hours, the two who had arrested her stormed in. They dragged the remaining chairs around the table

416 | DOUGLAS L. FIELD

opposite her and flipped on the light. One of them had a folder that looked to be filled with police documents.

"I am Detective Flórez," said the one with the folder. "This is Detective Arias."

"Why am I here?" Ariel managed.

"Silence! We will ask the questions, and you will provide the answers," said Flórez.

But no questions were forthcoming. He paged through his folder, stared at her several times, pointed to one or two papers, and looked at Arias.

It was Arias who spoke, "Describe your relationship with the man known as David L. Fordham."

Ariel had started out paralyzed with fear. Now she had relaxed a little and was able to start to think. "A friend." *Cooperate, but don't elaborate*, she told herself.

"A friend? What kind of friend?"

"I don't understand, officer. What kind of friend? He's American."

"It's 'Detective,' and do not be facetious."

"I had no intention of doing so. I don't know what you mean."

"How close of a friend? How long have you known him? What is the status of your relationship?" Flórez jumped in.

"I don't remember how long."

"Where did you meet him?" Still Flórez.

"At a party."

"A party? Where?"

She saw a small opening. "At the Embassy of the United States of America."

Arias and Flórez looked at each other. Ariel thought this had come as a surprise.

"Is he an employee of the embassy? Does he have diplomatic status?" Arias again.

"I can't say."

"What were you doing there?"

MOSCOW GOLD | 417

"I'm not sure what you mean. I was drinking sherry and eating canapés."

Arias glared at her. "Why did you go to this party?"

"My patrón, Jaime Castellón, asked me to accompany him." Another opening.

"You are employed by Jaime Castellón?" the two detectives looked at each other again.

Ariel nodded.

"When did you last see David Fordham?"

"A week or so ago. In Santander." She decided to anticipate his next question.

"You stayed at the Hotel Sardinero." It was not a question. "Where did he stay?"

"I don't know. He didn't tell me."

"Did he stay with you in your room? Are you lovers? Did you sleep together? We find no record of his registry at any hotel in the area."

"Those are boorish and detestable questions. I will not answer them. I have no idea why you are unable to find his registration documents."

And so it went for three quarters of an hour more. Where did David live? Where did he work? Was he authorized to work in Spain and receive payment in pesetas? She was relieved to note that they failed to ask anything that would lead to DOCICA.

"Where is he now?"

"I don't know. Paris, I imagine."

"When does he plan to reenter Spain?"

A very precise question, to which she said, "He did not tell me."

"Where does he plan to reeneter?"

"I have no idea." So far, she was fortunate. The questions were not getting to Segovia.

Flórez threw down his pencil. "This man David Fordham is a potential enemy of the Spanish state. His whereabouts are a matter of national security."

418 | DOUGLAS L. FIELD

He handed her his card. "You are commanded to advise this office of any information that comes into your knowledge and possession as to his whereabouts in France or as to the date and place of his return to *la patria*. Do you have any questions?"

"None."

They got up and left.

After another hour, a different matron escorted her out. Ariel was told she could leave. She walked home to her flat on Gaztambide.

⌖

Up at the flat, she had to knock. She was too shaky to find her keys. The entire house was in an uproar. When Sagrario saw Ariel, she fell onto a sofa and appeared to faint. Smelling salts were called for.

"Ariel, Ariel my dear. What happened? Did they hurt you?" Sagra wailed when she had regained some of her composure.

"No, no, I'm fine. It was only an interrogation. I am not denounced. They are looking for David. They had dozens of questions about him. Nothing else. I think they have lost track of him."

"Do you have to return to talk to them again?" one of the others asked.

She held up Flórez's card, "No. Only that I'm to advise this detective if I learn when or where David is coming back into Spain. I don't have that information and doubt that I will be getting it."

"Oh, Ariel! They seized you right on the street. In front of half of Chamberí! *¡Qué barbaridad!*" keened Doña Sagra.

"Sagra, everyone. It's calm now. It was only for intimidation, I think. I need to rest and sleep," she said. "And decide whether I will be intimidated," she added under her breath.

MOSCOW GOLD | 419

CHAPTER 67

Madrid: Friday, May 19, 1939

All in all, it had taken Nacho and Nipi the better part of two months to get back to Madrid.

Nacho confirmed his initial impressions. Spain was a dangerous place for everyone and anyone during the early postwar. "Feels like the whole country, not just our old areas, is under foreign occupation," Nipi groused.

"It's a fascist dictatorship. Fascist, communist, socialist, whatever. Dictatorship's dictatorship. Look at this." Nacho pulled a folded paper out of his pocket. "It's Franco's declaration of victory."

The date was April 1, 1939, signed with flourish, rubricked, and officially stamped it read, "Today, the Red Army captive and disarmed national troops have reached their ultimate military objectives. The war is finished."

Nipi spat in the street.

"Careful with that sort of stuff, Nipi. You'll draw attention. I heard after Franco signed that paper, he got all sarcastic and said, '*Hemos pasado.*'" (We have passed).

MOSCOW GOLD | 421

"¡Cabrón!"

"He's not on a unity tour, Nipi. You gotta understand that. Be careful. Word is they've got thousands of our guys in labor camps all around. Summary trials for a lot of them. Almost always convicted. Some 250 to 300 executions a day. Death warrants to be signed by the Caudillo himself. Signs them en masse they say."

Along with tens of thousands of other madrileños, they lined the northern stretch of the Paseo de la Castellana, now renamed Avenida del Generalísimo.

It was victory parade day.

The victors had cobbled together a huge triumphal dais. It looked Roman and substantial, but that was superficial. It consisted of just wood and cardboard falseworks. Three stories high, "Victoria" was written above an arch, into which was inset a huge representation of the heraldic coat of arms of the Spanish kings. The coat of arms was flanked by the word "Franco" stacked three high on each side.

Along the street and under the viewing platform was drawn up the Caudillo's own Moroccan guard. Francisco Franco Bahamonde himself appeared resplendent in the uniform of a captain general. But beneath his tunic, there peeked out the dark blue of a Falangist shirt, and he wore the red beret of the Carlists. He was covering all his bases.

Well over a hundred thousand soldiers passed in review. Everybody was represented—regulares, legionnaires, Falangists, and *requetés*, as well as contingents of foreign troops, Portuguese, Italians, and finally Germans.

Now the parade was finished. It had come time for Franco's speech. This was preceded by several minutes of the crowd chanting, "Franco, Franco, Franco." Then the conquering victor took to the microphone. *"¡Españoles todos!"* He started with what would become his signature salutation.

As would prove time and again in ensuing years to be his wont, he went on to unburden himself of a full-throated stem-winder. The gist was that he had done Spain the enduring favor of rooting out all influence of the Enlightenment, the French Revolution, and all other accoutrements of modernity. The Second Republic had been rendered a mere interlude, an aberration in Spanish history. The proper balance of economic and social power in Spain had been restored. And on it went.

The air force arranged a ceremonial flyby. The aircraft in formation spelled the letters "V" and "F"—"Viva Franco." The commander of the Germans would later write home that, "The spectators go wild."

But not all the spectators.

"I survived the war for this?" groused Nipi.

Nacho looked at his companion. "Watch it. You'll get us in trouble again."

"Come on, jefe. A kid in colegio could see through this tripe. I don't want to have to listen—"

"What would you know, Nipi, you ingrate? You never went to colegio. I could have left you in Perpignan. Should have now that I think about it. Admit it. Even in its reduced circumstances, Madrid's better than St.-Cyp."

"Maybe. A little." Nipi pouted.

"*¡Bobo!*" (Fool!) "You would have died if I'd left you in St.-Cyp. At least you're alive here. You almost died anyway."

In this political climate, Nacho was worried about one or the other of them being arrested—a much more dangerous proposition if it were Nipi.

"If you get arrested, Nipi, you stay quiet as long as you can. I mean quiet. Keep your mouth shut and don't say anything. Clear?"

Nipi nodded.

"You're a talkative little shit, Nipi. Can you do it?"

"Yeah, jefe, I get it."

"I have some contacts. I can use them to get you out, but you must stay quiet. If they arrest me, you disappear and lie low for several days. Every day you pass through that subterranean passage that runs under

MOSCOW GOLD | 423

La Castellana at the Plaza de Colón by the National Library. I'll find you there."

Nacho then schooled Nipi in recognizing and avoiding Falangist patrols. He taught him how to spot and lose surveillance. Above all, he taught him how to be inconspicuous and appear innocuous in plain sight.

Nipi wanted to lose his sling. Nacho wouldn't let him. It was a convenient and simple distraction that might divert authority from having thoughts of questioning.

CHAPTER 68

Madrid: Wednesday, May 24, 1939

It was Nacho they arrested.

Nipi was alert when it happened. He made himself invisible and scuttled away. They were in Noviciados near the Glorieta de San Bernardo. A pair of Guardias Civiles hauled Nacho off to Tribunal No. 9 and then convened in the Palacio de Altamira.

"You're a soldier of the Republic, camarada." The one who spoke sneered, the last word dripping with sarcasm and condescension. "Pretty stupid of you to be wearing parts of your old uniform."

"Warm clothes are hard to find in Madrid now, *oficial*. I don't have political scruples about a warm coat and boots." Nacho tried to appear cooperative and reasonable.

"Maybe, but you look pretty beat up. Face is scarred, a couple of fingers gone. You've seen some action, and not with the good guys, I'd say. Tribunal will get the truth out of you."

Nacho spent a bad night in custody in the basement of the palace. Midmorning the next day, he was brought into a makeshift courtroom in the grand dining room. The prosecutor conducted Nacho's

MOSCOW GOLD | **425**

interrogation. There was a panel of what looked like three rather bored judges. No lawyer for the defense was in evidence.

"Name?"

"Ignacio Arjona Álvarez."

"Date and place of birth?"

"Here in Madrid, June 19, 1914."

"Occupation?"

"I'm a spy."

There was an *alguacil* (a bailiff) standing beside the prosecutor's desk. He stepped within range of Nacho and backhanded him hard across the face. The man was wearing a ring. It cut Nacho. He started to bleed. "You'll not disrespect el Señor Fiscal, camarada."

"No disrespect," Nacho persisted, glaring at the bailiff. "I am a spy."

The bailiff started for Nacho again, but the prosecutor raised a hand.

"Let us explore his claim a little. A spy for whom?"

Nacho told his story. The prosecutor was skeptical at first. Nacho meted out the facts with slow deliberation. He issued a cogent account. After some extensive questioning, Nacho was able to drop Ahumada's name and then later Cóndor's. As far as Nacho could tell, Ahumada was unknown to the tribunal, but Cóndor was. They threw Nacho back into the basement while independent investigations were conducted.

Late that night, he was brought upstairs, taken to the big portal on Calle de la Flor Alta, and shoved without ceremony into the street.

The next day, Nacho was waiting for Nipi in the underpass near Colón.

"What happened? I was afraid you were gone forever." Nipi's relief was visible.

"They wanted to shoot me, but I talked them out of it." Nacho tried to make light of it.

"*¡Mierda!* The crap you did. Look at your face. What happened?"

"I told them I was a spy. They let me go," Nacho quipped.

"A spy?"

"It's a long story. It's classified. I dropped a couple of important names. Then late last night, they kicked me out. Better for you if you don't know the details—if they pick you up."

"What do you mean you were a spy?"

"Let's find a bar. We still have some of Larrañaga's money. I'll tell you over a beer."

After they sat down Nacho did tell the whole story from his early fascist days with Cóndor, through Pindoque, Arganda, Teruel, and the Ebro—clear up until Saint-Cyprien. It took a long time. Nipi said nothing, and Nacho saw no emotional reaction.

"So, yeah, I started out Nationalist. Yeah, I was spying when I was with the Campesinos. It was around Teruel that I realized that the whole war, all the political theory, all the posturing, all the suffering and dying, all of it was nothing more than an absurd farce. I got out of it for any motivation other than that of keeping Nacho Arjona alive— me and one or two close to me. The fact that we're sitting here means maybe it worked."

Nipi still neither said nor showed anything.

Nacho went on, "By St.-Cyp, I didn't give a shit for Franco or the Falange or the Republic or any of it. All I wanted was to survive. Now we might—if we are careful. I can understand if you're pissed. I won't blame you if you leave."

A long time passed. Nacho said nothing more.

"You got me out of St.-Cyp. You knew I wouldn't last much longer. You stuck with me when I was sick and almost died. I don't care what you were. You're right; our job now is to live."

They clinked glasses.

"You headed back to Galicia?" Nacho changed the subject.

"Nothing for me there. Plus, less people. Not like Madrid. You can get lost here. Me and my sympathies are known there. Higher chance I get arrested."

"Guess we're going to have to find something here then," said Nacho

They were again silent for a while.

"Nipi, you know the story of our gold?"

"Gold?"

"Yeah, huge reserves of it that were in the Banco de España at the start of the war? Got ripped off from us—right at the beginning. I delivered part of it. Wonder if we could make something out of trying to get it back?"

"It's worth a look," Nipi agreed.

"Well, that's for later. For now, I know a baker. Down on Cava Baja. He's called Ahumada. Maybe he'll have something. People always need to eat."

"Including us!" Nipi enthused.

"Then I gotta look for one other guy. Named Beto. Beto and his aunt Lola," Nacho stated.

"Beto and Lola?" Nipi asked only vaguely interested.

"Yeah, Beto and Lola," said Nacho, his thoughts for a moment far away.

CHAPTER 69

Paris: Sunday, September 1, 1963

The month of August 1963 made serene passage into history.

By the time David left the Luxembourg, the sun was low in the sky. A balmy evening was in the offing. David was confident he had lost his surveillance—for now. They would find him again. It was just a question of how soon.

His job now was to get himself and his documents out of France and back into Spain without getting caught. He had Raúl's package in a small backpack, but the original receipt and his flea market purchases were at his hotel. He could live without the disguise, but he had to retrieve the receipt before he could get out of Paris. He had to get into the hotel and get back out without getting killed.

He decided to lie low and let his trail cool further. The Luxembourg Gardens led onto the Boulevard Saint-Michel. David hurried north on the great thoroughfare to the Boulevard Saint-Germaine-des-Prés where he jinked a bit east into the rue de la Harpe.

Where better to hide for a few hours than a French restaurant? He scuttled into the Maison Cluny. There was a table behind a pillar. He

MOSCOW GOLD | 429

could see the street and the front door, but it would be hard to see him. It was a straight shot to the kitchen and back door too—if he needed to bolt. Add to all of that, the place was teeming with people.

He dawdled over an aperitif and later ordered dinner. He worried about getting back to his hotel, and he wondered about Ariel. What was she was doing as this last day of August turned into September? He decided to write a letter to her that he would give to her from his hand to hers next week in Segovia. Would she even go to Segovia? He wrote his letter over a couple of cognacs as the crowds inside and out thinned a little into the night.

The night was bright, moving and still alive in the rue de la Harpe as David went back out onto it. Once he began to move down the rue Saint-Séverin it became quieter and darker—more so the further he went. It felt sinister and a little eerie by comparison to de la Harpe and the Champs. It was as if, with every step he took, he penetrated further back into the obscurity of the Middle Ages. The dark hulk of the Saint-Séverin church loomed ahead, brooding and shadowing the narrow street from the light of the city. David had a fleeting shiver across his shoulders.

The rue Saint-Séverin was not only dark but also narrow and lined with tall buildings. Sound echoed in this urban canyon. David was aware that someone had entered the street behind him. Footfalls rapid and purposeful. Catching up to him. One person. Not a woman.

Some one hundred fifty yards remained until he got to the corner with the rue des Prêtres de Saint-Séverin. A right turn there and a similar distance to the entrance to the hotel. He picked up his pace, subtly he hoped. Then another man, dressed all in back appeared ahead, entering off the rue Saint-Jacques, walking toward him. The distance to the entrance to Prêtres was about the same for each of them. He let the backpack slide off his shoulders and caught it by the straps in his left hand.

A nascent little fear grabbed him. He tried to recall what was there once into Prêtres. The main entrance to the church was on the left and, after that, an open square. Past the square on the right would be the entrance to the hotel lobby, on the corner with Parcheminerie. His best plan was to get inside the hotel. He should be safe if he could get in there.

David considered turning around, going back to de la Harpe, and then going around the block to come up on the hotel from Parcheminerie. If these were hostiles, he would have to fight his way back anyway. It was best to get to the corner. Then he could bolt past the church and into the square. The big front doors to the church were coming into view now. It was very dark in there. He put on a little more speed. He had to stay ahead of the guy behind and beat the one ahead to the corner. The worst thing would be to get cut off.

David remembered that Nacho had taught guile and bravado and to be confident.

The man ahead picked up the pace too. He had his hands in his pockets. Young and light on his feet, narrow waist, and broad shoulders, he was in good physical shape. A black cap with a brim was pulled well down over his face. Until now, David had resisted the urge to turn and look at the follower. Now he did. Same profile. David now began to hurry. He could forget subtlety now and would like to know what they had in their pockets.

David stuck his right hand in his own pocket. It would make them wonder too. He wanted to act nonchalant. Not make them nervous. Improve his chances to beat them to the corner.

The street corner was near now. It would be close who got there first. The three of them were converging. David tried to stay in the middle of Saint-Séverin. Make them think he may not make the turn. The man ahead was a little less cagey. He began to edge from the middle of the street to his left, positioning for the cutoff. Now David had real fear.

A stride or two from the corner now. It was time to run for it. David made a very fast feint to his left and then pivoted right into Prêtres.

MOSCOW GOLD | 431

The one ahead fell for it and moved to his right. This gained David a step and a half.

Everything went into slow motion.

David got to full speed within three strides. Centrifugal force made him take the corner wide. As he came around, he was facing the church steps. Out of the darkness, a third man materialized—fast. This one was armed. There was the glint of sharpened steel even in the dark. He held the blade low near his waist, ready to slash upward.

"Hold up, hold up." Like a stage whisper. Authoritative and demanding. Words in English. But odd. Not idiomatic. Accented. David had a lot of momentum. He ran straight for the knife. At the last instant he dove to the ground, tucking under and rolling over his right shoulder. His body somersaulted forward. He flung the backpack at the knife and then hit the man low, below the knees. David had gotten under the hostile's center of gravity. Bad guy was pitched forward. The shiv dropped with a clatter. David still had ahold of his pack.

Both David and his attacker were on all fours. The knife was behind the other man.

Both scrambled to get up. They were past each other. As the hostile propelled himself to his feet, he wound up farther behind David, who seized the knife with his right hand and scrambled forward. David sensed the first two were all but on him. He was back on his feet and surging ahead. Now he was armed.

Running on pure adrenalin, David flew into the square, hoping to jink back to his right and make for the door of his hotel. He could see light from the entrance spilling into the street. After the church came a masonry wall that had a little monument and statue set into it. Past the end of the wall was a small green garden with a large tree and park bench in the middle.

David was now ahead of his three pursuers. He had the faint hope of reaching his goal when, yet another figure materialized. Out from behind the monument. This one held a pistol in both hands, arms extended, the gun waving at all three.

"Stop this," he commanded.

One of David's pursuers shied away, giving the pistol a clear shot. The other was farther back. David charged forward; the gun still wasn't aimed. He flashed inside the gunman's reach and slashed at the left side of his neck. The knife was sharp. The edge bit in. Blood spurted. The gun hand flew to the wound. David was momentarily safe from the pistol.

David shouldered hard into the bleeding man and bolted past. He had the lobby door made. In his peripheral vision, he saw yet another black-clad figure appear. This one, from out of the garden. Then still more—four, maybe five. Two from each side of Parcheminerie.

David crashed through the hotel's entry door. His breath was fast and ragged. He tripped over the threshold and tumbled down. His momentum slid him across the polished floor, where he collapsed into the bottom of the stairs leading up. He scrambled to his feet and climbed, pack and knife still in his hands.

David was gone. The hostile from the monument with the pistol was holding his neck and bleeding through his fingers. He seemed surprised at the appearance of the men from the garden. A moment of confusion ensued. The original group was perplexed by the newcomers.

One from the garden circled his finger above his head and pointed back to Parcheminerie. His group melted up the street and into the darkness.

David's attackers rallied around their injured man and hustled him back the way they had come, up Prêtres and toward Saint-Séverin. The square became deathly quiet.

PART V
EL AQUEDUCTO DE SEGOVIA

CHAPTER 70

Paris: (Later on) Sunday, September 1, 1963

"He got away clean, Jack," Nick reported.

"He didn't need us. Sent one of the Ivans to the hospital with a bad knife wound—to the hospital if not the morgue. They saw us and split. Our team just melted away. As soon as we saw he was clear. We were never there."

"Subject injured?" Isham demanded.

"No. At least nothing serious. When we evacuated, subject was through the hotel lobby and started up the stairs. I'd say him and his stuff have Paris in the rearview mirror by now."

"It's good you were there. You chased off the Sovs. Gave him time to get away. What's your plan now?"

"Pick him up going back into Spain. He won't go in the way he came out. My instincts tell me he'll try for Port Bou."

"Find him again, Nick. Keep me advised."

MOSCOW GOLD | 437

Colone Vucetitch was apoplectic.

"Look at this, Pavel Leonidovich." He threw the flimsy at his aide:

57160 Vuceti MC

19630109

Operation journalist impeded stop Subject evaded at moment of arrest stop Current whereabouts subject unknown stop No friendly fatalities stop One injury mine serious stop Local authorities not repeat not alerted stop All friendly personnel accounted for and at embassy stop Await instructions stop

Myshnov

"An overindulged and glorified college kid 'evaded'?!? He evaded?!? The finest and most powerful security service in the world?!? *Evaded*?!? I'll have every one of them broken."

⌒⌇

"Speaking to you on an encrypted line from the secure communications room at the embassy, General."

"Go ahead, Sepp. It's safe."

"The Russians mounted a wet operation on Subject. He eluded capture," Staupitz reported.

"Really? Rare for them to lose one. Subject now?"

"Got clean away. No idea where he is now," said Staupitz.

"Scheisse! He'll head for the henhouse. You do likewise."

⌒⌇

David *was* putting as much distance between himself and Paris as he could. He had gone straight up to his room. After confirming that his injuries were minor, a bruised hip and some scrapes, he collected the rest of his things and checked out. He asked the sleepy front desk clerk to call him a taxi.

He remembered Nacho's admonition that they never give up. He knew they must have been on him most of the time in Paris. No matter that he had evaded capture in the square. They knew he was in the hotel. He would have to assume he was always under surveillance and vulnerable.

While he waited for his cab, he went into the hotel's darkened and curtained miniature dining room that looked out over the square. He was able to observe surreptitiously. After fifteen minutes had passed and by the time the taxi arrived, he had seen no movement or activity whatsoever.

He had the cabby take him out of the Latin Quarter by way of Saint-Jacques and Île de la Cité. Again nothing. He surveyed his suddenly silent surroundings. They had been so inviting and normal this morning. Now they threatened to suffocate him.

He gave instructions for the Gare de l'Est and went inside the terminal. Few people were about. He ran a few detection techniques that culminated in his grabbing another cab and going to the Gare d'Austerlitz. Nothing untoward caught his attention on the way.

More early risers and passengers on first-in-the-morning departures were in evidence. Still nothing. He bought a ticket to Orléans. Then he found the lost luggage office. It was closed, but its waiting room was open and unlit. There was a window that looked out over the platform from which his train would be leaving. He settled in to wait—and watch.

The train was scheduled to go at 5:47 a.m. It backed in well in advance of that time. A few people got on. The platform area began to fill up. More travelers were boarding the train. David continued to lurk in his darkened lobby until train time came. And went.

Just before 6:00, the train started to move. He tore out of hiding at a full gallop. His timing worked out. He was just able to jump onto the rear platform of the last carriage before the train accelerated away from him. He swung aboard and looked back at the platform. No one else was running to catch the train.

The Orléans train was an express. It took no more than an hour and a half to get there.

MOSCOW GOLD | 439

David now had a chance to think. He was enraged at last evening's developments. Not only did he have shadowers—he had known and expected that—but their intention was to kidnap him or, even worse, to kill him. He tried to believe it was the former, but he knew he had avoided being killed by only a narrow margin. He was in imminent, continuing, and mortal danger. Nacho had warned him.

Fierce resentment at Isham for compromising him and placing him at risk erupted to the surface. David no longer wondered whether he was being played by forces far beyond his ken. He now knew it and Isham had both hands in the pie. Then there was the exposure Isham had caused to Ariel. David promised himself that Isham's day of reckoning was coming.

⁂

David extracted Moscardó's packet from of his bag. The packet was the size of a large shoe box. David did his best to save Moscardó's wrapping. Inside were neat piles of what appeared to be chits of some sort—uniform chits, printed on forms about two and a half by three inches. There were hundreds of them. They were old, filled in on varying dates. The forms called for date, buyer, items sold, and amount received. They had been filled in with inconsistent degrees of willing compliance.

And then there was a small envelope. Pale gray stationery. Sealed tight. Addressed with a broad point fountain pen in blue-black ink. "To: My Cousin Carlos."

David studied the little papers. He began to draw conclusions. All were dated sometime during spring and summer 1937. He pawed through them but, after a moment, thought to be more careful. Better not to put them out of the order in which they'd been received. Not yet anyway. Perhaps they were, or maybe Moscardó had put them, in some special order.

They had been filled out by several different people. Those bearing similar handwriting were grouped together. Someone had arranged them in date order by writer. When he could get his hands on a 1937 calendar, David knew there would be no papers dated on Sundays. The gold merchants closed on Sundays.

The little slips were yellowed with time. Some were tattered and torn. Several were coffee-stained. One or two even had cigarette burns. David identified eight or nine groups. Some groups were easier to segregate and interpret than others.

He would need help deciphering the French handwriting. Yet some elements became clear. These were sales records documenting gold coin purchases from several of the Paris numismatic shops during 1937. Whoever the purchasers were, they did multiple deals per shop per day.

David guessed that some regulatory requirement had mandated that records be made—either the government or the dealers' own guild. Moscardó had implied that the dealers had collaborated and done it on their own.

The sums paid were large and almost always designated to have been in either British pounds or American dollars. A very few were denominated in francs, either French or Swiss. One was in Romanian lei and another in Turkish lira, but those were the two outliers. Pounds predominated by far.

The product descriptions left no doubt that specie was involved. He recognized reference to known varieties of large and valuable gold coin. The descriptions and amounts paid, compared and taken together, would go far in confirming that these records documented disposition of stocks that had been held in the Madrid vaults of the Bank of Spain.

Of greatest significance would be the list of buyers that could be assembled. Notations referred to companies, not individuals— those companies whose current identities, present iterations, and whereabouts would be ascertainable.

David placed his documents back into their box as close to how they had been given to him as he could. He took a moment to acknowledge his gratitude to Moscardó, who had given him a treasure of original source documentation. This was history certain not to be recorded anywhere else. Now it was in David's sole possession—along with what he believed must be the only remaining extant copy of the original receipt. The puzzle was coming together and, with it, David's ability to fight back.

✧

The gare in Orléans was much busier than Austerlitz had been. Rooting out any tails was more difficult, but David detected nothing. He knew his vigilance must not waver.

At Orléans, he switched from the express to a milk run local. He bought a ticket for Mâcon. The itinerary was Auxerre, Dijon, and Chalon-sur-Saône, with numerous smaller waypoints sandwiched between.

The locomotive on the Mâcon train was a coal-fired steam engine. It generated clouds of eye-stinging aromatic steam and smoke that reminded David of his first trip years ago—south from Paris to Madrid.

He bought himself a first-class ticket, thinking among other things that the carriage and its compartments would be less crowded. Surveillance would be easier to spot. His expectations were rewarded.

The first-class car was an anachronism. David thought it must have dated back to the era of the Great War. Rather than having an interior passageway with doors to the individual compartments, it had a long running board on one exterior side. Each compartment had its own door that opened onto the running board and the station platform.

David's instinct to get back into Spain was now twice as urgent. He needed to find Ituarte—without anyone else knowing about it.

As he mulled how best to do so, the little local eased into Chalon-sur-Saône. His ticket was good to Mâcon. It was time to do more evasion. If he was observed and followed in Orléans, they would think they had him till Mâcon.

442 | DOUGLAS L. FIELD

The stop in Chalon was twenty minutes. David busied himself with the normal preoccupations of the traveler. Check and organize his grip. Shift papers from one pocket to the other. Examine his passport. Verify he had his wallet. Francs in one section, dollars in another. Careful *not* to show any pesetas.

The locomotive whistle sounded. The train jerked forward. David leapt for the compartment door. To the astonishment of the others in it, he threw it open. He leapt onto the running board and then the platform. He batted the compartment door shut and watched the train pull out.

CHAPTER 71

Chalon-Sur-Saône: Sunday September 1, 1963

Chalon had a nice little promenade.

It ran along the north side of the river. At midday, there were a few retired people and a couple of nannies on it.

The Saône had formed the dividing line between German-occupied and Vichy France in the Second World War. That fact was advertised by signs along the river walk. He observed the riverine traffic, both docked and in transit. Its studied and practiced languidness confirmed that it was not the way for him back into Spain.

Tomorrow, he would go over this river—yet another crossing. There had been the Irún crossing those years ago. After that had been many more crossings. The Saône would be tomorrow. He reflected on what crossing the eastern Pyrenees in a few days might portend.

The old town square was a couple of blocks north of the river. He found a table in the shade at the corner of one of the establishments with outside tables. A few more people were coming out. It was the end of the first day of the week—time for a beer or a little wine. Nothing remarkable.

MOSCOW GOLD | 445

David needed to get back into Spain. He wanted to see Ariel. He was very worried she would not be in Segovia. Still, he had to try to make sure she was safe. He needed to talk to Nacho and contact Calvín and Onésimo.

He had to find Ituarte. Ituarte! That was the next big hurdle.

CHAPTER 72

Banyuls-sur-Mer: Monday, September 2, 1963

David took a night train out of Chalon headed south for Marseille.

He alighted in Avignon, again one major stop short of his ticket's stated destination. He later took another early-morning local through Nîmes and Montpellier. In the end, he arrived in Narbonne.

He put himself inside the heads of the bad guys. He concluded that they would have gathered their forces at various locations along the frontier, with the intention of heading him off going into Spain.

Over his croissants at the station café, he assessed how to get close to the frontier. Narbonne was not a large town. He made his way into the warehouse district. The germ of an idea had come into his brain. He could wangle a ride south, find someone at random. Random should be safe. Maybe some sort of a cargo van.

As David looked around, he feared that he had left it too late. There was no longer much activity around the area. The morning's loading and unloading, and, along with them, his chances to hitch had already occurred. Add to it that inapproachability seemed to be the character

MOSCOW GOLD | 447

of the place. He sidled up to several who appeared to be drivers. "Going south?" The replies were terse. Negative.

Not quite ready to give up, he saw a man humping flats of beer into a bobtail truck. Kronenbourg advertisements were splashed on its sides and back.

"Headed south today, mon ami?"

"Yeah. And I'm late."

"Give you a hand loading up?" David offered.

"What? For a ride to Perpignan?"

"A little further." David's expression said, *Sorry to press my luck, but if you're late ...*

The driver looked hard at David for a long moment but then hopped up onto the floor of his truck. "Toss those flats up. I'm Yves." He looked to be in his forties, well-built and robust.

With help, Yves was soon loaded and threading his way out of town. He had little to say until he had found and took what appeared to be a secondary road—one that meandered at once toward the coast and then away.

"What kind of trouble you in? Not French, are you?"

"Need to cross into Spain. Don't want to bother with passports, border posts, the Guardia Civil. None of those, uh, technicalities," David confided.

"Ah, oui? For sure? You Spanish?" Yves asked.

"The truth? No. Lived there a long time though."

"There's a backstory there. I can tell. None of my never mind though. I can get you to Banyuls. I turn around there."

The truck was a vastly underpowered Citroën. Yet Yves's adroit maneuvering got him in and out of tight spots at his delivery locations. Once back out on the highway, he managed to extract maximum performance without abusing the vehicle.

"You're a skillful driver." David complimented him.

448 | DOUGLAS L. FIELD

"Good jobs not easy to find down here, even less easy to keep. My truck breaks down less than, say, Pierre's. I keep driving. He doesn't."

It developed that Yves was a Catalán Nationalist. He waxed with fondness of his dreams of a traditional and historical Catalunya—one that would extend from Tarragona in Spain all along the Mediterranean to Marseille. His contempt for the governments of Spain and France was unrestrained, more so for Spain's. He accused it of overtaxing Barcelona and Gerona, in fact all the Catalán provinces, to finance its projects in poorer parts of the country.

The Franco government repressed Catalán nationalism and separatism. David's education and experience had not included most of what Yves was telling him. Not knowing what to make of it all, David nevertheless expressed interest and sympathy. Yves's good favor was secured.

Not too long after Leucate, Yves ran out of appetite for political talk. They drove along a coast-side road that passed through all the beach towns and villages—Port-Leucate, Port-Barcarés, and Canet-Plage. Yves had customers in each of them. David had opportunity to look round some and take the places in. For unknown reasons, he savored Saint-Cyprien and Areglès-sur-Mer. Both were decorated with gay, bright-colored beach umbrellas and cabañas that contrasted with the cerulean Med.

Banyuls, when they got there, was still basking in the glow of a good August holiday season plus some of the best weather southeast France had seen in years. Yves serviced two bars in Banyuls, L'Ours d'Or and La Goélette—the Golden Bear and the Schooner, the latter being a play on words, as *goélette* was also slang in France for a long, tall cocktail.

When Yves came out from La Goélette, he said, "This is where I turn back. Spanish frontier's four, five kilometers down the road we've been on—at Cerbère. But don't cross there. You'll get caught."

"I'll send you a postcard from Madrid."

MOSCOW GOLD | **449**

"You do that. You'll get there." Yves's handshake was firm, very un-French. And then he was gone.

⁊

David walked back toward L'Ours d'Or. It was ironic to him how the French were adept at disdaining their English neighbors yet admiring and imitating English culture. Thus tried the Golden Bear to be more English than if located in Old Blighty itself. It fronted on the wharf and had a nice view of the town's principal landmarks, an arcaded stone viaduct that led up from the shore to a promontory on the north side of the city and the lighthouse beyond.

L'Ours had a large wooden sign painted dark red and hung outside perpendicular to the street. The sign was replete with a gilded walking grizzly and gold letters announcing the establishment's name to go with the bear. The bar itself was wooden rather than zinc and fitted out with high barstools that had small backs for customer comfort. Wall decorations emphasized a British theme. There was a liberal variety of beer and ale on tap.

The English motif aside, the music in L'Ours d'Or was all European. From somewhere he could hear the song "Senza Fine" playing—"Senza Fine" and others, like "Al Di Là," "Volare," and "More," David called Italian joy music. They were good songs, tuneful and happy, modern-day iterations of Puccini arias he would guess.

David sat at the bar and ordered a Kronenbourg. Why not? He'd been bouncing around in one of their trucks all day.

It was quiet in the bar, and no one else had come in. David decided it was time to chat up the bartender. He ordered another beer.

"Speak Spanish?" David began.

"Sure. Most everyone around here does." The barman didn't much want to talk.

"Pretty quiet place, Banyuls," David continued

"Now, yeah. More action in August." Barkeep was still circumspect.

450 | DOUGLAS L. FIELD

"May cross over into Spain, maybe not until tomorrow. Gotta kill some time."

David felt he had planted the seed. He went back to his paper and beer. The bartender pottered around. He went out into a storage area behind the place. He appeared to do nothing other than continue his regular activities.

Not so in the event. About a quarter of an hour later, just as David had hoped, a young woman came in. The bartender had to have alerted her.

She was taller than average, had long legs and an athletic figure. In a sky-blue spaghetti-strap party dress with a rather daring neckline and a slit up one thigh, her startling figure was displayed to admirable effect. She arrived together with a cloud of loud perfume but no discernable makeup. She did not need it.

Face and form were one thing, but this person had radiant and smooth skin of a tone David had never seen before—not brown or olive or white or even tan. Along with the rich tone of her skin, there were unsettling tiger eyes and golden-brown hair to her shoulders.

She came straight in and sat next to David. She looked him over as thoroughly as he did her.

"Can I buy you a drink?" he asked, still taking it all in.

"Cinzano. With lemon."

"Barman, would you be so kind? A Cinzano for the lady. With lemon, if you please!" David ordered.

"How are you called, pretty lady?" he asked.

"Ambre."

He put it together—Ambre; Ámbar in Spanish; and, of course, Amber in English. She was just that, amber.

"Where are you from?" David tried getting a little personal.

"Here. Mother's Syrian, father was French. If that's what you mean."

"That *is* what I mean. Nice combination."

MOSCOW GOLD | 451

Ambre gave him a smile that seemed both grateful and wistful. "Looking for a date?" she asked.

David continued. "What's a date run these days?"

"Hundred."

"A hundred. Well, I'd say that's fair, but I'm not looking for a date."

A one-hundred-franc note appeared in David's hand below the level of the bar, where the bartender could not see. It was folded on the diagonal, and David held it between his middle and ring fingers.

"Rather than a date, how about we talk a while?"

She reached over with a gentle movement, took the money, and touched his hand for a fractional second. "I think that would be nice."

David and Ambre chatted each other up. Banalities for the most part. He noted, to her credit, that she never asked his name. He never mentioned it either. Then it came time to do business.

"Ever been to Spain?" David got down to it.

"No, never have. Would like to someday. You?"

"Yeah. Live there."

"You're very close to home then. Here in Banyuls." Ambre stated the obvious, inviting David's explanation.

"Close, but not *there*, am I?"

David saw her assessing him. Critical and serious. Then he saw that she caught on. "Oh, of course. I get it."

"Something told me you might. You seem very smart."

"You're not Spanish, are you?"

"Now why would you ask that?" David smiled at her. "Do I have a heavy accent?"

"You don't have any accent at all. I imagine you know that. But you're not Spanish. The business I'm in, here in this town I'm in ..." She paused for a second, "Well, you could say I *meet* a lot of Spaniards. You're not like them."

"Don't you like Spaniards?"

"No, it's not dislike. They're just Spaniards—a little brittle, I guess, inflexible. Tense and pessimistic too. You, handsome young fellow,

452 | DOUGLAS L. FIELD

have problems. I can tell that, but you're not brittle or pessimistic about them. Admit it. You're not Spanish."

"OK. No. Not Spanish," David admitted. "I'm American, but I've lived much of my life in Madrid. I need to get into Spain, but I don't want the authorities to know I'm back."

"Sounds complicated. I imagine that there's a girl involved. What's she like?"

David laughed out loud. "Like I said, you're smart. Her name's Ariel. *She* is Spanish—for dozens of generations. Not brittle or tense though. Different than you. Taught by the nuns—"

"Taught by the nuns?!?" Ambre scoffed. "Yes, then she's way different than me! Tell me more."

"Dark eyes and hair but very fair skin. Beautiful face. More beautiful smile, but still a serious person. Very smart and capable. Tender and kind. We have lots of fun. I hope she's meeting me on Saturday. She might not. I have to get there to see."

"You're in love!" Ambre pronounced. "That's for sure. I know someone. Have another beer. Don't go anywhere." Ambre stood up and drank off the last of her Cinzano. "I enjoyed our 'date,' Señor. Safe travels back to your Spanish lady." She then got up, shook David's hand, and vamped out of the bar.

The wait was not long. "Someone" turned out to be a man—one about a decade older than David. He walked in with evident purpose and sat on Ambre's stool. He pulled out a box of Players Navy Cut cigarettes—a box, not a pack. A box with the portrait of a Royal Navy matelot, a little lid, and silvered wrapper. British smokes, thicker than American, unfiltered and very strong. Not to mention expensive.

He looked hard at David and then fished one out. After that came a much smaller box that slid open to reveal a pile of wax-stemmed and blue-headed matches. One flared. He lit the smoke, which he then hung in a corner of his mouth. It bobbled up and down when he started talking.

"You the Spanish package?"

MOSCOW GOLD | 453

David nodded.

"I'm Andrés. It's going to cost you."

"Mmm."

"Two large. Half before we leave. The rest when I get you there. We'll walk. It's a tough slog. Lots of up and down. You a hiker? In good shape?" Andrés had a lot of concerns.

"I just gave Ambre a hundred. Do I get a credit?" David asserted himself.

Andrés did not respond at once. When he did, "Ah, a humorist. You will not be joking by the time we reach Spain. Please consider your decision. Once we start, we will maintain a steady and brisk pace. If you are not up to it, I will not be able to delay my own progress. You will be left to your own devices."

"Leave me up there to die?"

"Business is business."

David rehearsed his alternatives. He had already almost died in Paris. Now this. His choices were poor. His need to get across was urgent. Caution was a commodity he could ill afford. At least the guy was honest. The candor tipped the balance.

"I'm in."

Andres got up to leave. "There's a sporting goods place in town. Find it. Get yourself a good rucksack, straps for both shoulders. You can't go up there with what you've got. Get it big enough. You're going to carry something for me. I'll look for you in the town square at dusk. Except for buying the rucksack, stay out of sight."

David *supposed* it was still dusk when the battered Peugeot 404 taxi stormed into the square. It screeched to a stop in front of the fountain. Andrés appeared in the passenger-side window and stared out. David walked toward the car. Andrés motioned him to hurry. The back door opened. David followed his new rucksack in.

"You got the rucksack. Good. It's a thousand down."

David handed over the bills, which disappeared.

"He's Jacques." Andrés jerked his head toward the driver.

David knew it wasn't his real name, but they were not going to find time to become pals.

"Jacques" beat it out of town and up a paved but not major road. They seemed to be going away from the coast and climbing some. Jacques and Andrés made offhanded chatter in some patois that David could not understand. After some twenty-five kilometers, Jacques slowed down—looking for something. He found it and turned left onto a dirt track that led to what David thought was south, further, higher into the hills.

They pulled up in front of a darkened cabin.

Andrés hopped out. "Jacques has done what he can for us. We walk from here. Grab your stuff."

David alighted, dragging his rucksack out after him. Andrés gave Jacques what sounded like some curt instructions. The taxi turned around. It disappeared down the dirt road as fast as it had come up.

They had the benefit of a near full moon, so it was not pitch-black. It was stone quiet. Just as David was thinking this, Andrés confirmed it. "Good night for us. There's a moon. Harder without one. You can fall. Could get hurt. Long way to hike back on a broken leg." So went his lugubrious comment.

Andrés picked up David's pack. "How much junk you got in there? Not too bad. Wait for me a second."

A miniature flashlight came out. Andrés went inside the cabin. In no time, he came back out with an armload of cigarette cartons— American cigarettes. There were Marlboros, Kents, Parliaments, and Camels.

Andrés had a small pack of his own. He filled it with cartons. There were some left over. "Here you take these. They're not heavy. Help make the trip over worthwhile. Besides, it'll give us something to bribe the border guards with if they catch us." He laughed at his own joke—as if they would ever catch him.

MOSCOW GOLD | 455

During all this, David had a chance to observe and assess his guide. Andrés looked to be shading into his late thirties. He was about David's own six-foot height but very slim. He had long hands, arms, and legs; a square face and high forehead; and deep-set, dark blue-gray eyes that were adorned with rimless glasses—glasses he off and on polished with deliberate care and attention.

He dressed the part of a professional smuggler—a heavy flannel shirt tucked into wide-wale corduroy pants themselves tucked into thick, light-gray socks jammed into stout hiking boots. The socks were rolled down over the tops of his boots. In the moonlight, they looked like white rings around his lower legs. He'd be easier to follow in the dark.

He's nothing but two legs and two lungs. In another place and time, he might be a competition bicycle racer or swimmer, David thought

"Here's the rules: I lead. We'll break for five or ten minutes every hour and a half or so. The pace won't be killer, but don't let that fool you. We have about twenty-five kilometers to cover, but we'll climb about two thousand meters and descend almost that much—not quite. Lotta people find the going down the hardest part. Hurts your knees. And that's at the end. Be careful at the end. That's when you're tired. That's when you can get hurt. There are stretches where we can talk and stretches where we can't. If I raise my fist, you shut up. You can start talking again when I do. My fist goes up, you stay quiet till you hear from me. Questions?"

David thought about it for a second. Andrés was talking about a fifteen-plus mile march in the dark with some six thousand feet of climbing. "No. Let's go."

The early going was a steady uphill. They soon picked up a noisy flowing stream that rustled by. Andrés took the opportunity to socialize. It turned out that he was Spanish—from Valladolid. He spoke the clear, precise, and elegant Castilian for which that city is noted.

As was the case with so many of his generation, he had immigrated to France in hopes of securing gainful employment—employment that would pay his expenses and allow him to send extra money home.

"I found some acceptable jobs, but it was all menial stuff. Waiting tables, driving, cleaning up after people. Money was good enough, but it was dull. I can't abide dull. Decided I was tired of working for tips in tourist traps in Arles and Avignon, so I came down here. Now I'm in international transportation if you take my meaning."

They both were amused at that.

David added, "Plus the health benefits of exercise. Working outside. Not to mention the intellectual challenge of interacting with governmental authorities. On both sides of the border."

"You've caught the vision. And the girls down here are more down to earth. Pretty stuck-up they are up in Provence."

"Uh, Ambre being what you might call exhibit A?"

"Ah, yes, the fair and exotic Ambre."

Now more serious climbing started. They were still alongside the stream, but the path was much steeper. There were places where steps had been fashioned out of pieces of wood, chunks of granite, and thick tree branches. They got a little winded. Andrés's glasses fogged off and on. David noticed that, with care and patience, he cleaned them, never complaining.

After a bracing climb, they ascended to what seemed to be sort of a landing or plateau. The trail wound among huge stones and outcroppings. At one point, they came into a little clearing among the rocks.

"Let's have a break," offered Andrés. He pulled a metal flask out of his hip pocket and unscrewed the cap. "Try some of this. It's French. Way better than that Fundador swill that you're used to back home."

"I like Fundador." David feigned defensiveness. But when he tasted what Andrés had, he added, "Oh, yeah. This is just the ticket!"

"Of course, you like Fundador." It was an amiable comment by the guide. "All of us *gachupines* do. Reminds us of home. Being in France

MOSCOW GOLD | **457**

has refined my taste in brandy anyway." Out came the Players again.
"¿Fumas un pitillo?"

Back on the trail for about three miles, it was a little uphill, but the trail was sandy. Their feet sank in. The going remained difficult. Talking was still permitted. At least there had been no raised fist. The trail was wider. They could walk side by side. Andrés held forth on a wide range of topics.

David found it interesting that Andrés's great passion was to establish and operate a business. In David's experience, this aspiration was rare for a Spaniard. Most of the kids David's age had wanted to become intellectuals, poets, artists, university professors. or government workers. Andrés wanted to own and run his own *negocio*."

"What kind of business?" David asked.

'Doesn't matter. A bodega filled with fine wines, a car dealership, cheese wholesaler, coffee merchant. Whatever. Something that people always need. Easier to survive the hard economic times. We always have more than our fair share of those in Spain."

"Set up a medical clinic. Or a chain of optical shops. People will always get sick, and they always need glasses. Call it Óptica Andrés."

"¡Precisamente!"

It was notable to David, and fortunate he reflected later, that Andrés was knowledgeable on a range of other topics as well. And he was a bit of a philosopher. They were able to make progress through miles of interesting conversation. The distraction of it eased the way for David.

"How's our progress?" David wondered at one point.

"Acceptable. Some of the hardest climbing is just coming up. We'll take another break," Andres decided.

They sat on a couple of fallen logs, and Andrés probed a little. "None of my business why people want to make this hike with me. So, I don't ask. Not going to ask you. Under certain circumstances, ones we hope will never come to pass, it's better if we know less about each other rather than more."

458 | DOUGLAS L. FIELD

David said nothing. Andrés offered David another cigarette. They smoked for a time in silence.

After a while, Andrés started up again. "You're not the typical package, you know. You're too young to be a returning exile. You're not dour enough to be a communist. You're not some Latin American dictator seeking asylum. You've made me curious."

"That so?"

"This particular trail has some history and notoriety to it." Andrés tried a different tack.

"Has it now then?" David avoided a direct answer.

"It has. Around eighteen to twenty years ago, it got a lot of use smuggling downed American and British airmen out of Europe. World War II. Americans more than any other though. The Comet Line they called it. It was started by some Belgian woman. Dédée she was called, I think. They would get them through here into neutral Spain. If they weren't caught and interned by Franco, they got back to the war."

David then said with a wink, "The Americans are an interesting people, Andrés. Lots of them fought and died in France—twice in the space of twenty-five years in this century. There's great affection in the United States for France and, as details have gotten out, great admiration for the French Resistance. Not the least of reasons is for getting all those Americans flyers out of occupied Europe—out and back into the fight. It's talked about over there. To this day."

Andrés stuck out his hand and shook David's. "I thought so. Don't know why, but I thought so. Following where *those* Americans trod perhaps will make your little walk tonight all the more personal, no?"

"Well, yes. It will."

Andrés had not exaggerated. Until now, it had seemed to David that their way had been southward. Now the trail wound, twisted, and turned back on itself. He lost his sense of direction. It was, in places, very steep and primitive. They had to thread their way through boulders and tree roots that wanted to trip them up. It was necessary

MOSCOW GOLD | 459

often now to find handholds in rocks and branches at the side to keep their balance.

They had long since left the first stream behind. The path made an abrupt sharp left turn and ended at the edge of another stream.

Andrés looked a little sheepish. "I never tell my, uh, clients in advance about this part. We have to cross. It's dangerous—slippery and cold. Tie your shoes on your pack. Put your socks where they'll stay dry. Roll up your pants as far as you can get them."

David did so and observed Andrés to do likewise.

Andrés went first. David followed.

Glacial, or maybe polar, would have been the word for it. The water was thick and frigid. David could not imagine how it stayed liquid. It took his breath away. It interfered with his concentration. It was about knee-deep but was running so fast that, once David was in, it splashed up on him and soaked his lower body.

The stream was about twelve feet across. They had to pick their way on large rocks that were below the surface. Out in the middle, there were no handholds. Andrés stumbled at one point and went down. He popped back up cursing. David got almost to the far side without falling, but within eighteen inches of the bank, his right foot slipped. He splashed into the mud and dirt on the far side at the water's edge. Andrés's backpack was water-resistant, and David managed to keep his dry. Otherwise, they were soaked through.

Andrés had a towel in his pack. They dried their feet and then continued, soggy and cold. But their feet were dry. About a mile away from the stream Andrés raised his fist. They were coming out of the tree line. The trail circled over large rounded white granite. Sound carried far out here in the open. They would be easy to spot against the light-colored stone.

On they went and always upward. Andrés now called no breaks. The walking was strenuous, but their exertion kept the cold at bay while their clothing dried. They just hiked in silence, mile upon mile.

David sensed that they had started down. Again, Andrés raised his fist, but he followed that by stretching out three fingers of his left hand behind his back and parallel to the ground. David puzzled over this for a few hundred yards. Then he got it. An "E." España. They were in Spain.

The walk down was as represented. If not worse than the hike up, it was as bad. David became weary. At times, he walked in a stupor. Andrés had them on silent running the whole way down. The Spanish, David thought, must patrol their border with greater diligence than the French do theirs. David had never imagined that a person could fall asleep walking. It was his aching knees that kept him from doing so.

The mindlessness was interrupted when Andrés dove into the foliage at the side of the track. His sudden movement brought David back to full awareness. They burrowed in under what smelled like a large juniper bush. Andrés put his mouth right up to David's ear, "¡Guardia Civil! Patrolling the border. Pray there's no dogs."

David did so. At first, he saw and heard nothing, but soon came the distant sound of voices, maybe laughter too. David figured they must not be expecting to find anything. Otherwise, they wouldn't be talking, giving themselves away.

Andrés gave it plenty of time before they started again. There were then no more stops. The downward path leveled a little. Right after that, the new day started to dawn. Without warning, they popped out of the forest into a little town. It was just waking up. The place was in a swale between higher hills. Morning mist mixed with stove smoke gave it an ethereal look in the invasive pink-and-orange light of advancing day.

"This is Requesens. You are in Spain. The bus to Figueras should pass through the *plaça* around 10:00 hours. Best you and I aren't seen together. Thanks for carrying those smokes."

David opened his backpack and gave Andrés back his cartons— that along with the rest of the money.

"My feet hurt. You owe me a rebate."

MOSCOW GOLD | 461

"You'll get over it. By Figueras, I imagine. You got good Spanish papers?"

David nodded.

"You better. Guardia Civil aren't stupid. They suspect our little evening strolls. You aren't home free. They're good at recognizing new faces. Get caught and you're in for a stretch in the *bote* and deportation. Stay out of sight till you jump on the bus."

David just looked at him.

Andrés punched David on the shoulder. "Go on now. Get back in the fight!"

Then he left David and walked over to a café that was opening.

CHAPTER 73

Cerbère: Friday, September 6, 1963

It was a job of work for Nick to find a phone in this little backwater, much less one with any line quality.

One was at last located at the post office. The call was operator assisted. Her "assistance" took thirty-five minutes. Even so, the result was suboptimal. Through the scratches, hisses, and static, "I haven't seen him yet. On the bright side, no Russians yet either."

"He went through Irún." Isham's snarl was clear even over the bad connection. "I told you he would. He's dodged you again."

"No, Jack. He's too smart for that. He's coming this way. Or he already came."

"No Russians, you say, Nick. And no kid. You think the Russians have given up? They haven't. They never give up. They're on to him on the west side."

"No, the Russians ran off. There's temporary confusion in their camp right now."

MOSCOW GOLD | 463

"There's confusion in *our* camp. It's past temporary. Pick him up before they do. They'll kill him. Then you won't ever find him or your job. And I won't get what he's got. That's not acceptable."

Then the line, which had been marginal all along, went dead. Barnickle did not seek to reconnect.

CHAPTER 74

Madrid: Tuesday, September 3, 1963

Ariel's encounter with Detectives Flórez and Arias crystallized her thinking.

She had been timid and reluctant to assist David. Natural prudence and reticence had urged her toward caution. After the humiliation of being picked up by the police on a crowded public street, she had begun to understand David better. She became aware that it was not only David's future being leveraged but hers as well. She found herself developing a satisfying resistance to living in fear and intimidation. And with it came a new and strong bond of affection with David they had not had before.

She went and saw Nacho. He gave her a knowing look and then a little lecture on hiding in plain sight.

She went to Jaime, and he activated one of his many connections.

And she went to the makeup counter a Galeras Preciados on Fernando el Católico.

CHAPTER 75

Segovia: Saturday, September 7, 1963

Ariel was up early.

She hopped on the Metro and got off at Sevilla station. After the Metro, she went down la Carrera de San Jerónimo toward the Neptune fountain and the Palace Hotel. There she found the Madrid offices of American Express. She went straight to the busy counter and had a brief conversation with the attendant.

After what seemed like only half a minute, a young man approached. "Señorita Muñiz? Friend of Señor Castellón?"

"Yes. That's right."

"We have been expecting you. My name is Jorge. Please follow me." He led her down a wide staircase to a windowless lobby. Several American Express–related businesses had their entry doors there. Jorge paused in the lobby area for some seconds.

"Good," he said. "We are alone." He led her to and through the door marked Viajes Bailén. Ariel knew that Viajes Bailén was a prominent Madrid travel agency and tour company.

MOSCOW GOLD | 467

Once inside, Jorge pointed to a neat pile of clothes and said, "That is your uniform. You may use the ladies' room to change." He pointed. "The tour today is to Segovia, is it not?"

"Exactly."

"Right. Well then, the guide is Don Telesforo. You will act as escort. The tour is almost full. Americans and Brits with, I think, one German couple. Telesforo will do it in English."

"Very well," Ariel agreed. "My English is a little rusty. I'll get some much-needed practice. About what time does it arrive in Segovia?"

"At 11:00 hours, Don Telesforo will meet you and your companions there. At the bus terminal."

"Perfect."

"As escort, your role is to assist in keeping the group together. Round up stragglers—that kind of thing. Telesforo will do the talking. So, no worries for you there. You will find sufficient time to wander off on your own for a few minutes from time to time if you wish. Please feel free to make connection with the customers and spread goodwill if you can." He looked her over, smiled a little, and added, "I doubt you will have any trouble."

"I doubt it."

"Before you go and change, you'll need this." He reached into a corner where there was a stack of sticks with blue and white discs containing the Viajes Bailén logo and handed her one of them. "Your paddle. Makes it easier for the chicks to find mother hen and all that. Have a good time."

Ariel took her uniform and paddle into the ladies' room. She reappeared wearing the uniform, which fit, her hair pulled into a tight bun in the traditional Spanish style. She had applied rather heavy makeup more suited to one somewhat older than she that also darkened her fair skin a little. The final touch was a very red lipstick. She was ready.

They left a little late. It took about an hour and a quarter to drive up through the northern suburbs of Madrid, past the Valley of the

468 | DOUGLAS L. FIELD

Fallen and El Escorial to Segovia. Ariel had a good time chatting up her charges and pointing out the sights.

It was right on 11:00 when they arrived.

It was narrow and tight inside the city of Segovia. As advertised, Telesforo met them at the terminal. They walked a block to the wide Calle de Fernández Ladreda, which descended to the north and had an exquisite view over its entire length of the ancient Roman aqueduct, which towers above the bottom of the street at the Plaza de Azoguejo.

"The Romans built this acueducto in the first century AD. It stretches three thousand feet from the lower slopes of the Sierra de Guadarrama to the walls of the Segovian old town," Telesforo intoned. "For centuries, it brought, and could still bring, water from mountain streams to thirsty Segovia."

There were facts, figures, architectural particulars, and anecdotes in profusion, but Ariel's mind was elsewhere. She did note the day was glorious and the temperature mild. The blue sky and white clouds behind the light sienna stones of the great span were nothing less than a photographer's idyll. It was perfect for her rendezvous.

※

David looked down on the Plaza de Azoguejo. The square, which was by no means square, was teeming. Some locals were doing their Saturday business, but mostly it was tourists there to see the aqueduct on a fine day. There were two or three separate tour groups, identified by their leaders' uniforms and the little signs they carried.

Headed out of the plaza on the west side, under the aqueduct and perpendicular to it, was a switchback stone stairway that led to the upper city. At the top of those steps, some seventy-five or eighty of them, there lay a medium-sized landing that was protected by a chest-high parapet. The landing and parapet had an expansive view of the aqueduct from near its top, all along its length and down over the plaza and all the activity of Segovia below.

MOSCOW GOLD | 469

David was twitchy with nerves over whether Ariel would come. After all that had happened, he wouldn't blame her if she didn't. It had occurred to him to skip the meet and evolve a different plan. But he couldn't bring himself to do it.

He had installed himself on the landing. He was wearing a brown Spanish Republican Army overcoat and the tasseled forage cap typical of that service. He had a couple of weeks of scruffy attempt at a mustache and beard. He wore a pair of horn-rimmed glasses and had dark curly hair that looked to be going gray at the temples. Leaning against the wall was a makeshift crutch. Its cross piece had been padded with a folded and soiled chunk of old bath towel. On the ground was a brown beret that had a few coins in it. He wore a baleful look.

It was just coming up noon. This was the place where David, two Saturdays ago now, had asked Ariel, without fail, to meet him. She had said she knew where he meant.

There was no Ariel.

On the platform were two Asian girls twittering away in a foreign language and taking each other's pictures. They ignored the war-wounded soldier soliciting people for small change.

David looked over the parapet, down the steps, and into the plaza. It was crowded, but he knew he would recognize her, even at distance. One of the female tour guides was coming up the stairs—no doubt to meet her group who would come up after her. She climbed sedately. He saw she was pretty, just short of middle age, and trim.

The street that led to the cathedral and the Alcázar meandered away to the west off the landing. David looked up it. No Ariel up that way. He was realizing his worst fears. He looked back down the stairs. The tour guide was nearly up.

Still no Ariel.

The guide arrived at the landing panting just a little. It was straight-up noon. The Asian girls moved on.

Now it was only the guide and the soldier on the landing—no one else. She looked up the street toward the Alcázar and then back over

470 | DOUGLAS L. FIELD

toward the square. Both could see that no one else was approaching. They were alone.

David looked hard at the guide. He felt faint stirrings of recognition. The bearing. The straight posture. How the woman held her head. How could it be? Dressed up as a tour guide? Relief and disbelief washed over him.

She was continuing to look around, confused and starting to appear worried. She looked up toward the cathedral again and then over the rail into the square. Now he knew.

They were about five feet apart. It looked like she was going to go back down the stairs, away from the soldier-beggar. He said sotto voce so no one other than she would hear, "Hey, beautiful! Got a duro for a guy with a game leg?"

Every Spanish woman grew weary of piropos and unsolicited approaches. It never did to acknowledge them. It did not surprise David that this one put on her best hauteur and ignored the oaf. She turned to head down.

"Not even one solitary little duro?" This time a little louder, more urgent.

Now it penetrated. In spite of herself, she turned and gaped at the man.

Recognition flashed. "David!" It *was* him! She ran the step and a half to him and hugged him—hard, really hard.

He picked her up off the ground a little and kissed her face, "Sweet baby, you do look good to me! You look about forty, and you do look good. What a perfect cover. I knew you would think of something."

"I *looked* at you, but I didn't *see* you, David. I'm so sorry." She said in his ear. "You are so different. But it *is* you. I knew you would make it through safe. I *knew* you would be here!"

"And, Ariel, I hoped you would be here too. I counted on it. No, I've lived for it these last days."

They kissed and she ran her hands through his hair, and his cap fell off.

MOSCOW GOLD | 471

"You changed the part on your hair! Where'd you get that stupid hat? And those dopey glasses?" Her questions poured out.

"The Paris flea market. The cap's very valuable. Genuine Spanish Foreign Legion or some such. Like my cover?"

"It took me in. *You* took me in." Then she socked him in the chest but not all that hard. "I was beginning to be afraid—afraid that something terrible had happened to you. That you were hurt. Or worse."

"I'm OK. There's a story."

"Oh, David, I'm sorry. I've been so anxious to see you."

"It turns out I need not to be recognized for a couple of weeks. I wanted to see if my disguise worked. If anybody in Spain would recognize me, it would be you."

"It worked. I looked right at you and stood up here with you. I wouldn't ever have imagined that it was you."

"It's called hiding in plain sight."

Ariel gave him a grin. "I've heard of that. Nacho told me."

He stood back away from Ariel and took her in. "I like how you look in plain sight. You do all that for my benefit?"

She just made a flouncy little curtsey. "It worked. But you figured it out."

"We both almost went away from here very unhappy," David said

Then they started laughing, and once they got started, they could scarcely stop.

Ariel moved over toward the parapet and said, "Let's check down below."

"What for?"

"My tour. Here they come. That's how I came up here to Segovia today," Ariel explained, "on an excursion that originated in Madrid. I'm an escort, they call it. I left them to come up here and find you. They're headed up now. To get the view. Take their pictures with the aqueduct."

"I knew you'd figure some kind of cover, but you came to Segovia as a fake guide, with a whole group of real tourists? To distract attention?" David asked.

"*Claro está.* That and I calculated that it would help not drawing attention to us being together so you could tell me all that has happened. We can drop in and out of the tour group as it goes along. I didn't imagine that you would be disguised. I should have thought of that. It won't matter. There's always congregating around tourist groups. It'll still look natural. We can hide in plain sight together, I suppose." She was pleased with herself.

"Well, I suppose we can, Mata Hari, the spy. It's brilliant! I read somewhere, by the way, that she was very seductive. Mata Hari that is," David continued, ogling at her.

"Behave. Here they come. Don Telesforo, he's the guide. What a name, huh? Said we would be going to the cathedral and then to lunch and, after that, to the Alcázar. I figure there'll be plenty of time for us to talk."

"I have lots to say to you." David was still leering, playful.

"¡*Delincuente*! Bad boy! Control yourself for a second. Ignore me. As soon as they go up the street, we'll follow. Then we can talk."

David could think of nothing else than to go back to his wounded-soldier act. The tour group straggled up to the landing. There was, of course, protracted marveling at the aqueduct. Ariel socialized with one or two of the others and even tried out her prep school English on a couple in their mid-sixties from California. They asked her to take their picture overlooking the aqueduct.

Don Telesforo regarded David with undisguised contempt and initiated an attempt to run him off—that was, until they made eye contact. Then the little man thought better of it and retreated. Otherwise, David kept his eyes down and said nothing. He didn't need to, as several people contributed to his beret—a few with paper money even.

MOSCOW GOLD | 473

As the group moved off, David put his caps in the coat pockets. He folded the coat inside out over his left arm and his crutch. Then he hastened after Ariel.

"Weren't they a cute couple, those people from California?" Ariel gushed. "I couldn't understand all of what they were saying, but I liked them. But then as a rule, I like Americans! And look at you, you got a lot of money didn't you, poor gimp. You now can afford to treat me to a copa."

"I didn't know you spoke English, Ariel," David said in his native language. "Jou haccent ees praychous."

"Now you are making fun of me."

"No, it's enchanting." He switched back to Castilian. "The California people had been here before—a long time ago, some forty years, when they were students, or maybe right after. Anyway, when they were newly married, they came to Segovia and had their picture taken there at that spot. They wanted another one after all these years—to compare and for sentimental reasons. They told you that, after they get home and whenever they look at the picture you took of them, they will think of you. They reminded me of my parents."

"I want a picture of you and me there, David. And then maybe in forty years ..."

"Do let's, Ariel."

Now they were approaching the cathedral. Everyone, including David, went inside. Ariel and David sat down in one of the pews while Don Telesforo went on at excruciating length about the distinctives of the great church. It was dark and cool inside, fusty.

As they sat, Ariel said, "We'll be here for a while. You have a story to tell. So do I, David. You go first."

"What story, Ariel?" David became concerned.

"I'll tell you, but you first. Go."

David gave Ariel the condensed version. He started with Mrs. Negrín, the Soviet receipt, the failure with Portillo, Méndez Aspe, and finding Moscardó and his documents. He told her of the attempt on his life and then crossing the Pyrenees with Andrés.

474 | DOUGLAS L. FIELD

"What's your story?" he said before she had time to process all that he had told her.

She took a deep breath. "I have a confession to make to you, David. After Santander, I was angry with you. I thought you were selfish and reckless to have pulled me into all this. I understood your motivations—your need to get free—but I couldn't share them. I wasn't going to come today."

"But you're here. What happened?"

"Last week. I was out on Fuencarral with Sagrario and another girl from the flat. We were seated in a terraza. It was the height of the paseo. Everyone was out. The police came and arrested me, David. They hauled me up and threw me in a car. I was taken to the comisaría, and they left me in a room."

David gritted his teeth as his anger rose.

"Two of them interrogated me. It was all about you. It seemed to go on forever. They threatened me and told me I had to inform on you. They demanded to know if we were sleeping together. They then left me alone and let me stew for a long time before they threw me out in the street to walk home—showing me their disdain and disrespect, I suppose."

David's face flushed red. He started to speak.

"No, David. Let me finish. They tried to leverage me to get to you. You could think that such an experience would have frightened me into not coming to you today. But it enraged me. I understand now. You must get free. So now must I. I got a little help from Nacho and Jaime. I'm over the moon to see you today. Now I know."

She reached up and touched his face and smiled into his eyes. "The gold story wanted to separate us, David, but it didn't. It's brought us together. I'm so sorry that, at first, I didn't understand. Oh, look! Telesforo is ready to go."

∽

David watched from a distance as Telesforo led the group back through the upper city to the Plaza de Azoguejo. Ariel prattled merrily with her little group, he saw, as they moved through the ancient streets. Once back in the plaza, the tour chattily installed itself at several outside tables that had been reserved for it at La Amapola de Castilla.

David took a seat alone at the edge of the crowd. He watched Ariel take a place at the next table. They would be able to talk, but not appear to be a couple. La Amapola's service was leisurely, pleasantly so. Their mood lightened and they had ample time to continue catching up as they worked their way through drinks and a traditional Castilian dinner.

"I have something for you, Ariel," David said when they were settled. "Two things to be precise." He produced a box about the size of a small paperback book. It was wrapped in the violet paper of Joyas "Castilla la Vieja" of Segovia. Then there was a letter envelope that had "Ariel" written on top.

"Open the box first," David suggested.

"What is this? It's for me? ¡Ay! ¡*Qué emoción!*" Ariel unwrapped the package, conserving the paper. Inside was a necklace on a silver chain. On the chain hung a Sterling pendant, about the size of a large postage stamp. It had tiny, raised nail heads on its four corners, and the edges were daintily ruffled. There was an inscription. The tiny letters were centered and stamped out. The negative space said, "+ que *ayer*" and below that, " – que *mañana.*"

"More than yesterday! Less than tomorrow! David, it's exquisite." She took it out of the box. She turned her back to him. "Help me put it on."

He took the ends of the chain from her fingers and hooked them for her. Then he kissed her on the neck. "I hope you like it."

"Like it? I love it! I will never take it off!"

"You'll have to take it off some time."

"Quizás, but not for many months. What's the second thing?" she asked eagerly.

476 | DOUGLAS L. FIELD

"There was a note that I wrote to you while I was in Paris," David told her. "Before I was attacked, by the way. I was missing you. But I tore it up. It was too mushy."

"I like mushy. Too bad you tore it up. What did it say?"

"How nice it was in Paris. But how much nicer if you were here with me. How I would like to touch your hair and breathe you in. To look into those dark brown eyes and hear the low sound of your voice. If you were there, how we might join all the other lovers walking along and holding hands. Maybe I could steal a kiss or two of yours in the dark along the river. Stuff like that."

"I like it so far. What else?"

"Well, I was afraid you might not like it if I called us lovers," he looked a little embarrassed.

"But do go on. There was more, no?" She smiled sweetly.

"Well, I've had an old US dollar bill that I sentimentally carried around—since I first came to Spain. I tore it in half. I decided to enclose for you one half, keep the other, ask you to promise to meet me in Paris one year from that day, August 31, 1964? Then we could put that old dollar back together again."

He handed her a small envelope that she hurried to open. Inside was her half of the dollar bill.

Ariel started to cry, "Mushy? I'll show you *mushy*." Heedless of whomever among the tour might be watching, she fell on his neck and held on to him. "And, yes, I will be in Paris. One year. Under the Eiffel Tower maybe, yes?"

After a while, he put his hands on her shoulders and pushed her away from him a little. He looked at her face and then saw that his necklace was cosseted and comfortable in the "V" of her sweater.

After lunch, they went to the Alcázar.

Telesforo displayed good knowledge of the place. Built in the 1300s but remodeled a couple of times since, it was filled with stained-glass treasures, tapestries, ramparts with excellent views of the surrounding *paisaje*, countryside, and secret passages and stairways.

As to one large room, the guide noted King Ferdinand and Queen Isabella had used it as a bedroom. "Ferdinand and Isabella. Now there was a hot couple," David commented.

"It's not for nothing that we put them on our money," Ariel agreed. "Sister Clara, my history teacher, said they ran away together and eloped."

"Bet that caused a furor around the royal family dinner table."

They stood looking out a large open window over the Castilian landscape and a little round Romanesque church. Telesforo called it la Iglesia de la Vera Cruz and said it had been finished in the year 1208 for the Knights Templar. One of the oldest active churches in Spain, said the guide.

As they enjoyed the view, David put his arm around Ariel and held her close, "Once, when I was here as a kid, they told us that the queen's maid was standing by one of these windows, perhaps this one, looking out at the view way down below. She was holding the newborn baby prince, the heir to the throne. She leaned out to see better and, by accident, dropped the kid."

"Oh, David, that's awful. What did she do?"

"Jumped right after him. Didn't want to face the king's wrath, I guess. One of the Enriques I think it was."

She shivered a little and pulled him tighter. "That story can't be true. It must be, what do they call it, apocryphal."

"Could be." David enjoyed her discomfiture for a second. Then he turned serious. "But as we're learning life can be dangerous, uncertain and short."

As he could, mixed in among the wonders and the lore of the ancient castle, David explained his thoughts about the immediate future.

"Can I give you Mrs. Negrín's receipt and Raúl's chits? Keep them safe for me. Doña Sagrario will have someplace."

"Better than that," she said, "Gestoría Afán, my old escrow company employer. My girlfriend still works there. She'll put the papers in their safe. No one will know that they're there. Secure from theft, fire, and other risk of loss. Gestorías specialize in that sort of thing."

"I'll follow you day after tomorrow to Madrid. I can't yet go back to Vallehermoso. Tomorrow's Sunday. I'll figure a way to make contact on Monday."

They held hands back up Fernández Ladreda to the bus terminal. It was getting late in the afternoon.

About to go on the bus, Ariel took hold of her necklace. "I was afraid of this day, but it's been a *maravailla*. And, yes, David," she said, "we *are* lovers."

PART VI
CARABANCHEL

CHAPTER 76

Madrid: Monday, September 9, 1963

¡Ay, Madrid, con tus virtudes y tus defectos, pero siempre tú! (Ah, Madrid, with your virtues and your faults, but always you!)

David had been gone for only a couple of short weeks. Yet he had missed his city. It was still hot, the sunlight still intense. But in the first week of September, a hint of the more moderate days of fall was discernable—if nothing other than in its anticipation by the populace. It, by now, had had its fill of high summer.

The war-wounded cover was efficacious. David attained fluidity in getting around with his crutch. The disguise was proving to be natural and convincing. As he moved about the city, he encountered compadres who themselves had suffered from injuries and disabilities, ones for them that were altogether real. When they saw David, an immediate soldierly connection existed. This was never spoken. He could just see it in their eyes. David made no greeting to the several genuine ex-soldiers that he encountered whom he silently, and by *simpático* eye contact, acknowledged as he limped about his business.

The Diego Campos Lázaro identity was serving its purpose. On those few occasions when he was required to produce his documentos, it had proven itself. No further questions asked.

This morning, David had taken an early bus into Madrid from Segovia. The terminal was in Moncloa. This suited his purposes, as he had business in Vallehermoso. First, he went past Gaztambide and left a note for Ariel asking her to meet him this afternoon during the paseo on Fuencarral in front of the Cine Conde Duque. Next, he hobbled over to Arapiles to check in with Onésimo.

David stood in the shade in front of a storefront opposite Onésimo and his easel. He observed the surroundings for a good while. He noted nothing out of order. Onésimo was well occupied with his usual activities.

Not leaving the shadows, he said in a strong voice directed straight at the blind man. "Have you missed me?"

"Missed you?" Onésimo didn't miss a beat. "I was hoping I would never see you again."

"Always the joker! What's new?" David asked.

"People are looking for you, machote."

"People?"

"Police people, that's who."

"They talk to you?" David pressed for details.

"Nah, they don't know we are acquainted. But you're hot."

"Tell."

Onésimo obliged. "Well, first, your buddy Buitre was by. Late last week. Wanted to know where you were. When he could see you. I couldn't help him. Did say I thought you'd make contact whenever you got back. So, he says there's something called 'Room 11' looking for you. Very interested in you they are. He didn't know who they were, but he's working on it. They *are* government though."

"Room 11? Never heard of it. You?"

"No. No idea."

484 | DOUGLAS L. FIELD

'No, wait come to think of it I have," David recalled. "I need to remember. It'll come to me. Over at the Banco de España, I think. What else?"

"A couple of detectives. I think they had been over to your flat. Pumping the portero," Onésimo continued.

"They from Room 11?"

"Nope. More like Cuerpo," Onésimo thought.

"Working together?" David wondered.

"Might be." Onésimo had even more information for David. "The slew foots were canvassing the barrio here, checking with your regular haunts. The sereno from this block was out. They talked to him here on the corner. The lowlife's on the take from them, I think. Anyway, the talk was soft, but my hearing's good. I got most of it."

"And most of it was what?"

"You left Spain a couple of weeks ago—up in Irún. Somehow, they caught up with you in Paris. Some contention up there. It was vague. No details. After that, no David. They figured you'd have crossed back into Spain by now, but the Guardia Civil has no record of you. Sounds like they want you bad."

"And 'they' are this Room 11 group?"

"Seems like it. They are considering the possibility that you sneaked back in. So, they are asking around if anybody at all has seen you. Nobody has."

"No, no one has, and no one will. I have that covered," David assured the blind man.

"Covered by some kind of disguise?" Onésimo divined.

"Let's just say I'm hiding in plain sight. I'd explain, but it might put you in jeopardy."

"No worries. The cops think I'm stupid. They never talk to me. If they did, you know what I would do?"

"What?"

MOSCOW GOLD | 485

"Act stupid. Let them see what they want to see. Make them think that they're the smart ones. They fall for it every time. Then they move on. Wouldn't bother with me anymore," Onésimo explained.

"That's a good way to put it. I'm doing that to them now. You ought to be a spy, by the way," David told him.

"I *am* a spy. But only you and a few others know it. It should stay that way."

"OK. That all?"

"Heard they went over to the MonteAzul. Leaned on the Italian guy over there pretty hard. He told them he hadn't seen you, and they could kiss his backside. Been the talk of Quevedo for a couple of days. Has some guts, that boy."

"It's good to have friends you can rely on, Onésimo. I never forget that. Anything you need?"

"Nah. Life is good. About time for it to cool off a little."

David shuffled across the sidewalk to Onésimo and began talking to him openly. Once in front of the easel he leaned on his crutch. "Give me twenty pulls, *ciego*" (blind man). "Make 'em good ones." He faked harshness. Then he pulled out of his pocket a one-thousand-peseta note that he had folded in advance. "Ferdinand and Isabella send you their love," he said softer. "Keep the change. I'll be checking with you. Please ask Calvín, er, I mean, Buitre to meet me 8:00 day after tomorrow afternoon, Plaza de Santa Ana, over in Las Letras."

"You gotta be hot in that coat," Onésimo remarked.

"What would you know about any coat?" David challenged.

"I can hear you flapping the front of it. Fanning yourself like."

"¡*Increíble*! Unbelievable! Please, tell Buitre. And forget you ever heard the word Calvín," David shook his head in disbelief as he turned to go.

"Sí, mi jefe."

David was tempted to get into his street clothes, to try on the sly to infiltrate his pensión on Vallehermoso, but it was too dangerous. He maybe could have gotten past Don Alonso and Doña Mari, but the

486 | **DOUGLAS L. FIELD**

porteros were another matter. Now he knew the sereno was lurking about.

After Onésimo, David went around to Magallanes and into the MonteAzul. All appeared normal. He asked Victorio for a beer. Not a glimmer of recognition. He took it to a table near the back for a little quiet reflection.

One more piece of the puzzle, he thought. One more element, and he could deal with Isham and Room 11 and anybody else. It would be the toughest piece, he feared.

༺

David arrived on Fuencarral under cover. The Cine Conde Duque was showing *The Great Escape* and proclaimed it to be in its sixteenth week. Advertisement was by huge paintings that depicted principal actors and scenes, paintings on canvas rigged from scaffolds that rose as high as the third floor above the sidewalk.

The paseo was in full swing. Most of the Trafalgar District was out socializing and enjoying the balmy evening. There were other movie theaters on this stretch of Fuencarral. Their collective lavish signage contributed to a carefree, almost carnival atmosphere.

As he limped up, he saw that Ariel had found a table at the Café Comercial just up from the Conde Duque. She had ordered *un refresco,* a soft drink. It had just come as David approached. He came to her table, took off the coat, and folded it at his feet. Then he hid the crutch under the table. Under the coat, he was wearing normal summer street clothes. Sitting there, he and Ariel looked like a typical young couple.

"You have the limp down. It looks like you've had a bad leg for years," she said as he settled in.

They were delighted to see each other and made sincere but proper display of their affection. Ariel was still getting used to David's beard and mustache and the glasses.

MOSCOW GOLD | **487**

"It's amazing how small details can change appearance. The beard and mustache and the glasses work. You don't need the coat. No one would ever recognize you."

"You've changed your look too. You look fantastic!" David replied.

Ariel had her hair looser than usual. One long lock hung down over her left eye. She was wearing a starched grey pinstriped shirt with the cuffs turned up, and a dark blue skirt. The shirt complimented her silver necklace that, good to her word, David was pleased to see, she still had on.

"Everything OK?" David asked as he settled in.

"No problems at all. Just got here. You picked the right location. What a mob! But hard to spot us out," Ariel said, looking around.

The waiter came up. David looked at Ariel's drink," "I'll need something stronger than that. ¿Una jarra, sí?" He noticed that Ariel was watching him and smiling, but when she saw him look at her, she stopped.

They prattled away about banalities and office gossip until David's beer came.

"Thirsty work limping all over town in this heavy coat," David said.

David saw that Ariel continued to be amused about something. "What's so funny?"

Ariel tried to stop laughing but couldn't. "It's your beard!"

"My beard? What about it?"

"It's, well, it's just that, I don't know. It's just that, well, it's almost not a beard at all."

"Why not?" David touched his face.

"A beard should, uh, well, it should *cover* your face, but yours, it's five random little tufts. It's kind of sparse. It makes me laugh. I'm sorry. I wasn't going to tell you."

"I'm part native American Indian—on my dad's side. Great beardless warriors, we are, Ariel. In our culture, making fun of a man's beard is a serious offense." David put on being annoyed.

488 | DOUGLAS L. FIELD

Ariel cracked up again. "A serious offense, then? What's the penalty?"

"You have to sleep outside the wigwam," David intoned gravely.

"Oh dear!"

"For a whole week."

"Even worse!"

"With the kids," David added.

"¡*Santo cielo!*" (Good heavens!) "How many kids?"

"Seven, ranging in ages from nine to three months."

Ariel was in stitches now. "Not that, Oh Flaming Arrow! I'll be good. I promise."

Now they were both amused.

"You need another drink," David observed.

"I do. All that laughing. Besides we're calling attention to ourselves." She put her hand on his arm. "We need to be all prim and proper out here in public. But I love you, David. You know that don't you?"

"I do. But you show it in strange ways sometimes." He grinned at her. "Must be a cultural thing. Spanish."

"Afán?" David changed the subject and was referring to Ariel's old employer.

"I talked to Emejota today." Emejota was Ariel's former colleague and still girlfriend, María José Gutierrez. "MJ" for short or /eme-jota/ as the Spanish pronounce the letters. "Everything is secured. No one else knows. No one else will ever know. Emejota's a professional *gestionista* (escrow officer), David. She's consummately discreet," Ariel assured him.

"That's a relief. I went to a lot of risk, as it turned out, to get that material."

"Also." Ariel had more. "She and I went through Moscardó's chits. We put together a list of all the companies and individuals who received gold. The *gestoría* has indices and other resources to locate them and suss out their histories. She and I will work on that process together in the next few days."

MOSCOW GOLD | 489

"Isn't that a lot to ask of her? I've already asked too much of you. Emejota too," David worried out loud.

"She's intrigued by your investigation, and she's a conservative patriot. How would I put it? We're both motivated. But for different reasons." She favored him a fetching look.

"This is becoming *our* investigation, Ariel."

"Well, along that line, I mentioned Ituarte to Emejota," Ariel said. "She's going to see if she can find him. We had some back-channel police contacts when I was there at Afán. Doubtless they still do. She says it may be a needle in a haystack, though."

⁘

"He's not in Madrid, Chema. He's not even in Spain." Zapatero was exasperated. "Monge's checked every border post and port of entry in the country. Even down south. He's not here. We've turned over every rock there is."

"Details?" demanded Jaso.

Monge and Zapatero looked at each other. "Tell him," Monge said. "Don't leave anything out."

Zapatero did as instructed.

"What about the *girl*, detectives? The girl!" Jaso barked at them. "That's where he'll go. That's where you'll find him."

"We detailed that to Javi," Monge offered, looking at Zapatero.

"Javier García is borderline inept. Who's he related to? Otherwise, how did …? Ah, never mind. I'll get myself in trouble. What intelligence has Javi the Great for us?"

"Miss Muñiz hasn't seen the American. He hasn't been near her. In fact, Javi just saw her out on Fuencarral—with someone else, a Spaniard. They were having a good time. Javi's trying to get an ID. Looks like she's moved on," Monge summarized.

"No." Chema thought for a moment. "He paid his rent in advance, you say? He's here. He's here already. Throw out a dragnet. Random checks. Anybody suspicious or unusual. Work out a profile. Concentrate

490 | DOUGLAS L. FIELD

it in his home barrio up there. That's where he's comfortable. It'll be something obvious that he's doing. That we're comfortable with. That we're used to. Use your heads."

"We're on it, boss." Zapatero spoke up.

"You'd better be on it. Room 11's all over us. They want to get their hands on what he's got before the Americans do."

❧

"No, Jack, he hasn't chickened out. No, he isn't still in Paris. No, he didn't run home. No, you didn't misplace your trust in him. He's here. Back in Spain, in Madrid, right under our noses," Barnickle replied to Isham's torrent of frustration.

"And the hard evidence upon which you base your oh-so-confident assertions is just what? That you've, with your own eyes, seen him here? Running around? Doing his thing? Working on my project? Gathering the evidence we need? Come on, Nick, you're the best. Or so you tell me. But you don't have jack."

"Hee, hee. Good pun, Jack."

"Find him," Isham brayed. "Or you're going to have more jack than you ever wanted. Jack, Nick. That's Jack with a *capital* 'J.' You know who I mean."

"What do Jaso and them have?" Nick ventured, deflecting.

"Nothing. No better than you," Isham snapped.

"Well, look at the bright side."

"And that bright side would be, Nick?"

"Well, when you tell them we don't have anything, you won't be lying to them. Be a relief to your conscience," Barnickle quipped.

"I don't *have* a conscience, Nick. And that makes me more than willing to put you out of a job and on the slowest freighter I can find back to the States."

"I figure it this way," Nick said. "He sees old Negrín's wife. Why go to her? Maybe she's got proof that Stalin got the goods. Then it's Portillo, Méndez Aspe, and the gold dealers. Why them? Get proof of

MOSCOW GOLD | 491

where the goods were disposed of—that they're not still in Moscow—try to find out who got it. So, let's say that he can prove that Stalin got it and who got it from him. All that's left is where it is now."

"I want what he's got before Room 11 gets it. They get it first, and it'll cost me to get it from them. I don't want to have to pay."

"He may not have it all. Not yet. What does the mighty Company know about where that gold is now? Figure that out, and we won't need to know where he is. We'll know where he's going."

⁓

David invited Ariel to take in the 10:15 showing of the movie. She accepted, eager.

"We did the dubbing last year. Before you came," she said.

The theater advertised being air-conditioned. And so it was—cool inside. They bought loge seats and were shown to them by a gray-headed usher in a formal uniform, who gratefully collected a couple of pesetas from David. Before the presentation began, another usher went through the entire auditorium with a squeeze bottle of room freshener, giving the entire place the scent of a lemon grove.

They were able to talk before the show and during a rather long intermission. Now that Emejota was researching the identities of the parties that got the gold and the process of finding Ituarte was started, David had some practical considerations.

"I have a room in a little fleabag down in La Latina, but I have to get out of there. Too exposed. Cops come around too often. Even a place like that," David told her.

"What about taking Jaime into your confidence?" Ariel offered.

"Been thinking about that. Need to talk to Nacho too," David agreed.

"Come out to Carabanchel tomorrow," Ariel instructed, "around 11:00. I'll let you in. Jaime is here till late in the week. And Nacho's always there. He'll be glad to see you. He already suspects that you have a story to tell."

492 | DOUGLAS L. FIELD

"Well, I do, don't I?"

"Nacho loves you, you know. Like a son," Ariel said.

"No, he doesn't."

"Oh, but he does. Women know these things."

After the movie, they went into the theater's little café for a nightcap and spent a while enjoying each other's company.

"You never told me what happened after you got out of the mountains. How did you sneak back?" Ariel asked.

He filled her in on how he'd ridden the bus down from Requesnes to Figueras. "That was the diciest part. Andrés said the Guardia Civil are alert up there. Figueras is pretty big. Once I got there, I made friends with a group of US Air Force officers, on leave from Torrejón and vacationing on the Cost Brava. They were headed into Barcelona for a night on the town. Gave me a lift that far."

"How did you get the rest of the way to Madrid without being seen?"

"Long story short, I took the train."

"The train? But that's very public. They watch the trains."

"Not the freight trains so much. I hopped a freight."

"¡No, señor!" Ariel exclaimed.

"Yeah. Right out of the Barcelona marshalling yards. The trick is, well, there are two tricks. The first is not to get run over by the train getting on and off. Then you have to find the right train."

"You caught on to the first trick. You're here."

"You find an empty goods wagon, door open. Train has to be going slow. You look up the tracks for obstructions. Then you throw your stuff up. You run alongside and grab the rear of the door; there are handholds. Swing yourself up. You go for the rear, so if you stumble you can push yourself away."

"How do you know these things?" She shook her head.

"Tried it a couple of times. Back home."

"Why would you do such a thing?"

MOSCOW GOLD | 493

"A cure for boredom. Out of money and needed to get somewhere. Stupidity. Who knows?" David had no rational answer. "It's not all that uncommon in the States, but there are cops to prevent it. Must not be common here. Nobody bothered me. Didn't even see anyone, but it was night."

David watched Ariel's eyes. She was processing. Her expression gave nothing away.

"I hung around the train yard." David continued. "Found chalk markings on some of the cars that said 'Ato.' Figured it meant 'Atocha.' I swung aboard. The car was empty except for a few big sacks. I piled them up, had a nice little bed. I went to sleep to the rhythm of the rails. Sun came up, and we were rolling through Aranjuez. Train slowed way down by Getafe. I jumped off and hitchhiked into Madrid. Here I am."

"You could have been killed."

"Nah. I could have been killed in Paris. That train ride got me and now 'Emejota's documents' back in Madrid undetected. If they had caught me, those documents would have been gone. They're our future."

She shook her head.

"It was worth the risk, Ariel. And the risks aren't over."

They caught a cab back to Gaztambide. David paid the cabbie to park and go grab himself a coffee. He and Ariel enjoyed a few intimate minutes together in the car—before she went in alone.

CHAPTER 77

Madrid: Thursday, December 12, 1940

The almost winter's day dawned late.

It was so cold in the Plaza de Cánovas del Castillo that the Neptune fountain, its edges rime rimmed, was not playing. In mufti, Wilhelm Canaris strolled outside of the Palace Hotel for a breath of somewhat less than fresh air.

Although the sky was clear, the atmosphere out across the Paseo del Prado from the great art museum was hazy and heavy with the acrid but somehow sweet pungency of coal smoke. Even in cold time, the meseta sun is intense, and on this morning, it turned the morning haze crystalline and shimmery. The aroma, more than merely molecular, fell particulate on the German's olfactory sense. It wrinkled his nose, and it delighted him.

The Palace's footprint was a truncated pie shape with its narrow frontage on Cánovas but widening up the Carrera de San Jerónimo and Calle de Velázquez radials that run down to the fountain. The grand entrance was half a block up San Jerónimo toward the Cortes. Atop the roof fronting the plaza was a large steel latticework that supported

MOSCOW GOLD | 495

the hotel's name written in outsize letters that were lit flamboyantly at night.

Canaris had breakfasted, Spanish style, inside the Palace at the Café del Tridente. The entrance to the café was marked off by a rank of double French doors. Once inside, breakfasters were invited to sit at round tables set with white linen tablecloths and napkins, silver flatware, and elaborate floral centerpieces. The room was finished in dark walnut paneling relieved by gilt accented borders and large and colorful Chinese dynasty vases set at eye level on gray marble-topped mahogany sideboards. Brass sconces lit the room to the perfect level for a genteel morning repast.

After thick and rich coffee, for which the Tridente was famous; croissants; and orange marmalade, the Abwehr chief made a leisurely but complete circuit around the plaza. Back inside the hotel, despite scarf and gloves, his face was reddened by the cold. He felt braced and invigorated. As he came back inside, the German's aide was waiting for him at the side. "Where is your overcoat, sir?"

"I left it in the room. I like the cold. More so here in Spain. It's very dry. Makes me feel like a new man. Where's the car?"

"Should be out front now."

Canaris was in Spain on a delicate diplomatic mission assigned by the German Führer himself. He was also in Spain to advance purposes and interests of his own and those of a small cadre of associates. It was a high-stakes game. He planned to enjoy every minute.

"Off we go then. This should be an adventure." He rubbed his hands together in anticipation.

Outside a Grosser Mercedes W150 from the embassy was, indeed, waiting at the curb. Canaris and his aide settled into the commodious and elegant leather seat. The car was stuffy and over warm, so Canaris put the window down for a moment. He wanted one last whiff of the city.

A chase car fell in behind them, and they drove fast around Neptune's fountain and headed up the Paseo del Prado. The small

496 | DOUGLAS L. FIELD

convoy flew by the Plaza de España and up Princesa, past the Puerta de Hierro and onto the broad *avenida* of the same name. Within a very few kilometers, the cars turned north onto the C-601.

The persisting ravages of civil war included many conditions in Spain, not the least of which was roads of indescribable poverty. The C-601 was a notable exception. Wide, divided, and with fresh pavement, it headed knife-straight up beside the Manzanares River to its singular destination, the Palacio Real del Pardo, home of the newly installed Jefe del Estado Español, Generalísimo Francisco Franco, Caudillo de España.

The German mini motorcade was expected. It was waved through the security gates and roared up to the main entrance. They pulled into the ceremonial Patio de los Austrias entrance to the palace.

Waiting for them was a diminutive and portly little man in full-dress Spanish army uniform with a purple sash and very dark sunglasses. "Admiral Canaris, welcome back to Madrid. How long has it been?" The voice was a reedy first tenor.

"Too long, Caudillo. I took a walk around downtown before coming out here and was delighted to be back. The sights, the sounds, the smells, all of it—I have the greatest fondness for Madrid as well you know. All things considered; the city looks good. The postwar cleanup is a herculean task."

The mutual adulation continued for a few minutes. Franco's hairline had started to recede. His graying mustache tried to offset a less-than-prominent chin. His face was distinguished by somewhat wide-set and liquid dark eyes with heavy and arched eyebrows.

He had a wide and engaging smile that was on full display this morning for the honored German guest. Standing at Franco's side was another man, this one in the dark uniform of a senior officer in the Falange.

"Admiral Canaris, I believe you know my Interior Minister Ramón Serrano Suñer."

As Canaris was not in uniform, he shook hands with Serrano Suñer.

Franco went on still wearing the smile at its most ingratiating, "What you may not know is that Ramón and I literally are brothers-in-arms. He is married to Zita, my wife Carmen's sister. We are fond of calling him el Cuñadísimo, the Brother-in-Lawísimo. What do you think of that, Admiral?" Franco raised an ironic eyebrow.

Canaris fished for a humorous reply, but Franco stopped him. "No need to answer that question, Admiral. It was facetious. Ramón has my full trust and confidence. Come, come, let us go inside. It's warmer, and we may even find a hot drink."

This was not the first time that Canaris had met Franco. In fact, Franco was well known both to the admiral and in the upper circles of high German officialdom.

Back in July, the German High Command had planned an operation to seize British Gibraltar. Canaris had traveled to Madrid for talks with Franco, who was hesitant to enter the war. The German military planning had gone forward anyway.

The Abwehr chief was playing a duplicitous game. He had privately discouraged Franco from joining the Axis and warned the Caudillo that if Spain joined the Axis, the Spanish Atlantic and Mediterranean islands, the Canaries in particular, and even mainland Spain itself, would be vulnerable to successful British occupation. Canaris also allayed Franco's fear of a hostile German invasion of Spain if he refused to cooperate with Hitler.

Franco had stuck to his extortionate demands for allowing Germany access to Gibraltar through Spain. Canaris knew that Franco would do so again today.

The social banalities among Canaris, Franco, and Serrano Suñer continued for the time necessary to satisfy the Spanish ethos for such things. Time had come. The preliminaries were done. They got down to the business at hand.

"Caudillo, the Führer has asked me to advise you that our High Command has now completed Operation Félix." Canaris rehearsed the now finalized plan to take Gibraltar.

Franco listened. When Canaris had finished, Franco looked at Serrano Suñer, who commented, "Admiral, you know Spain's concerns. The British will respond by the seizing the Canary Islands. Even if we gained Gibraltar, we would be no better off, perhaps even worse."

"The Führer believes that German armed forces are up to the task."

"We are persuaded that it is problematical whether they are, Admiral," Suñer responded. "If I may be blunt, Gibraltar is easier assaulted than taken. The Wehrmacht would be constrained to attack over a very narrow land peninsula—one that is mined. Your troops could not be brought in secret to their jumping-off point. The British would take notice."

"The attack would not exclusively be across the land frontier but with naval and air operations as well," Canaris objected.

Serrano Suñer ground forward. "The winds around the Rock are capricious. Paratroop attack would be impossible. There is no open space to land gliders. The winds also render amphibious attack dubious of success."

Franco now entered the conversation. "Admiral Canaris," pronounced /Kah-*nah*-rees/, "Let me comment on a more visceral level. I have specified the stocks and quantities of food stuffs, military supplies, and hardware and petroleum reserves that Spain would need even to begin to contemplate going forward with an operation such as Félix. I have had no definitive reply from my friend in Berlin. Do you bring one?"

"Caudillo, the Führer is committed to supplying all reasonable Spanish requirements. May I carry back to him your commitment to lead Spain into the war and to facilitate the invasion of Gibraltar via Operation Félix?"

"Admiral, it is difficult for me to feed Spanish children on promises," squeaked Franco. "The ships carrying what we need have not yet arrived in Spanish harbors. Are they in route as we speak?"

"The Rock is Spanish, Caudillo. The wrongful English occupation has continued since 1713. Gibraltar is an integral part of Spain. Its sacred destiny is reunification. The current moment represents the best opportunity in two and a quarter centuries to right this wrong."

"My dear Admiral, the British would like to be rid of me. From time to time, they try to bribe one or the other of my generals to betray me. I am made aware of these contacts. We play London along. We take their money and make promises to act. Various impediments arise. 'The general is considering it.' 'The general is willing to act.' 'The general is fearful.' Additional inducements flow in. You, of all people, Admiral, will understand that process."

Canaris said nothing but gave the little Spanish leader a knowing look.

"While it may not be as satisfactory as actual occupation of Gibraltar, the worry, concern, and investment of time and resources that we are causing London are significant. Besides, the English pay in hard currency. My generals only accept dollars, pounds, and Swiss francs." This was Franco's limp attempt at humor.

The colloquy went on for some time. Parry and evasion, the conversants talking past rather than with one another. It was highfalutin twaddle. All three knew it. The moment came when Canaris felt that he could, in truth and good faith, represent in Berlin that the discussion had been full, frank, and candid.

"Generalísimo Franco, what position of the Spanish government shall I report to my superiors in Berlin?"

"I cannot agree to enter the war at the present time." Franco made his position clear.

"The Führer will be disappointed."

"Yes, and he will understand the realities under which I am laboring."

"I will do my utmost to represent to him the accurate details of our meeting." Canaris smiled.

"My good friend," said Franco, pulling himself to his full height and puffing out his chest, "I know that you are a longtime and loyal ally of Spain. We value that friendship and hope to see you often here in the months and years to come."

Canaris had himself driven back to the city. By suppertime, he was dining on the fast train to Barcelona.

All in all, a most agreeable and satisfying day. Gibraltar's secured. Franco will never go. Germany will lose the war. The Abwehr has safe haven for its assets.

CHAPTER 78

Berlin: Wednesday, December 18, 1940

"Are you ready for the Christmas holiday, Sepp?"

"As much as can be, Admiral. Yourself?"

"Oh, yes. At this stage, it's a gift for my wife. Little for me to be ready for."

Canaris stared out his office window. Snow was falling in fat wet flakes. It was filling the streets and pedestrian paths of the Tirpitzufer. "Look at that. Getting home will be a snarl. It was cold in Madrid but no snow, of course. It's rare down there. Sometimes though."

"Never as far down as Gibraltar, sir." Sepp smiled.

"Quite." The admiral smiled back. "My report from Madrid is dispositive. The comments I am about to make are of the highest classification. They are for your ears only. The decisions to which I refer are final. Any leakage of them would be prejudicial to the Reich. Understood?"

He nodded.

"And, moreover"—Canaris regarded him with raised eyebrows—"*existentially* prejudicial to any leaker."

MOSCOW GOLD | 503

Sepp continued to meet the admiral's gaze.

"The armed forces of the German Reich will not attack the British at Gibraltar, much less wrest it from their control. To be succinct, Generalísimo Franco does not believe that an attempt on the Rock would be successful. I have communicated to him the German government's extreme disappointment with his decision. I have also communicated my personal agreement with his evaluation and intentions."

Canaris let his information sink in.

"Practical implications," the Abwehr chief went on, "are that there will be no Spanish distractions from the preparation for and execution of Operation Barbarossa. The attack on the Soviet Union will proceed late this coming spring or early this summer."

Staupitz's face remained expressionless as his admiral continued.

"We have disguised the true ownership of the Abwehr's gold holdings in Gibraltar. From our parochial perspective, since the British will continue in possession of it, any Abwehr deposits reposing in vaults and deposit boxes there will remain safe and secure for us under their jurisdiction. I assume there are no questions."

Sepp had none.

"A very happy Christmas to you then. May it not, as I fear it will, be the last happy Christmas that we will have for many years to come."

CHAPTER 79

Carabanchel: Tuesday, September 10, 1963

It was little short of a plenary meeting of the DOCICA brain trust.

Jaime *was* in town and tacitly committed his support. Nacho acted his sober and unemotional self, but Ariel thought she could see that he was proud of David and that Nacho even envied David his exploits a little.

David told the story. Efficient. Clipped. Judicious. He included or left out details as best suited the coherence and cogency of his telling.

Once he had finished, David added, "So, the investigation's in as good a place as it can be for the moment. The people on earth who know where I am are those in this room. As soon as Ariel and Emejota can give me some leads on Ituarte, I'll go and find him, secure his cooperation. Then, when we have identified the current iterations of the receivers of the gold, we should be left with one last piece of the puzzle."

"Verifying the exact current location of the stuff," murmured Nacho.

MOSCOW GOLD | 505

"I get that, and I can write the story. It should make a big splash and be a significant help to Spain," summarized David.

Jaime had said nothing until now. "What a story! I'd love to see a Spanish production company make it into a film. Then *we* could set it into English. Dubbing rights in reverse!"

No one said anything for several moments. Then Jaime looked at Ariel, "And you've been in the middle of this all the way along. *¡Brava mujer!* But then I would have expected no less."

"Well, almost all the way along. David first took me into his confidence not long before Santander," Ariel explained.

"Ariel, you're a natural spy. You do it instinctually. I'm proud of you." Nacho spoke up again. "And you, David. You paid attention when we talked."

"I owe you a lot, Nacho. I'd have gotten nowhere without your help and advice." David gave it up to the older man.

Nacho smiled, a rare occurrence for him, but he said nothing else.

Jaime again took the floor. "All right, people. We're all interested to know who attacked David in Paris, but that doesn't matter for now. What matters is how we help him get the remaining elements of the story without getting caught."

Nacho spoke up. "He can't go home to Vallehermoso yet. What he needs now is a safe place to sleep—a base of operations for his next steps."

"You're thinking the chabolas?" Jaime asked.

"I am."

"You know those shacks? Across the alley behind the production building?" Jaime continued.

David and Ariel both nodded.

"I have, how shall we say, 'jurisdiction' over them. They're useful from time to time. Odds and ends. No need to bore you with the details. Nacho 'administers' them for us."

"There's a couple of them empty." Nacho again. "I've pirated electricity into them, so there's light. I think there's a cot over in

506 | DOUGLAS L. FIELD

the storeroom, and we can round up some bedding. They all have government-issued plaques, but the cops never bother our, eh, 'tenants' anyway. It won't be cold for a couple of months yet, so our 'refugee' should be able to stay comfortable."

Jaime said to David, "We'll 'hire' you in your disabled soldier persona. We'll make you our *conserje*. It'll look natural for you to come and go, natural for you to be over here all the time. You'll run errands too. It'll give you some freedom of movement. Maybe you can even continue with your translations."

He fixed a steady, but good-natured gaze on David and Ariel. "And here's a tasty irony. I'm sure Ariel will be able to find menial tasks for David to do—all for show, of course. Take out the trash. Go over to the post box. Bang around a little. 'Do this. Do that.' You'll *both* enjoy it."

Nacho approved. "It's the perfect cover. Unremarkable. No one will suspect, not if you continue to make a show of the limping, David." Then Nacho continued. "I suggest David stays here in the offices this afternoon. Ariel and I will set it all up. After that, David can take up residence."

❧

David went over for a reconnaissance late in the day.

Nothing could be stowed and be safe in the chabola, so he left all his important items in his office. It was a twenty-yard gimp from the rear door of the production building to his new home—a home that was as represented. It had cinder block walls and a corrugated roof. A single lightbulb hung suspended on its wire from the underside of the roof. There was an old window that someone had scavenged from some building remodel site closer in and a metal door that, after a certain fashion, locked with a padlock. The dirt floor had been compacted rock hard by unnumbered predecessor occupants.

Ariel and Nacho had, indeed, found a cot, a couple of wool blankets, and an old feather pillow. It wasn't the Palace Hotel, but it would do as a safe house. David would tolerate it well enough until the weather turned cold.

"You'll be long since finished with this project before the cold happens. You won't be shivering in the winter out here," Nacho commented.

After he had done what he could, Nacho left.

David and Ariel stood alone in the little hovel. He could see that Ariel was distressed at the poverty of the place. "It's *primitive*, David. You can't stay here after all. We'll have to think of something else," she said.

"No, Nacho's right. It's ideal. I'll be fine. It'll take me back to happy times I had at summer camp, where we bunked in Indian tepees. It'll be my first experience with a dirt floor, though."

"*¡Qué barbaridad!*" (How awful)! Ariel lamented. "I won't be able to sleep thinking of you suffering out here."

"*I* won't be able to sleep—thinking of you in your warm bed on Gaztambide. All cozy," David lampooned.

Ariel cuffed him on the upper arm. "*No seas impertinente.*"

"How about supper in town?" David switched topics. "La Playa. On Magallanes across from the Bar MonteAzul. 9:30." He caught her around the waist and pulled her close. "How's this for *impertinente*?" He kissed her on the mouth.

She wrapped her arms around his neck and kissed him back.

"You taste good, Ariel."

"'*Sabor a Mi?*' Like the old song says. 'The Savor of Me?'" Ariel purred.

"Just that. *Sabor a ti.*"

"Mmm. David, you taste good too."

Then both at the same time said, "Makes me hungry for La Playa," which got them laughing and horsing around again.

Then Ariel said, "I've been over here a long time. Tongues will be wagging if we're not careful."

"I think they already are," David replied. "Did you see Jaime's expression this morning? He knows."

⌖

David limped around Quevedo and turned into Fernando el Católico. He was passing a foosball arcade at the head of the street. Two plainclothes stepped out of the doorway just as he had almost passed.

One blocked his path and straight-armed him on the chest. "Documento." Not even a *por favor*.

David wrestled with his crutch and made as if to stumble and start to fall. The other grabbed him and kept him on his feet. David then muttered as if talking to himself and began fumbling through the various interior and exterior pockets of his greatcoat.

When he thought his timing was perfect, he produced the counterfeit DNI out of a breast pocket.

The cop fingered it and turned it over. He held it into the light of the arcade and studied it for a long moment.

"Where are you going?"

"Over to the Guardia Civil barracks on Vallehermoso. They give us soup and bread on Tuesdays."

"Walk on." The DNI was handed back.

David affected care in putting it away and mumbled to himself a little more before limping off.

"What a messed-up war," he heard one of them say just as he got out of earshot.

⌖

La Playa was jammed, every table full. Visibility was near zero due to the cigarette smoke. The crowd was drinking hard, loud, and boisterous. Madrid's rugby team was having a dinner with their girlfriends and fiancées. Everyone was in a festive mood.

MOSCOW GOLD | 509

"Cops stopped me just now. Over by the foosball," David said as they got settled.

Ariel had reprised her traditional look with the bun and darker makeup. "Fake DNI worked, *obviamente.*"

"Yeah. I think they were a little ashamed. I started to fall over. One of them caught me. Would have hurt if he didn't."

"So far so good. Nacho knows what he's talking about."

"How's about a jug of sangría? Celebrate moving into new quarters," David suggested.

"I still feel terrible about your staying there."

"Some sangría will salve your reservations," David reassured her.

"I didn't know we had rugby in Madrid," Ariel said.

"I didn't either, but if they play as hard as they party, they ought to win," David replied.

Restaurante La Playa had been there since the '30s. The dining room was open and bright. Mammoth amphorae doubling as planters were home to little palm trees and succulents in keeping with the sand-and-sea theme. There were, placed to good advantage thin, glass partitions with more palms etched in their surfaces.

The rugby players and their ladies were seated at long tables in the middle of the room, but the maître d' found Ariel and David a table for two at the front window—one that looked out over Magallanes toward the MonteAzul.

After sangría, they went for one of La Playa's specialties, *pollo al aljillo*, chicken roasted in garlic, lots of it.

Their quiet enjoyment was interrupted about halfway through when a pair of fit-looking men banged through the door and into the dining room.

They made a quick survey of the dining room and then split up, one taking each of the rugby tables. They were demanding identification.

David got out his fake DNI and put it in his lap in anticipation of their coming to his and Ariel's table. He had his military coat and

510 | DOUGLAS L. FIELD

crutch hidden beneath the table. He did not want to have to rummage around in it with them watching.

The older of the two finished his ruggers first and went up to David and Ariel. David handed up his DNI without being asked. The man scrutinized it and then stared at Ariel.

"Your mother's very beautiful, Diego," he said abruptly.

His partner was now finished. They left.

"We need to go to the gestoría tomorrow. Plan out the attack on Ituarte," David stated as their tension abated. "Hiding in plain sight seems to be working, but that was close. Onésimo says they want to find me. If they do, the game's over. We'll never find Ituarte. We'll never get free."

"Emejota will be there. I'll set it up with her in the morning."

"We better go separately. Fix it with the portero too, yeah. He'll be suspicious," David worried.

"Let's plan it for eleven o'clock. I'll get there early. I know the portero. He won't like it. You're right. I'll take care of it."

As they continued to decompress, they enjoyed a sherry in their own little space—a small and quiet world in the raucous universe of Restaurante La Playa, on a busy late summer's night.

"Ever been in the old MonteAzul?" David reached for her hand, gazing across the street.

"Not any sort of a place a respectable girl goes in, David."

"S'pose not. I go there a lot, but you're right. Mostly men. Been a haunt of mine since school days. I'm a valued customer. My *cole,* Carlos Primero, is about half a block down Fernando el Católico there."

"You can't let your editor get you thrown out of here, can you?" Ariel laid her head over on her shoulder and looked at David with affection.

"How do you mean?

"You love this place, David. I just live here. Madrid's a fact of life. For you, it's a surprise discovery—an unexpected gift."

"More so since Madrid gave me you. Our conversation has turned serious again," David said.

"You're flippant and cynical and edgy, David, but certain things are utterly safe and secure in your loyalty and devotion."

"And if I offered you my loyalty and devotion?" David smiled.

"Too late." Ariel was serious.

"How so? Too late?"

"You've already offered them, David. And I've already accepted. Now I'm guarding them in my heart." She reached up and touched her neck.

Later, David put Ariel in a cab back to Gaztambide. Before he closed the door, he leaned in, kissed her on the cheek, and said, "G'night, Mom!"

CHAPTER 80

Madrid: Wednesday, September 11, 1963

David found Calle de Salustiano Olózaga.

It ran for two quiet and short blocks from Recoletos to the Puerta de Alcalá. It was bordered by ancient leafy trees and lined by buildings of consummate category. Anchored by the French embassy at number 9, its buildings exuded stability and permanence.

He saw the buildings were populated by prestigious offices of lawyers, notaries, high-end accountants, and escrow firms, offices that were denoted from the street by understated yet highly polished brass plaques.

The little street suggested calm and steady. Calm and steady was what he needed.

He found Gestoría Afán at number 19. Number 19's portero appeared to David as more of a beefeater than a doorman. Stiff and turned out in tailcoat and gray striped trousers, he advised David that he was expected. David knew that, if he weren't expected, he wouldn't be getting into the building today.

MOSCOW GOLD | 513

"Segundo piso, señor. The elevator opens straight into the office," the man said colorlessly.

It was an office, it turned out, upon which a fortune had been expended in luxurious tenant appointments. It featured dark paneling and furniture; priceless tapestries hanging on many of the walls; and, where there were no tapestries, excellent copies of famous Spanish paintings.

Ariel was already there. She gave a demure peck to David's cheek. He then had a closer look around.

"What's with the paintings?"

"They're done by copyists from the Prado," Ariel explained. "Come on. Emejota's waiting for us."

Ariel took David by the hand and walked him back into the interior of the office. "This was my old office, and that was my desk." At a second desk in the office sat a young woman Ariel's age, maybe a little older.

"Emejota, this is David. I've told you about him."

"Yes, you have." Emejota regarded David. A little upturn showed in one corner of her mouth.

"Emejota's mother is Rosalinda Suárez Barba," Ariel went on.

"Of course, 'Rosi La Dinamitera.' She's well, I hope."

David was aware of this person. Rosi had been, at the age of seventeen, one of the first women to join the Republican militias and was one of just a few women on the front lines defending Madrid. After the siege, she became the single female in the dynamiters section. Thus, the sobriquet, Rosie the Dynamitrix.

An accident occurred in the trenches while she was fabricating explosives. Rosi's right hand was blown off. She recovered and went back to the fighting. She enjoyed notoriety throughout the war. To the current day, she continued to be a darling of the leftist press worldwide.

"She is well," Emejota responded. "Spent a few years in jail after the war. Now she has that all in the past."

"What's she doing?" David asked.

514 | DOUGLAS L. FIELD

"Has a little cigarette stall in the grand hall of Atocha Station. Good location. Pays the rent," the daughter said.

"You look a lot like her, Emejota, at least as I recall her pictures," David stated. A book had been written about Rosalinda's wartime exploits. Photos had been in all the papers.

For her part, tiny as a doll, Emejota had dark curly hair, bright eyes, and a happy gap-toothed smile—not beautiful, but definitely cute. Emejota produced a framed photo that showed a slender and smiling teenager in Republican fatigues and tasseled cap. The young woman was holding up what looked like a six-month-old blonde baby girl.

"And these ladies would be the *la famosa Rosi* with baby Emejota." David made it a statement not a question.

"Yes, Mami and me."

David looked back and forth from Emejota to the photo, "You look exactly alike. Could be twins!"

"Strange, isn't it? I guess we share the looks and the passion but not the politics. She's as much a leftie as she ever was. Not me though." Emejota shrugged.

"Collectivist idealism dies hard sometimes," David observed. "Hard evidence notwithstanding."

"It was those leftist *cretinos* that lost us that gold you're looking for, David. Spain needs it back. You'll have my full cooperation in finding out where it ended up."

"He'll find it, Eme. He's hardhead. And stubborn."

"Good." Emejota grinned. "Let's show him what we've got. I think we can have confidence he'll make use of it."

What they had was a typewritten list. All the recipients of gold from Moscardó's chits were set down in one column—one hundred forty-eight entries. The second column was a work in progress. Opposite some names were other names. Next to others, the original name was repeated. Next to still others, there was nothing—nothing yet, anyway.

MOSCOW GOLD | 515

Now Emejota was all absorption in the task. "This should be self-explanatory. First, we've done a recapitulation of the universe of recipients including all data contained on the chits. That data is, in most cases, limited."

David read the list and commented, "Looking at the amounts of gold documented in this list, it does not account for the disposition of the entirety of the gold reserves that the Bank of Spain held in 1936."

"Correct. I consider, however, that the data contained in the list is, from a statistical point of view, valid." Emejota's response was cogent. "We have sufficient source material for it to be legitimate to extrapolate that the remainder of the gold was disposed of in similar fashion."

She raised an eyebrow and looked at Ariel and David. There was no response, so she hastened on. "A small number of the recipients persist in the form they had back in 1937. Although locations and addresses may have changed, they appear still to be in existence and viable. For example, this one, The Shiloh Corporation. Its official domicile is in the United States, the State of Delaware."

"Shiloh was a famous and bitterly fought battle in the American Civil War," David explained.

"Right," Emejota agreed. "I think this name is a feint—to make it appear American, which it may not be. For its corporations, the State of Delaware has disclosure requirements relating to officers and directors. In the case of Shiloh, the current ones are listed—Conrad Ciliax, Otto Seldenreich, and Georg Thaler."

"Germans!" David observed. "East or West?"

Emejota nodded. "Looks like West. Wait till you see. This one, Onderhoud Friese Visserij, N.V. It's Dutch you would guess, and you'd be right. Something about fisheries in Friesland. Well, Dutch companies are designated either 'N.V' or 'B.V.' B.V. companies are not allowed to have bearer shares. This is an N.V. It can have bearer shares. Much more anonymous an N.V. is. But it has a parent company, Nordsee Gerät und Apparatur, GmbH. A GmbH is not Dutch but *is* German—West German as you noted."

516 | DOUGLAS L. FIELD

"What about all these entities with Spanish names like this one, Minas Atacama S.A.? There are several. They're not German, are they?" David was catching on fast.

"Whoever set this up was very cunning. The list does have several corporations and partnerships organized in Spanish-speaking jurisdictions. Atacama is Chile, but there are also Argentine, Paraguayan, Mexican, and Bolivian entities. None are Spanish."

"And do we find a consistent German connection?" David expected he knew the answer.

"We do. The Germans have always been very active in Spain and Spanish America, even more so in World War II and the years leading up to it. All the details are on the list. They are Spanish names but German ownership."

"So, *Germans* were behind the purchase of the gold?" David summarized. "Do you think it was the government?"

"Almost had to be, didn't it?" Emejota agreed. "There was a lot of money involved here—too much for all but a very few individuals or any but the very largest companies."

"Germans! I wonder which branch of their government?" said David.

Ariel now spoke up. "We still have more than half of the entities to research, but at this juncture, almost all trace back to West Germany in one way or another. I don't expect that to change as we finish the list."

"Adds an entire dimension to the story, I'd say," Emejota put down the list of companies and picked up another one. It was also neat and typed. "Since we're adding dimensions, David, here's what we have so far on Ituarte."

She handed him the paper. There were dozens and dozens of entries—more than a hundred.

It was Ariel who continued. "The Spanish state keeps detailed and careful records on its citizens. Through our sources in the *Dirrección General de Seguridad*, we located one hundred thirty-six Carlos Ituartes in metropolitan Spain and in the colonies. Addresses and other contact

MOSCOW GOLD | 517

information are on the list. We speculated before that finding Ituarte might be a big challenge. It looks like it will be."

"Have to hope he's here on the peninsula, not in one of the colonies," said Emejota.

Ariel cocked an eyebrow and said, "I don't know. A trip to Ifni or the Spanish Sahara would broaden David's horizons. He could ride a camel."

"You could come too, Ariel, except you might wind up in the Sultan's harem. Ladies, you've done yeoman's work. I'm impressed and grateful—to both of you."

Emejota seemed pleased, and Ariel explained. "I'm the little organizer in our partnership; Emejota's the ferocious and dogged researcher. We'll finish checking out the recipient entities and give you the new information."

Emejota offered the obvious. "You now need to find Ituarte."

⧉

David and Ariel made their separate exits from Afán and their separate ways back to Carabanchel. David analyzed the Ituarte document on his commute. He went into his office and flopped down in a big easy chair. He had installed it in a corner for when he tired of sitting at his desk.

Ariel had gotten back to DOCICA first. Aware of David's return, she slipped into his office, leaving the door half an inch ajar.

She was dressed as she had been at the gestoría in a long and full, half-calf-length, light taupe skirt; perfect, pressed, and matching blouse of the same color that buttoned at the elbows; and unadorned cordovan pumps and belt.

Unbidden, she sat down on David's lap and smoothed out her skirt. Then she threaded her right arm behind his neck. She draped her left arm over his shoulder.

"The sultan's seraglio, is it?" she whispered in his ear.

518 | DOUGLAS L. FIELD

"You'd fit right in. All those exotic and dusky doxies, with you, their chatelaine. You yourself said you're a great little organizer. You could wear those trousers with the super poufy legs and a turban." David put his arms around her waist.

"The harem I'm getting in is the one where you're the pasha, and I'm the single occupant," Ariel murmured into his ear.

"Idle and all day long at our leisure—just you and me. Sounds perfect. Genuine indolence. Think we could keep from getting bored?"

"No doubt whatsoever." Ariel vamped.

"Develop a long attention span."

"Long." She continued to hold on tight.

"We're not on a path that's conducive to your becoming a nun."

"Hmm." She was still nuzzling his ear. "Maybe I've caught another vision."

"Shall I encourage you?" He traced his fingers down her neck, past her shirt collar and toward the top button that he tenderly undid. "You're wearing the necklace."

"Mmm. Yes." It was a very low hum—like a contented tigress.

After a pleasant interlude, Ariel got back to her feet and did her blouse back up.

"I think I need to send our new conserje downstairs for some food," she said archly. "A tortilla sandwich, for me, I think, and a nice cold bottle of San Miguel."

She got out her pocketbook and held out a couple of bills to David. "Of course, he should get something for himself—whatever suits his fancy."

"Put the money away, Sultana. It's on me."

❧

After David came back up with their lunch, they discussed the Ituarte question.

David paged through the list. "I think you can conclude that the Ituarte family is madrileña. General Moscardó's mother, Raúl's

MOSCOW GOLD | 519

grandmother, was an Ituarte. Out of the names that you and Emejota came up with, half are in Madrid or its suburbs. Another thirty are in the provinces that surround the capital, Toledo, Guadalajara, Ávila, and Segovia. The rest are further afield, with seven in the possessions. Most of those are in Ceuta and Melilla."

"A series of concentric circles," Ariel mused as she envisioned the map of Spain. "Start in the center and work outward."

"Only logical way."

❧

"Where'd you catch it, soldier?"

David kept silent.

It was the convention in the Plaza de Santa Ana, as in many plazas in Spain during the paseo, for the younger men to circle in a counterclockwise direction and for the women to do the opposite. That way, everybody saw everybody else. If there was any interest, that could be telegraphed, after the third or fourth pass, by one kind of look or another. Then one of the interested parties could pause in the shade out of the way of the circling masses. When the other arrived, they could talk for a few minutes. It was an effective, convenient, public, and noncommittal way to get acquainted. Who knew what might follow?

David had been circulating with the men. Fitting in. Limping. Appearing to be older than most. Waiting for Calvín to show.

"Where did it happen, *mi viejo*? Somosierra? Brunete? The Ebro?" There were two of them. They had come up behind and fallen in a little behind him. He could just see them—dim in his peripheral vision. Sounded to be about his own age. Not in uniform.

Undercover cops again for sure, but this was different.

"Come on now, tell us where?" No choice but to answer.

"Teruel. With El Campesino." What was it Nacho had said about it?

"With *el distinguido* Campesino? I thought his pinko buddies left him and all his commie underlings to die in the cold there in Teruel. That's what he's always claimed."

"A few of us got out," David said, thinking furiously.

"A few? How many?"

"Don't remember—seventy-five, eighty." David was making this up as he went along.

They stayed right with him. Just out of real sight.

"That many were you?" one of them asked. "We heard it was a lot fewer than that. You wouldn't be fibbing to us, would you now? Where were you hit?"

"In the knee. Right one."

They were approaching one of the exits from the plaza. David thought about making a sudden bolt for it. If they believed he was hurt in the legs, they might not expect him to run.

"Bet that was painful. The knee. Even though you limp a little, don't be thinking about taking off on us. We have guys at each of the exits, so you won't get far. Besides, we don't want anybody to get hurt." Each one grabbed an arm.

"I'll just take that crutch for you there," said the one on the right. "We've got a hold of you, so no need for it at the moment." They were herding him out toward the Calle de las Huertas and the Plaza del Ángel.

They stopped in a darker spot, still staying behind. It was dusk, night coming fast. "Where are your documents?"

"Left breast pocket of the coat," David said.

The one on the right reached in and pulled them out. "Diego Campos Lázaro. And where do you live, Dieguito."

"Albacete. I'm in Madrid for medical treatment. On my knee," David claimed.

"Yes, of course you are. See that car up ahead? Let's just head over there and check in with the jefe. He's going to find your little history very amusing."

There was a polished, all-black SEAT 1400C saloon parked at the edge of the Plaza del Ángel. It was the preferred vehicle of Spanish government officials of some distinction and, of course, of the Cuerpo.

When they arrived at the car, they frisked David, found no weapon, and put him in the back seat. The doors were closed and locked. The sole occupant of the car sat in the driver's seat.

"Here are his documentos, jefe. Says he's from Albacete." The arresting officers recounted the other details David had given. Then they moved off.

The driver continued to look forward. There was a wire mesh between him and the back seat. He had the mirrors adjusted so that a passenger could not see him in their reflection. "From Albacete are you, Señor Campos, aka Paladín?"

"¡Buitre! You guys scared the crap out of me!" David burst out.

"Couldn't be helped. Continue to act like you're being interrogated," Calvín instructed. "You're wanted, and we had to maintain our cover. And yours. Where'd you come up with all that Teruel, El Campesino hokum?"

"True story. Just not mine," David replied.

"Well. You need to get the details right. Your legend's got to be down perfect. There still are lots of people around. They know who was there and how many. And from Albacete, are you?" Calvín sniffed.

"It's the first place that came to my mind."

"You've never been there in your life. Hot, dusty. Everybody who *is* there wants to be *from* there. Let's see your papers." Calvín studied the Campos DNI. "Wow, Paladín! This is a nice forgery. Where'd you get it?"

"Paris," David replied. "The giant flea market they have down on Place d'Italie. All the rest of this rig too. You can find pretty much anything you need. Counterfeit DNIs must be popular. They're all set up to do them. I got the impression that the guy had a stack of genuine blanks. Just filled in my specifications. Same-day service and all that."

"Looks like it. Overall, your cover's good. We picked you up because we knew when and where you'd be. The coat and cap look genuine. You've even made yourself up to look to be about the right age," Calvín commented.

522 | DOUGLAS L. FIELD

"Lots of Republican soldiers fled into France. They ended up having to sell uniform items for food."

"You were a busy boy in France. Tell me details."

David did so. "So now the priority is to locate Carlos Ituarte," he concluded after finishing by telling Calvín about Emejota and the gestoría.

"Everybody's looking for you, David—Seguridad, Guardia Civil, Cuerpo, all of them, even la Policía Municipal. How did you get back into Spain without them knowing? Wait. No. Never mind. Don't tell me. It's better if I don't know."

"Better, yeah." David didn't know what else to say.

"What I have is this," Calvín went on. "There's something called Room 11. It's very hush-hush. I can't find out a lot about it without making my interest known. It wouldn't be at all wise to do that. I did get that it's connected to the Banco de España. Some banking security, financial stability activity. Whatever it is, it has an office in the main building on Alcalá. The name associated with it is one Sáenz. Don't know him and can't find out anything without giving myself away."

David then added, "Onésimo mentioned Room 11. It all started to come back to me. I know that guy. I've met him. Ran into him by chance. After Isham gave me the gold investigation assignment, the first thing I did was go over to the bank. I stumbled by pure chance onto Sáenz and his office. First name Federico. Real bureaucratic type he was. Filled me in on a lot of background. Helpful to be honest. Bet if I check back, he was in a Room 11."

"Well, here's the interesting part," Calvín added. "While I can get that Room 11's interest in you and where you are is intense, their interest does not appear to be hostile. Normally an all-hands-on-deck effort like this is antagonistic and angry. Not this one. Room 11 wants you, but I don't have the sense they want to hurt you—not yet anyway. Maybe not until after they catch you."

David was absorbing Calvín's information, "*Someone* wants to hurt me. Tried to kill me! Is it about my investigation? The gold?"

"Gotta be."

"Do they want to stop it?" David wondered.

"That's the odd thing, David, it doesn't seem like that at all. All I hear is that they want to know where you are."

"Then why was I waylaid in Paris?"

"Why were you followed to Paris in the first place? And who knew you were there?"

"If they don't want to hurt me, should I let them find me?" David asked.

"I wouldn't go that far." Calvín mulled it over. "A couple of things you need to understand. You've lived here a long time. But you weren't born here. Living under dictatorship, even if by now it's a 'tender tyranny' as some say, isn't in your blood like it's in ours. They can make mistakes all day long, and it doesn't hurt them. You make one mistake and it's fatal."

"I have another Spanish friend who says that. I don't think I've made any mistakes so far," David said, defending himself.

"Well, don't make the mistake of trusting Room 11 or any of them," Calvín counseled.

"You think Room 11's been in on it from the start? They instigated the gold investigation? That it wasn't an accident that I stumbled onto them in the bank?"

"And they want to keep other people off of your back who would rather you not get the story." Calvín followed David's reasoning.

"After Paris, they've lost me and now they're panicking?"

"It fits." Calvín shrugged. "What you don't know is what their attitude will be when you have everything they want. From what you tell me, you're close but not all the way there. Once you've got it all, their favorable interest in you may turn unfavorable."

They sat in silence for a while.

Then Calvín spoke. "My colleagues are going to return in a second. They'll escort you back to the Plaza de Santa Ana. They will give you

524 | DOUGLAS L. FIELD

some attitude. It's for show. Keep your head down and act submissive. Then we have to get this car back to the ministry."

"What a great ruse you pulled off, Buitre!"

"Don't quote me, but all in a day's work for us in the Franco regime. Two more things. If they have already found you and are watching tonight, I will hear about it. It'll come out of Room 11 that some other agency picked you up. They'll want to know who it was, and we'll have a good clue that they saw us, and they've got you under surveillance. If that happens, I'll tell Onésimo."

"Perfect. What else?" David asked.

"Room 11 is interested in a woman. I'm not sure on the name or if there's any connection to you. Márquez, Meléndez, Montáñez. Something like that."

David started to explain, but Calvín stopped him. "Don't say anything. That's another thing I don't need to know, but it sounds like you do."

Back in the Plaza de Santa Ana a "chastised" civil war wounded veteran decided to shamble another couple of circuits around the plaza. By now, night had fallen. He went counterclockwise, of course. But if there were any pretty girls, he didn't notice.

CHAPTER 81

Moscow: Thursday, September 12, 1963

Colonel Boris Vucetitch was apoplectic.

"It's two weeks and they have *nothing*?!?"

"Nothing at all, Colonel. I'm sorry," replied his chief of staff in the merest whisper.

"*What*, Pavel Leonidovich? Gone? Into thin air? Eluding the mighty KGB? People can now just disappear on us? Where are they looking?"

"Paris and environs."

"Why not Spain? Wasn't the gold he's after Spanish?"

Each question was louder until Vucetitch was screaming, red-faced, and pounding the conference table with such force that the others' briefcases and teacups were bouncing up and down.

"Spain's a difficult environment for us, Comrade Colonel. Regime's hostile. Tolerates nothing from us. Risk of losing assets is high."

With effort, Vucetitch controlled himself. "Vladimir Yefimovich is inquiring. He speaks more softly than I, but do not be taken in. He understands the urgency of this—*and* what a fiasco it is. You can

MOSCOW GOLD | **527**

rest assured that the matter is the subject of discussion where the atmosphere is very rarified—discussion that has been embarrassing to him." Vucetitch then uttered a string of curses.

His fury abated. "Pavel Leonidovich, encode, and transmit the following cable. 'Locate subject now stop Complete mission forthwith stop Activate Spanish assets stop Report success immediately.'"

"Yes, Colonel. They should get the message."

"We shall hope that they do. Report developments to me twice daily, Pavel Leonidovich. Also hope your reports will be very few in number until you advise that the mission is complete."

CHAPTER 82

Pullach: Friday, September 13, 1963

Sepp Staupitz was back in Germany for consultations.

He was happy about it. Although a seasoned Spanish hand, he had grown weary of the country. Everything was cooked in olive oil and washed down with wine. He was ready for some hearty German food, laced with butter and chased with some real beer.

Gehlen came out of his office and showed Sepp in. "It's Friday the thirteenth, Sepp. Bad luck day if you're superstitious."

"I'm not, General."

"I'm not superstitious either, but you know, many Americans are. I hope that, in the matter of their little gold investigation, today we are confirming their worries." All broad smiles, *gemütlich* in every respect.

"If you mean, have we found the journalist, no. I'm sorry, we haven't," Sepp replied.

"Gibraltar?"

"Just got back, General. I contacted our several banks there. All is well. The accounts and vault deposits are up-to-date and in good standing. I inventoried several. All applicable fees have been paid.

MOSCOW GOLD | 529

Signature cards and access codes are current. I reviewed security with each of the general managers. It is tight. The coins, by the way, are a thing of beauty—breathtaking. Admiral Canaris let me keep one that I filched. It was nice to see some of the others again!"

"I expected no less. Ours is all but a thirty-year relationship with Gibraltar. It's been mutual and satisfactory."

"Add to it, General, that the Gibraltarians are shopping their banking services around the free world. It is essential to them that they be considered safe. 'Impregnable as the Rock itself' as one of our managers told me. Any problem with our deposits would generate disastrous press for them. They are motivated."

"Any indication that the young man's investigation's gotten down there?" Gehlen asked.

"None. They monitor who goes in and out of the crown colony. There has been no one nosing around, nothing unusual or alarming in any manner," Sepp replied.

"Good. But we're not safe—not until his investigation is ended, ended definitively. You understand me, Sepp?"

"I do, mein General. Is there any new intelligence here at headquarters?"

"No. No, there isn't. That worries me. The Russians have lost him. No idea where he is. It's giving them serious indigestion. The Americans think he's in Madrid, but they are just guessing. The Amis have a good man working the case, so it's a fair bet they find him first. I don't know what the Spanish know or don't know. But, Sepp, in the end, he may not be found. He's quite clever."

"I see, General. No choice but to continue our vigilance in Gibraltar."

"No choice at all. The fox will go for the henhouse. That's what foxes do."

"I'll be back there by the first part of the week," Staupitz assured his chief.

530 | DOUGLAS L. FIELD

"Perfect, Sepp. I'll have the consulate there alerted. But I'd stay away from it if I were you. Except for communicating with Pullach. Oh, and Sepp, it may turn out that you need some firepower."

"In the old days, we used some Bulgarian connections that we had," Staupitz recalled. "Kept *our* fingerprints off of things."

"Those contacts have been preserved and cultivated; you'll be glad to know. I'll get you what you need. But Sepp?" Gehlen paused.

"Ja, mein general."

"If you need to do what needs to be done in person, you are authorized to do it."

CHAPTER 83

Carabanchel: Thursday, October 10, 1963

Finding Carlos Ituarte had been more than a difficult challenge.

It had been impossible. The concentric circles worked well enough for eliminating Carlos Ituartes from Ariel and Emejota's list. *The* Carlos Ituarte remained, thus far, unlocated.

The search was time-consuming. All the while, David and Ariel were exposed.

David had been into and out of the barrios of Madrid in detail he had not experienced since his first days in the capital. Unsuccessful in the city itself, his search had then widened to the *alrededores,* the outskirts—Getafe, Majadahonda, Vallecas, Alcorón, and Móstoles. When there had been no joy there, on to Toledo, Alcalá de Henares, Guadalajara, Ávila, and even to Salamanca he'd pressed. It had gone on and on. Numerous leads were found and followed up on with no progress toward locating Moscardó's relative.

David and Ariel saw each other almost every day.

He ran street detection routes as a matter of routine before they would meet. There was never anything. He was sure Room 11 had no idea where he was. Onésimo had nothing from Calvín.

Ariel had developed a genuine talent for street craft. The two succeeded in being inconspicuous and in concealing their relationship and connection to each other. Often, they would meet in very crowded locations—Puerta del Sol on Friday evening or Sunday at noon on the Calle de Bailén in front of the Palacio Real. Or they would seek out quiet and intimate places, a shady lovers' glade in the Retiro or El Campo del Moro or a back corner in the *cafetería* at the Facultad de Filosofía y Letras out in University City.

David appeared in one or the other of various personae that he had developed in addition to the wounded soldier. Ariel somehow managed to be the pharmacist's assistant in a white smock, a uniformed hotel maid, or the chic Madrid office worker. To the watcher observing at a distance, they were always a different yet unremarkable couple.

On one occasion Ariel had shown up pushing a stroller with a life-sized infant doll swaddled inside. David was at once admiring of her initiative and taken aback by its implications.

"Little boy or little girl?" David played along as they moved off together down the street.

"Boy. He looks just like his father."

'Then he's *muy bien guapo*" (handsome).

"Of course!"

"I'm afraid to ask his name."

"Why? Do babies make you nervous?" Ariel punctuated her question with a bemused expression as they walked on, looking every bit a young Spanish family.

Today, David was in Carabanchel and on his way to meet Ariel. His midmorning trek from his chabola had taken him up the dusty Paseo de Nuestra Señora de Fátima. He headed for the Metro.

Two stops toward the center of Madrid from Carabanchel was the Lago Metro station. The Lago station was one of the few in the entire system that was above ground and in the open air. It had a quaint little station building in something of an Alpine style that led down to a medium-sized lake. *Lago* meant lake. The lake was known simply as "Lago." Lago had a fountain that spouted high in the middle. The Palacio Real and the Cathedral of Our Lady of Almudena overlooked it from the bluffs above the Manzanares.

Lago at noon on a workday was a quiet and serene place, considering it was so close by the city. There were terraces offering drinks and a light lunch, along with a rowboat concession off to the side.

In Madrid, the early days of fall were glorious. The baking heat of summer had abated, but skies remained cloudless and clear. There were often gentle breezes that gave just a vague whiff of winter to come. These were perfect times for enjoying the out of doors. David took a table at one of the terraces and ordered a *caña*, a small beer, and settled in to wait for Ariel. Soon she appeared, walking down from the Metro station in a bright print dress, a floppy sun hat, and the usual sunglasses.

"Buy you a beer, pretty woman?"

"A Negroni."

"A Negroni? Sounds exotic. And you look exhilarating."

"You're sweet." She bussed him lightly. "Exhilarating?"

"I'm serious." He indulged in a long and appraising look. "I'm thinking *curvas peligrosas*. Exhilarating."

"¿Curvas peligrosas?"

"Yeah. Curvas peligrosas. Dangerous curves, like the highway signs say. Like up at Altamira." He ogled her again. "Exhilarating and dangerous. Man's gotta be careful."

Ariel blushed.

"You're blushing. That's rare for you."

"Like I said, you're sweet," was all she could manage.

"Want to rent a boat later?" David proposed.

The rowboats at Lago were medium large. They had cushions on duckboards at the bottom. That and the thwart could be removed so

MOSCOW GOLD | 535

that the occupants could relax and be at their leisure. David rowed out to the middle near the fountain and took out the thwart. He stretched out at the stern, and Ariel did in the bow. They dipped their hands in the water, splashed each other, and enjoyed each other's company.

Then David said, "Being with you has improved my mood, Ariel. I woke up frustrated over the Ituarte search. I've contacted over one hundred five of the names on the list you and Emejota developed."

"You have to think that the odds are not good that any of the remaining few will be our man. Something's wrong," Ariel agreed.

"My exact thought. I'm discouraged."

"Are you in a dead end?"

"I'm resisting temptation to think that. If Ituarte were dead or never existed, why would Raúl have sent me to look for him?"

"We need a new idea, David, a new approach."

"Mmm." They relaxed in silence for a long time. Then David said, "Do you know the surname Ibarra?"

"Of course, it's Basque, not common, but on occasion encountered."

"We have a small Basque community in Missouri. I've known some Ibarras, but they spell—"

Ariel almost jumped out of the boat. *"¡La 'Y' griega en vez de la 'I' chiquita!* David, he uses 'Y' not 'I.' Why didn't we think of that before now? He's spelling it *Y*tuarte. Has to be. Let's get to the gestoría right away."

David already had the thwart back in place and was rowing for the dock.

Once on shore and on the way to the Metro, Ariel was very excited and asked, "Have you got a ficha? I'll call Eme and get her started."

David had one.

⁓

Emejota had found six names. "I should have thought of an alternative spelling. People using the 'Y' are much less common."

David scanned the list. "Look at this one. He lives at Paseo del General Martínez Campos 37. That's not far from the Castellana. High-rent district. Fitting for a banker. We'll do him first."

David and Ariel went out onto Recoletos and ran for the first tranvía headed north.

Ytuarte's *was* high rent. Number 37 was a large Italian Renaissance–style mansion, set well back from the street. Passage inside was through a red brick arch in an ivy-covered wall. David explained their business to the gatekeeper. After disappearing for about five minutes, he returned. They were admitted.

"You are in luck. Señor Ytuarte is at home this afternoon. He is willing to give you a few minutes."

They passed through a cool, shaded, and leafy garden. Sculptures and a bubbling hexagonal fountain suggested the Patio de los Leones in the Alhambra and created near total serenity—all just steps from one of Europe's busiest boulevards. Entry to the house was through an atrium. David and Ariel were conducted upstairs to a large salon furnished with heavy sofas and chairs. Even more, it was hung with original artworks.

"Thank you, Genaro." The gatekeeper turned on his heels as a small man appeared from a side room. He was turned out in a dark suit, white shirt, and conservative tie.

David remarked to himself that it looked like he sat around the house all day dressed up like this. He hadn't had time to change. He and Ariel just arrived.

In his late 60's, the man was of under-average height. His features were well proportioned with intense but sad eyes and a straight nose set off by a droopy moustache and longish goatee. "I am Carlos Ytuarte. It is my pleasure to meet you."

David took the man's proffered hand. "My name is David Fordham, *International Herald Tribune.*" He made to produce his credentials.

"There is no need for that, Mr. Fordham. I trust you to be who you say that you are." Ytuarte then looked at Ariel.

MOSCOW GOLD | 537

"This is my novia, Ariel Muñiz. She is assisting me with my investigation."

Ytuarte smiled at Ariel in a very courtly way. "*Encantado*, Señorita Muñiz. You are a very lucky man, Señor Fordham." He smiled holding Ariel's eyes all the while. "Genaro tells me that you are acquainted with my cousin Raúl Moscardó."

Eureka! Found him at last. With effort, David controlled his exuberance. "I am. I met him last month in Paris. He gave me a note to be given to you." Against the chance that he might at any time find Ytuarte, David kept with him the gray envelope that Moscardó had given him. He produced it.

"Come. Come. Let us find a more suitable place for our talk." He led them into a comfortably furnished, airy, and brightly lit study. "Please sit." Ytuarte indicated a pair of leather chairs. He then took his own seat across from his guests.

"Let us see what my cousin Raúl has for me." Ytuarte slit open the letter and read it. "You made quite a favorable impression in Paris, Mr. Fordham." He handed the note to David.

The note vouched for David, told Ytuarte what Raúl had done for David, and asked him to help David determine where the gold had been placed and secured after Paris.

Ytuarte said, "Please, Miss Muñiz, you should read the note. You'll find it interesting."

David handed it to her.

"We had a great difficulty locating you, Señor Ytuarte," David said to their host. "I had it from Raúl that the family name is spelled with an 'I.' You might be interested to know that there are dozens and dozens of Carlos Ituartes in Spain today. I have spoken with almost all of them. They are an interesting and varied group."

"In all candor, Mr. Fordham, the proper family name has the 'I.' I substituted the 'Y' for the sake of security and anonymity."

"It works. We came close to giving up on locating you. Allows you to hide in plain sight, if you know what I mean." David raised an eyebrow towards Ariel.

"A most apt and polished formulation of the matter, my good young man. I'm beginning to understand my cousin's appreciation for you. And, yes, it is, for the most part, effective. But may I say that I am in one sense content that, in the end, you did manage to find me. It is instructive to me that you were able to do so. There are all manner of strategies to maintain anonymity. Some would leave me much easier to find. Others would provide total effectiveness. The fact that you found me, although at the cost of intensive effort, means to me that my current strategy is well balanced." Ytuarte expanded on his position.

"In other words, unless you get an occasional speeding ticket, you're not sure that you're driving as fast as you can get away with?"

Ytuarte gave a hearty laugh. "I don't drive an automobile. But, yes, in very pithy and practical terms, you are right. You will concede, will you not, that the change of one simple letter has proved to be a simple but workable expedient for protecting my identity?"

A brief silence settled over the room. Ariel was entranced. She looked back and forth from David to Ytuarte.

"Would you like to meet my wife?" Ytuarte asked. "She may have a bit of refreshment for us." He led them back into the main salon where he had first greeted them.

Mrs. Ytuarte was on her feet, waiting for them in one corner of the room. "Mi amor, I would like to introduce you to Señorita Ariel Muñiz and Señor David Fordham. Miss Muñiz and Mr. Fordham, this is my wife Evangelina. Evangelina, these fine young people are looking into the notorious Moscow Gold."

"It is a pleasure to know you both. Won't you sit down?" Mrs. Ytuarte invited. "If we were in Britain, it would be teatime, but I've asked Concha to bring us a coffee. More in the Spanish custom, no?"

MOSCOW GOLD | 539

They were in one corner of the large room. Concha appeared with an elaborate silver coffee service and some decorated petit fours. "Do you take your coffee with sugar, Miss Muñiz?"

The questions surrounding the gold faded into the background, absorbed by the big room, and attention turned to an agreeable afternoon coffee.

"As you can see, I have an interest in impressionist painting," Ytuarte commented, moving his head in a circle as if to point out the many paintings that adorned the walls of the salon. "You will find works of Laureano Barrau; Meifrén; Joaquín Sorolla, of course; and Maurice Utrillo in our collection here."

Ariel stood up and made close examination of some of the frames. "I love impressionist painting. Your collection is magnificent. I would never have imagined that it existed here in Madrid."

"Well, we don't advertise it. The French claim Maurice Utrillo as their own. He *was* born there, but I believe his father was the painter Miguel Utrillo, a Spaniard, so I choose to number him as one of ours."

"Who is your favorite painter, Carlos?" asked Mrs. Ytuarte by way of encouraging her husband.

He didn't need it. "I wouldn't say I have a favorite painter as much as favorite paintings. Muñoz Degrain's *Chubasco en Granada*, Utrillo's *Casa de Berlioz en Montmarte* and *Paisaje de Mallorca*. And then which of the Sorollas? *La Hora del Baño, The Wounded Foot, Women Walking on the Beach* as the latter are known in English? Who could choose?!?"

And so it went, a cultured and successful man indulging his great passion. After an hour had passed, Ytuarte made reluctant return to the business at hand. "Thank you for permitting me to show you my collection. I've talked on far too long. Our little interlude has given me time to consider the position that your request and that of my cousin has put me in."

Ytuarte paused for a long moment and then continued, "I am a banker and so am constrained to exercise the highest level of discretion on behalf of both my depositors and the banking industry at large."

David feared that a refusal to cooperate was forthcoming. "I understand, Señor Ytuarte. We journalists labor under our own code of conduct and ethics, which is quite restrictive and jealous of the confidentiality of our sources."

"Good. You understand my position then," said Ytuarte. "But my cousin is correct. I have professional acquaintanceship with banking in Gibraltar. Gibraltar desires to establish itself as a banking center, so it needs to perfect an unassailable reputation for secrecy and security. The Switzerland of southern Europe, they hope."

After having listened in silence for some time, Mrs. Ytuarte spoke up. "Oh, Carlos, don't be an old foof. You know that nothing would please you more than for the involvement of the treacherous English with Spain's money to become known."

He smiled at her, "If I knew that the Moscow Gold were in Gibraltar, I would not be able to confirm it. If I knew who the holders of the depository accounts that contain the gold were, I would not be able to tell you. While I cannot tell you much about the Gibraltarian banks, I may have an interesting fact or two concerning the British government."

"Since the British *government* is not in the banking business and has no depositors, your fiduciary obligations do not extend to it?" David prodded a little.

"Correct. I have loyalty to my profession, not the government of Great Britain. The Gibraltar banks believe that they keep confidential their depositors' information, even from the authorities under whose aegis they operate and prosper. But their information is of use to Whitehall, so it spies on its own banks. Quite apart from the efforts of the Gibraltarian banks, London aggregates and keeps any information it can get."

"Husband, do get to the point. Tell them. For no other reason than that if she won't give Gibraltar back to its rightful owners, England should pay a heavy price for keeping it."

"Very well, my dear. There is a nondescript activity in Gibraltar gloriously called Her Majesty's Office of Data Development and Information Processing. By intention, this office is little understood. And by intention, it goes unnoticed. But not to be fooled. Behind the front of innocent bureaucratic activity, it gathers information on both the identities of major depositors in the banks there and the details of their holdings. It engages in industrial and economic espionage. You will find it tucked away, with consummate British illogic, in the Registry of Marriages Office on Secretary's Lane."

David noted these details.

Ytuarte looked at his wife for a long moment. "That, *mes enfants*, is the best I can do for you, for my cousin, for my family, and for Spain. I have told you where the information you need may reside."

"Thank you, sir. You have helped us immeasurably," David said.

"You surely are, at this very moment, planning an excursion to Gibraltar. But let me ask you a question. Do you love this young lady?"

"Yes, sir, I do."

"Good. If you love her, do not go to Gibraltar. It will not go well for you there. You will leave her grieving and brokenhearted."

David and Ariel looked at each other.

"Gibraltar is wide open and full of intrigue and deception. Extracting what you want will not be possible. The British are not a people to be trifled with. They may seem often to fumble and bumble along, but they are calculating and ruthless, experts at protecting their own interests and at any cost. They always win. Look how they have managed to keep Gibraltar for two and a half centuries against all efforts to extract them. The only chance against them is to take advantage of their arrogance, and that is unlikely to avail you in Gibraltar."

Mrs. Ytuarte nodded, a resigned expression on her face. "Can't you drop the story, pursue your affair and live, as you say in English, 'happily ever after'?"

542 | DOUGLAS L. FIELD

Before either David or Ariel could answer, Ytuarte went on. "That great limestone rock is full of tunnels and secret chambers and dungeons. The Soviets and the American CIA and maybe even Franco's people would not hesitate to kill you. The British are capable of worse. They would throw you in a hole in that rock and let you rot."

The Ytuartes got to their feet. It had come time to leave.

David shook the older man's hand. "Thank you, Don Carlos. Thank you for everything—not only the information, but also for a fascinating afternoon. You also, Doña Evangelina."

Ytuarte turned to Ariel. "Let us end on a more encouraging note. You are captivating, Miss Muñiz. If this attractive young American has indeed stolen your affections for himself, then today hearts are breaking all over Madrid!"

Ariel flushed—for the second time that day.

PART VII
MONTIS INSIGNIA CALPE

CHAPTER 84

Madrid: Sunday, October 13, 1963

From the first that David approached him, Nacho had been eager in embracing the whole Gibraltar proposal.

"Go to Gibraltar and screw the British? Let's head out tonight. I've been itching to do something about that gold since I helped drive it to Cartagena," Nacho had urged.

"Don't you think we should do some advance planning?" David was pleased at Nacho's enthusiasm, but Ytuarte's admonitions urged caution.

"We can do that on the way down. Plenty of time to plan. It'll take us a while to get all the way there. Ever since I got back to Madrid after escaping from Saint-Cyprien, I've dreamed about doing something to get that gold back. I've never had any opportunity till now."

David redirected the conversation. "Ytuarte assures that the information is there. Find someone to give it to us?"

"*Give* it? No, the limeys are too 'honorable,' David. And there's no time to set up a bribe or blackmail."

"But, Nacho, it's the executives who are British. We can find somebody in middle management who's Gibraltarian. Not the same level of loyalty."

"Don't kid yourself. The Gibraltarians are more British than the British. We'll never find a traitor—not without more time and enough money to set up an attractive *mordida*. We have neither."

"Well then, what if we forced it out of one of them? At the point of a gun or a knife or spear. Something like that."

"Way too messy, David, and very risky. We need not to call attention to ourselves. You *know* the answer. The only way."

"Steal it?" David had to concede.

"Yep. Good old-fashioned larceny. Do you know the exact location of the data?"

"A little office on a little street called Secretary's Lane," David said. "They say everything's little in Gibraltar. The whole place is about two and a half square miles. Lots of people are packed in there though. Dense population."

"Well, that's good for us," reflected Nacho. "Everything we need will be close at hand. Easy to lose ourselves among the locals. The tactical situation could be worse."

"And they can't know they've been hit." David was catching Nacho's vision.

"Cannot," Nacho agreed. "They find out, they will take steps. It'll spoil the impact of your story. We'll have to create some sort of diversion—a ruse that's believable, one that's easy to mobilize and carry out."

David thought for a moment. "Churchill, I think it was, said the truth is so precious that it needs to be protected by a bodyguard of lies."

"He's smart. Even if he *is* English. Not just a bodyguard of lies but a bodyguard of liars. We're going to need a couple more guys."

The conspirators then fleshed out their plan. Nacho gathered his troops and left for Gibraltar. David decided to delay his departure.

❧

On that same Sunday, Nick Barnickle found himself on stakeout on Ribera de Curtidores. Barnickle had no history of doubting his skill and ability. But he doubted himself now. Isham was out of his mind. Nick had never considered giving up on a surveillance. Today he was tempted. Isham's harangue from earlier this morning was still stinging his ears.

"Nick, you're a loser. You told me you'd find him. You told me he's here in Madrid. That was weeks ago."

"He's good, Jack. What do the Germans have? What do the Russians have?"

"Nothing. Nothing, Nick. Nothing. Just like you. They have bupkis."

"What's that tell you, Jack?" Barnickle argued.

"It tells me that they are worse losers than you are." Isham was screaming now. "Of course, *they* can't find him. That's why I have *you*. You talk a game, Nick, but you're nothing but a second-rate shamus. An eighth-grade girl could do better," Isham raged.

"What are the Spaniards saying?"

"The Spaniards? The Spaniards, Nick, are questioning my manhood and your manhood. And I'm having trouble defending yours."

"Well, *their* manhood hasn't found crap either, Jack. Remind them of that," Barnickle snarled back.

"I can't remind them of anything. They're every day reminding me that I promised *we* would find the guy. I told *them* that because you told *me* that," Isham screamed.

It had been hard to fight back. Nick had promised to deliver the goods—repeatedly. But the guy was gone. "Nobody eludes Nick Barnickle. Not for long," he'd proclaimed.

MOSCOW GOLD | 549

"What's Langley say about where the gold went after Paris?" Barnickle demanded.

"They have no idea. Does this surprise?"

"If we knew that, we'd know where to find him," Nick persisted.

"You have till the end of the week," Isham had growled. Then he'd left the office and kicked the door shut so hard that the walls shook.

❧

The plan for this Sunday had been to hang around Curtidores, a street that, on Sundays, was closed to traffic and became the huge Rastro flea market. The big draw, in Nick's mind, was that tens of thousands of people swarmed around the kiosks and stalls from morning till early afternoon. The upside for spotting Nick's quarry was good.

On this good weather morning in October, La Latina and the Rastro were mobbed. Still smarting from Isham's diatribe, Nick was lounging in the doorway of a pastelería that was closed—watching the crowd for anyone unusual, out of place. But he saw nothing unusual.

No. Wait. Working her way up the street was a pretty young nurse—wearing her cape, white shoes, and a starched hat. She seemed to have a little bit of an odd gait. "Maybe unusual for a Sunday, maybe not," he muttered to himself. "Hospitals and clinics stay open on Sundays. Have to. But still. Out in her full regalia?"

His attention almost waned. Then he saw the doctor. Making his way across the up-and-down flow of the people. Young guy also. Glasses and a beard. White coat and a stethoscope clipped to it. Nick tried to remember if there was a hospital nearby. The doctor and the nurse saw each other. Their eyes met, but they didn't talk. It seemed odd. Even if they don't know each other, you'd think they would at least speak. Professional courtesy.

The nurse continued uphill. Nick moved into the stream. The doctor started uphill too.

❧

David passed Ariel without speaking to her. He hiked up Curtidores, onto Calle de Toledo and into the Plaza Mayor. The doctor and nurse idea had been hers. He found a spot in the shade at a terraza in the southeast corner. Ariel found him. They embraced—a light public embrace, an embrace lasting for just that additional moment that distinguishes between acquaintanceship and intimacy.

"Where'd you get the uniform?" David did not even try to disguise his admiration of her.

"Marisol. She's a friend from school. Now a nurse at the British-American Hospital over by Moncloa." Ariel struck a sexy pose. "Her tunic is a little small for me."

"Not for me."

"Marisol's got big feet," Ariel continued unabashed. "Her shoes are too big. They make me walk funny."

"So, Marisol's feet are bigger than yours?"

Ariel looked suspicious.

"I think I've stumbled on a *norma,* a maxim, a postulate, a theorem," David continued.

"What *maxim* would that be, my love?"

"*¿Es obvio, no?* The larger the shoes, the smaller the tunic, and the smaller the shoes, the larger the—"

Ariel whacked him before he could finish. Then she stood up and adjusted Marisol's tunic. She pulled the collar forward. Inhaling, she smoothed it down in front and retucked it.

David's breath caught in his throat.

"You seem distracted, David," she said, all innocence.

I'll take that image with me all the way to Gibraltar. "Speaking of funny, I'm *feeling* funny." David tried to recover.

"Are you sick?" She responded in kind.

"I think so. My heart." David looked down at his chest.

Ariel took his arm. "Your pulse is strong but a little fast." She concentrated for a few seconds and then looked satisfied. "I think your heart's OK, though."

"I'm not so sure. It feels inflamed."

"Inflamed?"

"Yes. Inflamed with passion."

"For real? Well, that does sound serious." Ariel looked concerned.

"It *is* serious," David agreed.

"Do you have a fever?" Ariel leaned over. She brushed herself provocatively against him. She touched his forehead. "You do. You have a high fever. I'll get the orderlies to give you a cold shower."

And on it went.

After their persiflage petered out a little, David filled her in on his and Nacho's plans for Gibraltar.

"Are you taking any weapons?" Ariel inquired.

"Too dangerous. Easy to get caught going in and out of Gibraltar. The British are quiet but competent about border security there. We have to be clean."

"Remember Paris, David. They haven't given up. They're looking for you—if they haven't already found you. Give thought to defending yourselves if you need to."

"Stealth and guile, Ariel. It'll have to be that." Then he added, "We'll be getting down there the middle of this week and hope to be back the week after that. Twenty-second, twenty-third. Along in there."

Then they arranged for their own next meeting.

⁓

Barnickle decided to stick with the doctor. He and the nurse were familiar in the Plaza Mayor. When they got ready to leave, they exchanged a passionate kiss. Her hat fell off, which amused them both. She headed out of the west end of the plaza towards Ópera and the Plaza de Oriente. He went the opposite way towards Sol.

The young doctor hurried down Carrera de San Jerónimo. As he did, he engaged in several surveillance avoidance techniques. It was not what Nick would have expected from a doctor. Once he got to Neptune, the doctor grabbed a cab. He had himself delivered to Atocha. Nick followed. It was easy.

Once inside the big train station, Barnickle's quarry went to a public locker, where he dropped off the medical disguise and picked up a small backpack. After that, he hid out in a café by the departure platforms. Nick had time for a ten-second call to Isham's line—before he followed the "doctor" onto an express headed south.

Now Isham's gonna get what he wants, Barnickle thought to himself. *And he's gonna get what I want him to have on top of it.*

He also had time for a second ten-second call.

CHAPTER 85

Algeciras: Wednesday, October 16, 1963

"Windy," observed Nipi.

"It's a Levanter," commented Nacho. "Strong east wind. Forms up out over Mallorca somewhere and then picks up speed as it funnels through the strait. It's October. Late in the year for a Levanter."

The bar of the Hotel Reina Cristina looked out over a large pool and patio, where the grass was dry and turning brown. The wind was very steady, strong, not gusty. It picked up dust and all manner of paper detritus that littered the patio. It riffled the surface of the pool.

"I like flags." The younger man's answer was incongruous. "I wonder what the yellow and blue one is."

"City's flag, I guess."

There was a mast installed in the patio that had a yardarm rigged to it with different flags run up its halyards. The flags were standing straight out—no fluttering and no flapping—like they were starched flat.

"We were talking about flags this morning on the train. I like them," the little fellow continued. "I think I'll start a collection."

MOSCOW GOLD | 555

"You do that. Then I'll buy you a French tricolor for your santo. Remember how brightly it fluttered over the beach when we were there?"

The Reina Cristina is not *on* the water, but it's close. From certain vantage points, Algeciras Bay can be seen beyond the cracked and brittle streets of the town. The Levanter was raising whitecaps out on the bay waters.

"See that cloud over the Rock?" Nacho gestured with his beer. "That hot wet wind hits the cooler limestone of the Rock, and it makes that cloud. Looks like the Rock is on fire."

But now interest in geology and the weather waned. Nipi nodded toward the lobby and the guest rooms of the hotel, "What's with your friend?"

"What's *with* him?"

"You know. Why does he talk that way?" Nipi said as he massaged his left shoulder.

"Now *that's* your most intelligent question of the day, Nipi." Nacho turned truculent. "For the same reason that you're so short. Stuff happens in life. Sometimes it's not all that pretty."

"*Cálmate, macho!* I didn't mean any offense; I was just curious."

"Well, here's what you do." Nacho gave vent to his impatience. "You direct some of your curiosity to observing him. He's very intelligent. He's a genius mechanic. He can fix anything. He will be an asset to us. Just doesn't talk very good. Not his fault. That's just how he is."

"Grouch!"

"Listen to him. You'll learn to understand him. On a job like this, a guy like him is invaluable. People think he's an idiot. He knows that, and he knows how to manipulate them. You won't believe what he can get away with."

Nipi had celebrated his recent retirement after a quarter century as a firefighter in the Madrid Fire Department. "You got good at fighting fires, Nipi?" Nacho said. "Beto's like that. He's good at what he does. Known him longer than you. First met him in the war. Ciempozuelos.

556 | DOUGLAS L. FIELD

That's where he's from. I knew his aunt. He stayed there after. Became the town's jack-of-all-trades and fixer. Everybody down there knows him and trusts him. They all also *respect* him, Nipi."

"Want another beer?" Nipi tried to mollify his friend.

"Yeah. You can pay me back for the history lesson I gave you on the train on the way down."

The three had this morning come down from Córdoba. There was a long layover in Málaga. Plenty of time for talk. Nipi knew little of Gibraltar and its history. Nacho had read Nipi in. Beto had busied himself on his own.

"David thinks the gold's in Gibraltar and that some Germans put it there to keep it safe. Gibraltar's a British colony," Nacho had explained. "Going over there is like going to England. We're leaving Spain. The official language is English, but everybody speaks Castilian. You'll *feel* at home, but you're not. They have British laws there, not Spanish. That's why Spain can't just take the gold back."

"We ran into some Englishmen in the war," Nipi recalled. "International Brigadiers. England's way up north—past France they said. Why would the English have a colony near Spain?"

"It's not *near* Spain. It's *in* Spain. The bastards stole it, and they won't give it back. It's a strategic spot. Controls entry to the Mediterranean from the Atlantic. The water between Spain and Africa there is only nine miles wide. The Rock juts up 1,400 feet. It dominates the land and the sea all around."

"If it's ours, we should have it back." Nipi was indignant.

"You know the coat of arms on our flag? It has those two pillars?" Nacho continued. "One of them represents Gibraltar, and the other is a mountain on the African side. Jebel Musa, I think it is. The Greeks called them the Pillars of Hercules. Greeks had it that their god Hercules stood astride the 'pillars' and guarded the entrance to the known world."

Nipi took it all in. "Why would the English steal what belongs to us? How could they get away with that?"

MOSCOW GOLD | 557

"It goes back two hundred fifty years. The Hapsburg family were kings of Spain. To make sure it was always someone from their family who was the king of Spain, they married their own cousins. You shouldn't do that. It's unhealthy. Pretty soon, along comes one king by the name of Charles II. Because of the intermarrying, he had all kinds of health problems, including that he couldn't have any kids."

"So, the whole plan backfired?" Nipi was tracking.

"Yep. Charles dies, and he has no heir. A war starts to see who gets the Spanish throne. Distant Hapsburg relatives wanted us, and so did the royal family of France. England jumped in on the side of our guys, the Hapsburgs. So did the Dutch. As part of the war, the English and the Dutch sent a fleet and occupied Gibraltar. In the end, the French royalty got the Spanish throne, but the English refused to give Gibraltar back. Then, while Spain was still weak, they convened a big meeting in Holland somewhere and sneaked through a treaty that gave them the Rock 'in perpetuity.'"

"Jerk Brits!" Nipi reacted.

"Spain's been trying to get Gibraltar back ever since. But it's not so easy," Nacho continued to explain. "There's information over there that proves who has our gold now. David has to get that proof so he can finish his story and expose to the world all that happened. But we're going to have to be careful because, if we get caught, Spain won't be able to help us."

Nacho looked up. He murmured to Nipi. "Here comes Beto. Try to remember what I said."

Beto came up and took a seat. "Have a beer, Beto? Nipi's treat," Nacho said in greeting.

"Aahseeaah, Ni'i." Beto said.

Nacho turned his face away from Beto and hissed at Nipi, "What'd I tell you?"

"*De nada*, Beto," Nipi replied while still holding Nacho's gaze.

The Spaniards left the Reina Cristina but not together. Nacho had ordered, "Split up. Watch for anyone taking unusual interest in us and anybody you think is following us. Anybody you see more than once. Don't look at or talk to each other. Or to me."

"Who's following us?" wondered Nipi.

"Maybe somebody. Maybe nobody. Maybe Russian spies. Maybe Spanish cops. Maybe the British Secret Service. Whoever they are, you won't know them. You catch them by watching how they act."

The wind continued very strong and steady. It messed up Nipi's hair, and dust blew into his eyes. He squinted at Nacho and looked sorrowful.

"You can handle it, Nipi. Just stay alert. Do what I tell you."

Then Nacho looked for Beto. The wind was blowing full in his face too. But Beto had a twinkle in his eye. He was enjoying this.

They made a circuitous path down to the marina. Once there, Nacho wandered a large open area that led from the quayside highway to the slips. He stood and looked at a couple of monuments and displays that had been placed there. He next had a stare at Gibraltar five miles across the bay. The Rock looked from Algeciras like a sleeping mastodon—just preparing to wake up and rise. The turbulent waters were agitating the pleasure boats. As Nacho had hoped, the Levanter was keeping most people inside.

Near the top of the hour, Nacho walked over toward the wharf used by the larger boats. What looked like a small red-and-white ferry had just pulled in. She disgorged half a dozen passengers—a small fraction of her true capacity. Nacho went to a shack that adjoined the landing area. The shack also was painted red and white. The wind was rattling its roof, oftentimes with violence.

"Algeciras Bay Cruises. Aboard the luxurious *Kon-Tiki*. Every 90 minutes," said a sandwich board that was held down by a lanyard tied to a big cobblestone.

Nacho bought a ticket. After that, he went to sit in the shade on a bench that was under cover and shielded somewhat from the wind. He

MOSCOW GOLD | 559

was pleased to see that first Beto and then Nipi followed his lead and bought their own tickets.

"Good boys," Nacho said into the wind. "I knew you could figure it out."

Beto went over to the quay and sat dangling his feet over the edge, observing operations on the wind-tossed water. Nipi hung around the shack. He started chatting up the ticket salesgirl, who looked one-third his age.

Now the *Kon-Tiki* was empty. Time to board her new group. The mate stood at the gangplank and waved everyone forward. Everyone consisted of very few people. Nacho surveyed them.

An American college couple, well known to each other, playful and animated—holding hands, bumping each other, and laughing. Both were around twenty and mutually enthralled. They were speaking English, with many Castilian words and phrases thrown in. Their coats and shoes weren't Spanish. You can always tell by the shoes, Nacho knew. Dead giveaway every time.

Then there was a middle-aged Spaniard and his wife, with one who seemed to be their teenage daughter.

Last of all, there were three elderly ladies. Northern European, he thought, by the paleness of their skin, British or Swedish. Quiet, stolid, and reserved, yet not deterred from the day's intended activities.

Beto hurried forward and boarded first. He climbed to the upper deck and staked out a place where he thought there would be the best view. Nacho followed the Americans on. They were conversing excitedly and kept looking and pointing at Gibraltar. Nipi ambled aboard and sat in the stern.

Just as the mate was about to pull in the gangway, a man with glasses and a beard appeared from behind the shack and hurried forward. No one else came after.

❧

560 | DOUGLAS L. FIELD

"Weather's on our side today."

"Perfect. Not much of anybody interested in a harbor cruise in these conditions. I taught Nipi and Beto some street surveillance. They didn't spot anything. Neither did I."

"No bad guys got on the boat," David reported. "Even if we're under surveillance, they figure to pick us back up on the dock. Should be safe to talk here." Not only did the wind make overhearing conversation difficult, but also the captain was going through his regular harbor cruise patter over a loud but scratchy public address system.

"I wondered about the two Americans," Nacho responded. "Nipi talked to them. Students from Madrid. Say they are going over to Gibraltar tomorrow to get married. Guess there's little or no waiting period over there."

"They look happy. Ariel and I could do that," David muttered to himself. "No fuss, no muss."

"Say what?"

"Oh, nothing. Let's get the others. We'll go over the details of our plan of attack."

CHAPTER 86

Pullach: Wednesday, October 16, 1963

General Gehlen shouted for his aide.

"Make a secure message to Staupitz. 'Subject located, Madrid. Headed south. Suspect destination G. Advise status Bulgarian initiative.' Get it out. 'Most Urgent, Eyes Only,' priority."

"Yes, sir. It's on its way."

CHAPTER 87

Moscow: Wednesday, October 16, 1963

"Ah, Pavel Leonidovich."

Colonel Vucetitch regarded the younger man through vodka-blurred eyes. "Join me for a short one?"

It was getting late in Moscow. The colonel was deep into tonight's bottle. Heavy consumption was becoming a nightly practice. He had quit going home nights. He was disheveled most of the time and seedy. Pressure from above, together with naked fear had all but undone Vucetitch. His fate was clear. It remained merely to discover the specifics of the date and manner of its execution. That revelation, he knew, would come in due time.

"Thank you, Colonel, but no."

"Well, be that way. I'll just have another little bit. If some is good, more is better, right?" Vucetitch slurred.

"Colonel, listen to me. The Americans appear to have located the subject," said the underling.

In that instant, Vucetitch's mind cleared. "How? Where? How valid is the information?"

MOSCOW GOLD | 565

"In Madrid. The Americans were looking for him. We have occasional informal contact with the guy they have on it. Hates his boss, I guess. It's confirmed in that they told the BND. We have BND penetrated. The Americans have him headed to Southern Spain. BND thinks he's making for Gibraltar."

"Gibraltar!? Why Gibraltar?"

"No idea, sir, but that's what the Germans think. And it appears they are acting on it."

"All right, we will too." Vucetitch tried to get himself together. "Alert the team. Have Myshnov take over. Cover all points of ingress and egress to Gibraltar. There can't be that many. They are to execute on the subject's way in or out. They are not to risk getting caught by the British intelligence services *in* British territory. Francisco Franco, the leader of the Spanish state is a fascist and an enemy of the Soviet Union. To the extent that it is an annoyance to Franco, the Soviet government supports England's continued possession of the colony. Let us not annoy London over this."

"Understood, sir. I will instruct them forthwith. In your name. Will you advise Vladimir Yefimovich?"

Vucetitch appeared to gaze into a far distance. "Yes, Pasha, yes. For whatever good it will do me—do us. I'll advise him. Get my orders out now."

CHAPTER 88

Madrid: Wednesday, October 16, 1963

Isham had calmed down a little.

Now he could face Chema Jaso and his people. "Nick's caught up with him, Chema," Jack reported. "We're back in business. This is going to have to play all the way out for us to get what we want. I sense we are getting close. The Germans think he's headed for Gibraltar. They're responding. KGB has Pullach penetrated, so they will be responding too. German and Russian intentions are hostile. We need to protect him till he gets us what we want. Then I don't care."

"We'll have to stay in Spain, Jack," Chema had advised. "Foreign Ministry is unwilling to risk any sort of incident with the Brits."

"You got enough horsepower to cover both the frontier and the ferries?"

"More than," Jaso stated.

"We'll be good then. If he leaves Spain for Gibraltar, there's little for him to do but come back into Spain.

Jaso called in his people. "We have to deploy again—this time down south, to La Línea. Somebody thinks he's going to Gibraltar. We'll meet Nick there. Isham has it that both the BND and the KGB are onto the subject's movements and want to do him ultimate harm."

"Same rules of engagement as before?" asked Zapatero.

"Yes, but we don't leave Spain under any circumstances. We won't need to. CIA is aware that the subject needs protection until he gets what they want. Room 11 agrees, except that they want what the subject gets before CIA gets it. Questions?"

There were none.

CHAPTER 89

Gibraltar: Thursday, October 17, 1963

David and the team took the 9:00 ferry from Algeciras to Gibraltar.

Myshnov and the Soviet wet operations group had driven all night from Madrid in a quartet of embassy Mercedes 220s. The N-IV south to Córdoba was two often-narrow lanes. Progress was retarded not only by a multitude of slow and heavy trucks, but also by Despeñaperros and several other narrow and winding mountain passes.

The sun was well up by the time they reached San Roque. There he detailed two cars down to La Línea and the land frontier. The other two he had continue around to Algeciras and the ferry dock. Myshnov stayed with the La Línea group.

The Algeciras group went straight to the ferry dock. They fanned out and started their search. One of the team members noted a ferry headed east about a quarter mile from the shore. He assumed it was the harbor tour boat and thought no more about it. But the harbor tour boats and the Gibraltar ferries looked a lot alike.

∾

Casemates Square and on up into Main Street was teeming with humanity. David noted that "Forever British" had been scrawled in several places on the walls leading to the tunnel that gave onto to the square.

Team Zeta, as David, with a tinge of sarcasm, had taken to calling them, meandered with no apparent coordination around the souvenir and jewelry shops and sidewalk cafés. They let themselves be accosted by the upper rock, meet the Barbary apes and dolphin tour operators. But in the end, they were not buyers.

The ferry was a straight shot from Algeciras leaving from the dock right by where the harbor tour boats also tied up. No tails or surveillance were detected.

They would need fast and nimble transport in Gibraltar, so David had hired two Bultaco Sherpa-S motorcycles from an agency in Algeciras. The bikes rode over on the ferry with Team Zeta.

The ferry landed at Glacis Road. David had them park the Bultacos and lead them on foot through the West Bastion into Gibraltar Town.

"Today's plan is to reconnoiter our objective and assemble equipment and supplies," David said as they meandered through the square. "I have already been to Sheppard's Marine Supply in the Waterport. They have some of what we need for the op and have put me on to where to get the rest."

David sent Nipi and Beto up Main Street. They mingled and threaded their way towards the convent that now was the governor's residence. Nacho and David took the parallel but far more plebian Line Wall Road in the same general direction. Both thoroughfares passed through different sides of John Macintosh Square. David caught a peripheral glimpse of Beto there inspecting the British War Memorial.

570 | DOUGLAS L. FIELD

Not far past the King's Bastion, David walked Nacho to a narrow road that led to the left and to a small but intense and busy street called Secretary's Lane. They found Secretary's Lane to be impacted with vehicular traffic of all sorts.

"Main Street's one-way south from Casemates to Governors' Lane," David said. "Besides, Main Street is so crowded, it's impassable in any direction. Traffic headed northbound to town from the south part of the colony is funneled down Governor's Lane. Then it's forced to make this narrow ninety-degree left turn north onto Secretary's Lane.

"This is perfect," commented David over the din. "Look at all the traffic that runs by here."

It was true. There was a steady, swirling gusher of cars, bobtail trucks, motorcycles, motorbikes, and bicycles all gunning for position and advantage as they worked their way north. It was impossible for anyone on foot to cross the little road. There were no breaks in the flow, and no one was in any mood to stop or extend courtesy.

"I like it," Nacho agreed. "All this *tumulto* will give us good cover."

They looked around. At the intersection of Governor's and Secretary's to the left there was a twenty-yard stretch of Secretary's that ended in a dead end. On the west side of Secretary's, they found a neat, two-story, white stucco office building decorated with simple, blue-painted windowsills and shutters.

"That's it. Look." David nudged Nacho with his elbow. And then, as if contemplating how to cross, he concentrated on the traffic hurtling toward them.

"Right. Somebody could park a vehicle there in that little dead end." Nacho also avoided staring at the building.

Here was their objective. In front stood a neatly lettered sign. At the top was the Gibraltar castle and key coat of arms with the colony's Latin motto, *Montis Insignia Calpe* (Badge of the Rock of Gibraltar). Centered below appeared:

HM
Registry Office
-Marriages-
-Passports-
-Vital Statistics, Births, and Deaths-
-Office of Data Development and Information Processing-

David and Nacho's only route back up to Main Street was a narrow sidewalk along Governor's Lane. So narrow it was that they had to turn their shoulders sideways. Even then, they were brushed back by the wider of the passing vehicles.

"Office of Data Development and Information Processing. Would be Dirección General de Desarrollo de Datos y Procesamiento de Información in Spanish," David opined.

"Not very descriptive, is it? Look. There's Nipi! What's he got?" Nacho walked off toward the little Galician.

"Trying to call attention to yourself, Nipi?" Nacho nodded derisively at a very dark-colored and fat but stubby cigar that Nipi was smoking.

"I got it at La Casa del Habano. Back up the main drag there. They take pesetas. It's Cuban. You can't get them just anywhere. Lots of people have them here. I'm fitting right in."

Nacho looked around for Beto to see if he had participated as well. Beto was draped like an old rag over a nearby park bench. No cigar but looking conspiratorial. The two had made friends.

"Vosotros me estáis poniendo de mala leche," grumped Nacho.

"You guys are pissing him off." David grinned. He liked the two that Nacho had added to the team, and they were getting on well.

"You think that's it? In the Marriage and Passport Office? And the name. It doesn't tell anybody anything," Nacho questioned.

"That's it. No doubt in my mind. One of these days, I'll explain about British understatement. It's an article of faith with them. Besides,

572 | DOUGLAS L. FIELD

considering what it is, you'd expect them to give it a meaningless and, if possible, misleading name."

"If you say so. We need to get inside the office if we can."

"Right," David acknowledged. "I have a possible plan. Come on, Team Zeta. Let's head back to the bikes."

⁓

The Bultacos' "Sherpa" designation implied they could carry a load. They could. They were 200 cc and very loud. They had ample capacity for riding double.

Having reconnoitered the registry office, David and Nacho wanted to have a look around this British overseas territory of Gibraltar. The idea was to familiarize themselves with the roads and terrain, to understand traffic patterns, and maybe even locate a bolt hole or two. Just in case.

David drove with Nipi in back, and Beto took Nacho. They headed south on Queensway and weaved through the truck and automobile traffic inching along that route.

They drive on the right-hand side in Gibraltar. Like Spain and the rest of Europe. How very un-British! David mused.

He drove briskly past the Wellington Front and took the roundabout at Ragged Staff Gates to the east toward Trafalgar Cemetery and the Europa Road. He then led the way to Europa Point and the Trinity Lighthouse.

He pulled up at the point and stopped to have a look at Africa across the strait. Nacho hopped off Beto's bike and came and backhanded Nipi on the shoulder.

"Get off, Nipi. You're riding with Beto," Nacho ordered. Then to David, "I'm not afraid to die, but not today. Not riding with Beto. He's insane."

"¿A sí? Not a good driver?" David suppressed a smile. "I didn't see. Guess my mirror's a little floppy."

"Liar. But yes, dreadful."

MOSCOW GOLD | 573

They then went back to Gibraltar Town, the long way through Dudley Ward Tunnel and past Sandy Bay on the east side. The tunnel, David noted, was long and dark. There were pullouts and clefts in the dripping, slimy limestone.

"With enough of a lead, we might waylay or evade pursuers in there," David shouted back at Nacho as they pulled out of the tunnel and back into the light.

After circling the colony, David and Beto stowed the bikes at a car park near Casemates and the team headed, with no evident coordination, back down Line Wall toward the registry.

⁓

"Mr. Nigel A. C. Punton," announced an understated plaque on the man's desk.

David was looking at a man who was crowding fifty and had a strawberry comb-over and mustache. Small and active blue-gray eyes dotted his sun-blotched face. They added little animation as they regarded David.

Time is short, thought David, *before portliness turns to fat. His complexion is going from ruddy to rubicund. And he's got the telltale spider veins high in his cheeks. Likes his pink gins, I'll bet.*

The man was overdressed for Gibraltar—beige seersucker suit, pale green shirt, and what David imagined to be a school or regimental tie. His coat was draped over the valet stand by his desk. A battered Panama graced a hook behind his desk.

Punton's speech was clipped, affected, and wordy. He more talked, it seemed, to himself than to his guest. He was a man self-absorbed of both demeanor and deportment. David realized they had gotten lucky with Punton. He impressed David as the perfect caricature of the British colonial civil servant. His desk was empty of any ongoing work, papers, or projects. David imagined it stayed that way.

David recalled what Ytuarte had said about British bureaucratic arrogance. Punton gave every evidence of having set up his operation

574 | DOUGLAS L. FIELD

in accordance with accepted norms and of having supreme confidence in it and in the bureaucracy that had birthed it and now sustained it. Punton now sat back, David imagined, and watched it run with no thought for breakdown or breach.

David flashed his *Herald* credentials. "Thank you for taking the time to speak with me, Mr. Punton. It's most kind of you."

"Not at all, not at all," came the preoccupied and not very sincere response. "Always a pleasure to render all possible assistance to our cousins from 'across the pond,' as we like to say. How precisely may I help you?"

"My paper is preparing a series of articles on economic development in Europe and the British Isles, as we are getting toward twenty years after the end of the Second World War. My beat is Spain. Been there for several years now. I'm looking into the situation there. Out of that, I learned that Gibraltar has a budding and burgeoning financial services sector. So, I came on over to have a look for myself."

"Well, quite right you are." Punton allowed himself a little preen. "Gibraltar's always been a commercial center in this part of the world, but we like to think that, from rather humble beginnings, we are on the point of making a plausible contribution—not the least in banking, I might add."

Now that he had Punton talking about himself, David took the opportunity to look around the office. There were no personal effects to lend the man any humanity or to provide insight into his personality. Like his desk, everything was empty of any clutter— all buttoned down. There was no freestanding safe in evidence, and there were no frames hung on the walls. David concluded that Punton had no wall safe. What he did see were two large and fireproof filing cabinets. Both were tidy and secured with heavy metal straps and one large Yale padlock each.

"Is it the brief of the Office of Data Development and Information Processing to look after the financial solvency of the Gibraltarian banks?" David feigned a callow ignorance.

"By no means. That is the purview of my colleague, the Commissioner of Finance and Banking. He has offices over in Government House. You and he have not yet had the pleasure."

"No, indeed. Perhaps I'll go there from here. It's a short walk, I gather."

"Quite. One might say that any walk in Gibraltar is short, eh?" He was amused at his little verbal flourish. "We're a tiny colony here. But to answer your question, the Office of Data Development and Information Processing monitors the physical plant and tangible facilities of the institutions under our jurisdiction."

"You look after the bank buildings and grounds, whether the doors lock tight? Are there places where a thief could hide until after dark and then run amok?"

"It's rather more vault security, proper operation of the time clocks, and avoiding vulnerability to after-hours breach—all that sort of thing."

"Have you a large staff to assist you?" David fanned his ego.

"None at all. It's yours very truly, all on his own, I'm afraid." Punton was warming up now, and he prattled on.

"In addition, this office is charged with verifying the adequate protection of what may be the hard assets holdings of our banks. This includes specie, gems of all kinds, bearer bonds, and gold and silver bullion. The security of those holdings indicates stability and solvency. And as go her financial institutions, so goes Gibraltar. Don't you agree?"

"And you follow the status of the personal holdings of the depositors as well, I imagine." David tried to make his comment innocuous, innocent.

"Well, it's a perceptive and interesting question, but Her Majesty's Government is jealous of Gibraltar's banking secrecy laws. I'm not at liberty to comment in any way on individual deposits or depositors."

Now there's a poorly crafted answer, Nigel, David said to himself, *and a definite yes.* "Oh, of course not. It was silly of me to have asked."

576 | DOUGLAS L. FIELD

David went on for several minutes more with questions designed to flatter the man's self-importance. While he did so, he continued to case the office. It was as bland as its occupant—off-white walls and a brown carpet, green metal desk, and a couple of spartan chairs. Punton did have a large window. It looked over the King's Bastion, across the Bay of Algeciras, and through the brown haze that hung above the water generated by the bay's namesake's many oil refineries.

"It's been most gracious of you, Mr. Punton, to take the time. I'm grateful. If you have access to the old *Herald*, watch for our series. I trust you'll find it to be factual and well done."

"I'll do that. And a good day to you, sir."

David had taken a seat in the little park in front of the Eliot Hotel on Governor's Parade. It wasn't long before Nacho found him and slipped in beside.

"That's the place. Run by a guy named Punton. Classic English clerk. Got his little fiefdom and fancies since, in his brilliance, he's the one that set it up, it's safe and secure. Never gives it a second thought. One medium-sized office. Standard lock on the door. No safes. Just a couple of stout filing cabinets. The information's in them. I'm sure of it. Two big Yales."

"Elementary. People think the bigger the better, but when it comes to picking them, it's the bigger the easier."

By now the others two had filtered in.

"You guys found out what we need?" Nipi asked.

"We cased the registry part," David advised. "The plan should work. They issue marriage licenses and passports in there. Typical administrative office. Pretty quiet. Government workers proceeding at government speed. Long lines of resigned but impatient customers. There's good access around the outside of the building. The lines, meter, master valve, and equipment—all are accessible."

"We go tomorrow," Nacho proclaimed, "right before lunch. Right now, we'll go and have a look at the apes."

❧

Alois fidgeted. The airport terminal was all but empty. Most flights in and out were on the weekend. The original intention had been that his guests would arrive then, fitting in among the press of coming and going. But there had been issues of some kind at Heathrow. It had taken until today to clear them up. So now the arrival would be conspicuous.

A narrow strip of flat ground connected Gibraltar to Spain just north of the Rock. The frontier ran west to east and was just a skosh over three-quarters of a mile in length. When it had been determined that Gibraltar needed an airfield, there had been but one suitable location—that flat ground just south of the frontier. First the colony's horseracing track, the space had been too short for any but the smallest aircraft. Additional length had been added on landfill to the westward extending well into Algeciras Bay.

The runway crossed the main road into Gibraltar from the Spanish mainland. All inbound and outbound vehicular traffic gave right of way, by force of an elaborate crossing gate control installation, to arriving and departing aircraft. Having yielded and once the gates were again raised, traffic tumbled straight across the runway into the swirling restlessness of the colony.

As he waited, Alois thought back to the earlier time when he worked with these particular people. They had seemed capable. He supposed their sickly leader had not survived the war.

Alois searched to the east for a glint off the approaching plane. So far, no plane, just fidgeting. Then he saw it. He moved to the windows and watched it come in. It was bounced around by the winds and made a rough landing.

The plane was full for a midweek flight, but they were distinguishable from the rest of the passengers.

"Agent *Ponasya?*" (Bear?)

"Yes. Alois?"

"Good flight? The landing looked rough."

"Terrible, but we're here."

The ground crew today was very efficient. Baggage was already coming through.

"As you are able to do, grab your bags and equipment. I have a jitney bus outside to take us to the hotel."

It was Ponasya and a dozen others. They looked like the refugees from far eastern Europe that they were. Alois had them taken to the Rock Hotel. The Rock would be their base of operations.

"I well remember Vratska. From Paris. We ran an operation there in '37. An excellent operative Vratska, but he seemed unwell," Alois stated.

"He *was* unwell. He passed in the fall of 1939 just as the Germans were invading Poland. That Paris operation is well remembered in Bulgaria. I was a participant in it, as were Auloy, Boyko, and Petar, the senior operatives on this team."

Alois had noticed that some were older. As their little bus made its way up to the big white hotel on Europa Road, Alois offered a briefing to his hired muscle.

"In the simplest of terms, we will locate and eliminate an American journalist," he said. "I represent parties with interests in several Gibraltar banking institutions. The journalist is here investigating those parties, with the intention of making a journalistic exposé, the details of which would be prejudicial."

He then went on to describe David. Last, he provided the names and locations of the various governmental offices and bank branches that were the object of David's interest.

"The Paris operation in '37," observed Ponasya acerbically, "involved high-value assets that were moving through the French capital. Such assets are, shall I say, very durable. They never disappear. Please do not feel the need to respond, Agent Alois, but my instincts

MOSCOW GOLD | 579

tell me that our presence here in Gibraltar concerns the same, shall I say, materials."

Alois said nothing but leveled a steady look at Ponasya. Alois continued, "Our mission is to find the American and remove him from Gibraltar. Permanently. We have no desire that he should ever return."

"Have you confirmed that he is here in the colony?" asked Ponasya.

"He has not yet been seen here. We know he left Madrid headed this way. He's here. Or soon will be."

Alois divided the group into teams of two and assigned them strategically around the town and at the ports of entry. When the American was spotted, one would tail him, and the other would report in. The troops would be rallied. The assignment would be carried out.

Alois had rented a pair of Vauxhall Crestas to give himself and the Bulgarians ready freedom of movement and so that the subject could be transported as and where needed—when time came. One car they parked on Line Wall near John Macintosh Square, and the other, on Queensway at Ragged Staff Gates.

"Tonight, we will disperse around the shopping, restaurant, and hotel areas in hopes of spotting the subject. Tomorrow morning, you start on stakeout as assigned," Alois ordered.

CHAPTER 90

Gibraltar: Friday, October 18, 1963

Team Zeta met on the sly in Commonwealth Park.

They parked the Sherpas for easy access and a fast break.

"Gibraltar's impregnable in a lot of ways," David said. "But one weakness is fresh water. They don't have enough reliable, clean supplies of it. Water will be our point of attack on the registry building. It used to be brought by donkey cart or by hand. There was a lot of disease. They have desalinization plants and catchments for rain runoff. That's why there are great sheets of concrete on the east slope. They're still nervous. Now Franco has cut their supply from the mainland. They take water protection seriously. We are going to exploit their fears."

Alois had already figured that the Office of Data Development and Information Processing might be a high priority target of the American. He assigned Auloy and Boyko, two of the senior men, to it. Alois hadn't anticipated that there would be a team. They were looking only for David.

The two Bulgarians arrived early. Now they were getting bored. The registry had opened at a leisurely 9:30. After that, there had been a steady flow of ordinary people who appeared to have ordinary business. The American was nowhere in evidence.

Boyko left for takeaway coffees. While he was gone, a somewhat strange man had come into the area and looked all around. The man approached a couple of individuals who were walking in the vicinity and made conversation with them. He gestured overmuch when he talked. It was evident to Auloy that the people he approached had trouble understanding him.

Boyko promptly brought the coffees.

⁊⁊

Nipi and Beto were detailed to reconnoiter the objective. After about half an hour, Nipi came back and reported that the registry office was open and that all appeared normal. Not long after, Beto reappeared, looking concerned.

"What is it, Beto?" Nacho demanded.

There was a lengthy exchange between them. Nacho then translated. "He identified a man hanging around the registry area with no apparent business there."

"Can you identify him if you see him again?" David asked. Beto said he could. "Let's leave it for now. We'll deal with it if we need to when we arrive on scene. All of you scatter around the park here and wait for me. I'll be back at 11:20 on the nose. You won't have any trouble recognizing me." Then David trotted off toward Queensway and the commercial buildings and offices down at the port.

Nacho saw it first. A quintessentially British olive-green Austin A 35 Racevan, no identification markings on the side, right-hand drive, David at the helm. Nacho gestured for the others. David stopped at the side of Queensway, hopped out, and opened the rear door. Beto and Nipi piled in back. Nacho got in the passenger side.

"Where did you get this?" Nacho said as David pulled back into traffic.

"Cowperthwaite's Tools and Equipment, down in the port," he replied as he turned right at Ragged Staff Gates and headed for the water, where he parked.

"There are monos and berets for everyone in the back. Get them on. There are also a couple of tool bags that Beto and Nipi can sling over their shoulders. It's time. Let's go."

After they were suited up, David drove back through the Ragged Staff Gates roundabout, past the Queen's Hotel, and up Boyd Street, where he headed back into town on Town Range. He joined the crush of traffic headed down Convent Place and Governor's Lane. Instead of making the right on Secretary's Lane with everyone else, he drove into the earlier identified little space to the left in front of the registry. Everyone but David jumped out as traffic continued streaming past.

Boyko and Auloy's boredom was interrupted just before lunch. A commercial van drove into the space in front of the registry. Three workers exited it. One of them went around the back of the building. The other two went inside. A fourth worker waited in the vehicle. It was dark in the van. The Bulgarians could not make out much about the one who stayed with it.

"Some kind of a work project?" postulated Auloy, suspicion not yet arising.

"I'd say. Two of them have tool bags. Utilities? Gas or electric? Maybe there's a fault in their service," Boyko continued the thought. They were looking only for a single person.

Occupants started leaving the building, office worker types plus one man in a summer suit and hat. "A gas leak, maybe," continued Boyko. "Looks like they're evacuating the building. This is odd, Auloy."

Beto ran around the registry building to the Line Wall side and shut off the main water valve that served the building. He next undid the coupling that attached the building service to the main.

Nacho and Nipi went inside to the small lobby. Nacho flashed fake credentials. Loud and with authority, he announced, "AquaGib. We have potential contamination in this sector. We need to cut off your service, drain and secure the building."

Nipi went into the public restrooms off the lobby and opened the valves in the fixtures there.

"We will require that you secure your offices and evacuate the building," Nacho continued. His talk was urgent, the entire building aware of the commotion.

Nipi went to Nigel Punton's office, pounded on the door, and opened it. "AquaGib, sir. Evacuation order. Should be just an hour or so."

Punton was already up and in the process of locking his filing cabinets. "I'll just be having an early lunch, then," Nipi heard him mutter to himself.

There was a lavatory near Punton's room. From that vantage point, Nipi observed that Punton had donned his coat and hat and then locked and left his office.

Back in the lobby, Nacho was herding the clerks and secretaries out of the building and assuring them that there was no danger, and that the evacuation was precautionary. It would be short.

"The Englishman's gone," Nipi told Nacho.

"Go and get David," the older man ordered. "Then find Beto. You two watch the entrances."

❧

They saw the driver get out of the Austin and head for the door.

"Shit." Auloy woke up to what was happening. "That's the American! Hard to recognize him in the work clothes, but he's the right age and height. There's no gas leak or whatever over there. It's a

584 | DOUGLAS L. FIELD

ruse. The American's got himself some help, and they're raiding the data information office, whatever it is."

"Gotta be," Boyko said looking at the description he had of David.

"Go and get Alois, Boyko." Auloy pushed him back up Governor's toward Main Street. "Now! I'll stay here and see what happens, where they go."

David came running in, and he and Nacho went to Punton's office. Nacho had his lockpicks out. In a flash, he had them inside the office. Now the Yales. Nacho chose one of his heftier picks. He felt inside the lock. There it was—just like all of them—the sensitive spring mechanism. Careful now. Just the right touch. And *click*, the lock fell right open.

While Nacho did the second lock, David opened the filing cabinet and began to look for want he needed. Everything was well organized and labeled.

Nacho had both locks open now. For the moment, his work was done.

He shouted for Nipi. "Have Beto button the lines back up. You go and close all the valves inside the building. Get the water back on. Then you two watch the area. See if the guy you saw this morning is still hanging around."

David had not found what he needed in the first filing cabinet and was now going through the second. It was all very tidy—file folders all neatly named. No effort had been taken to mislead with the titles. There it was!

"Institutional and Industrial Inventories—By Location." The file was not large. Its pages were laid out in columns under main titles, one for each of the locations in Gibraltar offering vault services. The columns went: Box Number, Contents, Titular Depositor, Depositor Details.

MOSCOW GOLD | 585

"Here it is, Nacho. He has everything—all the boxes, what's in them, whose they are, and notes on who's behind the named title holders."

"Get your pictures. Hurry up. We've been here too long already."

David pulled out a Minox B—a subminiature "spy" camera he'd acquired before leaving Madrid for just this moment. He started photographing the pages. The device was four inches long and under an inch wide. He held his breath and squeezed the shutter. He didn't flinch. He had only this one chance. Methodically, he went through the pages. The film cartridge held fifteen exposures. He had to reload— once. And then again.

After forty-three shots, he had the whole file. He placed the jacket back in the cabinet and secured both locks just as they had been found. Then he closed Punton's door, leaving it locked. Punton would never know.

Nacho was down in the lobby. David rushed up to him. "I'm done. Let's go."

Nacho grabbed his arm and held him back. "No. Wait."

◦◦◦

Beto *was* a good mechanic. He had the registry's water service hooked back up and operational again in moments. He gathered his tools and left. There would be no trace of his having been there. Coming around the building toward the van, he heard Nipi from the shadows inside the lobby alert him to the presence of a man across the street.

"Go over and talk to him, Beto. I'll follow," Nipi ordered.

◦◦◦

Auloy was maneuvering for a better view when he saw the same man from earlier coming around the building, now dressed like the other workers. The man had seen him and was approaching. He walked right into the stream of traffic making the turn onto Secretary's and approached Auloy. He was talking, but Auloy didn't understand him.

586 | DOUGLAS L. FIELD

He was making gestures, and Auloy could hear him, but the words were strange and made no sense.

Then the little guy came over.

❧

Nacho gripped David's arm as they watched first Beto and then Nipi cross the street.

"That'll be the guy Beto saw this morning, David. They may be on to us."

Then they saw Nipi getting close. "Watch this," Nacho said. "Nipi has very fast hands."

❧

Nipi had never grown tall. He didn't bother with theories as to why. It was what it was. He had come to understand, nonetheless, that there were benefits to not being tall. He was, by now, expert at using those benefits to good advantage.

The little Galician watched Beto cross the street. Beto was chatting up the guy as he went like they were old friends. They guy looked confused. Beto did that to people. Beto was gesturing and smiling, sucking up the man's attention and concentration.

Nipi started across after Beto. Nipi pointed straight at the driver of a small truck and stared him to a stop. Beto was close now to their adversary. The man was defensive and retreating a step or two. Nipi covered the intervening distance and shot ahead of Beto. Taking advantage of his speed and small size, Nipi got inside the larger man's reach and delivered a vicious uppercut to the underside of his jaw. His head snapped back, and he crumpled.

Nipi didn't have to say anything. Beto jumped forward, and they dragged the limp form to the side of an adjoining building. They turned and ran back to the van.

❧

MOSCOW GOLD | 587

Nacho and David ran for the van and started it up. Nipi and Beto were barely back in before David had careered into the stream of cars on Secretary's. The little Austin, its four-banger shrieking, was all the way into traffic before they even had the rear door shut. David headed for the Sherpas.

❧

"Get to the cars!" Alois ordered as Boyko came running up. The pair of Vauxhalls were already forcing their way down Governor's and on to Secretary's as David pulled away.

"There's Auloy!" Boyko saw him leaned against the wall.

"Leave him for now," ordered Alois. "We'll come back for him."

"It's the green Racevan." Boyko again.

"Right. We're on it. Aleksandr!" Alois yelled at the driver. "Get closer and don't wreck us."

❧

David forced his way into the stream. He stayed on its left side. Coming to a left turn, he took it one block west to Line Wall Road, where he turned left again and headed south. He had to get back to Queensway. It would be a circuitous route.

"Get out of your monos and back into street clothes," David shouted at the others.

He could have saved his breath. They were already in the process. He weaved his way to the end of Line Wall and turned left up to Main and right through the arch at South Bastion, hooking back onto Ragged Staff and then right on Queensway. Now he was headed north.

❧

Aleksandr and the driver of the second Vauxhall were having trouble keeping up with David. They caught a quick glimpse of olive green going through the arch, but they were not there yet. They lost sight of

588 | DOUGLAS L. FIELD

the van. Coming through, they had a clear view to their left up through the traffic circles headed toward Europa Road. No sign of the van that way. Alois jerked his thumb to the right. Aleksandr turned onto Ragged Staff. Once down to the gate, there still was no sign of the American and his friends.

"Where now?" Aleksandr asked circling the little glorieta.

"That big road. Back up toward town." Alois pointed at Queensway.

⟋⟍⟍

Team Zeta had arrived back at Commonwealth Park. They ditched the van out in the open in an illegal parking spot next to Commonwealth House.

David stripped off his mono and tossed the Minox to Nacho. "You take this. It's me they're after." Nacho caught it and shoved it deep into his pants pocket.

They retrieved the Sherpas and were preparing to mount up and head for the ferry dock when a pair of passenger cars rolled up.

⟋⟍⟍

Queensway had been the right guess for Alois. Just as they were passing a park, they spotted the green van left by the side of a building. Then Todor saw one of the people who had been with the American. He was getting onto a motorcycle. One of two—four men in total.

"There! Alois! The motorcycles!"

⟋⟍⟍

David saw that the occupants of the cars had spotted the green van and were staring at it, gesturing. Then one of them saw David and shouted at the others.

David ripped off fast—south on Queensway. Beto followed close behind. David regretted that he had not hidden the van better. He weaved in and out of traffic. The cars had to turn around to follow.

MOSCOW GOLD | 589

That let David and Beto get well ahead. The Bultacos blew through Ragged Staff Gates and into Rosia Road through Keightley Tunnel and onto Europa Point.

David stopped for a look back. No cars. He took off again toward the east side and flew into Dudley Ward. It was dark and dank, just as he remembered it. They found a service area that had been hewn out of the limestone. They hid themselves and the bikes in it and then settled in to wait.

⁓

The Vauxhalls could, at best, follow in the motorcycles' general direction. They went all the way south through the residential areas on Rosia and out to the lighthouse.

"Go up the east side, Aleksandr," Alois instructed. They came to the tunnel and drove through it—slowly—letting their eyes acclimate to the dark. But they saw nothing. Alois had them continue through.

Alois had the cars come into town the back way. "They can't get out of Gibraltar without coming through the town. Let's get back there and spread out."

⁓

The Zetas saw the Vauxhalls roll slowly past. The occupants were searching the tunnel, but the cars did not stop. After they had gone out of sight toward the north end of the tunnel, the Zetas mounted back up and drove fast south out of the dark.

The challenge for David was to get the Zetas back into Spain unseen and unmolested. Team Zeta had created a good deal of commotion in the past hour. Getting out of Gibraltar unscathed and unnoticed would be dicey at best.

⁓

590 | DOUGLAS L. FIELD

David knew that his coordination would have to be spot-on accurate.

Earlier, the team had figured they would return to Spain the way they'd come, on the Algeciras ferry. After they eluded their attackers, they went back south out of the tunnel to Europa Point and, by as circuitous a route as they could find, back into the center of town. They remained vigilant for their pursuers but saw nothing of them. They had stashed the Bultacos in a small corner alley off Bayside Road.

Nipi volunteered to recce the ferry dock. "Let me go, David. I'm the last one they'll recognize. They have your description, and they know Beto from in front of the registry. The single one of them that's seen me is the guy I hit, and he was paying attention to Beto."

"They don't know me," Nacho said. "I'll do it."

"Nacho, if they catch me, what's the difference? You and David need to get the film to Madrid. Besides I'm faster and nimbler than you." There was more argumentation. In the end, Nipi went.

After about three-quarters of an hour, Nipi rematerialized at the alley.

'They have the ferry staked out. One of their cars is there and about half a dozen men. They're easy to spot. They don't act or dress like us. I couldn't tell if they have weapons. Didn't want to get that close."

"I'm guessing they're from Eastern Europe," David said, "Hungary, Serbia, or Romania—somewhere out there. Those countries have a long history of clandestine activity. Maybe not that much else to do. Not only that, but they are also historically tight with the Germans."

Nacho added, "They're dirt poor there. Communism has demolished those countries. Like David says, they're good at secret operations. Rumor has it they hire themselves out to Western agencies to do dirty work."

"Who hired them to go after us?" Nipi bridled.

"Whoever will be most hurt by the pictures I took in Punton's office. We think it's Germans," answered David. "Let's go. We'll have a look at the land frontier."

MOSCOW GOLD | 591

"Split up and fan out. See what you can find," David ordered. "I'm going to try to figure us a way out of here."

Nacho went back into Casemates Square. He crossed it and exited through the archway in the north corner. He went through the pedestrian tunnel that led back out into Corral Road.

It was Nacho who located the second Vauxhall. He found it lurking in a corner of the last petrol station before the frontier. The driver was alone in the car. That meant the others were nearby, out looking for Team Zeta.

Like everything in Gibraltar, the access road was densely busy at all times of the day and night. Beto had spotted the car too, and he had Nacho in sight. Beto had found a bicycle cabled to a streetlight. The cable was long enough to have let him flip the bike over on its seat. Beto was making like he was working on it. He looked quite natural. He located two others from the Vauxhall. They were not making serious efforts at concealing themselves. Beto concluded that there were others loose in the area as well. If Team Zeta were spotted, they would have some prearranged signal to gather everyone to the car.

Beto saw Nacho reverse and return toward Casemates, so he flipped his adopted bike upright and headed there himself.

"At least we know where they all are," Nipi commented when they were back together. "We're safe enough here in the square while they concentrate on the borders."

"I've been watching the frontier road. I think I have figured a way for us to get out of here. Let's go and get the Sherpas." David went on to explain his plan.

Tension grew as they waited. The Zetas were behind a glass bus stop enclosure on Glacis Road. David felt that concealment was not a high priority, as the opposition was deployed closer to the frontier. The bus stop location, on the other hand, did afford an excellent field of view across the frontier area past the north end of the Rock and toward Spain.

"Patience is a virtue, Nipi." David noted the little man's agitation. "Shouldn't be long. Gotta be something soon."

In truth, David was feeling the pressure himself. Nacho remained calm and cool—to outward appearance at least. Beto was unflappable as always.

Another half hour went by. Uncertainty as to whether the plan would work came over David and the team.

'There!" David elbowed Nacho. He was looking toward the Rock. "Our timing will have to be perfect." He continued to look east.

Then Beto saw it too. He backhanded Nipi on the shoulder and pointed to the sky.

An aircraft, a large one, was on approach to the Gibraltar runway. The whole team had it spotted now, mesmerized, watching it grow.

David continued to wait. Cars, trucks, motorcycles, bikes, and walkers—all continued to flood past on Glacis and onto the frontier access road. The stream had not been stopped—not just yet.

"Wait. Wait. Not yet. Not quite yet. Now!" David kick-started his Sherpa. "Go, go, go!" he yelled at Beto and blasted into the river of traffic.

Beto stuck like glue. They were very conspicuous, but it didn't matter now. The Bulgarians were vigilant. They took immediate notice of the two Sherpas that had eluded them for some hours now.

David was concentrating on the approach of the plane, a gawky Lockheed Constellation, full dirty, wheels and flaps all the way down. In his peripheral vision, he saw men running toward the petrol stop. The Vauxhall was already in motion toward the access road. Slow. People were jumping into it on the roll.

David and Beto were weaving heedlessly between the crush of vehicles headed to Spain and, when necessary, were intruding into oncoming traffic. They screamed past the Vauxhall that was now gaining speed but was not as agile in contending with the other traffic.

MOSCOW GOLD | 593

The aircraft floated in fast. David could hear throttled-back engines. Backfiring. It was still far enough away that the runway crossing was still open. A second or two more. Now the large red-and-white diagonally striped crossing guards were coming down. The signal lights at the crossing had turned red. A loud warning bell had started up.

One or two last vehicles for Spain pressed on through, but now the stream stopped. Then it compacted. The Sherpas were ahead of the Vauxhall. David and Beto kept on squeezing in and out and between the other vehicles. Then the oncoming traffic ended as the gates on the far side began to lower.

David and Beto drove on the wrong side of the road up to the gates on the Gibraltar side that were lowering slower than those opposite. One or two in the Vauxhall had gotten out. They were running forward. The plane was close to its flare-out point.

David's timing had been superb. He and Beto flew through on the wrong side of the road as the gates neared horizontal. The one on his right hit Nipi on the shoulder and tried to knock him off the bike. Beto recovered artfully.

He and David ripped across the runway. The giant aircraft and its whistling slipstream, just inches above their heads, cast Team Zeta for the briefest moment into shadow. They caromed obliquely and rapidly through the far side gates, hearing behind them the bark of the Connie's big tires as they kissed the runway tarmac.

They busted through and pulled into the Spanish border post. Back in Spain. But not yet out of trouble.

594 | DOUGLAS L. FIELD

PART VIII
THE SUNSET CLUB

CHAPTER 91

La Línea de la Concepción: Friday, October 18, 1963

The guards on the Spanish side had not yet been alerted to the Zetas' exploits on Gibraltar.

The Spanish border post at which Team Zeta landed after their flight across the Gibraltar runway consisted of a two-story yellow stucco structure that held *Inmigración y Aduana* (Immigration and Customs) and a single-story, two-lane, covered vehicular breezeway that led from the frontier into the town and the rest of Spain beyond.

David and the Zetas were subjected to only the most cursory border check. The bikes were registered in Spain, so the team showed their documents and were passed right through.

Nick and Chema were lurking at the far end of a wide plaza that was closed off at the other end by the Spanish customs and border post that led to the frontier with Gibraltar behind. They and several additional Spanish operatives had been on station for two days. Good detective work in Algeciras had developed that David was with three companions on two motorcycles in Gibraltar.

"What do we hear from Algeciras?" Nick asked.

MOSCOW GOLD | 597

"*Sin novedad*" (nothing new), Jaso answered. "Like us, they have seen nothing so far. I took the precaution of sending an agent over to Gibraltar to watch the ferry dock—just in case they tried for Tangier. Tangier's the one other destination there is out of Gibraltar. It's a single ferry a day. Nada."

'They're coming out through here. La Línea," declared Nick.

Unperceived, the shadows began to lengthen. The sun inched toward the hills behind Algeciras. Nick, Chema, and Chema's people were restless and bored. It was still hours until closing time.

Then they heard the blare of a pair of light motorcycles in the near distance, charging over from the British side.

"*Alertos todos*" (Everybody awake), commanded Nick. "Each of you pick up your man. If it's them, the others will make their move. You know what to do."

Nick could dimly make out a pair of motorcycles in the dark of the customs shed. Their engines had been shut off.

❦

The control passageway gave out onto a wider plaza. David and Beto kicked the Sherpas to life. Sedate now, they moved forward.

"We're not in the clear yet," David said as they started to move. "At every chance, there will be more attempts to stop us. Our best assets are these bikes. If the bad guys are in cars or on foot, we evade easy. Better hope they don't have bikes too. Let's go. Beto, you did superbly on the runway. Stick close again now. Once we're out of La Línea it'll be safer."

❦

Nick saw the Bultacos move out into the plaza—two of them, riding double and moving slowly. It appeared that the lead driver was vigilant, looking for the correct exit that would take him out of town.

"Looks like our boys, Chema."

❦

As the motorcyclists appeared to settle on their exit road and headed to it, a dark-colored Mercedes moved toward the same exit as if to block the motorcycles' path. Then a second similar car started in motion. As the first car moved on the exit, a synchronized automobile evolution unfolded. The lead car's rear doors opened. Two occupants alighted. The doors were left open. The two on foot moved on the motorcycles. No one got out of the second car. It rolled forward.

David saw the little ballet unfold. "Go for the ones on foot, Beto!" he screamed as he opened his throttle wide. The Sherpa burst forward. Nacho held tight. David headed straight for the lead walker, who tried to run. David kept the bike pointed at him. Beto aimed at the other. They missed their marks by millimeters.

The cars had insufficient time to react. David and Beto blew past the ambush and onto open road running out of town.

"They were going to grab your *compatriota*, Nick," Chema hissed. "But he broke it up. He's the one they want. Not the others. They were going to throw him in the back seat. The second car would block his retreat and then provide cover as they made their getaway. He saw it coming. Brilliant move to use motorbikes—very maneuverable."

"Go! Now!" Chema shouted at his troops. "Let's arrest these assholes. We couldn't do anything with them in Paris. But this time, they're in Spain."

Five plainclothes Spanish operatives sprang into action. All had their credentials out and on full display—one each on the two who'd gotten out of the lead car, one on that car's driver, two on the second car.

"Border police!" shouted Monge. "Everyone out of the vehicles, please."

The occupants were reluctant. Slow to react.

"Move your asses!" Rude shouting by Monge now.

Someone jerked the driver's door open. "Your documents. Out of the car! Quick!"

Passports began to be produced. Chema moved out into the open, the obvious commander of the team. "What have we here, Inspector Monge?"

"What appear to be Russian diplomatic passports, sir."

"We are accredited diplomats of the Soviet Union," snarled the driver of the first car. "We have immunity. You are not permitted to detain us. We are leaving now."

"These vehicles are blocking access to the plaza. That cannot be tolerated. You are going nowhere. The validity of your papers must be verified."

Chema Jaso gathered up the passports. He passed them to Nick, who scanned them.

"My people will move the cars. Follow us across the plaza to the immigration office. We will carry out the necessary checks there." Chema pocketed the passports.

Livid and fuming the Soviet team leader nodded his head toward the yellow building. His recalcitrant troops followed him toward it.

❧

As they drove away from the border post, Beto and Nipi caught up to David and Nacho.

"Who the hell was that?" Nipi yelled over the noise of the bikes.

David did not answer. He accelerated fast through the rest of La Línea to San Roque, flipped a left onto the N-340, and crossed the marginally wet Río de la Miel.

"Honey River! What a name for such a dirty little creek," he shouted back at Nacho. "It wasn't Honey Creek we've been up today."

Nacho laughed. "I have the last piece of the puzzle in my pocket. Now you do the story."

"And get free," David added.

In twenty-five minutes, they were back in Algeciras.

❧

600 | DOUGLAS L. FIELD

Jaso took over a pair of rooms in the border post. He and Nick divided the Russians up. Jaso took their leader. Nick got the troops.

"Interrogate them a little. See what we can find before we have to let them go, yeah," Jaso said as he closed his door.

"So, who have we here?" Jaso said to the leader. Passport says it's Mikhail Myshnov. You're KGB or GRU, Misha. Which is it?

"KGB, and its Major Myshnov."

"Maybe not for long. You got your team caught here today. Moscow Center is not going to like that. What was you mission?"

"You know I'm not going to tell you that. We are all attached to the Soviet embassy in Madrid and have diplomatic immunity. You are required to free us. All we have done is drive around in this little Spanish dump of yours. Might be stupid, but it's no crime. Let us go."

"How is it that you happened to pick La Línea, Major?"

"Normally I wouldn't tell you that either, but my service is interested in sowing distrust between you and the main opposition with whom your service is in bed. We have one of them on our payroll. He drops us a tidbit now and them."

Jaso handed Myshnov the stack of passports. "Get out of La Línea."

"Nick!" Jaso called into the other room. "Let them go. They have immunity. We know who they are. Not much good to their bosses now that we have seen them."

It didn't take Chema long to figure out that Nick was the mole—or to decide what to do about it.

MOSCOW GOLD | 601

CHAPTER 92

Madrid: Monday, October 21, 1963

Nick Barnickle was summoned to the San Bernardo Comisaría.

He was directed to Chema Jaso's office. There were no preliminaries, no pleasantries, and no offer of refreshments. Jaso started out by staring at Nick

"Nice to see you, Chema. What brings me here?" Nick was unsettled.

"We have a score to settle. You are aware that I had a little talk with the KGB major in La Línea," Chema started. "He says someone on our side tipped his people off that your journalist was in Gibraltar and would be coming back into Spain."

"No surprise there. Everybody's got one kind of connection or another." Nick shrugged.

"I think it was you, Nick."

"What if it was? No harm no foul. The kid's safe, and you and Isham are going to get your story."

"Room 11 wants influence with Isham on the details of the publication of the story. Where's the kid?" Chema pressed forward.

MOSCOW GOLD | 603

"Unknown. Probably in Madrid. He won't meet with Isham. Says he'll be in touch when he's got the story done. Isham has me looking for him."

"That's what Room 11 wants too, Nick—for you to look for him. And keep looking for him until the story's done. The kid stays disappeared, and Isham doesn't learn about your extracurricular contacts, Nick. Have a nice day."

CHAPTER 93

Madrid: Wednesday, October 23, 1963

"How did the tradition of tapas get started?" David asked.

"Theories abound. I think nobody knows," Ariel replied.

"Which story is your favorite?"

David was sitting with Ariel in El Schotis Restaurante down from Plaza Mayor on Cava Baja in the old city of twisted and random streets. Cava Baja presents as one of a few lanes in Madrid called *cava* rather than *calle*. The cavas trace the outline of and are filled-in sections of the old moat that, in medieval times, protected the town.

David had picked Ariel up at Gaztambide 67 earlier in the evening. They had barhopped their way down the Gran Vía onto Calle de Preciados, through Sol and into La Latina. It had taken a few stops, a few drinks, and a few tapas for him to tell the whole story of Algeciras, Gibraltar, and La Línea.

It was dark now. Madrid had cooled off some since fall had arrived. It even rained a little. The terrazas had all been stowed till spring. Everyone was jamming inside the bars, cafés, and restaurants.

MOSCOW GOLD | 605

Once seated in the restaurant, Ariel had draped her calf-length and close-tailored coat over her chair. As they chatted, she left on a matching very broad-brimmed and stylized trilby. She had dressed for David in a sleeveless green party dress with a swishy skirt.

"Oh, I'd say the King Alfonso XIII version. He's in Cádiz, so it goes. That wind that they have down there is blowing up a gale." Ariel started the story.

"*El levante*. There was one last week in Algeciras."

"There was, yes," Ariel said. "And Cádiz, I guess, is on a long sandspit, so all kinds of dirt and grit is being kicked up. The king goes into a bar and orders a wine. Barman brings it to him with a slice of salted ham set on a thick paper disc on top of the glass. 'To keep out the sand, Your Highness.' Alfonso drinks it down and orders another '*con la tapa*' (with the cover). People liked to curry favor with the monarch in those days, so everybody started putting 'tapas' on their glasses of wine."

"That *is* a good one. How about the one that, in the eighteenth century, way back in the day, there were so many fruit flies all around Spain that the barkeeps would give you your drink with a round paper cover on so the flies couldn't dive-bomb it. Then they figured out, if they put a few bits of very salty food on the cover, you'd stay thirsty and drink more."

David saw her cock her head to the side and lifted her eyebrows. "Mine is more complementary to the general Spanish character. Not so cynical."

"That's a cute hat. Where'd you get it? The old man's?" David reached across the table, slid his hand across hers, and took hold of her wrist. She was wearing a delicate filigree gold bracelet.

"It's a little too *de moda* for Daddy. A little haberdashery over by Quevedo. I'm glad you like it." Coy. Seductive but understated.

"You look good in hats. You look good anyway. In fact, you're *all* color and motion tonight." She was wearing the Segovia necklace, he saw. "You doing that on purpose?"

606 | DOUGLAS L. FIELD

"Who me? Never. I'm just a retiring little thing that was taught by the nuns. Incite a man's passions? Now, David!" Ariel put her other hand up to the neckline of her dress and looked at David—openly and boldly.

"You're blocking my view, Your Coyness," David's said, favoring her with his best lupine expression.

El Schotis was a steak place, but they didn't cook your steak. They cooked your plate. The raw meat was delivered to your table on a heat-stained ceramic plate that had been fired in the oven—one that was often still glowing red-hot. You couldn't eat right away. There was a minute or two to wait while your dinner sizzled and steamed before your very nose and eyes.

Ariel didn't take down her hand, not just yet. "I believe I'll have the *solomillo*," she continued, blasé.

"Me too. I need sustenance. I'm breathing heavy. My energy is being sapped."

"I can't, for a moment, imagine why." A corner of Ariel's mouth turned up as she changed the subject. "So, Nacho says someone was on to you?"

"On the Gibraltar side. That's for sure. We were vigilant. We spotted them. They were aggressive and chased us, but we got away— by the skin of our teeth. An airplane tried to land on my head!"

"Whose idea was that? Nacho's? To rush the runway. He's still crazy all these years after the war." Ariel shook her head.

"Nacho's idea? No. He was on board though," David admitted.

"So, it was *your* idea. You two should never be trusted in public without adult supervision."

"It worked out. Nacho sneaked the Minox into Spain no sweat. Now the film has been developed. All is good, which is a surprise. I was afraid some of them would be shaky. The negatives and prints are with Emejota now. They're safe."

"And the British are none the wiser?" Ariel ventured.

MOSCOW GOLD | 607

"Not so far as we know," David confirmed. "That'll all change when the story comes out. All the research and background are done, except for you and Emejota following up some of the entities we turned up at the registry."

"Your antagonists from the Gibraltar side you haven't identified?"

"No."

"They could still be following you?"

Dinner came—with simmering flourish. Both plates were still rubrous, just as advertised. David and Ariel watched their steaks cook. He started eating first.

"Like mine rare. American style," David said a little sheepish. "But could they still be following me? Sure. We got away from Gibraltar clean."

"What happened on the Spanish side?"

"People in cars and on foot tried to stop us. I saw it coming. Beto and I drove right at them. They scattered. We got away."

"Who?" Ariel asked.

David cocked his head. "You know the old saw, 'Follow the money.' The parties interested in the gold are the Spanish who lost it; the Russians who stole it and fenced it; the Germans who bought it and, we now think, still own it; and the British. We've verified it's still in English custody."

"No offense, David. But what about the Americans?"

"I've thought of my beloved countrymen. But why? What interest does the US government have in the Spanish gold and its story? So far, I haven't been able to imagine the connection."

"If the British knew you were there and what you were up to, they would have stopped you, no?" Ariel reasoned.

"There was no such effort. They were clueless. Besides, they could have acted openly on their own territory. They wouldn't have needed to skulk around. It's not the Brits."

608 | DOUGLAS L. FIELD

"What about Spanish agencies? They arrested and leaned on me," Ariel noted.

"None of that makes sense," said David. "I've checked in with Onésimo. He hasn't heard from Calvín. That means Calvín has no indication that Room 11 is on to me, aware that I'm back in Spain—at least not as of last month when Calvín 'arrested' me. But they could know by now and Calvín just hasn't found out about it. Whatever Room 11 is, they must be involved at some level, but why would they attack us?"

"So that leaves the Soviets and the Germans," Ariel decided.

"Right. I've done some checking, Ariel. The Russians do their own dirty work. They have a huge intelligence apparatus. They're paranoid. Don't trust anybody else. On the other hand, the Germans earlier and now the West Germans, what with their history, like to use surrogates."

"These are dangerous people, David."

"My best guess is that the people in Gibraltar were a team working for the West Germans—West Germans who don't want their interest in the gold to be revealed to the world. Then it was Soviets in La Línea who tried to stop us and whom we evaded."

"David, why wasn't it the Russians who tried to waylay you in Gibraltar?"

"The enemy of my enemy is my friend. Franco and the Soviets are enemies. Franco and the British are quarreling. Moscow doesn't want to annoy London while they're giving Madrid a bad time." David shrugged. It was as good a theory as any.

"And the Germans have no such scruples, since they get others to do their dirty work. Then they have no fingerprints on anything." Ariel brought the conversation full circle.

"Right. There's one remaining and burning issue."

Ariel required no time to think. "How the Russians and Germans knew about you but the British not know about you or the Germans and their pals?"

MOSCOW GOLD | 609

"Smart girl! Haven't worked all that out yet."

"There's no guarantee that you're out of danger, David, none at all," Ariel proclaimed.

"No, Ariel. I'm still in danger. Until the story is done. I'm avoiding Isham till then. I don't trust him. Even finishing the story won't make us safe. I'm developing a backup plan—one that preserves the leverage we need to get out of this mess."

They went back to enjoying their evening out. After they had eaten, David ordered a couple of *cafés solos*. They soon came. While Ariel was busy with her coffee, David appropriated the opportunity to take in the view.

She's good at her attire, David commented to himself. *Understated sexy. How does she manage that? Not obvious, just suggestive.*

She caught him looking.

"Thanks," he said, now his look arrant. "I enjoyed that. You're a good dresser. Beautiful package. One I'd like to unwrap."

"You're frisky tonight."

"Are you objecting?"

"I am. My virginal integrity is at stake."

"OK. I'll stop."

"No particular hurry." Ariel was enjoying being admired. David was enjoying admiring her.

"You're still worried about my safety." David went back to their earlier discussion.

"More than worried."

"I'm happy that you worry about me."

"My worry makes you happy? Is that nice?"

"Well, if you are worried, maybe it means that you like me just a little." David fished.

"I do like you."

610 | DOUGLAS L. FIELD

"Just a little?"

"More. Way more." Ariel gave him the big smile.

◦◦◦

After David paid and back out on Cava, they walked along *côte á côte*, as they say in Paris, she off and on putting her hand in his coat pocket. They wandered through very narrow and twisting streets and hooked back up toward and across the Calle de Segovia.

"I missed you while we were in Gibraltar." David started off on a different track.

"Did you?"

"I wished you were there with me, Ariel. Have you ever been to Gibraltar?"

"No, never. Not that common of a destination for us Spaniards."

"If you had the chance, would you go?" he asked.

"Maybe. If I didn't have to crash the airport runway." A soft smile at David.

"I found out something unusual about Gibraltar that I didn't know."

"Mmm." Ariel wondered where all this was going.

"You can get married there with just a one-day waiting period. No banns. No priests. No fuss. People from all over Europe do it."

'They do?"

By now, they were in the small streets that lead to Calle de Bailén and Plaza de Oriente. David looked up at a street sign, high on one of the corners.

"Look, Ariel! This is the Calle del Cordón" (Street of the Knotted Rope). David stopped and faced Ariel. He threaded his hands and his arms inside her coat, around her waist; pulled her close; and looked at her steadily.

"Will you marry me, Ariel? I don't have money or possessions to offer you, but I will always love you and care for you with all of my power and might."

MOSCOW GOLD | 611

Ariel didn't breathe before answering. "Yes, David, yes I will. And I love you and I will always love you. With everything I have."

Then, there on Calle del Cordón, on the mildest of October nights, they embraced and kissed for a long time, touching each other's faces.

When, well into the early hours of Thursday, they moved on, Ariel said, "Are we formally engaged?"

"Formally and irretrievably."

"David, did we become engaged on the twenty-third or the twenty-fourth?"

"I'm not sure. Somehow I didn't look at my watch."

"How will we know which day to celebrate?" she wondered.

"Well, we never will. Have to celebrate them both, I imagine."

"Was it just an accident that we wound up on the Calle del Cordón?" Ariel raised an eyebrow.

"No. I nudged us toward it. I've known about it since I was a kid running around here."

"What a memory you have created, David. I will guard it in my heart always. It's a very beautiful gift."

Once back at Gaztambide and before she went in, David suggested, and Ariel agreed that they would meet for lunch the next day out at Lago.

CHAPTER 94

Madrid: Thursday, October 24, 1963

David took the Metro.

They had settled on 1:00. He was early. He chose a table at the Bar Vista del Lago. It had a good view of the access road and the path that came down from the Metro station. He would have the intense pleasure of watching her walk up.

"What's on tap, joven?"

"Mahou, of course."

"Bring me una caña, sí?"

Ariel floated into Doña Sagra's large, white-tiled kitchen for breakfast. She was determined to keep her secret for herself. For just a little while anyway. She thought she could just act normal. Do what she always did. No one would know.

"Coffee's almost ready, mija," Sagrario advised. "Would you like a little marmalade with your roll?"

"I would. I'll get some for both of us."

MOSCOW GOLD | 613

"No, no. You sit." Sagra pointed to Ariel's usual place at the table that dominated the center of the big room. "Going to Carabanchel this morning?"

"'No. I'm going to ask for the day off."

Sagra let a faint slyness color her countenance. "Are you? Not much notice for poor Don Jaime. Going shopping? Lunch with school chums?" She continued to act the ingénue, her expression soft, her eyes finding Ariel's.

Ariel began to wonder. *What does she know? How can she know? It happened last night. She was in bed when I got home.*

"Oh, no, Doña Sagra, nothing like that."

"No? It's just that you seem content this morning. I just imagined you might have an appointment with some couturier downtown." Sagrario kept probing.

Ariel couldn't help herself. She started grinning. "No, no dressmakers, no girlfriends."

"Well, you look beautiful this morning. Forgive me, but I thought it must be something." Doña Sagrario was laughing now.

Ariel gave up the charade. "Oh, it is, Sagra. It is! More than just 'something.' David asked me to marry him. I'm just hugging myself."

"I *knew* it, my girl. I could see it. You're radiant. Let me hug you too, child." Sagra did so with strong and ample arms. "Your young American will make us an excellent addition to our informal family here. And even more, you will to his!"

"How did you know, Sagra?"

"If you could see your own face, Ariel. Its beatific."

Breakfast somehow did not come together. Ariel shared the details of last evening.

"That young man has the touch, Ariel. You are beyond fortunate. You have left out one important answer though."

Ariel looked confused. "I have?"

"Did you accept?"

Her eyes glistened. All she did was nod.

614 | DOUGLAS L. FIELD

"Where are you meeting him?"

"Lago."

❧

Ariel's street was a one-way street that shot straight down from Cea Bermúdez to Alberto Aguilera. The portal of number 67 was set close to the sidewalk. The steps from the lobby were steep. Ariel greeted Don Hilario as she all but skipped though the lobby. Ariel had to concentrate on the steps going down. This put her already out on the sidewalk before she was able to take in the situation ahead of her.

Ariel had on a light blue silk blouse, straight khaki skirt, and brown tassel loafers—all pressed and polished to perfection. She knew she looked good. Ariel's usual pattern was to cross the street and go toward downtown on the side opposite from her building. This avoided walking past the cervecería located on the corner and all the inevitable piropos.

Today, in her exuberant state, she found herself in the mood for one or two unsolicited compliments from the beer drinkers. She didn't cross.

As she started off, Ariel pulled her dark sunglasses down from her forehead. Some sort of work was occurring on the sidewalk near the corner. Several tiles had been removed from it. She saw she would have to weave her way through. Her attention was fixed on conditions at her feet as she got to the corner.

She vaguely noticed the open rear door of a large SEAT taxi as she came abreast of it. Out of the shadow of the cervecería, two men materialized, one behind her and the other to her right.

'Taxi, lady?" said the one to her right in accented Spanish. She turned her head toward the sound. Then she felt herself grabbed behind and thrown through the open door and into the backseat. Her other attacker stood back, intending to block the view of any watching bystanders.

MOSCOW GOLD | 615

There was a third man inside the car who seized Ariel. A calloused and grimy hand clapped over her mouth. The original assailant followed her into the car. The man still in the street slammed the door. The cab sped away fast from the curb, headed toward Aguilera.

Ariel struggled inside the cab. She was viciously restrained. Terrible fear rose in her throat. The abduction had taken mere seconds. She knew there was little hope that it had been observed by anyone in the vicinity.

∾

One o'clock came and went out at Lago. The day was one of Spanish perfection. Deep blue skies backed huge pure white clouds behind the Madrid skyline. The sun was bright, yet the temperature was mild, ideal for meeting your novia on the morning after making your engagement.

David had just ordered his third caña. His concentration was shifting from the beauty of the lake and the city behind to the Metro exit and access road and back.

It was not like Ariel to be late. She never was. She never would be on a day like today. She would never spoil the *ilusión* of this day of days.

As David watched a gentle breeze ruffle the lake, a tincture of disquiet riffled his own surface calm. He sensed the first whispers of anxiety.

Ariel, where are you? He looked again up toward the Metro.

∾

By the time Ariel was an hour late, David had become frantic. Following his first impulse, he went to Gaztambide. The portero confirmed that Ariel had left the building. He could not be exact. But, yes, it would have been in plenty of time to make it to Lago by 1:00. After David explained Ariel's failure to show up at the lake, Hilario agreed to escort him up to Doña Sagrario's flat.

Sagrario was appalled, but she kept her emotions under control. She did her best to help David. Sagra confirmed that Ariel had left on her way to see David. She was taking the day off. Lago had been mentioned as the place of their meeting. She had helped Ariel get ready. She was able to describe in detail how the younger woman had been dressed.

David used Sagra's phone to call Nacho. He confirmed that Ariel had spoken to Jaime earlier in the day and asked to be excused from work. David asked Nacho to reassemble Team Zeta and meet him at Gaztambide.

"It's the same bastards from Commonwealth Park, Nacho."

"Right. The La Línea mob would kill you in an instant and dump you in Algeciras Bay. But they would never risk a lower-level crime like kidnapping—not here in the capital, not in broad daylight."

"Muster the troops, Nacho. I'm going to go downstairs to see what I can find out. We need to find her—before they get her well-hidden."

"On my way."

Before David left the flat, he made one more call, this one to Calvín.

"Surprised to hear from you by phone, Paladín," he remarked obliquely. "I saw Onésimo yesterday. There was nothing from you."

"In Plaza Santa Ana you mentioned the involvement of a girl. Remember?"

"I do remember."

"Her name is Ariel. She's been kidnapped, Buitre."

"When? Where?"

"Around midday," David gave the information he had. "Don't know where they grabbed her from yet. Must have been near her flat in Vallehermoso. I'm there now. Her landlady and the portero confirm she went out about that time. She was on the way to meet me. She never showed."

"You tell the cops?"

"Not yet. Wanted to talk to you first."

MOSCOW GOLD | 617

"Good call," agreed Calvín. "They're not going to be that interested this soon. And you'd have to say whom you suspect and why. I'm pretty sure you're not wanting to divulge all those details."

"I figured to leave the cops until tonight. My team from Gibraltar is on the way."

"Paladín, a kidnapping in our ordered and law-abiding dictatorship is super rare. The franquistas have informants everywhere. Little escapes their notice. If this lady's been taken, they have to hold her somewhere while they run the ransom piece of it."

"I assume it's me they'll approach, but nothing yet," David said.

"Right. And I doubt they'll move her too far away until they start on that. They know you will demand proof of life, David. What are they going to want?"

"The research I've done on the gold—at least that. Me for her. None of us has money, so I doubt that's any part of it."

Calvín said nothing for a long moment. Then, "I don't have much for you, Paladín. Just this. A lot of people these days say that our Spanish dictatorship has gone soft. Maybe, but everything that goes on in Spain is still known and reported."

"Then it should be easy to find her."

"*Quizás*," Calvín cautioned. "The exception to, what I call, our 'information management,' is the brothels. The creeps that run them have the authorities bought off. Franco tolerates it tacitly. They act as a sort of pressure relief valve, I guess. The government sees them without seeing them. They are free to do what they do unmolested. Unless it's egregious, what goes on in the cathouses is left alone. Great place to conceal an abducted lady. If you ask me anyway."

"The brothels! Holy shit, Buitre."

"The good thing is that we do know who and where these, ah, 'institutions' are. It's a limited number in any Spanish city. Madrid's no exception."

Calvín then gave David five names and addresses.

❧

618 | DOUGLAS L. FIELD

While he waited on the others, David did a little investigation on Gaztambide. No one at the schools across the street had been aware of anything. Likewise, the other porteros in the vicinity came up empty. A barbershop kitty-corner from Ariel's building had large storefront windows with a good view of the intersection. But there was no success there either.

He went into the cervecería. Neither the barman nor the waiter was any help. He asked the patrons at the bar. This he did rather loudly. No one knew Ariel. No one had seen a woman of her description that day. No blue blouse. No large sunglasses. No pretty girls that day. Not even any piropos. But they were facing the bar, not the street.

David headed down the street. There was a little *libería* next door to the bar. David went in and approached the proprietor, a wizened little man of about seventy. David described Ariel and said he was looking for her.

"Young man," he replied, "I am a resident of this barrio for many years—this very street. I'm well familiar with it and the people who live here. I know this young woman. I know her by sight. She lives a little farther up the street. I have never met her. I would like to. She appears to be a lovely person."

"Her name is Ariel. Did you see her today?"

"Yes, not long before siesta."

David felt huge relief. "When, Señor? She may be in danger."

"I had left my shop for a medical appointment, after which I stopped for a bit of refreshment at the cervecería next door."

"Yes, yes, of course, but as to the matter of my friend?" David endeavored to maintain patience.

"I have a fine memory, you know. I also have keen powers of observation. That is why I stayed at the cervecería longer this afternoon than I had intended. I wanted to reflect on my earlier observations, you see."

"And those observations were?" Davis encouraged him.

"Your friend, well, in all candor *joven*, she's more than a friend, no?"

MOSCOW GOLD | 619

"Yes, she's my fiancée. She was here in this vicinity this afternoon?"

"I knew there was more to it than friendship. My ability to see what others do not, you know." He touched his upper cheek just under the eye with his index finger. "But as to your immediate concern, Señorita Ariel, may I call her that?"

"Of course. Do go on." The waiting was becoming excruciating for David.

"Well then, this is how it went. Señorita Ariel came down, on this side of the street. From the area of her building. She was neatly, but plainly dressed—light blue shirt with no sleeves and a tan-colored skirt. She had on her sunglasses. She's fond of sunglasses you know."

"Yes, I do know that."

"She was walking with purpose. It was as if she had somewhere to go. To meet you, I imagine." He gave a conspiratorial look. "I was in the cervecería. Sitting at one of those tall tables that they have by the windows. I could see the entire corner of the street."

The little man proceeded to describe Ariel's abduction in detail. When finished he added, "Señorita Ariel may have been kidnapped."

"That's my great fear, "said David. "Can you identify who did this?"

"Not Spaniards. I could tell by their shoes and socks. And the cut of their trousers. They wore the cuffs of their trousers higher than we do here in Spain, and both had poor shoes and holes in their socks. Spain may be a poor country, but we have sufficient for decent shoes and socks."

The little man paused for effect.

"They are from communist east Europe somewhere. But Slavic. Yugoslavia or Bulgaria. Not Romania or Hungary. Not Russians, I think."

"Why not Russians?" David asked.

"In Slavic languages, including Russian, the word yes is 'da.' They said that. I heard it. But Russian for no is 'nyet.' They did not ever say that. What they did say was similar but different, along the order of

620 | DOUGLAS L. FIELD

'ne.' I observed, as well, that when they would say what I thought meant yes, they would shake their heads and when they said no, they would nod. Just the opposite from us and everybody else in the world. It may seem an odd fact for me to have in my brain, but I believe there is one single place in the world where that is done—Bulgaria."

"I'm grateful to you. I have some friends on their way. We are going to do all that we can to find Ariel."

"One more thing, if I may. It will not surprise you that, along with my other faculties, I have a photographic memory. Do you have a paper?"

David pulled out a small notebook and the little Spaniard wrote, "M350061."

"M350061?" David was perplexed.

"*La matriculación*—perhaps it will be of assistance."

It was the taxi's license plate number.

Nacho and the boys met David at Ariel's building. He filled them in on his investigation so far.

"Bulgarians?!" Nacho was muttering to himself, full of questions. "I had an experience with a group of Bulgarians in Paris during the war. That bastard Alois. You think it was Bulgarians who chased us out of Gibraltar? No time for that now. Let's get our plan together."

David spoke up. "My analysis is that the two best bits of information we have are the list of brothels and the car license. There are five locations. I'm saying we each take one, fan out, and check them. It'll be no surprise for a few men to be hanging around some whorehouses. Chat up the girls. Buy them a drink. See if there's anything unusual, any foreigners around. Then, too, look around the area. Maybe we'll pick up the cab."

The five names were Orange Blossom Ranch, Cíbola, La Torre Tolteca, Ariadne, and the Sunset Club. David assigned the first four. "We'll leave the Sunset Club for last. Most of these addresses are near

MOSCOW GOLD | 621

La Castellana. Meet at Café Colunga on the Plaza de Colón in three hours."

⁓

At Café Colunga, there was no progress. Nothing out of the ordinary. No foreigners. No taxi. "Just business as usual, you could say," Nipi said salaciously. Nacho and David ignored him. Without success Beto tried to cover up a laugh.

"OK. Our last best possibility is the Sunset Club. It's at General Yagüe 9. General Yagüe runs into Generalísimo near Santiago Bernabéu Stadium. Here comes a streetcar. Let's go."

⁓

General Yagüe was a broad and leafy street in the newer residential areas north of the center. It was lined with modern high-rise flats and corresponding high-end businesses at the street level. Number 9 was but a block and a half from Generalísimo. You climbed about a dozen steps to the main portal, but the Sunset Club wasn't there. The Sunset Club was at the street level. You entered through a windowless, dark red painted door to the left of the steps to the portal. The place was identified with a small brass plaque announcing its name. It was all very understated.

"We three will go in separately. Beto, you scout the area for the cab. Then come in and find us," David ordered.

Beto jogged off.

David entered the Sunset Club first. Once inside there was a lobby area. The lobby was a balcony with a modernistic chrome rail that overlooked a large discothèque on the floor below. To the right was a wide curving staircase that led, together with a blue backlit balustrade, down to the dance floor and tables below.

The disco below was very plush, white leather chairs at thick round glass tables that themselves were also lit from below with soft blue lights. In front of the tables was a polished hardwood dance floor that was well patronized, the music all current and popular, selected by a disc jockey. Behind the tables was another observation area. The patrons there stood, either along an elbow-high glass shelf that ran the length of the area, or at tall tables that had no chairs.

David went down the stairs and to the observation area in the back.

He ordered a gin and tonic. As he watched, first Nipi and then Nacho filtered in. Nipi took a seat in the front row by the dance floor. Nacho found an empty table in a back corner. David concluded that the three had the location well covered. There were numerous couples, along with knots of single men. At first it seemed like all the girls were accompanied. He noticed as he observed that several couples both came and went by way of the staircase.

David was confused. The place looked like a normal but elegant and expensive disco bar. There didn't seem to be any pairing up. Couples were coming in from outside already together. As he watched, though, the situation became clearer. His eyes adjusted to the low light. He now saw a heavily curtained doorway at the end of the area where he was standing. Not long after, a young woman approached Nipi and spoke with him. He signaled the waiter, and the girl sat next to him. In quick succession, a couple came out from the curtained area. Soon after, another went in. David could not see what was behind the curtain.

Now he had it. The whole disco was an elaborate cover for the Sunset Club's elicit activities—a legitimate business fronting, with evident popular support, for the darker side.

Now Nacho was talking to another man—well dressed in a coat and tie. David's immediate impression was that the guy was the club's bouncer. It was just like Nacho to probe the opposition.

"You bring your girlfriend tonight?" A young woman slipped up next to David. She was tall and willowy. Jet-black hair and evening makeup. She wasn't pretty but interesting looking and had a good figure.

MOSCOW GOLD | 623

"No," David said. "She's a little under the weather this evening."

"Buy me a drink?"

"You bet. I'm having gin and tonic. You like that?"

"Prefer rum and coke." It was she who summoned the waiter, and he came right over.

"A rum and coke for the lady. Another of these for me," David ordered.

"I'm Miranda," she cooed as the waiter hurried off.

"Diego."

"You don't look like a Diego somehow."

"I'm not. You don't look like a 'Miranda.'"

"I'm not either."

They had a little giggle over that. Then the fresh drinks came.

David indicated he would pay on the spot. *"¿Cuánto es?"*

"A hundred fifty."

David pulled out a thousand-peseta note. The waiter gave him his change in a little white dish.

"Drinks are reasonable here."

Miranda looked at the ceiling. "Well, I guess it's obvious, the bar trade is not our main source of revenue."

"Not so obvious," David said. "The disco's a pretty good cover."

David's change was in paper money. There was a blue five-hundred-peseta note included. He separated it from the rest with his finger and slid it toward Miranda. "In the mood to answer a couple of innocent questions?"

The five hundred pesetas disappeared.

"Tú dirás,", Miranda said.

"How long you been working here?"

"Around five months."

"Gotten familiar with the routines?"

"I'd say so, yes."

"What's business like tonight? Same as usual?"

"Strange you would ask that," Miranda commented. "Not like usual."

"How not?" David asked.

"Not sure. Some foreigners. Maybe half a dozen. In the back where the rooms are. You know the ones I mean?"

"What kind of foreigners, Miranda?"

"Not sure. Odd ones. Not your typical Italians or Germans or Americans. Different looking. Darker skin. Mustaches some of them. Speak some strange language."

"How many rooms?"

"A couple. Makes it tougher for us girls, y'know. Slows production."

"Sure, I do."

"The other strange thing, Diego, or whoever you are. They brought their own girl."

David's stomach lurched. He tried to keep his composure. "How long are they here for?"

"All night. Or so we hear."

David put his arm around her waist and kissed her cheek. "Thanks, Miranda. You take care of yourself."

He looked over at where Nacho had been. The bouncer was gone, but Beto was there. David went over to them.

"Look at what Betito's got here, David," Nacho said dryly. Under the table at Beto's feet were two pieces of white metal with black raised letters and numbers, M350061.

"You found the cab. Genius. Where?"

Nacho responded for Beto. "He says it's just half a block down Yagüe. Very close. Positioned for a quick departure if needed."

David looked at Beto, "Did you do anything other than grab the plates?"

Beto straightened out his fingers and then squeezed them slowly down on his thumb.

"You flattened a tire. Good work!"

Beto shook his head and held up all the fingers of his other hand.

MOSCOW GOLD | 625

"You flattened *all* the tires?"

Beto shrugged his shoulders.

"Like I said, genius! Go and get Nipi, would you? He's chatting up that hooker in the front row there."

Nipi and Beto came back to Nacho's table, and Team Zeta debriefed each other.

"She's here," David said.

"Yeah, she is," replied Nacho, "But how are we going to dig her out without getting her hurt or worse? Bastards."

David made his decision.

"Beto, go through that curtain over there and find the back door to this place. Don't let anybody out."

David marched over to a fire alarm that was located near the bar. He punched it hard with his fist. Glass flew everywhere and chaos erupted. Strobe lights throughout the entirety of the Sunset Club's space began to flash. The fire alarm horn started its piercing two-pitch whoop.

The effect was unnerving. Bewildered patrons began exiting the premises.

David ran behind the bar and began rummaging for what he knew had to be there. Mere seconds and he had it—the bouncer's billy club.

"Come on. Let's go and find her," he said to Nacho and Nipi. He ran ahead of them into the curtained area.

It was a long hallway with room doors on either side. The upheaval was tremendous. Men and women in the hallway tumbled into their clothes. The hookers were resigned, the men mortified. A mass of people moved through the heavy curtain and into the discothèque.

"Break into the rooms. She has to be here," David shouted.

Agents Alois and Ponasya had Ariel in Room 15, on a bed, tied hand and foot. The lights in the room were flashing and the warning horns howling. Ariel got off the bed. She hopped toward the door. Amid all the rest of the uproar, she started screeching at them to let her out. The rest of the Bulgarians had been detailed to positions around the Sunset Club as security.

Alois took charge. "It's a fire. Stay calm. We'll find the back way out."

"We'll have to cut her loose," Alois shouted. "Hold her close. Act natural like you are out together but hold her close. We will get outside as fast as possible and head for the cab."

Alois reached for the door, which was violently kicked in before he could touch the handle.

David followed the flying dust, wood, and metal into the room. He was screaming profanities and had his club raised high in his right hand, which was bleeding from hitting the fire alarm. The effect was unnerving.

Ariel still was yelling. Ponasya was holding Ariel with one arm and showing her what looked like a stiletto. "You *will* behave, lady, or I *will* cut your pretty face."

"Drop the knife, asshole," David shrieked and swung his club with all his strength at Ponasya's head. It was a tremendous shot that caught Ponasya full force on the right temple and raked him down the cheek. The man staggered back but did not drop the knife. David swung again, this time with both arms—backhand across his body. He connected with Ponasya's neck and jaw. David recoiled and raised the club high above his head and brought it down with a loud grunt on top of Ponasya's head. Ponasya went down for good. The knife clattered away.

David turned his attention to Alois just as Nacho tore into the room.

"Get her out," Nacho commanded. "This one's mine. Leave me the stick."

MOSCOW GOLD | 627

David tossed it to him. He used the stiletto to cut her loose and shouted "¡*Córrete*, Ariel!" David grabbed her hand. He pulled her out of the room and ran for the back door. Beto let them out. David headed them for La Castellana.

⁓

Nacho squared off with Alois. "I wondered if it was you, Alois. Bulgarians involved. That's what tipped me."

Alois looked puzzled as he maneuvered for better position. "How do you know this name?"

"Have you forgotten? Ah, but it's me. Agent Aníbal. Paris in 1937. You betrayed me. To these stinking Bulgarians. Then to the Soviets."

The dawn of remembrance broke on Alois's face. He lunged at Nacho, but Nacho was too quick. He hit Alois on the nose, and blood flew. Alois grappled and tried to take the club from Nacho. But as they wrestled for it, Nacho kneed Alois in the groin. Alois grabbed for Nacho's neck, but Nacho pummeled the side of Alois's face with the butt of the stick. Alois fell back.

"I've longed for this day for a quarter of a century, Alois," Nacho said calmly. And then he proceeded to use David's club to leave Alois with several permanent remembrances of their latest meeting.

CHAPTER 95

Madrid: Friday, October 25, 1963

By the time David and Ariel fetched up onto Generalísimo, the calendar had turned to a new day.

They turned right off Yagüe and headed down toward La Castellana and the center of town. It was a perfect late Indian summer night in Madrid. After several blocks, they pulled up out of breath and panting.

They were in front of Nuevos Ministerios. David backed them into the shadows. He reconnoitered the street back up toward Yagüe. Nothing. He also watched for any stopping cabs or vehicles, but traffic was hastening south with no interruptions discernable.

The huge Nuevos Ministerios government office building complex stretched four long blocks from the top of La Castellana down to Plaza de San Juan de la Cruz. The monolithic structure was set far back from the street. Along the sidewalk was a high arcade that extended the length of the buildings. Between the arcade and the buildings was a long, narrowish, but cool and pleasant park adorned with statues, monuments, and public exhibits.

MOSCOW GOLD | 629

David backed them into the darkness of one of the arches. "Are you all right?" David touched her face first and then slid his hands over her shoulders, arms, and hips. "Did they hurt you, Ariel?"

"You came for me, David." Tears were coursing down her cheeks. "You came for me." She slumped against him, still short of breath.

He held her away a little so he could look at her. "Of course, I did. But are you injured? Did the cabrones hurt you, Ariel?"

"No. No. I'm fine. They didn't hurt me. I was very frightened, but I tried to fight back."

Then she saw David's hand. "You're bleeding, David. Your hand."

It *was* bleeding. He had gotten blood on Ariel's clothes. "I got you dirty," he said. "I wrecked your blouse. I'm sorry."

"How did that happen?"

"I punched the fire alarm box. It had glass. I should have wrapped it up, but I was in a hurry, so I just hit it. I'll wrap it up now. I'm fine, but are you hurt? Did they mistreat you, Ariel?"

"No, no. I was afraid they would, but they didn't." Her story started to tumble out. "I was on my way to meet you at Lago. I was so happy. They surprised me and grabbed me almost in front of my building. I tried to fight, but they were too many and too strong. It was you they were after."

She started crying gain. "You came for me, David. Thank you for coming for me. I knew you would. That hope sustained me. But I was afraid. I didn't know how you would find me. But you did find me. And you came. Thank you." Her arms were locked around his neck.

"Of course, I came for you." David tried to back away to look at her, but she held on tight.

"How did you find me? It's a miracle."

They moved further into the park in front of the darkened offices and found a bench.

David recounted his anxiety when she didn't show up at Lago, his visit to Doña Sagrario, his call to Calvín, the interview with the man from the bookstore. "We were lucky, Ariel, very lucky."

They began to decompress and relax. Their conversation slowed.

"Do you think the police will be involved?" Ariel asked.

"I left them out unless we couldn't find you fast. So, no. The cops won't act right away on missing persons. Calvín had good information. He agreed that we should act on it first. We found you. I'd say we continue to leave them out of it."

"Better that way," she agreed.

David said, "We should get you home. Doña Sagrario will be worried."

"I'll call her once we get back out on the street," Ariel promised.

David walked them back toward the lights of La Castellana. As he did, he said, "Do you still want to marry me, Ariel? I would understand it if you felt after all this that you've made a bad decision and—"

Ariel interrupted him. "David, David, stop. I want to marry you now more than ever. Don't be silly." After a very long and freighted moment, she added, "We'll have a unique story to tell people about how we got engaged."

CHAPTER 96

Madrid: Friday, November 22, 1963

The gold story was done.

It had taken time to finish it. David batted out his first draft on the old maroon Smith Corona. Then there were refinements and redrafts that had been required. Now that was all done. The exposé had been written.

David's efforts resulted in a 9,500-word story.

The *Herald* was giving David's exposé significant advance play. It would appear in serial form. There would be two long installments, starting tomorrow, Saturday, and culminating in the Sunday edition.

Interest inside Spain, had been piqued. Rampant speculation was ongoing as to what the story would contain. In anticipation that the story would undergird Spanish claims for recompense, the Madrid stock market had moved upward for some days now.

Known only to David, his back-up plan was done as well.

David felt he now was able to return to the pensión on Vallehermoso. In the morning, he had picked Ariel up at Gaztambide and they'd ridden out to Carabanchel together. After the intensity of Gibraltar and the Sunset Club, their lives had settled some.

It had been a routine day out at Carabanchel. David and Nacho talked. Beto had gone back to Ciempozuelos. Nacho thought he might go down to the little suburb for a couple of days and visit with Beto and his aunt, who Nacho indicated he also knew. Nipi was enjoying his retirement, advancing his standing in Madrid's café society.

It clouded up during the day and was threatening rain when David and Ariel left Carabanchel on the tranvía for home. By the time they got back into the city, it was raining—oily, cloying rain, falling in soft plops, not wind-driven like it would be soon enough in January. The trees were getting bare. Piles of their leaves gathered. They were tramped into an auburn porridge that collected in the gutters and storm drains.

David and Ariel holed up in the Café Palomita on Alberto Aguilera, hoping it would stop. It didn't. They had to walk. David left Ariel a little wet and bedraggled at Gaztambide. He would pick her up for supper later in the evening.

He returned to Vallehermoso. Life was returning to normal. With the publication of his story, serious and studied indolence was again on David's horizon. He sat down and put his feet up.

He flipped on his old portable radio. It was tuned to Radio Madrid, the volume low. The announcer intoned, his voice soothing, *"Está lloviendo en Madrid."* Then he played Tommy Edwards', "It's All in the Game," A perfect soft and nostalgic choice for this evening. David picked up a novel, but, after shutting off the radio, he dozed.

Doña Mari knocked at around eight and woke him from his reverie. "You have a visitor, Señor David."

David was not expecting anyone, "Who?"

Doña Mari smiled and shrugged. "A young lady."

David found Ariel at the door. She was crying. "Ariel what's wrong? What has happened?"

634 | DOUGLAS L. FIELD

She threw her arms around his neck. "I'm so sorry, David," she managed through her tears.

"Why? Why are you sorry? Come in. Tell me."

"It's President Kennedy."

"President Kennedy? I think I read he's in Texas today." David looked at his watch. "Should be not long after lunchtime there."

"Yes, David, Dallas." She pronounced it /Dahlahs/. "That's in Texas, no? He's been shot, David. In Dallas. President Kennedy is dead."

After they regained some of their composure, David and Ariel went downstairs to look for a newspaper. They found a late edition, *Madrid: Diario de la Noche.* Its headline blasted, "Kennedy, *Asesinado*" (Murdered), with the secondary lead, "A Communist, Apparently the Killer, Is Arrested." Details were still scarce. Early Spanish reporting had two Secret Service agents also killed and the governor of Texas gravely injured. The vice president had taken the oath of office.

They had a subdued supper. David took Ariel home.

On arrival back at Vallehermoso, he was handed a summons from Jack Isham to appear at Isham's office at nine in the morning.

David sent word to Ariel of the meeting. He asked her to accompany him.

CHAPTER 97

Madrid: Saturday, November 23, 1963

David was up and out early.

Despite yesterday's devastating news, he didn't want to admit it, but he was excited to see his own story—in print at last, after all that had happened.

He headed up Vallehermoso toward Fernando el Católico. He carried a sealed manila envelope. Onésimo was already on scene at the corner. David did the dozens with the blind man for a moment. After, he went around the corner to a large kiosk that sold the *Herald*.

He tucked the envelope in the paper and shoved both under his arm. He went around to the MonteAzul. "Gimme a Fundador Victorio, would you?"

He opened the paper. It wasn't on the front page. Of course, it wasn't on the front page. Kennedy was all over that. He looked all through the interior pages. No gold story. No David L. Fordham byline. No nothing. He checked again. Page by page. Nothing. It wasn't there. He folded the paper, put the manila envelope back inside, and headed for Gaztambide.

MOSCOW GOLD | 637

By the time he got to Ariel's, he had become irate. "Look." He held out the paper. "They didn't print it!"

"Of course, they did. They advertised it. Let me see." Ariel didn't find it either.

They left for Calle de Narváez in a state of perplexity and frustration.

⁓

Jack Isham was waiting for David. He was not alone. David and Ariel were shown in straightaway.

The older man looked at Ariel and evidenced mild surprise at seeing her. "Would you care for coffee?" It was all laid out on a large tray.

David was not in the mood for social amenities. "My story didn't run, Jack." He held up his copy of the Saturday edition. "Why not?"

"We'll get to that, young man. But first, I think, we have some introductions to make"—he smiled at Ariel— "one more than I had planned. This is Nick Barnickle, David. He is on special assignment with me here in Madrid. He has, in that capacity, shall I say, followed your activities and movements relative to the gold story with interest. And this is Inspector José María Jaso of the Cuerpo General de Policía. I think, David, you have encountered them now and then since you've lived in Spain."

Isham did not wait for David to answer. "And you, fair lady, are?" He reached out to take shake her hand and took it in both of his, putting on what, for him, was maximum charm.

"She is Ariel Muñiz, Jack, my fiancée."

"Your fiancée? *¡No me digas!* Indeed! I had no idea," Isham said in his stilted and mildly accented Castilian and trying for uncharacteristic courtliness. "My heartiest congratulations."

The remainder who were new to each other shook hands. The Spaniards did their perfunctory air kisses on each cheek. Everyone

638 | DOUGLAS L. FIELD

was invited to sit. David and Ariel sat in front of Isham's desk. Jaso and Nick stayed back, off to the side.

"Let's dispense with all the bullroar, Jack. What happened to my story?"

"We're coming to that, David. I need to tell you that, in a conversation such as this, I would in normal circumstances ask Miss Muñíz to excuse us, but not today. Ariel, may I call you by your given name?" Isham had no evident intention of doing otherwise. Ariel was watchful and said nothing. "Good. So then, David and Ariel, we are aware, have been for some time, of the fact that Ariel has been of some assistance and, uh, has been involved in the research and development of the gold story. In view of all of that, I think today we can make an exception"—Isham looked at Barnickle and Jaso—"and invite her to stay with us." He gave Ariel an unctuous smile.

Isham plowed forward. "I don't know if you figured it out, David, but newspaper editing is not my main vocation here in Madrid. My primary work is for a division of the United States government known as 'the Company.' The Company in fact is—"

"The CIA," David cut in.

"Quite right. The CIA." Isham cast a curt glance at Barnickle. "Nick here works for the Company too. Inspector Jaso and several of his detectives, along with a department of the Bank of Spain called Room 11, were seconded to us here at the Company during the time of your investigation."

David was both assimilating Isham's information and whispering summary translations to Ariel. Isham was enjoying his notoriety to the fullest. The cadence was slow—slow enough to give David the time he needed.

"Now to get to the point of our meeting here this morning. David, m'boy, I'm sorry to have to inform you, but your story has been spiked. It did not run today. It won't run tomorrow."

Isham looked again at Barnickle and then went on. "There are two reasons. The first is obvious, the second not so much so. The first

MOSCOW GOLD | 639

reason is the horrific assassination of President Kennedy yesterday. The assassination has changed everything."

"Our colleague"—Isham raised an eyebrow—"over at the FBI, J. Edgar Hoover, is convinced that the Soviets are behind this hideous act. Hoover intends to pin this crime on the Russians. Word has gone out that nothing will be done that distracts from the FBI's efforts.

"Your story would divert attention from the scrutiny on Moscow that we want now. Your story's publication would prejudice the Brits. We need them in the coming days and weeks. It would expose the BND. We need them right now too."

David tried to make his expression vacuous and said nothing. Isham paused for emphasis and to allow Ariel to be brought up.

In his own time, Isham continued, "Your story cannot be allowed at this time. In fact, I need to tell you now that it will not ever be allowed to go to publication. It has been declared classified. It is now *by law* off limits to you, David, and to everyone else."

Isham now looked at Jaso with a pained expression. "In addition, you will turn over all your original research and any historical documents that you have collected to Inspector Jaso, who will receive them on behalf of Room 11. The Company felt those items should remain with it, but after discussion, it has been determined that they will stay here in Spain."

The CIA man came around to the front of his desk and leaned against it. He was warming to his task. "The second reason is nuanced. Please indulge me as I explain." His explanation took a few minutes.

The Spanish Civil War was a disaster for the Spanish economy. It took until 1955 to return it to prewar levels of 1936. Loss of the gold reserves was financial calamity. Return of the gold would help, but not solve the entire problem.

An epiphany had been appreciated. The gold remaining unlocated and the periodic subject of inquiry better served Spain than finding it would. If the gold were found and if it were returned, two big ifs, there would occur a one-time benefit. But if the gold remained the

640 | DOUGLAS L. FIELD

subject of uncertainty and controversy, it provided the opportunity for repeated periods of confabulatory excitement, which, when artfully timed, would weigh favorably for Spain time and again.

The mere conduct of David's investigation had done more to serve both Spanish and American interests than the actual publication of his piece, or the repatriation of the gold for that matter, ever could.

Ariel now noted that David's jaw was clenching. She knew him well enough to know that he was not pleased. "Was it your intention, Jack, to spike my eventual story from the beginning? Clear back to our pleasant little meeting at Café Gijón? In August, was it?"

Isham ignored the question and pressed forward.

Not only that, but also the entire exercise had exposed very meaningful intelligence about each of the interested nations. Aside from the Spanish, none of the players in the drama of the gold looked at all good. This included the Soviets, the Germans, and the British.

It was now confirmed that the KGB was very active in Spain. Defensive steps could be taken. The Soviets were well informed, through the BND primarily, as to activities in Spain that involved Soviet interests. The KGB had proved itself willing to take action to protect what it saw as Soviet interests within Spain and France, but not in British territory. They had proved themselves to be sanguine relative to wet operations. Finally, the Company now knew that the Spanish gold was an issue of significant sensitivity. Opportunities to exploit that sensitivity would be arranged.

The BND had proved to be penetrated by the Russians. Whether this was known to the BND remained undetermined. The BND was now seen to be well connected to its Nazi past and capable of craven behavior in its own parochial interests. BND operatives could be counted on to look to their personal interests at least as much as Germany's. Excellent exploitation opportunities would follow going forward.

MOSCOW GOLD | 641

It was BND who had hired a team of Bulgarians, of all people, to do their dirty work. This was an old relationship forged in the Second World War but one now likely to be finished.

As to the kidnapping, the rescue operation was well done and congratulations to all hands, including Ariel for her bravery.

The British were not penetrated. The measures they had taken since the Kim Philby debacle were working. The Company could trust MI6 more than it had been willing to do in recent years. However, the British were not getting very good information from their own sources, as evidenced by their total unawareness of David's activities in Gibraltar.

Isham acknowledged that his whole game had been to capitalize on the gold story to tweak the Company's opposition and induce it to expose its methods and its sources—to drag the cockroaches out into the light; to paint their radars, make them react, and observe what they did; and to determine how best to penetrate and manipulate them in return.

There was stellar cooperation between Spain and the Company. He nodded to Jaso. But the gold investigation needed to have been done by an "agency" whose independence was unassailable. Neither the Spanish government nor the Company could have any part. David, the ambitious young journalist, had been the ideal choice.

Several months ago, Isham had enlisted the Cuerpo's assistance to make occasional contact with David as a sort of preliminary job interview. The pretext had been working illegally in Madrid. They had turned nothing up. Isham's inclinations to get David involved were confirmed.

Under the protection of the Company, Room 11 and the Cuerpo, David had been always safe—well, except for once or twice when David's well-developed street craft has caused Barnickle to lose track of him. The disinformation correspondence to Ariel had been a deft touch.

642 | DOUGLAS L. FIELD

And David's having managed to sneak unnoticed into Spain after Paris! Isham looked very much forward to debriefing that part of the whole adventure at leisure over dinner.

Ariel studied David. From his expression, she saw that such a dinner would not be occurring.

David had eluded Barnickle, the Spanish authorities, the Soviets, and the BND. The details and effectiveness of David's avoidance techniques would long be remembered and used as teaching tools for CIA recruits. Isham looked with mild derision at Nick, who mouthed the words, "Screw you, Jack."

Isham apportioned praise upon himself. Approaching David had been an excellent decision. One after the other, David had made right choices, and his decisions had, right along, conformed to the needs of Isham's grand strategy. That had been gratifying—and, he added, with mild self-congratulation, not unexpected.

At last, he was done.

David exploded. "You used us as bait," he snarled first in English and then in Spanish. "You scheming, smarmy son of a bitch. All the way along, you asshole, you let Ariel and me walk right into danger, mortal danger. You risked our lives and played us as pawns in your lousy, filthy little game of spies. You don't give a shit that Kennedy died. That's just a dodge. You planned this all along. You're thanking your lucky stars that JFK got shot. His getting killed has just made your job today easier."

Before Isham could draw breath to answer, Ariel, fast as a cheetah, leapt at Isham. With remarkable force, she slapped his face with her right hand. The report cracked like a pistol shot in the quiet office.

Isham staggered back against his desk. Ariel appropriated the advantage of his confusion. She hit him again with her left. Just as hard. David jumped up to restrain her.

"¡Sinvergüenza!" (Shameless miscreant!) she swore.

Barnickle laughed uproariously, and Jaso tried not to.

"Wow, she's strong! Are you OK, little lady?" Nick said, barely able to talk.

"Ouch, she hurt my face, Nick, you jerk." It was Isham who answered.

"*¡Malvado!*" (No-good creep!) Ariel wasn't finished.

David grabbed her before she could do any more damage. He hauled her back to her chair and stood between her and Isham. "Are you OK, Ariel? Will you be calm? No more outbursts?"

Ariel nodded. "My hands hurt."

"Do they now?" David asked, bemused.

David let the room settle a moment. "Ariel, do you have control of yourself?"

She nodded.

David turned back to Isham. "Do you know what a gestoría is, Jack?"

"Of course, it's like an escrow company. Who cares?"

"Well, Jack, *you* are going to care—starting now. Yes, gestorías are the Spanish version of escrow companies. They're even more discreet, even more trustworthy. They're loyal to their clients and jealous of the preservation of their integrity to a fault."

David looked at Barnickle and Jaso and let the drama build. He reached into his folded copy of today's *Herald Tribune* that had failed to run his article and pulled out his sealed manila envelope.

"I have a copy of something for you, Jack. You are a devious, conniving, disagreeable bastard. You are untrustworthy. I began to suspect you way back when you called me over to Café Gijón back in August. I came to suspect that you would spike my story. I didn't anticipate the Kennedy assassination yesterday. No one could have. You thought you got lucky with that, but you didn't.

"This, Jack, is a copy of a second gold story"—David put the envelope on Isham's desk—"the *whole* gold story. I wrote it along with the one I submitted to the paper. That's why it took me so long. Knowing you, I figured I needed an insurance policy. So, I thought I

644 | DOUGLAS L. FIELD

ought to do two stories. It looks this morning like I was right. You can read the whole thing at your leisure. But as we're all here together, I'll give you a summary."

David looked around the room. Jaso deadpanned. Barnickle suppressed amusement. Ariel was intrigued. Isham was fulminous.

"It details all your machinations in the matter of my investigation of the Moscow Gold. All your prevarications and schemes are included. The way you manipulated Ariel and me is in there. I included how you, deliberately and for your own advancement and benefit, put us repeatedly in mortal danger. It's there, Jack. All of it."

David returned Isham's withering look with one of his own. "I don't trust you. You tooled me and my lady and my friends—when we thought we were working for you and that you were looking out for us. You betrayed us. You don't give a shit for anything but your pathetic career and advancement in your 'Company.' You are a self-centered, narcissistic prick. Now it's going to cost you."

"He's ready to kill you, David," Ariel whispered in Spanish.

"Don't worry. There are witnesses. That's why I'm doing this now. He can't kill us all," David answered. "Just listen. There's more."

"Here's the deal, Jack. The original of my second story, a copy of which you have in that envelope there on your desk is being held by a licensed, experienced and dedicated *gestorista* somewhere here in Spain. This gestorista has instructions to submit this story to *ABC*, the other principal Madrid dailies, and a careful selection of leading American papers that I have specified. This will be done ten days from today on December 3—that is unless I, both alive and in person, instruct to the contrary."

"So, you're blackmailing me?" Isham blurted out.

"Spare me the moral outrage, Jack. You're not even in the same universe with any standards of morality. You tried to leverage me. Now I'm leveraging you. This is how it feels, Jack."

Barnickle sniggered.

MOSCOW GOLD | 645

"Here's what you're going to do to prevent the release of the story you have there, along with the evidence that backs it up. You are going to get together with your perverted spy buddies in the KGB, the BND, MI6, and Room 11 and arrange the following: You will have deposited in safe-deposit accounts at the banks listed in your envelope the following amounts in gold coin from the German vault deposits in Gibraltar. The deposits will be in the amount of $5,000,000 each in gold coin, not paper money, in the names of David Fordham, Ariel Muñiz, and Ignacio Arjona. In addition, you will deposit $2,000,000 in gold coin each in accounts in the names of Junipero Contreras, Juan Miguel Calvín, Onésimo Menéndez, and Roberto Torres, as well as a sixth nominee account for my gestorista whose name will, for obvious reasons, remain undisclosed. All the details are in your envelope there. It's very straightforward. I've made it simple for you."

"You won't get away with this shit. I don't control those agencies. You can't dictate like this to me, you little pissant!" Isham snapped.

"Oh, but I will, and you do, and I can, Jack. Let me explain. You made a big mistake. You didn't consider the original historical documentary evidence of the entire gold story that I succeeded in collecting. First, I have the original receipt for the gold signed and acknowledged by the Soviets. Next, I have the original chits from the French coin dealers that document that it was the Germans who bought the gold and the detailed investigative information tying the purchases back to the wartime Abwehr. Last, I have copies of the British Government's secret and ill-gotten, in violation of their own privacy laws, list of all the German vault deposit accounts, their German owners and their contents."

David looked at the CIA operative, who would not meet his eyes. "Shall I go on? There's only a little more."

Isham made no reply.

"Here's what else you are going to do, Jack. In exchange for the Soviet secret services agreeing with you guys at CIA and at the other agencies that Ariel, Nacho, Nipi, Beto, and I are henceforward in every

646 | DOUGLAS L. FIELD

respect untouchable, they may have their original receipt back. In exchange for the British government granting total immunity from prosecution for any alleged crimes committed by me and the boys in Gibraltar, they will have the copies of their files back. In exchange for their release of the gold coin requested, the Germans will get the original French chits and all the information I developed concerning their continuing and embarrassing ownership of the gold. My requirements won't even make a dent in their totals, I can assure you."

David now looked at Jaso. Jaso appeared to know what was coming. "Then there is Room 11. Room 11 and the Spanish government will make no effort to obstruct or publicize any of the payments and agreements that will occur here. They will waive any claim to the gold being transferred to the specified accounts. They will immunize me and my team from prosecution. They will then be free to achieve their goal of keeping the gold controversy alive from time to time as it suits their purposes. However, Inspector Jaso, the original documents will not be turned over to you or Room 11. Their disposition will be as I have indicated. Actions have consequences, Inspector. Consider it a small recompense for your agency's mistreatment of Ariel back in September."

Wrapping up, David smirked at Isham. "And, Jack, you and the Company get the original of my full story and this fiasco covered up. Neither of you will suffer the embarrassment of having the details of the mess you created being made public. None of us expected the Kennedy assassination, but it will serve as cover for all of us in that everyone else will be concentrating on it and be distracted from impeding, much less even being aware of, our deal. Whether, when this all is revealed to your corrupt and immoral colleagues in the other agencies, your credibility as a clandestine will be so shot that your career is wrecked, I don't know or care."

David sneaked a look at Ariel and gave her a nod. "I gather that there are no questions. Ariel and I will be on our way now. When my gestorista is advised of the deposits and confirms them and the other

MOSCOW GOLD | 647

requirements are documented, the evidentiary elements in question will be released as agreed."

"A good day to you, gentlemen." He took Ariel's arm and left the office.

❧

The closing of the door reverberated in the room. Jaso endeavored to be the soul of discretion. Barnickle made no attempt to restrain his amusement. Isham was still furious.

"I'm not doing all that. I can't. I won't. It's a lot of money!" Isham raged.

"The hell you're not, Jack," Barnickle told him. "The kid's got it figured. He's outsmarted us all."

Barnickle looked at Jaso, who nodded. Then Barnickle went on. "The Sovs, the Brits, and the Krauts will be glad to cooperate. And, in the case of the Germans, they'll pay up to keep this little debacle of theirs and yours quiet. The Sovs are guilty of theft, fencing stolen property, and attempted and actual murder. The Germans are guilty of buying and holding stolen property and being accessories to kidnapping, attempted and actual murder. The Brits are guilty of facilitating and enabling the whole scheme, all in violation of their own laws against such things. And you'll be glad to set it all up since it will keep your ass out of a sling for botching this entire op. You're an embarrassment to the Company sometimes, Jack."

"He's not doing this to me, Nick. He's not!"

"Oh, yeah he is. He's screwed you, Jack. He fully, fairly, and flat-out screwed you. You thought you had screwed him, but he's turned it all around on you."

"Kiss my ass, Nick."

"Not a chance, Jack. You're gonna be kissing his. The whole setup is elegant. He's dividing up the evidence of the crime among the three perpetrators. Each one holds tangible assurance that the documents proving the crime can never be reassembled so the crime can't ever again be proved. Mutually assured protection, you might say."

Barnickle, dissolved in laughter, wiped his eyes. "It's priceless. Absolutely priceless. You should recruit him, Jack. Hell, you should recruit the two of them. The Company needs 'em both! What a pair!"

EPILOGUE

Madrid: Friday, April 1, 2005

Spring officially comes to Madrid on April first.

Back on November first madrileños had converted to winter. Today, as they had done for decades, they changed to summer clothes and had the heat in their buildings turned off.

And well they might have done. Vigorous spring was upon the Spanish capital. The plane and chestnut trees had set their leaves. Ornamental plants exploded in full flower. The air moved a little, comfortable and mobile. Not yet had come the stale and suffocating stillness of Castilian summer.

This fine morning, thoughts of his legacy agitated the old communist Santiago Portillo. He shuffled his way toward his flat from a light breakfast at the Café Noviciados. It looked to be a nice day, and he should have been content. This coming October, the Autonomous University of Madrid would accord him an honorary doctorate. After all those years in exile, now he was home—and the doyen of progressive society not to mention.

At ninety, he was one of the very few left from those heady days. Now, his life consisted more of memory than mission. And much there was to remember. There was the desperate defense of the city, the illusion of a new order, and the hope of revolution. But none of it had come without controversy, without expense.

Santiago's reveries had been roiled. In just the past week, his remarks at the launch downtown of somebody or other's new book had been interrupted and the bookshop ransacked by reactionaries. Santiago Portillo, hero of the Spanish Revolution, had been confronted and rebuked for his promotion and defense of it.

Young thugs in an apostate cause those.

And what complaint was theirs? After all his revolutionary fervor, his long lifetime of dedication, must it come down to dirty lucre, to a mere matter of *that* money?

Creaky, cranky, and reduced to using two canes, he turned right off Calle de San Bernardo into Calle de Daoiz and home. He struggled for inspiration that would right the wrong being done to his reputation.

Then he saw the graffiti. It was new overnight. Splashed on the wall of *his* apartment block. Big, drippy red letters for the convenience of the dim eyesight of age. It was meant for him, meant for him alone:

"This is how the war began and we won. Portillo, we know where you live."

And then, "Where is the Moscow Gold?"

Portillo knew then that he would be dogged to the end of the few days remaining to him by the Moscow Gold.

༒

Central Madrid remained a small community, so it was no surprise that David and Ariel were also walking around after breakfast, soaking up their springtime city.

Coy, Ariel took his arm, held him close, and asked, "When did you first love me, David?"

"That's easy. As soon as I found out you were rich."

"Naughty boy. *You* made me rich. You made us both rich. It was before that. When?"

"I know the answer to this question," David stated.

"Are you going to tell me?"

"What's in it for me?"

"Tell me." She elbowed him.

David gave in, "You're right. It *was* before you got rich. It was the very moment I saw your face and then the rest of you coming up out of the Ópera Metro, at the Teatro Real—the most beautiful thing I ever had seen in my life."

Ariel looked a little wistful, "Do you know when I first loved you?"

"When you found out *I* was rich?!"

"You are rich, but it was not then."

"Oh? Not then? Well, when?"

"The time Jaime took me to the embassy party, even before you first came out to Carabanchel. I said to myself right then, *I want that!* I was smitten, *perdidamente*, utterly lost."

"I never knew. You were cool to me that night," David recalled.

"You were without understanding," she explained. "I had to get your attention."

"Strange way to do it, but I'm glad you did. Very smooth. Very subtle." David gave her an affectionate and admiring look.

They went on a little farther without talking. Then Ariel continued. "David, do you remember the old people?"

"No. What old people?"

"We saw them on Gaztambide. We were walking home from the symphony performance. That was a beautiful night."

"Oh, they were blind. Each had a cane." David did remember.

Ariel searched his face and said, "Yes. I was moved. I have never forgotten them. It was if they had become as one. Have we become like them?"

"Well, I don't know," David said. "I can still see you. You look good."

"Of course, we can still see but—"

"I'll get you a white cane for your birthday. It's coming up next month. Then you can get me one for mine. Mine's in June, remember?"

"I remember you said that it was as if those dear little old people were as one flesh. Do you remember saying that? Have you and I become as one flesh?"

"Oh, yes. Yes, we have." David got serious for a moment. "*Más que ayer, menos que mañana*, my love. That's never changed. Never will."

Ariel's fingers went to her neck, to the necklace. Like they had done tens of thousands of times since she and David had met in Segovia after he came back from Paris.

"David, you act like a hard case sometimes, but you are a romantic at heart. I love you." Then she hugged and kissed him. Just there on the sidewalk.

They were in Noviciados on Calle de San Bernardo.

"Let's go up to Magallanes. Want to? See if La Playa's open. Have lunch?" asked David.

They turned off San Bernardo into Calle de Daoiz. They saw but paid little attention to an old man ahead walking painfully, bent over, and using two canes.

Then David saw the graffiti—the dripping red letters.

"Ariel, look." He pointed.

"This is how the war began and we won. 'Portillo, we know where you live. Where is the Moscow Gold?'"

"That'll be *Santiago* Portillo, the infamous communist, Ariel. Siege of Madrid in '36 and all that. Didn't know he was still alive. Gotta be ancient. He must be back in Spain, must live around here somewhere. I met him, remember? That time in Paris, in '63, with Mrs. Negrín, Méndez Aspe, and Raúl Moscardó."

"I wonder what has happened to the rest of all that gold," Ariel said. "We were correct, all those years ago, when we realized that the gold story will never go away."

654 | DOUGLAS L. FIELD

"Shall we go down to Gibraltar and nose around? See what we can find? We know where the registry is. Do you think they would be glad to see us?" David smiled at her.

"I can be packed and ready in fifteen minutes!"

Ariel took his hand and they scampered off toward Fuencarral. And Quevedo beyond.

HISTORICAL BACKGROUND AND CONTEXT

The epicenter of this story is the city of Madrid, Spain, in the summer and fall of 1963, where and when I spent significant portions of my middle and late adolescence. I first set foot on Spanish soil on August 24, 1963, at Irún. After attending the Colegio Carlos I in Madrid, I returned home in 1964. Almost exactly five years after first arriving in Spain, I returned on August 17, 1968. Three days later, I met Sandra Thaïs Soeder. We attended the University of Madrid together, dated, courted, and married on February 28, 1969, in Gibraltar.

This book is a work of fiction. A historical romance, it takes place in real times and places. While the scenes portrayed are, for the most part, imaginary, the narrative is played out in the context of actual events, localities, and personalities. In many respects, the typical disclaimer attached to most novels applies. Except for the principal historical persons and occurrences, most characters and their activities portrayed in the book are the fruit of my imagination. In those cases, resemblance to real people and events is coincidental and unintended, except those persons of public prominence who have been mentioned in their appropriate settings for purposes of verisimilitude.

However, this novel is also grounded in actual events which took place in Sandy's and my lives in Spain. I have taken the liberty of conflating events of the two times that I lived in Spain into a single whole. Nonetheless, the entire story of David's arrival in Spain; of his learning Spanish, adapting to and then adopting Spanish culture; of the development of his love for Madrid; and, finally, of David and Ariel's meeting and falling in love with each other is based on fact. Most of that did occur. Rather than write a memoir or autobiography, I have found it more interesting and more enjoyable to set my recollections of those seminal times in my life into novelistic form. I thank my readers for their indulgence.

No treatment of mid-twentieth century Spain is possible without reference to the civil war that occurred there between 1936 and 1939. Even as late as 1963, not to mention during the remainder of that decade, the memories and effects of that conflict were indelibly imprinted on the Spanish people and their culture. It is impossible to write about the first years of the decade of the '60s in Spain without extensive reference to that seminal event earlier in its history. For this reason, there appear numerous flashbacks in the story to that most essential of Spanish conflicts.

The events that led up to and that occurred during the Spanish Civil War are convoluted. The bibliography of books on the subject both in the English and Spanish languages is vast in the most expansive connotation of the word. The subject is huge. Any attempt in just a few words or pages to summarize it runs the risk of failing to do it historical justice. Nevertheless, the fictional story offered in this volume will be much better understood and enjoyed if it is accompanied by a brief recounting of the events that led to the Spanish Civil War; the unfolding of the war itself; and a description of what happened in Spain after the war was concluded, during World War II, and then in the first decade and a half of the Cold War. Such a recounting follows. I trust that it will be judged as fair, as it is succinct.

Civil unrest and even war were not an unusual occurrence in Spanish history during the several decades that led up to 1936. The conflict that occurred between 1936 and 1939 was the fourth that had taken place since 1830. Spanish history of the last two hundred years or so has often been characterized by lack of synchronization between social realities and the political institutions in place over them. Social and political development would be attempted. All too often, political and military power would rise to resist it. That, in turn, would give rise to explosions of revolutionary activity, all occurring in repetitive cycles.

Until the 1950s, Spain had an agrarian economy. Although by no means exclusive, the prevailing structure was the latifundio, the great agricultural estates that dominated the center, south, and west of the country. The landed oligarchy would for long periods enjoy political dominance. This would occasionally but regularly be challenged by the atrophied mercantile and industrial classes, along with the great hordes of landless day-laborer peasants, the *braceros* and *jornaleros* who worked the land under exploitative conditions.

Defeat in 1898 at the hands of the United States in the Spanish-American War, along with the concomitant loss of Spain's remaining colonies, Cuba in particular, produced upheaval. In the following two decades before World War I, interest in and participation in socialist parties and unions increased, particularly in Madrid, Bilbao, and Barcelona. Those cities, of course, dominate the northern, central, and eastern portions of the country.

Spain contrived to remain neutral in World War I from 1914 to 1918. It managed, in notable degree, to grow wealthy selling armaments and supplies to the belligerent parties. Much of the coin and gold bullion holdings that are the subject of this book were acquired and placed away in the vaults of the Bank of Spain during that period.

Frequent risings and strikes by a welter of groups—socialist, communist, and anarchist—characterized the years after World War I. A bewildering alphabet soup of names and acronyms, that to the current day vex the student of this period, identified these groups. The Guardia Civil (Civil Guard) and the army put down these manifestations with varying degrees of violence. Compounding the national malaise was a humiliating defeat of Spanish military forces in Morocco in 1921 by Rif tribesmen at a place called Annual.

In September 1923, Army General Miguel Primo de Rivera led a coup d'état and installed himself as dictator. Primo de Rivera had close association with industrial ownership interests in Barcelona but was himself descended from a southern landowning family. He, thus, was well cast as defender of industrial, capitalist, and landowning interests. At first, he enjoyed relative success in tamping down civil unrest and benefitted from a general upturn in the European economy. Nevertheless, he governed with an ad hoc, improvisational style that resulted in several political missteps. His blunders caused offense to every element of society. He resigned in January 1930. Ironically, in later years, Primo de Rivera's dictatorship would, with nostalgia, be remembered by many as a sort of "golden age" of the pre-civil war era.

Spain at the time was a constitutional monarchy. Alfonso XIII was king. The constitutional monarchy was antiquated and decrepit. Alfonso tried to maintain power and reestablish order. He was not successful. On April 14, 1931, he abdicated and left Spain for Rome, never to return.

The departure of Alfonso opened the way for the Second Republic. (The First Republic had been a short-lived and abortive attempt at democracy established in 1873. The army soon crushed it after two years in 1874.) The establishment of the Second Republic on April 14, 1931 was accompanied by widespread and general popular support and rejoicing. Few at that time would have imagined that five years later, large segments of the Spanish populace would believe that war was the only way the country's problems could be solved. In the years between

1931 and 1936, the advent of the Second Republic notwithstanding, political hatreds persisted and then flourished, highlighting the profound conflicts that continued to exist in Spanish society.

The creation of the Second Republic failed to satisfy the extremists. Republicans had their republic; now they wanted revolution. Unrepressed spates of lawlessness were compounded by unending, innumerable strikes, themselves accompanied by fierce quarrels among no fewer than a dozen political parties of the Left. This instability, plus administrative fecklessness and attacks against the Catholic Church, led, in November 1933, to a decisive defeat of the leftists in the first elections after the Second Republic's foundation.

The right-leaning government that followed had no greater success. In the period leading up to the generals' rising in July 1936, there were twenty-six changes of government, as well as several localized revolutions. The most significant and memorable took place in the northern mining province of Asturias.

The development of a workable constitution was an overwhelming challenge for the Second Republic. A viable one was agreed upon, but the left-wing parties sabotaged their own interests by insisting on a provision that held the inauguration of the new constitution in abeyance.

As a result of the persistent conflict during these years, the issues and parties began to crystallize. In January 1936, the twelve parties of the Left made common cause in the form of the "Popular Front" under the leadership of the talented politician Manuel Azaña. They managed a decisive electoral victory the following month. The home-rule parties of the Basques and Catalans joined the Popular Front to further their separatist aspirations. Some moderate elements, including the Republican Union, found themselves bedfellows with entities of bluntly communist inclination, including the Socialist Party and several fulminatory trade unions. Most of these had their own military forces that were often in open warfare with each other. The most radical union was the National Labor Federation, a party of

MOSCOW GOLD | 661

unbridled and passionate violence. To this volatile admixture was added the Communist Party, then small in Spain. Also added was the Anarchist Federation. It, on the contrary, was a large and menacing organization, whose contempt for life and property and desire for the dissolution of the state and breakdown of all administration was well known.

The 7th Congress of the Comintern met in July 1935 in Moscow and approved the tactics adopted by the Popular Front that, in turn, became the official policy of the Spanish Communist Party. As a result, the communists began to enjoy greater power and influence. They came, after the war began, to dominate the leftist camp.

On the right, there was a confused jumble of parties, including Radicals, Liberals, and the Carlist party of Navarre. Most important was the then nascent but soon to dominate Spanish Falange. (*Falange* is the word in Spanish for phalanx.) At the outset, the Falange, a fascist party, was small and unrepresented in the Cortes (the Spanish legislature). But Antonio Primo de Rivera, son of the aforementioned Dictator-General Miguel Primo de Rivera, had founded it. Like the communists, it was destined to experience meteoric growth in numbers of members and influence.

There were two other entities of interest—the Catholic Church and the army. The level of influence of the church had, by 1936, waned in comparison to what had existed in previous centuries. Persecution against the Church had mounted under the Second Republic. It increased exponentially under the Popular Front, such that the Church's authority and influence were crippled.

Not so the army. It exercised major influence in Spanish politics, both overtly and covertly. The army was small and not notably competent as a fighting force. Every tenth member was an officer, and every hundredth officer was a general. Since many officers had risen from humble origins up through the ranks, it would, however, not be considered a class-based organization. While class interests may not have motivated its many generals, the generals were aware of and jealous of the army's political power. The general bent of the army was rightward, but the Republican politicians on the left purposed to counteract that inclination by promotion of officers sympathetic to them, as well as through the posting of generals with undesirable political orientation to positions in the overseas colonies and possessions. Such was the case of General Francisco Franco, who had been sent off in February 1936 to command the garrison in the distant Canary Islands.

A leftist electoral victory in February 1936 raised tensions to critical mass. The Falange was banned. Jose Antonio Primo de Rivera was arrested. Institutions within the government whose role was to maintain stability and protect the persons and property of the citizenry instead took the opportunity of their accession to power to prey upon and exact revenge against their political enemies. Roving gangs broke into private homes and shot their inhabitants upon proclaiming them as "fascists." Peasants went on rampages, seizing land, mutilating and killing livestock, and destroying crops. Businesses and shops were looted at gunpoint. The sign of the raised and clenched fist was ubiquitous. People of rightist inclination holed up in their flats, going out only when necessary to buy food and, even then, carefully disguised. One favorite tactic was the release of political prisoners by the thousands, who lost no time in seeking retribution. The Church and its interests suffered. Priests and nuns were harassed, mutilated, and killed. Churches, monasteries, and convents were burned or appropriated. Strangely, it was found that these buildings made for good leftist prisons.

Supporters of the Right did not stand short. Outrage was responded to by outrage, murder by murder, mayhem by mayhem. Discipline and civil authority were nonexistent. During a four-month period in 1936, there were documented over 3,000 assassinations, 113 general strikes, and twice as many partial strikes. Hundreds of churches, clubs, newspaper offices, and other buildings were burned. When José Calvo Sotelo, leader of the opposition party in the Cortes, reported to that body the foregoing statistics, leftist ministers roundly criticized him. (The notorious Dolores Ibárurri, later to become known to the world as La Pasionria, rose in response and promised him ominously and prophetically, "You have made your last speech.") Two days later, on July 13, 1936, members of the communist-inspired Assault Guards and several other leftist organizations seized Calvo Sotelo in the early hours of the morning at his residence, killed him in a police truck, and dumped his body at a local cemetery. The Right was apoplectic. Madrid became a tinderbox.

The tornado touched down on July 18, 1936. The army garrison in Melilla revolted. General Franco was transported by an aircraft chartered in England from the Canary Islands to Morocco, where he took command of the Army of Africa. The rising had begun. The rebel forces enjoyed good initial success in the northwest and parts of the south, Seville in particular. By the end of July, Franco and most of his army had been airlifted from Morocco to metropolitan Spain. The rebels threatened Madrid from the north and west.

Among the many significant complicating factors in understanding this conflict is the plethora of names that are, in various contexts, given to the two respective sides. Those sides were (1) the duly constituted Spanish government and its supporters and forces known variously as the Republicans, the Loyalists, and the Communists and (2) the rebelling forces led by Francisco Franco and several additional generals of the army, known variously as the Nationalists, the Royalists, and the Fascists. Most frequently used are the Republican and Nationalist designations. They predominate in this book.

In Madrid, the Nationalists were poorly prepared and the rising there was not well coordinated. After two days of fighting in the streets and of mob violence, the rising was resisted by troops loyal to the Republican government and by armed workers. Nationalist troops, along with monarchist and Falangist volunteers, took refuge in the large Montaña Barracks in the northwest part of the city. The commander of the barracks dithered and kept his troops inside. The barracks were surrounded and stormed by an angry rabble on July 20, and their occupants led away, for the most part, to summary execution. Control of the city passed to socialist trade unionists that took over the homes of the wealthy, public buildings, restaurants, and hotels. They established street patrols and arrested, searched, and often killed suspects and opponents on the spot.

With a small and inexperienced force, General Emilio Mola arrived on July 23 at the Guadarrama Mountains north of Madrid and threatened the city. People's militias were formed. They went out and, filled with revolutionary ardor, resisted the threat.

Meanwhile, the southern part of the country had been won for and stabilized by the Nationalists. Franco organized an army of some fifteen thousand for a move eastward on Madrid. Franco enjoyed initial success and, by September 21, had reached the town of Maqueda some fifty-five miles from Madrid. At that point, he made a tactical error and redirected his advance southeastward away from the main attack vector on Madrid to Toledo, where he relieved a Nationalist garrison that had been besieged in the Alcázar there for many weeks. The detour to Toledo secured a propaganda victory for the rebels but allowed the defenders of Madrid to strengthen themselves and to hold the city later in the year.

In the north, General Mola, who disposed of four separate columns of troops, was asked during a propaganda broadcast which of the four would reach Madrid first. He famously replied that it would be the "Fifth Column" of clandestine supporters that he already had inside the capital. As a result, that famous phrase was added to the lexicon of political vocabulary. The leftist forces in control in Madrid went on a rampage of terror and killing, with the goal of rooting out and eliminating Nationalist supporters in the capital.

Nationalist forces continued to move up toward Madrid from the west and southwest. By early November, they were ready for what they hoped would be the final assault on the city. The Republican government fled Madrid on November 6. The attack began November

MOSCOW GOLD | 665

7 from high ground in the large parkland known as Casa de Campo west of the city. There was fierce fighting on November 8 and 9, including inside some of the university buildings. The arrival of International Brigade troops and a column of anarchists under Buenaventura Durruti was just enough to stall the advance.

The Siege of Madrid became perhaps the most renowned event in the war. It lasted from November 7 to 23, whereupon lines were established and then Madrid settled into a dug-in stalemate for over two more years.

The fight for Madrid was desperate and bitter. In University City, there arose pitiless contention for every path, every building, every house, every floor, and every threshold. The frontline sometimes went through valuable laboratories and libraries. Sometimes breastworks were constructed from huge volumes of the *Encyclopedia Britannica*. Starting in November 1936 and all the way until 1939, University City was the high watermark of the rebel assault on Madrid. In places, the Nationalists were three or five hundred yards from the nearest bar or café inside the city.

The struggle for Madrid resolved into a cold-starved stalemate reactivated by periodic air raids, artillery barrages, and infantry flare-ups. The lines split Carabanchel in half. A surreal and bitter battle for control continued there. It was complete with flame-throwing vehicles, snipers, and tunneling under enemy positions to set explosives.

Since it had become known from Franco's own lips that the Salamanca district would be spared, the area filled to overflowing. There were so many people that the streets were impassable. Franco's largesse evaporated. He now told a correspondent for *The Times*, "I will destroy Madrid rather than leave it to the Marxists."

The Soviet advisors and foreign correspondents lived in sumptuous luxury at the Ritz, the Palace, Hotel Florida, and Gaylord's. Daily sustenance for the rest of the population was meager. Voracious housewives stripped to the bone any draft animal killed by shellfire. Cat and rat meat flavored up thin lentil soup. The tranvías and the

Metro still ran. The Metro was safer because shelling affected surface traffic. Nonetheless, people preferred the tranvías. Tranvías had to stop at the frontlines. Many made mistakes on the Metro and wound up on the enemy side.

Exact casualty figures for the siege of Madrid are not known. Some thirty thousand to forty thousand fighters participated on each side, and total casualties are most often estimated at ten thousand.

Foreigners were impressed with the insouciance of Spaniards in the face of danger and death. One Serbian fighter observed with both articulation and prescience, "Spaniards are very brave in the fighting. But this courage, too, is of a knightly, poetical sort. It is hard for them to adapt to the volatile, pedantic and prosaic demands of modern war." The siege turned what was to have been a routine Spanish coup d'état into a full-fledged and vicious civil war—a civil war that would be grievously prolonged by the quixotic nature of the Spanish national character, not to mention the intense outside intervention that turned it into a world war in miniature.

Upon the outbreak of the war, European powers and the United States declared their neutrality and declined to support either side. This neutrality was, however, broken by both Hitler in Germany and Mussolini in Italy, who sided with Franco and his Nationalists and by Stalin in the Soviet Union, who sided with the Republican government.

The war after 1936, in summary, was characterized by torturously slow but inexorable eastward progress by the Nationalists. The conflict developed into a full-spectrum war with air, land, and sea operations carried out by both sides. In the end, however, it was the land war that predominated.

In 1937, the Nationalists continued their advance from strongholds in the south and west. The Republican Popular Army attacked at Brunete northwest of Madrid to relive the northern front on July 6. The attackers were successful and captured the town. But by July 26, the Nationalists had reorganized and reversed all their losses. The

Nationalists overran most of Spain's northern coastline in that year. They continued to invest Madrid from the north, south, and west.

Early in 1938, Republican efforts to take city of Teruel failed. Through the summer and fall, the opposing sides battled along the Ebro River, with the Popular Army conceding defeat in November and retreating to the north.

Early in 1939, Franco continued to strangle the Republicans and captured large parts of Catalonia. Important southeastern cities fell in steady succession. Madrid fell after prolonged fighting in March. Franco declared the war over on April 1. The United States recognized his government.

The end of the war resulted in the exile of thousands of leftist Spaniards, many of whom fled to refugee camps in southern France. During this time, Spain suffered the loss of professionals, businessmen, political figures, and artists by the thousands. Those who did not emigrate often lost their positions, privileges, or seniority. Spain was thus deprived of many of its best workers and educated professionals.

In September 1939, World War II broke out in Europe. Just over a year later, on October 23, 1940, Hitler met with Franco at Hendaye, France, just across the border from Irun, Spain. Hitler desired Spain's entry into the war on the side of the Axis. However, Franco made significant demands, which included economic assistance and Spanish control of Gibraltar. No agreement was reached. Gibraltar was not retaken for Spain and, to this day, remains in the hands of the British.

With the end of World War II, Spain suffered from the economic repercussions of its earlier support for the Axis and consequent isolation from the international community. Spain was ostracized by the rest of Europe and by the United States. This period is sometimes called "the Hunger Years."

The ostracizing ended and the situation in Spain began to improve when, in view of Spain's strategic location as the Cold War unfolded and Franco's success in parlaying his bona fides as an anti-communist to the Western powers, the United States entered a trade and military alliance with Spain. This historic alliance commenced with President Dwight D. Eisenhower's visit to Spain in 1953 that, in turn, resulted in the Pact of Madrid between the two countries. (Francisco Franco is credited by many commentators as having driven a very favorable bargain for Spain in those negotiations with the United States.) Spain was then admitted to the United Nations in 1955. (It is said that, by 1955, Spain had at last regained the economic prosperity and productivity that it had enjoyed in July 1936 at the start of the civil war debacle.)

Franco did prove himself to be stalwart, steadfast, and stolid as an anti-communist. He demonstrated good talent at rooting out and resisting all attempts by the Soviets and their allies to infiltrate Spain and its institutions and to conduct espionage against it and its Western friends there.

By the summer and fall of 1963, the West was assiduously prosecuting the Cold War against the Soviet Bloc, with the benefit of Spain as its new and effective ally.

ACKNOWLEDGMENTS

My sincere thanks to my daughter Julia C. Fikse of West Hills, California; my son David M. Field of Pleasant Hill, California; my late stepmother Lucille Reneiro Field of Santa Rosa, California; Russell W. Taylor of Oakland, California; Mac Erwin of Walnut Creek, California; and Sonia Lupian of Stockton, California, who graciously and patiently read and commented on the manuscript for this book. Their learning and input were invaluable to me in completing it to its final form. The description of the necklace that David gives Ariel when they meet in Segovia is gratefully acknowledged to have been inspired by a design of Molina García of Valencia, Spain.

ABOUT THE AUTHOR

Douglas L. Field, Esq. attended the Universities of Madrid, Spain, and California at Berkeley and was admitted to the practice of law in 1973. He has practiced civil defense law for over forty-eight years in California. He retired from active litigation practice at the end of 2011 after trying numerous jury cases to verdict.

His undergraduate major was Spanish-American economic history. He maintains his fluency in the Spanish language and has an enduring interest in history, particularly of Spain, Spanish America, and Portugal.

During the entirety of his law practice and in his retirement, he has indulged his avocations as not only an amateur historian but also an educator and public speaker.

He lived in Madrid from 1963 to 1964 and from 1968 to 1969. Since then, he has returned regularly to Spain and travels multiple times each year to Central and South America and the Caribbean.

Mr. Field has extensive experience as a cruise line destination and enhancement lecturer, has sailed with numerous cruise lines, and has made presentations on a wide range of topics. These include Spanish and Latin American history and culture, geology, meteorology, oceanography, volcanology, the Panama Canal, South American politics, Latin American political figures, and numerous Cuba and Caribbean topics.

He is the author of the 2013 book *The Expert Expert: The Path to Prosperity and Prominence as an Expert Witness.* He has two grown children and five grandchildren. He lives in Ripon, California.